THE BARBAROSSA COVENANT

Ian A. O'Connor

Pegasus Publishing & Entertainment Group

Pegasus Publishing & Entertainment Group
The Barbarossa Covenant 2015© Ian A. O'Connor. All rights reserved.
First Printing August 2015

This is a work of fiction.

Cover art by: SelfPubBookCovers.com/GoodCoverDesign

Visit the author at: www.ianaoconnor.com
Contact the author: ianaoconnor@ianaoconnor.com

ISBN: 978-0-692-47636-9

Manufactured in the United States of America

Ian A. O'Connor

To my wife and best friend, Candice Myers O'Connor

Fiction Titles by Ian A. O'Connor
The Twilight of the Day
The Seventh Seal
The Barbarossa Covenant

Nonfiction Titles by Ian A. O'Connor
With Howard C. "Scrappy" Johnson
SCRAPPY: Memoir of a U. S. Fighter Pilot in Korea and Vietnam

Short Story Titles by Ian A. O'Connor
The Last Grandmaster

THE BARBAROSSA COVENANT
PROLOGUE
THE PRESENT
Day 1. Rome. Monday morning

Justin Scott stood next to a Japanese foursome on the cold, windswept pavement of Rome's Leonardo da Vinci Fiumicino Airport. Winter had bullied its way into the capital city under the cover of darkness this sixth day of January, leaving in its wake temperatures more suitable to Oslo. Now, in the dawn's meager light, he thought the two men and two women seemed lost and confused as they shivered inside expensive, ankle length, leather coats.

Justin swung his garment bag up to his shoulder, stepped off the curb and headed toward the line of idling white taxis at the stand across from the International Arrival and Departure Building. Suddenly, a terror-filled scream split the air. Heeding time-tested instincts, he ducked while pivoting to face the unknown, only to see the building's massive plate glass façade crack, then disintegrate into a million shards. The scream died mid-octave, immediately replaced with a surreal staccato-like chatter.

Justin threw himself to the ground, using his bag as a cushion to absorb the impact. Once down, he abandoned the carryall and began rolling toward the curb, a singular thought crowding all others from his mind: *Take cover behind the row of taxis!*

His heart pounded in concert to the rhythm of the chaos around him. The firing continued unabated, filling the air with the pungent smell of gunpowder.

The racket ended abruptly. After a long moment, Justin peeked over the trunk of a Fiat, taking in as much of the scene as possible in one quick scan as he had been trained to do at the FBI academy more than a quarter of a century earlier. The seemingly lost and confused tourists of moments ago were now anything but. They had formed a solid phalanx and, with Micro Uzi SMGs drawn from inside their coats, had laid down a withering fusillade into a group exiting the terminal. Bodies lay atop bodies.

Justin reached for his holstered weapon only to remember he wasn't armed. He jerked backward, startled, as a police car fishtailed to a stop a couple of yards from where he crouched. *Godallmighty, I could have been run over! No siren, no warning, no nothing.* Two *Polizia di Stato* officers jumped out, drawing their Berettas as they tried to size-up the impossible scene.

"Get down!" Justin yelled at the top of his lungs.

The smallest Japanese woman wheeled, drew a bead on the two men and fired on full automatic. 9-millimeter Parabellum brass casings cascaded from her weapon like so many shiny trinkets, clinking as they hit the pavement and bounced into the gutter. The officers collapsed in unison. One Beretta went airborne, turning end over end before striking the ground and skidding to a stop within inches of Justin's feet. Out of the corner of his eye, he caught sight of what looked like a hotel courtesy van as it slammed into the rear of the police car, propelling the cruiser headlong into the side of a taxi, which in turn struck an aluminum light pole.

Pandemonium reigned.

Then, as if on some silent cue, the four lowered their weapons and sprinted in lock step towards the van. Suddenly, the smaller woman stopped mid-stride. She expertly ejected the magazine from her Uzi, slid her right hand inside her coat pocket and extracted a fresh 25-round magazine, all the while keeping her eyes riveted on a badly wounded, but still-alive officer.

Justin immediately understood her intention. In one seamless move, he scooped up the Beretta, held his breath, took aim at an invisible bull's eye in the center of the woman's chest and squeezed off two shots. The would-be executioner let loose a long groan as she crumpled to the pavement, her weapon falling from her left hand, the unspent magazine still clutched in her right. Her companions piled into the van and slammed the door. Because she was either dead or dying, she was expendable. Three pairs of hate-filled eyes glared at Justin through dingy windows and, as the van lurched forward, one of the men drew a finger angrily back and forth across his throat in a wild, slashing motion.

Justin became aware of the yelping and whooping from scores of sirens, all getting louder. He glanced at the gun in his hand then threw it down, knowing he didn't want to face an army of enraged Italian police officers. He hobbled over to the nearest downed policeman and probed the neck for a pulse. Open and lifeless eyes stared off into eternity. He made his way painfully to the second. Also dead. Ashen-faced, he straightened and turned toward the woman. She was on her back, limbs akimbo but her eyes were wide open, gazing up at the pewter-colored sky. Slowly, almost imperceptibly, her left arm moved, stopped, moved again. She was alive and searching for her weapon.

Ignoring a searing pain shooting down his left leg, Justin covered the distance in less than three seconds and kicked the Uzi out of her reach. She slowly turned her head and looked up at him, her powdered face an inscrutable mask. Satisfied she no longer posed a threat, Justin turned his back on her and went to offer help to the other victims.

"Welcome to carefree, not-so-damn-sunny-Italy," he muttered as several police cars converged on the corpse-strewn battlefield.

* * * * *

Throughout this brief reign of terror, a tall, regal blonde dressed in a three-quarter length Persian lamb coat followed Justin's every move from behind the safety of a new Volvo parked at the end of the line of taxis. She held a cell phone close to her ear.

"Make sure Tel Aviv understands that the civilian shooter is definitely Justin Scott," she said in a carefully modulated voice so there would be no misunderstanding by whoever was listening. She spoke in a Yiddish dialect that had not been in vogue for more than a century and, even now, was only understood by a smattering of people in Israel, Russia, Switzerland, and the Balkans. She hesitated for a moment, eyes riveted on Justin. "You know, of course, this changes everything, because his presence confirms our worst fears. War is now imminent, and either Rome or Moscow will survive, but not both." She severed the connection, climbed into the car, sat back against the cold leather seat and continued to study Justin as he limped toward to the expanding knot of police officers.

Oh, Mister Scott, she found herself lamenting, you should have just said no when Cardinal Kettering summoned you to Rome. But you didn't, and now you, too, will soon die, as will many others.

A sense of despair washed over the woman. No longer able to contain her emotions, she lowered her head and allowed the tears to silently flow. After a full minute, she wiped her swollen eyes and whispered prayerlike to the ghost of a man long dead. "Szűrös, you always insisted Winston Churchill had done something long ago which would one day compel Moscow to declare war on the Holy See, yet we all chose to dismiss that warning. What happened here moments ago proves you were right all along, and now the world is about to reap a terrible whirlwind.

CHAPTER 1
Wartime London. November 1940

Lieutenant Commander Ian Lancaster Fleming, RNVR, (Royal Navy Volunteer Reserve) was suffering from one whale of a gin-induced hangover. The party had lasted long past the witching hour, and he had no idea how he had made it back to his flat on Ebury Street. He slept through the alarm's raucous call to quarters, and when he finally struggled up and read the clock's face, he saw to his horror the hour was 9:15. He threw off the bedclothes and jumped into his uniform.

Exiting the underground twenty minutes later, Fleming scurried up Whitehall to his office in The Admiralty, scanning the buildings along each side of the street as he went, looking for signs of new damage. Not much, thank God.

Back on September seventh, the Luftwaffe had begun a strategic campaign of bombing high value targets, and London was at the center of the storm. Then in early November, Reichsmarschall Hermann Göring had upped the ante by sending an even greater number of his bomber formations over the capital in round-the-clock raids. Adolf Hitler was apoplectic that England had not sued for peace during the summer, and the reason for this British stubbornness had escaped him. In simple terms, Göring's Luftwaffe had failed to destroy the inferior RAF.

As Fleming double-timed his way up the street that bleak November morning, he tried to remember if there had been anything on the day's schedule with his boss, Admiral John Godfrey, RN. He didn't think so, but he wasn't really sure. His legs were still rubbery from too much gin and too little sleep.

Admiral Godfrey, Britain's Director of Naval Intelligence and a man with a well-deserved reputation for not suffering fools lightly, had announced early in the summer of 1939 that a thirty-one-year-old failed stockbroker named Ian Fleming was about to become his personal assistant. The news had caused many in high places to wonder aloud, *Ian who?*

Fleming held a reserve commission in the king's army as a subaltern, but Godfrey had pulled the right strings and turned his army reserve commission into a navy reserve commission. Godfrey then bumped his new assistant up a grade, and Fleming came on board as a full lieutenant. But not even Admiral Godfrey could turn the appointment into a regular navy commission, so Fleming sported two wavy gold stripes on his sleeves, branding him as a member of the 'wavy navy,' an appellation all similarly situated reservists loathed.

Within months, however, the special assistant was promoted to lieutenant commander. Even Fleming had secretly found himself somewhat bewildered with the offer for employment from the man responsible for all intelligence matters in the Crown's senior service.

On September 1, 1939, Germany attacked Poland, prompting England to honor a longstanding treaty with that country. Along with France, England declared war on Nazi Germany two days later, and everyone living on the Sceptered Isle wondered what was going to happen next—including Lieutenant Commander Ian Lancaster Fleming.

Fleming tossed his cigarette butt into the gutter and made his way around the wall of sandbags protecting the building. Every important structure in London was similarly safeguarded. He returned the sentry's perfect salute, then pulled open the massive front door. As he made his way into the gloomy recesses of the old, but still impressive edifice, he flashed his photo ID card several times before finally arriving at his desk in the ultra-secret area of the building known as Room thirty-nine.

"Well, well, nice of you to finally show up," a cadaverous lieutenant said from behind a mug of steaming tea. He shot Fleming a cursory glance as he spoke, then turned his eyes back to a huge aerial map covering his desktop. "You do look bloody awful, Ian, I must say."

"Blow it, Charles, I'm in no mood," Fleming replied, tossing his gas mask under the desk. He peeked at the opaque glass door separating his kingdom from the Old Man's on the other side. Admiral Godfrey's office was referred to by all as the *sanctum sanctorum*, and in order for one to enter, that person had first to get past Lieutenant Commander Fleming.

A regular navy commander leaned over Fleming's shoulder and rapped on his pristine desk. "You open for business, yet, Ian?"

"I am indeed, sir. Pull up a chair and tell me what's on your mind."

Instead of pulling up a chair, Commander Angus Brosnan, Godfrey's director of operations, tossed a packet held together by three rubber bands onto Fleming's desk. "This arrived yesterday from one of my agents, a woman in Lisbon. Came by way of Jamaica and Halifax. Don't know if it'll be of any interest to you, however, but she went to a lot of trouble to get it here, so we should at least give it the once-over."

Fleming lit a tailor-made cigarette from Morland, readily identified by his personal signature triple gold band and squinted at the bundle. "Why would you think I'd be interested?"

"Haven't the foggiest, but you do have a keen eye, so be a good chap and take a gander when you get a free moment. My lads have rather full plates."

The free moment did not come until the next day. During a relatively quiet spell, and while the admiral was out, Fleming began rummaging through the packet. He did have a knack for zipping past what he called bloody blather, and just as he was about to deep six the lot, several pages torn from a spiral notebook and paper-clipped together caught his attention. He adjusted his desk's lampshade and began to read the cramped but grammatically correct English, working his way to the bottom of the page. Now this was quite something else! He lit another cigarette and began again from the top.

The narrative spoke of a woman named Margaretha Zelle, better known to the world as Mata Hari, an exotic dancer caught spying for the Germans in Paris during WW I, and summarily executed by the French on October 15, 1917. But what this British agent in Lisbon was now suggesting was simply the stuff of fiction. Regardless, he found himself captivated by her yarn.

It is no mere coincidence Mata Hari was executed on October 25, 1917, because that same morning, General Henri Simonette, a member of the French general staff, received a cable from Petrograd at 3:00 a.m. informing him the czar's Winter Palace had just been sacked. It also advised Simonette that Czar Nicholas II, the Czarina, and their five children had simultaneously disappeared from their place of confinement in Moscow.

Fleming sat back, laced his fingers behind his head and allowed his mind to pull to the forefront certain historical facts with which he was quite familiar. Because of his new job, he had taken it upon himself to study the biographies of several of the most notorious spies from the Great War. None was more infamous than the woman known as Mata Hari. The French had long insisted she had been executed by a firing squad on October 15, 1917; yet here was someone now suggesting the deed had taken place on the twenty-fifth. Why such a discrepancy? Especially in light of the irrefutable fact that a British reporter, Henry Wales, had supposedly written an eyewitness account of the execution. As he thought it through, Fleming suddenly asked the question no one else ever had: why was a British reporter there and not a Frenchman? He shook his head. It was a real puzzler.

Fleming was also familiar with Russia. He had been sent to Moscow as a journalist for Reuters early in the prior decade, and although he did not speak the language, he understood a lot more than he let on. Because he was considered a harmless dilettante, he was able to uncover information regarding trumped-up charges of espionage levied against several British Royal Engineers working in Russia at the time. His behind-the-scenes efforts helped free the men, and the one lesson he learned from all this was to never trust a Ruskie.

Fleming continued to read.

Rumors swirled at the time that Mata Hari had shared her favors with both General Simonette and the mysterious Russian who had sent him the telegram from Petrograd that night. It has been further suggested that Simonette had been anticipating the arrival of just such a telegram, and that it was really a secret command for him to act. Whatever the truth, Simonette apparently decided Mata Hari could not be allowed to live, and ordered her to be executed before dawn.

Fleming paused long enough to lift a steaming mug from a tea trolley a young WREN had parked next to his desk. Her uniform was rumpled and her hair unkempt, but her bubbly, enthusiastic smile and was contagious. She offered him a scone.

Fleming smiled back as he patted his concave stomach. To be eighteen again, he thought. "Mustn't get fat, you know."

She laughed, then blushed deeply. "Not you, sir!"

Fleming returned her good-natured laugh and waved her away. He began blowing into the mug and continued to read.

General Simonette retired in 1928 and nothing more was heard from him, that is, until he surfaced a few months ago in Lisbon. The now-elderly gentleman began making discreet inquiries regarding a particular convent in the small Spanish town of Tuy, which lies just across the Minho River from Valença. He said he was seeking refuge for a certain unnamed woman. Impossible, he was told. Unwilling to take no for an answer, General Simonette approached the Patriarch of Lisbon, Cardinal Cerejeira, to intervene, who in turn requested the approval of Pope Pius XII. At this point, one could reasonably be moved to ask: why would a Portuguese cardinal and the pope become involved in so simple a request, especially since the convent was situated on Spanish soil? There were two reasons actually, but I'm getting ahead of myself.

On August 13, 1940, a substantial sum of money was transferred from the Credit Lausanne Bank in Lausanne, Switzerland, into the Vatican Bank in Rome, and under cover of darkness on the night of August 16, an unknown middle-aged woman took up residence amongst the nuns at the convent in Tuy. No outsider had gotten as much as a glimpse of her.

Fleming found himself hooked. This secret agent's report was riveting, and he couldn't begin to guess at the ending.

Personally, I believe the story. I say this because my family is close to Cardinal Cerejeira, and when I made inquiries about the woman, he said it was something he could not discuss. However, he did suggest Portugal needed to show its solidarity with those patriotic forces opposing the Russian communists; a foe the Virgin of Fatima had repeatedly called the scourge of the earth. The cardinal then said the following, which I found odd. 'One day, with the help of the Virgin, I pray a Romanov will again rule over a Russia dedicated to Our Lady.'

Fleming drained his mug. He glanced about the room but the happy young naval rating and her tea trolley were long gone. Damn! He lit another cigarette and read on.

This past October seventh, a local doctor was summoned to the convent to treat a patient said to be suffering from stomach cramps and severe pains in both of her big toes. He diagnosed Hallux valgus, a condition that causes the joint at the base of the big toe to turn outward while the top of the toe turns inward. He noted that such a condition rarely affects both big toes in the same person and prescribed a sedative for pain and, if necessary, surgical intervention. He wrote he was not qualified to perform such an operation. In a footnote, he mentioned that he had treated another nun during the visit. Her name was Sister Lucia, the same person who as a young girl in Fatima had seen the Virgin Mary in multiple visions over several months. Sister Lucia was now suffering from recurring bouts of pleurisy, possibly even pneumonia, but he had found her to be a cheerful and non-complaining patient. Nonetheless, he was worried over her inability to get well, and voiced a frustration that he had no medicine to cure her.

Fleming turned to the last page.

I took it upon myself to look further into these matters so I began to gather information. A source in Lausanne asked if I could confirm the birthday of the mysterious woman with Hallux valgus in the convent at Tuy. I did. It was June 5, 1901. I was then asked if maybe her date of birth could have been June 26, 1899 instead. No, June 5, 1901 was correct. Which calendar was being referenced: Julian or Gregorian? Julian, I replied. All of which leads me to feel comfortable in pronouncing the identity of the mysterious woman at the convent in Tuy.

She is the Grand Duchess Anastasia Nickolaevena of Russia, and I come to this conclusion for the following reasons. One: Of all the czar's children, Anastasia alone suffered from Hallux valgus in both her great toes. Two: She had a history of stomach ailments. Three: She was born June 5, 1901.

For the record, it should be noted that when I reference dates regarding events in Russia before the revolution, I use the Julian calendar—the norm in Orthodox Russia at the time—rather than the

Ian A. O'Connor

Gregorian calendar which has been in favor with most of the rest of the world since 1582. There currently exists a disparity of thirteen days between the two; a gap which will widen with the passing of time. This means the Gregorian calendar would show Anastasia's birth date as being June 18, 1901, and not the fifth. Likewise, the West favors using the date for the storming of the Winter Palace as being November 7, 1917, whereas Russian history books record the date as October twenty-fifth.

The idea that this could be the enigmatic Anastasia electrified Fleming. "I'll be a monkey's uncle," he whispered under his breath. Rumors had circulated for years suggesting that one of the czar's four daughters had escaped the firing squad. Some had said it was Marie; others claimed it was her younger sister, Anastasia. However, it was the Anastasia story that had gained traction and finally stuck. Indeed, a movie had been released in 1928 about the missing Anastasia, and although it made for good entertainment, most people did not believe any of it, himself included. But now he wasn't so sure.

What could all of this possibly mean? He hadn't the foggiest. But a nagging thought told him that despite his full plate, he should find the time to corroborate what he had just read. He at least owed that much to a superbly competent British spy in Lisbon.

Just then, the red scrambler phone on Fleming's desk began to ring. A momentary look of aggravation flitted across his face but he kept his voice professional as he identified himself.

"Ah, Ian, Commodore Paisley here. Admiral Godfrey says you're to pop over to Number Ten Downing Street right away and bring with you the 'eyes only' file on Pilgrim's Progress."

Pilgrim's Progress! His proposed secret operation to have Hermann Göring assassinated. Anastasia was quickly forgotten as he rubbed his hands together in anticipatory glee. It looked like Churchill was about to sign off on Pilgrim's. Good show!

CHAPTER 2
Oxford. November 1940

The young Englishwoman kept repeating to herself, *Mrs. Margaret Rivera Smalling*. Even after one week of marriage, it still sounded so strange to her ears. She had secretly wanted to stay at home this Saturday and enjoy a quiet day with her husband, but something kept telling her history was about to be made in the laboratory.

Hurrying up the stairs to the second floor of the Sir William Dunn Research Building, she turned the corner on the landing and bumped into her boss, Dr. Howard Florey, who was thundering his way down. Florey instinctively grabbed her arm to steady them both.

"You trying to run me over, Margaret?" Florey asked in his strong South Australian accent.

"Not a bit of it, sir. I'm dreadfully sorry!"

Florey smiled at the most junior member of the team. "You really didn't need to come in today, you know, newlywed that you are, and all."

"I wouldn't have missed today for anything, Doctor Florey."

"Well, I'm glad you're here, young lady. When you get upstairs, tell Ernst I'll be back within a half hour and we can all get started."

Ernst, was Dr. Ernst Chain, a German-born biochemist and second in command of the tight-knit team of chemists and biologists. A brilliant scientist in his own right, Chain had been at Oxford with Florey since the mid-thirties, both working tirelessly on refining and experimenting with Alexander Fleming's miracle discovery called penicillin. Margaret still pinched herself whenever she thought about the final interview she had had with the two men, and the invitation to join them.

While Florey was regarded as something of a generalist—but one with a superb handle on what the others were doing—he had already started to experiment in limited fashion on small animals. However, the major reason for a recent slowing down with these experiments was the effort it took to grow even the infinitesimally small quantities of the penicillin mold they needed.

Ian A. O'Connor

It was Chain's job to purify the penicillin, a time-consuming and tedious task. Fellow team member Edward Abraham helped him enormously in this endeavor, while another threesome concentrated on determining how the strange penicillin mold reacted with other organisms. Margaret delighted daily in being included.

Today was the day they all had been waiting for. Margaret removed her mackintosh and slipped into a white cotton lab coat, going directly to the small room holding the mice. Sidling next to two cages, each holding four of the creatures, she bent down and studied them. They were lethargic and shivering, none showing the usual interest they exhibited in her presence when they followed her every move in anticipation of being fed. Not today. All were mortally ill. She felt a special twinge of sorrow for four. The eight had been given lethal doses of *staphylococci* bacteria the day before. She had injected them, but hoped that history was about to be made this weekend at Oxford, home to the oldest university in the English-speaking world.

The rest of the team crowded into the room. Chain opened the door to a small refrigerator humming noisily against the wall and took out a chilled, but not cold, metal kidney bowl holding four syringes, the collective value of whose contents was truly beyond measure. It had taken many weeks of painstaking work to grow enough of the milky substance which now filled each small syringe with fifty milligrams of the treasure mixed with sterile water.

As Florey plucked the four mice one–by–one from the first cage, Margaret expertly inserted the sterile needle's tip under the skin between two muscles, and allowed the thick, cool liquid to enter the shivering bodies. Each mouse involuntarily stiffened, seemed to let out a tiny gasp, but that was it. A small square of exposed skin on their backs was painted with the germicide merbromin in order to identify the rodent as having received a dose of the precious penicillin. Florey wanted to make sure no animal was injected twice.

Chain then opened up the second cage, home to the other four mice. This was the control group. Margaret injected each with the same volume of sterile saline instead of penicillin, then Chain daubed each unshaved creature with a small amount of the merbromin on its belly. "Don't want to leave a doubt in anyone's mind this germicide had any effect whatsoever on the outcome of the experiment." He closed the door, making sure the latch was secure.

"Now comes the hard part," Florey said, "the waiting." He turned to Margaret. "And you'll let us know right away of any change in the mice?"

"Yes, Doctor."

By afternoon, all rodents were non-responsive, the only sign of life being a rapid, but shallow, in-and-out movement of their flanks as they struggled to breathe. At seven o'clock Florey suggested stopping for the day.

"Cover the cages and leave them some water, Margaret. If any survive the night, it's water they'll be wanting, not food."

* * * * *

Margaret was the first back on Sunday morning. She held her breath as she approached the side-by-side cages. With her face pressed up against the mesh of the cage containing the control group, she stripped away the cover and counted aloud: "one, two, three and four." She felt her heart pounding, and her ears filling with the sound of coursing blood. All four were dead.

She turned to the second cage, removed its cover and let loose an involuntary gasp. *All were alive!* Not just alive, but thriving. One, sucking on a tube connected to a water reservoir outside the cage, managed to cast a wary eye in her direction but kept on drinking. His three companions were busy rooting around in the sawdust.

"Well, what's the verdict, Margaret?" Dr. Florey asked as he sidled up next to her. His face broke into a grin as he looked inside the first cage, then the other. "Well, well, maybe there's something to this penicillin after all," he said, tongue firmly in cheek.

Ten minutes later the room was filled with excited chatter. This was a happening of historical proportions; something much more than each had secretly hoped for. Ernst Chain opened the fridge and pulled out a bottle of champagne. "I've been saving this since Nineteen Thirty-eight," he announced, "because I knew it had to get good and chilled before drinking."

The happy scientists toasted themselves and the four living rodents. Then they toasted the four creatures who had given their all.

"I can't wait to give Alexander a ring," Florey said, "he'll be delighted."

Alexander, was Alexander Fleming, the Scot pharmacologist who had discovered penicillin in 1928. He had isolated the world's first antibiotic found in the common mold *Penicillium chrysogenum,* and it had taken twelve long years of travel from there to here.

A half hour later, Margaret busily prepared the cadavers for examination. She knew what she would find. However, much more interesting would be the results of the blood analysis of the four thriving mice.

CHAPTER 3
London. November 1940

Admiral Godfrey read *The Times* while Fleming dozed in the back seat of the staff car.

One day had passed since the meeting with Churchill at Number 10 Downing Street and the discussion of Pilgrim's Progress. They had been delayed getting in to see the PM because he was busy with some scientists. As the two men and one woman came out, Fleming's eyes fell upon the woman. Her face turned scarlet as she noticed him giving her the once-over.

You're the cheeky sod, Margaret Smalling thought, as she followed Dr. Florey and Dr. Chain into the foyer. But a dashing one, nonetheless, she found herself adding as she buttoned her coat. There was something chilling and electrifying at the same time about the man.

"Come in, you two," Churchill called out in a booming voice, "I can only spare a few minutes." Before they had a chance to sit, he began telling them about the group that had just left.

"They're from Oxford, doctors on the verge of creating a miracle drug they've named penicillin. The stuff was actually discovered by a Scotsman, Alexander Fleming, back in the late twenties…" Churchill paused mid-sentence and looked squarely at Fleming. "Any chance he's a relative of yours, Ian?"

"None, sir."

"Well, anyway, they've been working round-the-clock with this stuff since thirty-eight," Churchill continued, "and they're calling it a miracle drug because they have high hopes it will save countless numbers of our soldiers' lives one day fairly soon. Men dying from battle wounds, that kind of thing. They tell me they need to find a way to produce it by the pound and not just the ounce." He harrumphed, then added with a twinkle in his eye, "But there's one thing I know for a fact, and that is Dr. Florey has excellent taste in picking his female assistants. Did either of you happen to take a gander at Doctor Margaret Smalling as she left here? Lovely lady," he added with an impish grin.

Fleming stifled a laugh. Here was the PM carrying the weight of the world on his shoulders yet still able to take the time to admire a beautiful woman.

"All right, why are you here, John?"

"Pilgrim's Progress, Prime Minister," Godfrey replied.

Fleming then gave the PM his plan to assassinate Goring.

"I like the idea of getting rid of that fat poofter, and I particularly like the thoroughness of your planning, Ian. You definitely think things through, so let me do the same. I have other more pressing matters to deal with at the moment, but I promise I'll get back to you on this."

Both men knew of Churchill's other pressing matters. They were privy to a tightly guarded secret, one the PM had shared only with his closest advisors. Simply put, Churchill had grave misgivings as to England's ability to fend off an invasion by Germany; something his spies on the continent had assured him would take place in the spring. He had tried to come up with a plan of action to either thwart, or at least blunt, any frontal assault on the homeland. Fleming had made a special note of the concern he had seen etched into that bulldog-like face.

However, this day, both he and the admiral had been up to Bletchley Park, a magnificent baronial estate some fifty miles north of London now home to a formidable spy center, officially called The Government Code and Cipher School.

They had spent hours attending classified briefings on the latest information gleaned from the highly secret decoding of Axis message traffic using a captured German Wehrmacht ENIGMA machine, a complex mechanical device used to encrypt and decrypt secret messages. ULTRA was the codename the British had given to this top-secret code-breaking program. Already ULTRA was proving itself a tool of unimaginable value for deciphering the radio traffic from German High Command Headquarters to all army and air force units, as well as to its ships and submarines at sea. The small cadre of Allied mathematicians working on ULTRA was the best of the best, and although Fleming could understand less than one percent of what they were talking about when they tried to explain the mathematics behind their achievements, he certainly understood 100 percent of the information they were getting. He had looked over at the admiral more than once to gauge his feelings and could almost hear the man saying: "Thank God for those brave Polish resistance fighters who smuggled this remarkable machine off the continent and into our hands."

This particular day, he and Godfrey had been briefed on a troubling Nazi scientific undertaking regarding stepped-up activity at the Norsk Hydro Heavy Water Plant in Vemork, Tinn, Norway. Whatever the Germans were up to, it had something to do with an arm of physics neither man knew anything about, namely, the production of nuclear energy. Both knew that some nuclear theorists said it was possible to build an atomic bomb capable of blowing up the world, while others countered that the sustainable, controllable fusion of matter from the nucleus of an atom was not a reality, and to pursue such an undertaking would prove to be a giant waste of time and money.

Apparently, the Germans were thinking otherwise.

The meeting ended at dusk with Admiral Godfrey thanking everyone for their hard work and asking them to stick with it. "Because if the situation in the fjords would ever come to warrant intervention by the RAF and the Royal Navy, well, rest assured, the PM will order all measures necessary to put Jerry out of business."

Godfrey finished *The Times* article he was reading and turned to Fleming. "You awake, Ian?"

"I am now, sir," Fleming replied, then covered his mouth to stifle a yawn.

"What do you know of a Sister Lucia and her supposedly seeing multiple visions of the Holy Mother as a child in Portugal? In a village called Fatima, to be precise."

That last bit about Fatima made Fleming bolt upright. Hello! Why that's the name of the nun being treated by the Spanish doctor in the convent where Anastasia was rumored to be hiding.

Fleming answered with a question of his own. "Why do you ask, Admiral?"

"I ask, because of an article in today's *Times*. It seems the good sister has been given the last rites because she's gravely ill with pneumonia. It then goes on about three secrets she supposedly was told by the Virgin Mother, and how none have yet been revealed. Anyway, the piece wraps by saying Pope Pius the Twelfth has asked Catholics everywhere to pray for her. Personally, I always thought the miracle thing at Fatima was just so much rubbish, but there are millions who believe otherwise. They could be right, I suppose. Wouldn't be the first time I've been wrong."

Fleming sat in silence; eyes closed, mind racing. A picture was unfolding like a cinema film. He turned oblivious to his surroundings, totally engrossed in the images bouncing off his shuttered eyelids. Finally, he asked, "May I see that article?"

"I thought you'd nodded off again," Godfrey said as he passed the paper to Fleming.

Fleming read the short piece and came to a decision.

"Admiral, I think I might have just found the answer to the PM's dilemma regarding Jerry's planned invasion," he said in a matter-of-fact voice.

Godfrey paused, his pen held mid-air over a report he was editing and peered at Fleming in the dim light. *The answer to thwart the German invasion of England?* Now this should be interesting. "Go on. Tell me what you're thinking, young man."

Fleming told Godfrey of the packet he had received from a spy in Lisbon two days earlier, which spoke of the possibility that the Grand Duchess Anastasia was purported to be in the same Spanish convent as this Sister Lucia, of Fatima fame. Then he said what he had in mind. "I don't know if I buy the Anastasia thing; it just seems like a huge stretch to me, something like your feelings about the miracle at Fatima. Moreover, I didn't see anything of value in the fact this Sister Lucia happened to be in the same convent, but now I'm thinking; this could be a bloody godsend! I mean, it could be a message from God. Literally." He wished he could light up a cigarette, but he knew how much Godfrey detested the smell.

"Go on."

"Here's what I have in mind," Fleming continued, gathering a full head of steam. "What if we somehow got to this Sister Lucia and had her write down one of the secrets, one we would make up for her, of course, then find a way to get the message into Herr Hitler's hands?

And what if the message from the Virgin Mary said it was God's will for old Adolf to forget about invading England and attack Russia instead? That God wanted him to get rid of the bloody Bolsheviks once and for all?"

"Quite a tall order," replied a dubious Godfrey. "Why wouldn't Hitler spot it as an English ruse; one with Churchill's fingerprints all over it? Moreover, how do you propose getting to see this Lucia person in the first place? You can't simply go up and knock on the front door of her convent. Especially not if that Anastasia woman really is in residence as well. And before I forget to ask, just how did you come across all of this information?"

"From an asset we have in Lisbon; a female agent controlled by Commander Brosnan's group. Angus dumped her packet on my desk because his team was swamped with other matters. Said I should look at it. Glad I did!"

"So what would be your pretext to get someone in there?"

Fleming understood that it was time to get out of turbulent waters. He would jot down his ideas at home tonight and present them to the admiral in the morning.

* * * * *

At noon the next day, and after a thorough going over of the audacious proposal, Godfrey told Fleming to leave the report with him. He was impressed. Godfrey thought the plan was doable. Of course, the PM would have to sign off on this one, and fast, because time was of the essence. He mentioned he would be at Number 10 later in the afternoon and would find the right moment to present it to Churchill.

"Meanwhile, get that Lisbon agent's radio contact schedule from Angus," Godfrey said, "and have her controller ask just how difficult she thinks it would be for us to get a female physician into the convent under the guise of treating Sister Lucia. That's if the good nun doesn't die before we can get to her. And the bit where you say there should be some penicillin to give to the patient? That could be a non-starter, at least if we're to believe what the PM told us about its scarcity."

"Agreed," Fleming replied, "but our success hinges upon three factors, all of which must come together seamlessly. One: we must have the penicillin to save Sister Lucia; Two: finding a female physician we can trust to get into the convent and do what needs to be done; Three: finding the means of getting the forged letter into Hitler's hands and having him believe it's a mandate from on high." He let loose a dry, humorless laugh. "I know I can make it work."

The set of Fleming's jaw confirmed to Godfrey the man indeed had faith enough to spare in his God-given abilities to move any mountain. What Godfrey didn't know was that Fleming still hadn't figured out just how he was going to get the message to Hitler.

"I hope you're right."

Fleming merely nodded, his mind already miles away. What was it the agent in Lisbon had written in her report? Something had struck him as profound, but he couldn't remember what. Yet he knew it held the key to his success.

"On second, thought, Ian, I want you to come with me and tell this to Churchill yourself. I'd probably completely muck it up and leave out all the important details."

Fleming couldn't hide his elation. "Aye, aye, sir!

CHAPTER 4
London. November 1940. Evening, the same day

Godfrey signaled to Fleming to follow him into his office. The admiral tossed his briefcase and gas mask onto the desk and nodded for Fleming to shut the door.

"It's a go! The prime minister has signed off on your plan. There is no higher priority, and he promised you'll get everything you need, including penicillin and a female doctor. In fact, he wants you to go up to Oxford immediately and speak with a Dr. Florey." Godfrey handed a letter to Fleming. "It's from the PM. It tells whomever you present it to that they must comply with all of your requests, and they should consider such as coming from Churchill himself." Godfrey lowered his voice. "For God's sake, don't lose it. And remember this: you will destroy it at the end of your mission, understood?"

"Yes, sir."

"The PM said you'll be in for quite the surprise when you get to Oxford tomorrow morning. When I tried to press him, he just laughed."

All the air raid sirens in the city suddenly began to wail. The noise started as a low-pitched hum, and as the electrically driven turbines spun faster and faster, the noise turned into an ear-piercing shriek. The Luftwaffe was on its way.

"Blast it!" said an angry Godfrey. "I was supposed to be at Charing Cross at seven for supper with Anthony Eden. Instead, I'll have to stay downstairs until the all clear, which could be hours away. Damn the bloody Hun!" He looked Fleming in the eye and his face softened a tad. "One last thing. Mister Churchill was curious to know if you've come up with a name for your little caper?"

"Barbarossa," Fleming replied without hesitation. "I want to somehow weave that particular name into the letter from Lucia, and have it done such in such a way Hitler will think it was chosen in heaven. If he falls for our stunt, then we'll know we've been successful when we hear from our spies in Germany, or through the ULTRA team,

that *Barbarossa* is the code name Hitler has chosen for his plan to invade Russia."

"*Barbarossa*," Godfrey repeated, allowing the word to roll leisurely off his tongue. "I like it. You've named it after Frederick Barbarossa, the German warrior king from days of yore. I know Mister Churchill will heartily approve and I suspect Herr Hitler will, too." He held out his hand and smiled a most appreciative smile. "Good luck, Commander. That's a devilishly keen mind you have. I really think you should consider writing books."

Fleming shook the proffered hand. "I'll give that bit of advice some thought, sir," he said, then came to attention and smartly saluted the admiral, just as he had been taught to do years earlier at the Royal Military College at Sandhurst.

CHAPTER 5
Oxford. November 1940

The first person Margaret Smalling spotted as she entered Dr. Florey's office was the cheeky lieutenant commander from Number 10 Downing Street.

Florey said, "Commander Ian Fleming, may I introduce you to Doctor Margaret Rivera. Margaret, please meet Commander Ian Fleming."

"Smalling. It's Margaret Smalling. I've been married a fortnight, Commander."

Florey turned a deep shade of red. "Talk about a faux pas! I'm so sorry, Margaret."

She laughed and held a hand out to the commander. *God, he looks so smashing in that navy uniform!* "How do you do, sir?"

"Seeing as how we're going to be working together, please, call me Ian."

"And I'm Margaret." She then turned to Florey, a puzzled look crossing her face. "I don't understand, Doctor. Did you forget to tell me about working with the commander?"

Fleming answered for Florey. "No, Doctor Florey only just found out about it himself a couple of minutes ago." He smiled, and asked, "Did you grow up near London, Margaret?"

She shook her head. "I was born in Rio, but I've lived here in the UK for ages, and I'm a British subject."

"Rio, as in Brazil?"

"Is there any other?"

"Do you speak Portuguese?"

"Eu falo Português fluentemente, Comandante. E também falo Espanhol. I speak Portuguese fluently, Commander. I also speak Spanish."

"And you're a medical doctor?"

"Naõ, na verdade eu sou uma doutora em biologia. No, actually I'm a Ph.D. A biologist."

Fleming turned to Florey. "Why didn't you say so?"

"Say what?"

"That Margaret here speaks Portuguese. Spanish, too, if I understood her correctly."

"You never asked."

Fleming's smile was dazzling. "Touché," he managed as he snapped open his soft-sided eel skin briefcase and pulled out a slim folder stamped Top Secret. As he watched the beautiful Margaret Rivera Smalling settle into her chair, it suddenly dawned on him why the admiral had said Churchill knew he was in for a huge surprise. Seated beside him was his ticket into the convent in Tuy, Spain.

For the next twenty minutes, he told Florey and Margaret of his plan to convince Hitler to change his strategy and attack Russia and not England with the coming of spring. At the end he asked, "Any questions?"

"I can think of a hundred," Florey answered first, "but ninety-nine are quite unnecessary because you won't be getting any penicillin. Which means the rest of your proposed undertaking must fail before it starts."

Fleming turned to his right and, putting on that dazzling smile again, asked, "And you, Margaret? What's on your mind?"

Gone was the awe and excitement she had felt mere minutes ago. *He really is quite ruthless, isn't he? I wonder how many people he's killed? Dozens, probably.* She shuddered. *And he wants me to go inside this convent; treat the dying Sister Lucia of Fatima with penicillin, then put some truly evil thoughts into her head about seeing a vision from the Virgin Mary. And after all that I'm to steal some of her writing paper, envelopes, ink, and anything with her handwriting on it, and leave. I'm to rush back to England where this monster will have forgers make up a letter for Hitler who will think it was written by Sister Lucia, telling him God wants him to attack Russia instead of England. The man must be mad!*

"Margaret?"

Margaret jumped up and made a brushing motion on her skirt. "What you are asking of me, Commander Fleming, is to take advantage of a dying saint like Sister Lucia and I shall have no part of this. Good day, sir!" She turned to Florey. "I've got to get back to work." She started for the door.

"Stop. Is that your final answer?"

She stopped as commanded. "It is."

"Very well, you're under arrest, Doctor Smalling. What you have just been told is classified well above top secret, and there is no way I can allow you to walk out of here knowing what you now know."

"You can't be serious!"

Florey remained silent and seated, his eyes darting from one to the other.

"I've never been more serious in my life," Fleming said in a wintry voice. "And you will go to prison until the end of the war. You signed the Official Secrets Act when you came to work here at Oxford in nineteen thirty-nine. You don't get to choose which secrets you'll honor and which ones you won't. The world does not work that way."

A furious Margaret Smalling turned to face Florey. "Howard, you've got to tell this to the prime minister." It was the first time she had ever used Florey's given name.

Fleming reached into his uniform jacket's inner pocket. The movement caused Margaret to flinch. *He's reaching for a gun!*

Instead, Fleming's hand reappeared holding an envelope. He opened it and took out a sheet of paper.

"I know you speak Portuguese and Spanish, but can you read English, Doctor Smalling?" Fleming's tone was most reasonable.

"Of course I can read English," she snapped back.

"Then read this," he said, handing over the letter from Churchill.

She read it once then read it again. She looked at Florey, her face reflecting an equal mix of alarm and awe.

"Doctor Smalling, sit down…please," Fleming said.

Margaret Smalling slumped into her chair.

"Let me share another secret with the both of you. Mister Churchill does not believe England will be able to repulse the Germans when they invade us in the spring. An advance man has been spotted in London. His name is Wilhelm Morz. This Morz chap was seen operating in Czechoslovakia and Holland just before those countries fell to the Germans. We had him and we lost him, and we've been searching for him since June, so far without any luck. His presence in England has the PM very worried."

Both scientists hung on his every word.

"Come spring," Fleming continued, "Jerry will swarm ashore in the hundreds of thousands and England will be defeated because we have neither the resources nor the equipment with which to fight. We left everything on the beaches of Dunkirk. As you know, we were able to evacuate our army, but we did so at a price that was simply too great. England is now bankrupt, and the only reason we are able to keep on fighting is because King Leopold the Third of Belgium shipped us some four hundred million dollars worth of his bullion reserves to use just before the Germans invaded his country. It's stored in the vaults of the Bank of England; but once that's gone…well, who knows what will happen then."

"You're serious, aren't you?" Florey asked, his voice a whisper.

"Very. And that's the reason we have to make this plan work, because failure is simply not an option. We must get Adolf Hitler off our back, and the only way to do that is to have him turn on the Russians. That will buy us the time we desperately need to regroup."

"So what you're really saying is that for the greater good of mankind…"

"What I'm saying, Doctor Smalling," Fleming interrupted, "is we are engaged in a war where civilization itself is at stake. Because if the Nazis defeat us, the United States will not be far behind."

"Commander Fleming, I mentioned a few moments ago we don't have the penicillin you need, and that's true I'm afraid," Florey said. "We just don't have it."

"You're telling me you have none? *None at all?*" Fleming was incredulous. "Does Churchill know this?"

"Well, maybe not quite none at all," Florey replied, "but let's say not enough for your needs and for us to simultaneously continue with our experiments."

"Doctor Florey, if you don't give me every drop of penicillin, then come summer, you'll be conducting your experiments for your new masters in Berlin."

Florey shot a look at Margaret then back to Fleming. "Your point's well taken, sir." He sat up straighter, his face transformed into a study of resolve and fortitude.

"Then I can assume you're with me, Doctor Florey?"

"One hundred percent."

And you, Doctor Smalling?"

"Of course I'm with you and, please, it's still Margaret."

Florey, coughed as if to clear his throat, then said, "Commander Fleming, here are some facts I think you need to know about penicillin..."

Ian A. O'Connor

CHAPTER 6
London. November 1940

Admiral Godfrey, Ian and Margaret were seated in a small hut owned by the British Overseas Airways Corporation. The hut was on the banks of Poole Bay, west-southwest of Southampton. There was a slight drizzle, and the early morning sky was overcast. The S.23 Flying boat christened *Ceres* was bobbing lightly on its mooring, and Margaret could barely make out the two mechanics going over their last minute pre-flight checks on long-range fuel tanks and the four huge engines.

She was about to be off to Portugal. Margaret was dressed from her skin out in clothes from either Portugal or Spain, and inside the Spanish-made suitcase she was carrying, everything originated on the Iberian Peninsula. Everything that is, except for a plastic box containing the world's entire supply of penicillin packed in dry ice.

For five hectic days and nights, she had prepared for this mission. She had been assigned the code name *Fantasia* by Fleming, and when asked what it meant, he had smiled a most enigmatic smile and replied, "Absolutely nothing, my dear. I just like the sound of it." In reality, he had pinched it from a Disney film of the same name that had just been released to theatres in America. When she had asked for his code name in case she had to contact him, he had replied, *Goldeneye* and not *17F,* his official intelligence community identifier.

"Time to board, folks."

They all stood at the plane captain's command.

"Right, then, Margaret," Fleming said. "The embassy's protocol officer will meet you when you land. Sign in at the embassy, act like the secretary you're supposed to be, and Ambassador Gibbons will link you up with your contact. We'll have you back here four days from now. Good luck." He winked his approval, and she found herself glowing inside.

Admiral Godfrey gave her a chaste kiss on the cheek. "Thank you, Margaret, and Godspeed, my dear."

* * * * *

Five and a half hours later the flying boat touched down onto a light chop on the Tagus River estuary in neutral Lisbon. The aircraft had not encountered any Luftwaffe interceptors over the Atlantic, but if it had, the hope was the civilian BOAC markings would show the enemy that the flying boat was a non-military craft.

Margaret was the eighth of nine passengers to disembark. Once inside the small terminal on the floating dock, a rail-thin customs agent glanced at her Foreign Ministry diplomatic passport as he affixed an entry stamp, lingering for a long moment on her flattering photograph. The man drew a large X in chalk on the side of her bag, and waved her through the gate.

She watched an impeccably dressed man approach a woman who had deplaned before her, say something, but the woman shook her head. He touched the brim of his hat by way of an apology and looked around. His eyes fell on Margaret. He made his way to her side.

"Margaret Smalling, I presume?"

"Henry Morton Stanley?" she asked in a breezy reply.

"No, Stephen Morris, actually," he said with a confused look, then a second later his face broke into a wide, toothy grin. "I get it! A play on words. The ultimate laconic greeting Henry Stanley uttered when he met the supposedly lost David Livingstone for the first time on the shores of Lake Tanganyika. Good show!" He snapped his fingers in the direction of a young man dressed in chauffeur's livery and a driver's cap who was deep in conversation with a flirtatious young woman. "José, please get Miss Smalling's suitcase and put it in the boot." Stephen Morris then took her by the arm and guided her to a waiting car parked at the curb. A minute later José jumped in.

Morris chatted nonstop all the way back to the embassy. He told her how delightful life was in Lisbon considering how the rest of Europe was at war. Like everyone else on staff, except for the ambassador and the intelligence officer, Morris had been told Margaret Smalling was a crackerjack secretary-interpreter who would be joining them for a few days to translate some agricultural manuals from Portuguese into English regarding the country's cork production. He also knew she would maybe have to return for a follow-up visit in early December.

"I don't really know how much time I'll have to sightsee," she said brightly, craning her neck to take in the activity beyond the window. "I'll be in the field for a day or two inspecting some cork tree groves...so, we'll just have to wait and see." She turned and gave Stephen Morris a wonderful smile.

This girl's quite the looker, Morris thought as he helped her out of the car. Why, if I wasn't a married man with six children, I just jolly well might...

She stood and waited for José to retrieve her bag. He looked confused for a moment or two, then turned a deep crimson.

"Mister Morris, I left the lady's luggage back at the terminal," José said, panic in every word. "It was a mistake. Please tell the English lady I will go back and get it and I will deliver it to her room myself."

Margaret froze. Her bag had been left behind? Left with the world's entire supply of penicillin sitting on the pavement? *My God, this can't be happening to me!*

She jumped into the car. "Back to the terminal," she commanded in Portuguese.

"Miss Smalling, really, there's no..."

"Get in, Morris, I'm leaving."

"Miss..."

Her face was suffused with anger. *"Shut the damn door!"* She turned to a thoroughly startled José. "Drive me back to the terminal at once."

This pretty Englishwoman speaks Portuguese! José found first gear and the car lurched forward, leaving a confused Stephen Morris standing alone on the curb.

Margaret was out of the car before it came to a complete stop. Her eyes swept the curb for the suitcase, but after being gone more than forty minutes she really hadn't expected to see it. Her heart tumbled to her feet.

"No, no, I left it on the floor. I never carried it outside, Miss." José led her back into the terminal. The crowd of forty minutes earlier had thinned out considerably; now there were only a smattering of people gathered in twos and threes. Margaret frantically looked around. Oh,

God, I've ruined the plan before it even got started. I just know Commander Fleming will think this was deliberate on my part.

Then she spotted it! A uniformed customs officer and a middle-aged man in civilian clothes were hunched down, studying the case's ID tag. The civilian said something in a snappish voice as he flipped the suitcase onto its side. He began to insert a key into the lock.

"Stop!" Margaret called out in English. Her voice was loud enough to cause several heads to turn in her direction. She crossed the floor rapidly, on over to where the duo had now risen up to their full heights. "That's my suitcase, thank you very much." She reached out to take a hold of the handle.

The civilian stopped her with a hand held up as barrier to her own and stared down at her with gimlet eyes. He sported a monocle, the first time she had ever seen such a device. "No, this bag has been here for quite some time. No one has claimed it, so we are going to open it to see if we can discover who the owner might be, Fräulein."

He's German! Margaret pushed the man's hand aside. "I'm the rightful owner. That's my name on the tag."

"Ah, and how are we supposed to know this, hmm?"

She whipped out her diplomatic passport. "Because I say so, that's why. This bag is the property of the British Crown. Now step aside, sir." With an impatient wave of her hand, she beckoned José forward.

People had now gathered around, silently curious as to what was taking place between the German and the attractive young lady. The German looked angry, but kept his composure. He glared at her for a long moment, clicked his heels and bowed slightly. "Then I'm glad the suitcase has been reunited with its rightful owner. *Auf wiedersehen, Fräulein.* Until we meet again."

* * * * *

Lisbon, later that evening

Margaret met with Ambassador Gibbons at 7:30 p.m. Most of the locals had left for the day and the legation's British staffers were readying for dinnertime.

"I heard about the ruckus earlier," Gibbons said, after welcoming his visitor, "but I assume everything is as it should be with your personal effects?"

"Yes, thank you, sir."

Gibbons smiled and handed her a photograph. It was the man with the monocle, and it must have been snapped earlier that day because he was dressed in the same suit and tie. She gave Gibbons a querying look.

"His name is Franz Kittinger," Gibbons explained, "but we at the embassy have taken to calling him Willy. He's a German spy, but not a very good one, I'm afraid. Even the local children snicker behind his back, and when they see him on the street, they pantomime wearing a monocle, dropping it on the ground then grubbing about on hands and knees looking for the silly thing. Willy is quite harmless, I assure you, but he does serve his purposes for the Reich, I suppose."

Gibbons picked up a pipe, and as he was about to strike a match, waited a moment, then asked, "Do you mind?"

"Not at all, sir. My husband enjoys a pipe every now and then."

"Ah, I didn't know you're married, nothing about that in the report which arrived with you today." He puffed contentedly, allowing the sweet aroma of the tobacco to encircle his head. Noticing her quizzical look, he smiled, and explained. "The diplomatic pouch came on your flying boat, and in there was a briefing paper from Admiral Godfrey and Commander Fleming about you and your mission. Of course, it took me a couple of hours to translate. Everything these days must be in code in case the plane crashes and Jerry gets his hands on the pouch. Don't want those blighters knowing our secrets, what?"

"I didn't notice a courier among the passengers," Margaret said, remembering what she had seen in the pictures at the local cinema where sinister looking men traveled with briefcases chained to their wrists.

"You wouldn't have," Gibbons replied. "The pilot had the pouch, and its contents are disguised as technical flying manuals, so it's an aviation-related code. He's really a naval officer; actually, most of our BOAC flying boat captains are navy chaps. They manage to see and gather a lot of useful intelligence as they fly about the world, and no one's the wiser. Works well for Admiral Godfrey, I must say."

Margaret saw the brilliance in that arrangement.

Gibbons took the pipe from between his teeth and put it on the desk. "Anyway, I know a little bit about your mission and, of course, I will help in any way I can. My staff has been told you're here as a secretary and interpreter to help us translate some technical Portuguese agricultural manuals. And we made sure Willy was duly informed of your visit so that he can tell his masters you're nothing more than a new secretary."

Margaret moved restlessly in her chair, causing Gibbons to correctly interpret the body language, which said, *get to the point!*

"Right, well, here's the drill. Tomorrow morning you will meet with the local contact at seven o'clock sharp at a café, and she will take you to the convent in Tuy. It's about a four-hour drive, and your route will take you through the cork tree growing regions, so that's good. Did you know Portugal accounts for over fifty percent of the world's cork production?"

"I do now, sir," she replied in a voice that fairly screamed, *who cares?*

"Yes, well…" Gibbons let loose a nervous giggle, and continued. "The Mother Superior is expecting you at the convent to treat Sister Lucia. It seems the woman you will be meeting tomorrow smoothed your way with no less a personage than the Patriarch of Lisbon, Manuel Cardinal Gonçalves Cerejeira. He is what my American ambassador friend would call a heavyweight, so may I suggest that your deportment tomorrow reflects your awareness of his prestige. It will impress the Mother Superior. Of course, it doesn't hurt that she's also keen to be having a British doctor treat Sister Lucia." He looked directly at Margaret. "By the way, when did you get your medical degree? I ask, only because you look so young."

Margaret chose to ignore the question and answered with a request. "There's one thing I do need, and that is some fresh dry ice to protect the medicine I'm carrying."

"Yes, the admiral did mention dry ice in his communiqué, but that's not going to be a problem. There's lots of it here in Lisbon because refrigeration isn't widely available. Remarkable stuff. All of the city's best restaurants and hotels use it. Portugal's still a poor country, you know. Did you also know it's manufactured by having carbon dioxide go directly from a gas to a solid without passing through a liquid state?"

"So I've been told."

"Yes, of course you would know." The ambassador picked up his now-cold pipe and poked a thumb into the bowl. Blast it, this woman was making him act like a silly schoolboy! He gave her a weak smile. "Can you think of anything else?"

Margaret rose and smiled back. "No, sir, you've been most kind. I think I'll retire early. I plan to stay at the convent overnight because I want to see how my patient reacts to the medicine. Could be I might have to stay two nights; so if I'm not back on Wednesday, don't be alarmed. But if I'm not back by sundown on Thursday, then send someone to come looking for me." She held out her hand and added, "Anyone but Willy, that is.

CHAPTER 7
Tuy, Spain. November 1940

Margaret tried to make herself comfortable in the cramped back seat of the 1934 Traction Avant IICV Citroën sedan. Her companion introduced herself as Delores de Gama, then insisted Margaret use her middle name, Olivia. She was also not sure whether Olivia knew the true purpose of the visit to the ailing nun, Lucia.

They conversed easily, ping-ponging back and forth between Portuguese, Spanish and English, and within an hour found they were completing each other's sentences. Both laughed like schoolgirls, and before they knew it four hours had passed and they were leaving the town of Valença and crossing the Minho River on Gustave Eiffel's magnificent Tuy International Bridge.

They were in Spain.

A few minutes later, they drove up to the convent and got out.

"We'll be a while, Antonio," Olivia said, "so go enjoy your cigarettes; or maybe you'll want to take a walk, just don't wander too far. I'll be going back to Lisbon with you, and I want to be home before dark."

The women climbed the steps and Olivia pulled on a rope hanging to the right of an ancient oak door. A bell tolled somewhere within. They waited. No answer. Olivia checked her watch. 11:30. Too early for the noontime Angelus Prayers she thought, then yanked the rope again, this time with more vigor. Again, the bell sounded and they waited. Margaret put her case down.

The door finally opened and a diminutive figure in a nun's habit appeared at the threshold. As the nun led them into the convent, Margaret looked around, guessing little had changed since it had been built, probably sometime in the early eighteenth century. Walls which once wore a coat of whitewash were now a dingy gray and in desperate need of a fresh application. The several mismatched, rickety chairs lining the perimeter of the parlor were obviously charitable donations.

What would possess a woman to willingly abandon the world to live such an existence behind these walls? Margaret wondered. Could it simply be ascribed to an absolute love of God?

Before she could form an answer, the door opened, and an older nun entered. Spotting Olivia, the woman's features softened in recognition.

"Mother Superior, this is the English doctor I told you about. Her name is Doctor Margaret Smalling, and she speaks Spanish and Portuguese. I really believe she has been sent by God to help Sister Lucia."

The nun turned to face Margaret. She drew the Englishwoman's hand up to her lips and kissed the palm. "The sisters have prayed for a miracle. Our dear Lucia is very ill and she is now slipping in and out of consciousness. I do not think she has much time left."

As they made their way into the recesses of the dank and gloomy convent, Margaret heard a bell tolling, summoning the community to noontime prayers. Shadowy forms crowding close to the walls slipped by her, all bowing their heads in respect.

Up to the second floor the trio went, then down a hallway lined on both sides with doors leading into individual monastic cells. They stopped before the last one on the right, which was slightly ajar. Hanging on the wall beside the middle hinge was a small ceramic font holding a square of sponge soaked in holy water. Mother Superior dipped a finger into the font and, following a timeless ritual, blessed herself as she entered the cell. Margaret and Olivia did likewise.

A nun rose from the wooden floor where she had been kneeling, reciting the rosary over her friend. She bowed to her Mother Superior and retreated into the shadows.

"You may leave us, Sister Maria."

Margaret made her way to the bed and looked down at the fitfully sleeping figure. Sister Lucia looked as small as a child bundled under a mountain of blankets, her cropped head propped up on three pillows. The rasping sound that accompanied each intake of air was ominous, as was the low whistle that came with each exhalation. The nun was emaciated, either sleeping or unconscious. The end had to be near.

Margaret set her suitcase flat on the floor, opened it and took out a stethoscope.

While the two women raised Lucia, she wrapped her hands around the metal disk at the end of her instrument to warm it. She took several minutes listening to each lung, moving the stethoscope around the pitifully thin chest. Then she repeated the procedure from the back. Sounds like winter thunder rattled inside the fluid-filled lungs.

She took out a thermometer and slipped it under the patient's tongue. She picked up the right wrist, which was not much bigger than a twig, found a faint pulse, and began to count. 148 beats a minute. This is a body on the verge of collapse. Holding the thermometer close to the light from a vigil lamp, she read the results. 104.5 degrees. Sister Lucia's brain was beginning to cook.

Mother Superior and Olivia silently followed her every move. Margaret extracted a plastic box from her suitcase, which she placed on top of a small wooden desk.

"I need a bowl and some warm water to heat up my medicine. Not hot, but it must be warm."

Mother Superior nodded and left the room to do Margaret's bidding.

"What do you think?" Olivia whispered.

"It's bad," Margaret whispered back. "Sister Lucia has late-stage pneumonia and her body is burning up. She should be on a continuous intravenous drip to hydrate and nourish, and she should have been hospitalized days ago."

Olivia sighed, tears forming. "These good sisters are the poorest of the poor, and they live in an impoverished country. Hospitalization is a luxury far beyond their reach. And if it's God's will to call this nun home to be with Him in heaven, then they accept that with grace and dignity, and pray for the quick repose of her immortal soul."

"Well, I'm going to fight to keep her immortal soul out of heaven for a while," Margaret vowed in a determined whisper as she busied herself by readying the first dose of penicillin. She noted the shards of dry ice were disappearing. They would have to be replaced.

The Mother Superior returned with a shallow bowl and pitcher of warm water. Margaret filled the bowl, tested it with her finger, then inserted the sealed glass vial of penicillin. She saw herself now very much alone; an explorer venturing into uncharted territory. Since those first heady experiments on the eight mice, the team had injected several larger animals with the *pneumobacillus bacterium*, a non-motile, gram-negative bacterium known to cause a severe form of pneumonia. They had treated their four-legged patients with varying doses of the scarce miracle drug. Their studies had shown that the efficacy of the medicine was time-constrained. Eighty percent was flushed out of the bloodstream by the kidneys within four hours, and because of the drug's scarcity, they had collected the animals' urine, extracted the penicillin and injected it again into those stoic subjects.

That scenario was not going to be possible here, she realized. Florey and Chain had determined Sister Lucia would need an initial dose of 400,000 Florey units, a measurement the team had invented, the equivalent of two hundred and fifty milligrams. They had reached this conclusion based on what they had guessed might be Sister Lucia's body size and weight. The plan called for her to follow-up with a second similar dose six hours later; then twelve hours after that, she would inject the last dose of one hundred milligrams—and that would be it. There was no more. If this did not provide enough relief for Lucia's body to marshal an army of its own antibodies to attack the foreign invaders, then her patient would succumb. She shuddered at the thought.

She then went about preparing the injection, drawing the thickish liquid up into the barrel, making sure the solution was thoroughly mixed. Florey had wrestled with the idea of using an oil-based injection, but finally settled on sterile water only because he thought it would be easier for Margaret to transport. She tapped the side of the syringe with the nail on her middle finger then nodded to the others.

"Mother Superior, I'm going to inject this medicine deep into Sister Lucia's buttock." She stepped up to the bed. "Please turn sister over on her side."

When the unconscious nun was ready, Margaret swabbed the site with alcohol. Then she expertly inserted the needle into the upper, outer quadrant of the buttock. She took special care to make sure it sank deep between the muscles and away from any nerves.

"What should we do now?" the Mother Superior asked as she stroked Lucia's feverish forehead.

"We pray, Mother Superior, and hope God hears our prayers."

CHAPTER 8
Tuy, Spain. November 1940

Margaret peered at the luminous hands on her watch. Ten o'clock. The inside of the convent wasn't merely uncomfortable; it was downright cold. The community of sisters had retired to their individual cells and every so often she thought she could hear the faint sound of voices floating from somewhere within, voices she suspected were praying for Lucia. The Mother Superior had kept a long vigil—as had Olivia, until it was time for her to depart for Lisbon. She asked if there was a message Margaret wished to send to London.

"Yes, tell London Fantasia is OK and that I've started my work."

Ten o'clock. Two more hours until Lucia's third and final injection. The Mother Superior had made the cell next to Lucia's available, and she had lain down directly onto the bed's wooden slats because there was no mattress. She had been provided with two threadbare blankets, which she had finally placed beneath herself.

The Mother Superior had brought an extra candle into Lucia's cell around eight for some added light, along with a small quantity of dry ice. She assured Margaret she would return at midnight to help with the last injection.

Margaret went into the next cell and studied the sleeping face. Was that a hint of color creeping into the cheeks? She wasn't sure. However, Lucia's temperature had dropped to one hundred and one degrees, a good sign. And her breathing didn't seem quite as ragged as earlier. Three times in the last two hours, she had sponged Lucia's face and wrists with cold water, and had left a cold wet cloth on her forehead. Yet she still felt so helpless, and found herself praying for God to save this special woman.

Through it all, her mind would not let her forget the real purpose for her visit to this convent and the bedside of the dying Sister Lucia of Fatima. Much as she dreaded it, the time had come to act upon Commander Fleming's plan.

She put her mouth close to Lucia's ear. The nun had shown signs she was no longer unconscious, but had transitioned into a deep sleep.

Every so often, she would make small whimpering sounds and try to cough. Her eyes would flicker between open and closed, and she would suck hungrily at a clean cloth soaked in cold water. Margaret was elated. Water as much as penicillin would save the woman. She cleared her throat and began to whisper in her native Portuguese. Commander Fleming had carefully scripted every word, which she in turn had translated and committed to memory.

"Be not afraid, Lucia," she began in a low murmur, *"for neither I, nor my only begotten son, Jesus, has forsaken you. I explained to you many years ago that you would have to remain on earth long after Jesus took Francisco and Jacinta to be with Him in paradise. Your time is not yet at hand, my child, and Jesus has sent me to you with this special message. Listen well, and remember it, for what I am about to say is the will of God."*

Then she whispered the words Ian Fleming had painstakingly authored in the hope of saving England.

"There shall spring forth from the land of Barbarossa, a king who will be blessed in heaven. He will obey my son, Jesus, and banish forever from the earth the scourge which is the communist unbelievers of Russia. The day of destruction..."

Three times, she repeated Fleming's words into Lucia's ear, then stopped. Once, the patient actually stirred, opened her eyes and looked Margaret square in the face. She smiled, then immediately fell back to sleep.

Sister Lucia heard me, she understands!

Margaret failed to hear the door open or see the figure slipping into the room. She was once more back to whispering into Lucia's ear, repeating the same message when she noticed a shadow moving on the wall. She held her breath.

"Ave Maria, cheia de graca, o Senhor é convosco, bendita es vós entre as mulheres..." she began in a loud whisper in Spanish. "Hail, Mary, full of grace, the Lord is with thee, blessed art thou amongst women..."

Mother Superior slipped up beside Margaret, blessed herself and began to whisper along with the English doctor, "and blessed is the fruit of thy womb, Jesus..."

Oh, God, that was close!

Margaret gave Lucia the last injection without incident at midnight, and after she had cleaned the syringe and packed it away, the Mother Superior suggested she get some more sleep.

"I will stay, Doctor. You are exhausted. And thank you for praying the rosary into Sister Lucia's ear. I know that has made her happy."

* * * * *

When Margaret slipped back into Lucia's cell at a little before six, the Mother Superior rose slowly and grasped Margaret's hands in hers. "I've witnessed a miracle this night," she whispered. "You are truly a gift from God. Dear Lucia woke, recognized me, said hello, then fell back to sleep."

Margaret tiptoed to Lucia's bedside and felt her forehead. The raging furnace of just a few hours ago had been banked. Her skin temperature was near normal. And there was color in the cheeks. She got her thermometer and took Lucia's temperature. 99.3. Wonderful! She carefully listened to the lungs. No doubt about it, there was a marked improvement!

"Have you said anything about me to the rest of the community?" she asked the Mother Superior.

The nun shook her head.

"I should have mentioned this earlier, Mother Superior. The Vatican does not want this information getting into the newspapers, and I assured Cardinal Cerejeira that you would honor those wishes. So please, don't say anything about my being an English doctor to the other nuns; just say I'm a friend."

"I understand," the Mother Superior replied in a voice that suggested: what nun would dare disobey a cardinal much less the Holy Father?

"One last thing," Margaret said, nodding in the direction of the small desk. "I need to write down some instructions for Sister Lucia's continued treatment after I leave. Is there some paper and a pen, perhaps?"

Mother Superior opened the lone drawer and peered inside. She reached in and shuffled the contents. "Yes, there are some unused sheets and some envelopes left. I also see a pen and a small jar of ink.

Ian A. O'Connor

If you need more paper, I have some in my cell. We all share. There's a stationery shop in town, which donates what we need. Most of the sisters cannot write well, but Sister Lucia writes all the time, especially letters. So, yes, use whatever you need." She made the sign of the cross and left for the small chapel and morning prayers.

Alone once more with Lucia, Margaret again whispered her command into the woman's ear. As she was finishing the message for the second time, Lucia's eyes fluttered rapidly, and then opened fully. As she struggled to focus, she reached out as if wanting to take hold of Margaret's arm.

"Oh Senhora mais Preciosa, eu obedecerei a vontade de vosso Filho. Most Precious Lady, I will obey the will of your Son." The utterance seemed to exhaust her because she immediately slumped back and fell into a deep sleep.

I will obey the will of your Son! Lucia had understood! Margaret's heart raced as she digested the enormity of the words the nun had just spoken. It meant Prime Minister Churchill and Commander Fleming were on the verge of changing history!

"Sleep, my child," she cooed into Lucia's ear. She donned a pair of cotton gloves and opened the drawer. She placed the meager contents on the desktop, four pages filled with what she had to assume was Lucia's handwriting. But nothing was written in Lucia's native Portuguese! She looked at each page again. All were devotional prayers to Our Lady, and the grammar was far from perfect. It was as though Lucia was practicing her Spanish. Commander Fleming had naturally assumed all of Lucia's writing would be in Portuguese. So had she. But she couldn't dawdle any longer so she chose two pages which held the most writing. She then scooped up four blank sheets, folded the six pages inside a clean envelope and slipped it inside her brassiere.

Having these handwriting samples from Lucia was crucial to the mission's success. Fleming's forgers needed them to recreate the handwriting so perfectly that Lucia herself would insist it was her own. Next, she took a small square of absorbent cotton cloth and poured some of Lucia's ink into it, which Fleming would have analyzed and reproduced. She folded the stained square to protect her liquid treasure then tucked it down the side of her suitcase. Was there anything else? Anything she might have missed? She frowned, then jumped. *Oh my god!* Yes, there was one last thing.

She searched the case for a small box holding ten strips of sticky paper and two larger rectangles. She carried the box to the bed and freed Lucia's right hand. She pressed the strips one by one against the tips of Lucia's fingers and thumb, then repeated the process with the sticky rectangle held firmly against the palm of the hand. She took Lucia's left hand and went through the procedure again. This would enable Fleming to transfer Lucia's fingerprints to the sheets of writing paper back in London so that in the event the pages were scrutinized by the Germans, there would be no doubt as to their origin and who had written the message. She had to admire his thoroughness to detail. Commander Fleming was a genius!

Her timing was perfect, because just as she finished writing her detailed instructions for Mother Superior, a young novitiate appeared carrying a breakfast tray bearing a mug of steaming black tea and a thin slice of plain bread.

* * * * *

"Just follow the instructions, Mother Superior, and Sister Lucia should make a full recovery," Margaret was saying. "It's important she coughs up the mucous from her lungs. Have her spit into the jar with some water, just as I showed you. That way you can monitor the color of the sputum as well as the volume. I'm hoping it will rapidly begin to turn clear. Also, give her all the fluids she wants; this will help flush the poison from the lungs. Lastly, I suggest you start out feeding her warm water mixed with honey. Then you can reintroduce her to solid foods."

"I understand. Will you be coming back?" Tears glistened in her eyes.

That really depended on how well things went in London. "It's my intention to come back," she whispered, "because I might have to bring some more medicine. I pray Sister Lucia won't need it, but yes," she continued in a firmer voice, "my hope is to be back within a week; ten days at the latest. Olivia will let you know, Mother Superior."

"Go with God. We're forever in your debt."

Ian A. O'Connor

While Margaret waited for Olivia, she kept asking herself one last question. How was Commander Fleming going to get the message supposedly written by Sister Lucia into the hands of Adolf Hitler? And have the Führer believe it was the divine word of God!

CHAPTER 9
London. November 1940

*F*leming met her at the BOAC flying-boat anchorage at Poole.

"Welcome home, Margaret."

"It's good to be back. We had a bit of a scare fifty-five minutes ago when two German fighters swooped down on us southwest of Ireland, but when they saw we were a civilian aircraft they just waggled their wings and flew off."

Five minutes later, they were in the car heading for London.

"The PM is anxious to get *Barbarossa* into play," Fleming said, as he stared out the window at a marching column of Home Guard recruits, men in their fifties and sixties. "The Germans upped the ante a couple of nights ago by giving the city of Coventry a bad pasting. The entire downtown was firebombed, and the great cathedral is now nothing more than a burnt-out shell. Worst of all, they killed thousands of civilians. I've never seen Churchill so angry."

* * * * *

Fleming spent the entire day conducting the debriefing. When Margaret came to the part where she had whispered into Lucia's ear, he wanted to know everything. Did the nun move? Did she make faces? Did she make noises? He finally noticed that Margaret couldn't keep her eyes open.

"In case I get too busy in the next few days, let me say this now. Thank you. You are the only person in all of England who could have pulled it off. I'm not sure if your country will ever be able to recognize you properly, but history will prove that your efforts over these past two weeks were pivotal in allowing England to remain a free society."

Thank you, Ian. I appreciate the kind words." Both realized this was the first time she had called Fleming by his given name.

* * * * *

Fleming waited patiently while Szűrös Havel, a displaced Hungarian master forger, studied the two purloined pages of Lucia's handwriting. His head bobbed from side to side as if on a spring, and while he

Ian A. O'Connor

inspected the sheets, he hummed an off-key rendition of God Save the King. Finally, he put his jeweler's loupe down.

"This should not be difficult to copy. I speak and write Spanish fluently, so I suppose I could do the job, but you say you want something written in this woman's native tongue, which happens to be Portuguese? So why didn't you just get me something in Portuguese? That would have made the job much easier."

"Couldn't," Fleming replied. "Maybe I'll get something in the next day or two, but don't count on it."

Szűrös frowned, picked up his loupe and peered at both pages again. His nose began to twitch. He smelled cigarette smoke.

Fleming dug into his tunic pocket, took out an aluminum cigarette case filled with his special brand of Morland cigarettes and laid it on the desk along with his Zippo lighter. "Help yourself, old chap. Sorry for my bad manners."

Szűrös Havel puffed and studied; puffed and studied. A couple of minutes later he blew out a final stream of smoke and announced, "Then I'll do it myself, Commander Fleming. Get me a Portuguese book or magazine and I'll start practicing." His eyes fell to the cigarette box. He deftly plucked out another Moreland and lit it.

"I do believe I can do you one better," Fleming replied. "The fact is I have an agent who speaks and writes fluent Portuguese and Spanish. I can't believe I didn't think about using her until this moment. I'll have my woman stop by and introduce herself in the morning."

As Fleming made his way across town, heading toward some of the world's most accomplished currency forgers and ink specialists, a daunting question continued to plague him. How was he going to get his bogus letter into Hitler's hands?

CHAPTER 10
London. November 1940

Fleming bolted upright in bed, his heart pounding. He had just seen in a dream how he would get his letter placed squarely into Hitler's hands. Through the offices of the Holy Roman Catholic Church and his conduit would be none other than the Patriarch of Lisbon, Manuel Cardinal Gonçalves Cerejeira! Who was more staunch an anti-communist than the patriarch reigning over Fatima? He was bloody perfect! Not only was Cardinal Cerejeira close to the Portuguese dictator, António de Oliveira Salazar, but he had also cultivated contacts in all of Europe's capitals, including Berlin.

Fleming arrived at his office just as the last all clear sounded in the heart of London. The non-stop pounding by the Luftwaffe formations was taking a toll, especially on the East End. Whole neighborhoods had been reduced to rubble, and the population was in a constant state of fatigue.

The Admiralty, however, never closed, never slept. This was an around-the-clock operation simply because British and Commonwealth naval operations were being conducted twelve time zones away, deep in the waters of the Pacific and the South China Sea. And even though hostilities had not yet broken out between them and any Imperial Japanese Forces, Admiral Godfrey's agents still kept vigilant ears close to the ground.

Fleming took a steaming mug of tea back to his desk, lit his third Morland of the morning and rummaged through the desk for the original packet from the female agent in Lisbon that had started this whole show. Thanks to a photographic memory, he knew which page to turn to. He placed his finger on the exact line and began to read aloud.

"Unwilling to take no for an answer, General Simonette approached the Patriarch of Lisbon, Cardinal Cerejeira, to intervene, who in turn requested the approval of Pope Pius XII. At this point, one could reasonably be moved to ask: why would a Portuguese cardinal and the pope become involved in so simple a request, especially since the

convent was situated on Spanish soil? There were two reasons actually, but I'm getting ahead of myself."

"I indeed thank God you were getting ahead of yourself, Olivia," Fleming said to the shadows, "because that last sentence of yours somehow stayed in my mind and nagged me no end." He stubbed out the cigarette, skimmed for the next reference to Cerejeira and continued to read.

"I personally believe the story. I say this because my family is close to the cardinal, and when I made discreet inquiries about the woman, Cardinal Cerejeira said it was something he could not discuss in any detail. He did say that Portugal needed to show solidarity with those patriotic forces opposing the Russian communists, a foe the Virgin of Fatima had called the scourge of the earth. He then said the following, which I found odd. 'One day, with the help of the Virgin Mother, I pray a Romanov will again rule over a Russia dedicated to Our Lady.'"

There was no doubt where this cleric stood. The man hated the Russian Communists through and through. Now all he had to do was learn as much as he could about this Prince of the Church who would pave the way to Hitler's doorstep.

* * * * *

Lt. Commander Fleming heard the excitement in Szűrös Havel's voice over the phone line when he asked if he could spare a moment. Twenty-five minutes later, he was seated beside the Hungarian genius.

"What have you got, old chap?"

"A bloomin' miracle, that's what I've got!"

Fleming allowed a hint of a smile to show. "Easy there," he teased, "miracles are only found in my bailiwick, not yours."

"Tell me what this is, then?" Szűrös challenged, as he handed over a photo of a page crammed with writing. "In case you don't know it, that's Portuguese you're seeing, and it's the handwriting of none other than Sister Lucia!"

Fleming said, "Good work. I couldn't tell it from an original."

"You're not listening to me, Guv'nor," the forger replied testily. "Get the wax out of your ears. I'm trying to tell you this is the woman's writing. Not mine. Hers! *The genuine ticket!"*

That got Fleming's attention. "But how's that possible?"

"You can thank that woman who brought back the paper samples from the convent, that's how."

Szűrös slid a piece of paper in front of Fleming, shielded inside a clear plastic sleeve. The page was blank.

Fleming gave the man a quizzical look.

"Now for my miracle," Szűrös said, as he slid the page under a black light. Suddenly, under the soft purple glow, the paper turned from a blank sheet to one filled with writing; faint writing to be sure, but definitely legible. In addition, the surface seemed to have taken on a mottled look.

Fleming peered closely. "Your loupe, Szűrös." With the ten-power loupe held firmly up against his right eye, Fleming slowly covered every inch of the page.

Szűrös' eyes crinkled in pleasure. "You've already figured it out, haven't you?"

"Yes," Fleming replied, "but my hat's off to you all the same. That was brilliant of you to look for impressions on a blank piece of paper. And then coax out an optimum image. Congratulations."

"Thank you, sir. By the way, would you happen to have a spare cig?"

Szűrös lit up and sat back, thoroughly contented to have nicotine once again course through his body. "More than enough here to write a letter the good sister herself would swear on her mother's grave was her own. All I need now is to practice."

Fleming stood, dropped half a dozen cigarettes on the table and held out his hand. "Thank you, Szűrös. You'll never know just what a great job you've done today."

"Ah, it was nothing," Szűrös replied, his face reddening in embarrassed pleasure. "You have a natural gift for this line of work. Not many do. England should be damn glad you weren't born a bloody Kraut."

* * * * *

When Fleming returned to his office, he found an envelope on his desk. Someone had written his name across the front in red ink, then in the lower corner had added three bold, block letters. I. I. D. This would be the special report he had ordered on the Patriarch of Lisbon from the Iberia Intelligence Desk at MI6. He had been told it would take six to eight weeks for such a low priority report to get back to him, but when the bureaucratic bearer of those bad tidings was shown a copy of Churchill's letter, that timeframe immediately plummeted to four hours.

Fleming began to read the terse narrative.

Manuel Cardinal Cerejeira: born 29 November 1888; ordained in 1911; elevated to bishop in 1928, and to cardinal in a consistory one year later together with his longtime friend Eugenio Giovanni Pacelli. Cerejeira's investiture as the Patriarch of Lisbon came concurrently with his receiving the red biretta from Pope Pius XI. Ten years later Cerejeira participated in the conclave which elected Pope Pius XII— his friend Eugenio Pacelli.

Three items vied for Fleming's attention. One, Cerejeira had a birthday coming up soon. Two; he was only forty-one when the pope had elevated him to cardinal. Three, his college roommate had been one António de Oliveira Salazar, the same man who was now the dictator of Portugal.

The report ended with an explanation of how the cardinal was in favor of authoritarian rule but seemed to appreciate the Italian model of fascism over the German one. Yet in spite of this, he continued to cast a wary and jaundiced eye toward Spain and Franco's regime.

Fleming had found his man.

* * * * *

Margaret was summoned back to London by no less a personage than Winston Churchill who wanted a firsthand accounting of her trip to Tuy. She went to Number 10, accompanied by the admiral and Fleming.

"I've heard nothing but good things about you from these two men, young lady," the PM began. "I'm told you'll be making a return trip to Lisbon soon, and I just wanted to pass along my personal thanks."

A return trip? This was news to her. She looked at Fleming. He caught her eye and made an almost imperceptible shake of his head.

"Will Sister Lucia live long enough for our purposes?" Churchill was asking.

Margaret told herself to concentrate on what the PM was saying. "Yes, sir, I believe she will. However, I can say unequivocally she would have died without the penicillin."

"Well, your next trip will be even more important, Margaret," Churchill was saying, "because all will be for naught if we fail to get our message into Hitler's hands before the end of year." The dark cloud that covered his face as he spoke his ominous words suddenly disappeared, only to be replaced with a beaming smile. "But these two fine officers assure me the plan is foolproof." He paused a moment before speaking to Margaret again. "One last thing. When you go back to the convent, I would like you to ask the Mother Superior about a certain woman who has supposedly taken up residence there, a woman we have been told is none other than the Grand Duchess Anastasia of Russia," Churchill said.

Margaret Smalling's eyes widened at the news. What was this all about? Anastasia? Was this entire phony letter thing with Sister Lucia and Hitler nothing more than a ruse to get to Anastasia? Was she really being used for a completely different purpose? Were these men playing her for a fool? The world collapsed on top of her.

Churchill read her face perfectly. "My dear, anything you would discover about Anastasia would be secondary to your mission. I want you to use your best judgment. We have it on good authority the Vatican and Cardinal Cerejeira were persuaded to make her presence there possible. However, if you do not find the right moment to make an inquiry, then don't. Your mission with Sister Lucia is the only thing I really care about. Clear?"

Churchill then gave Margaret a succinct summary of Anastasia's medical history, impressing Fleming with what he had retained about the woman's ailments. "I mention this only in case you should happen to see her. This way you won't be blindsided. You can safely look, touch, tut-tut and frown appropriately as you give her a cursory medical examination. You can end by assuring the patient her condition is not life-threatening and, from what I understand of her ailments, you won't be lying."

"Yes, sir."

"Splendid. Then I'll see you when you get back. Good luck, my dear."

* * * * *

Ian Fleming and Margaret Smalling had sequestered themselves inside the admiral's office. The door was locked and a sign hanging from the handle read: Do Not Disturb. Ring the Telephone in Case of an Emergency.

It took three hours to perfect the message for Hitler. The words had to mimic Sister Lucia's in both style and context even though the message was purportedly coming from the Virgin Mary. They now knew from a close study of Lucia's writings that the nun was prone to errors in grammar and punctuation, so it became Margaret's job to intersperse several small mistakes into the wording.

Darkness had long overtaken the city when Fleming looked at his watch. 8:00 p.m. He felt too keyed up with excitement and not anxious to return to his flat. "How about I buy you dinner, Margaret, and you can tell me about growing up in sunny Rio!"

* * * * *

Margaret accompanied Fleming on his visit to Szűrös Havel. Szűrös had fastidiously copied her work through several drafts until he could produce an exact replica of Lucia's handwriting. He now felt ready to tackle the real thing.

"Leave me some cigs, would you, Commander? I'll be able to better concentrate, that's a promise, mate."

Fleming shook his head. "There'll be no smoking anywhere near that letter, Szűrös, and I mean it. Admiral Wilhelm Canaris will soon have his Nazi intelligence experts poring over it with microscopes and chemicals, and if they find even so much as a trace of cigarette smoke on the paper, well, the jig will be up. Jerry knows that nuns don't smoke!"

Szűrös Havel shook his head in wonderment. Who but Commander Fleming would have thought about such an insignificant, but crucial detail? "You're absolutely right, of course. In fact, I'll scrub my hands and brush my teeth so as to not even breathe on the paper…better yet, I'll put on a surgical mask when I slip into my cotton gloves to make sure none of my fingerprints get on it."

* * * * *

Two hours later Margaret and Fleming returned to Havel's cramped kingdom. Upon inspecting the finished product under the loupe, Fleming declared it a masterpiece. Szűrös had also prepared an envelope addressed in Portuguese to *Sr. Adolf Hitler, Chanceler de Germany*. Fleming again thanked Szűrös for his fine work and left him an unopened box of Morland's.

Their next stop would be for a visit with the experts who would transfer Lucia's fingerprints and palm prints to both letter and envelope. As they hurried up the street, Margaret noted how Fleming was heeding his own advice. There wasn't a hint of cigarette aroma on his person or his clothes.

* * * * *

Later that night, Szűrös Havel returned to his flat in the heavily bombed section of East London and wrote down in a Yiddish dialect everything he could remember about his forged letter and a chronology of the history of events with Commander Fleming. It was a dialect that had been out of vogue for more than half a century, but still written and spoken by a tight-knit community of Jews in his native Budapest and a smattering of small villages in Switzerland, Russia and the Balkans. The task took him the better part of an hour. Then he penned from memory an exact copy of his forged Portuguese letter, and when finished, slipped all the pages inside an ancient prayer book and retired for the night.

CHAPTER 11
Lisbon. November-December 1940

The day was November 30, 1940, and this time Margaret was escorted to Poole Bay by Fleming alone. In the dead of night, Churchill had dispatched Admiral Godfrey on a clandestine assignment to Canada.

"This should pretty well be a repeat of your last visit," Fleming said as they sat huddled together in the BOAC shed. "The embassy staff thinks you're returning to clear up some odds and ends. Of course, Olivia will escort you to the convent as before, and the Mother Superior has been told it's simply a follow-up visit for you to check on your patient. All indications are that Lucia is recovering nicely." As he spoke, he handed her the sealed envelope in its plastic sleeve. "As soon as you get to the embassy, have the ambassador put it in his safe. When you return to Lisbon from the convent, that's when you'll deliver it to Cardinal Cerejeira. Olivia will set up that meeting as well." Had he forgotten anything?

"What about the Russian woman?" Margaret asked in a low voice, deliberately not using Anastasia's given name.

"If you can't get the Mother Superior to say anything about her, then don't press the issue. I don't want any alarms going off in her head; it's just not that important."

The flight was called and she held out a hand to Fleming. He ignored it and boldly kissed her on the cheek, just as Admiral Godfrey had done two weeks earlier.

* * * * *

The flight was uneventful. Indeed, Margaret had managed to doze off for fifty minutes, lulled to sleep by the throaty drone of the four Bristol Pegasus engines. She had some warm tea and soggy toast upon awakening, then spent the rest of the flight reading a Spanish printing of the year's bestseller, *How Green Was My Valley* by Richard Llewellyn.

She cleared Portuguese customs with a wave of her diplomatic passport and little fanfare. José was there to greet her and, after tipping his hat, latched onto her bag with both hands. "I learned my lesson last time, Miss," he managed in hesitant English.

Margaret led the way out of the terminal, trying not to look obvious as she nonchalantly glanced around for any sign of Willy. The German spy was nowhere to be seen.

At the embassy, she had the ambassador put the letter in the safe. As with the last visit, she would meet Olivia at seven sharp the next morning outside the same café and drive to Tuy. She had no penicillin this time, but she was carrying two doses of injectable multi-vitamins for the now-recovering Sister Lucia.

It was Fleming who had decided she make this follow-up visit, a necessary pretext to validate the reason for her handing over the letter from Lucia to Cardinal Cerejeira, and for him to forward it to Berlin. Fleming's plan called for the cardinal to be told the letter was, in fact, the brainchild of British intelligence and not from Lucia, but that a consequence of its delivery to Hitler would be the defeat of the Virgin Mary's mortal enemy, the Russian communists.

Margaret found herself agreeing the end here justified the means, and understood that Fleming felt confident Cerejeira was the right man for the job. She, however, harbored some serious misgivings.

* * * * *

Seven o'clock came and went. No Olivia. Then seven-thirty and eight o'clock, and still no sign of Olivia. What should she do? No one had thought of a contingency plan for such a possibility because this was neutral Lisbon, not occupied Paris. No Gestapo agents skulked in the shadows, men in long black leather coats with dark fedoras pulled menacingly over hidden brows.

Margaret realized she could not wait any longer. She hailed a taxi and directed the driver to take her to the British Embassy.

"My contact didn't show," were the first words out of her mouth to the ambassador. "Can you find out if she left a message for me with the switchboard?"

Gibbons picked up his phone and spoke to the operator. He stated his request and listened to the reply. He looked at Margaret and shook his head.

"I have a bad feeling about this, Mister Ambassador. Something has happened to Olivia. Maybe Willy is involved."

"Willy has proven to be nothing more than a petty nuisance in the past, so I'm disinclined to add nefarious conduct to his list of shortcomings. At least not yet."

"I need to contact London," Margaret said, taking a fountain pen and small spiral notepad from her purse. She began to write rapidly. Finished, she tore out the page and handed it to Gibbons. *Fantasia to Goldeneye. Pomba do Branco a no-show. Need instructions.* Below the cryptic message was the shortwave frequency to contact Room Thirty-nine in London.

"I'm hoping we'll get a reply within the hour. Commander Fleming is capable of making quick decisions."

The answer came fifty-five minutes later.

Goldeneye to Fantasia. Go to appointment tomorrow, December 2. Use embassy car and driver. Follow through with conduit as planned. No reply necessary.

If Ambassador Gibbons was curious as to the nature of Margaret's mission, he kept his interest in check. "I'll make sure the car is properly serviced and I'll alert José to prepare for a long day tomorrow."

* * * * *

Margaret was on the road by seven o'clock, seated beside José. The morning sun had turned the dewdrops on the lush green fields into acres of shimmering diamonds. She took note of the many shepherd children moving their flocks of sheep and goats from one pasture to another, a replaying of events unchanged in a thousand years. This had been Lucia's life as a young girl in Fatima, she thought, before her provincial world forever changed in 1917.

At eleven thirty, they pulled up to the front door of the convent.

With her small bag in hand, she waited for someone to answer the door. When it opened, she recognized the same novitiate from the last visit. She smiled.

"What an unexpected surprise," Mother Superior said as she took Margaret's hand five minutes later. I was expecting you and Olivia yesterday." She looked over Margaret's shoulder.

"Olivia fell ill, Mother Superior, and we had no way of getting a message to you yesterday."

"Nothing serious, I hope?"

"I hope not, too," was the most honest reply she could think of spontaneously. She changed the subject. "How's my patient?"

"Sister Lucia is doing remarkably well. She often asks me about the doctor who saved her life with some special medicine, and she believes it was a gift from God. But then, so do I."

Margaret followed the older woman up to the second floor and down the familiar dingy corridor to Lucia's cell. The door was slightly ajar.

"Sister Lucia, I have a special visitor, someone you've been wanting to meet."

Lucia was seated at her desk, but instead of being dressed in her nun's habit, she wore a simple cotton nightgown and a threadbare blanket covered her shoulders. Her only other comfort was a pair of thin socks to keep her tiny feet warm. Margaret's heart ached at the sight.

Lucia's eyes fell upon Margaret. She put down the pen she was holding and slowly rose. Her smile spoke volumes.

Margaret gathered the woman in her arms. She could feel the bones in the nun's back and shoulders as she held Lucia close. This woman can't weigh much over five stone, she thought, trying not to show the alarm she felt. She's as frail as a sparrow.

"I have prayed to the Virgin Mary every day I would get the chance to say thank you. Now my prayers have been answered." Sister Lucia lowered her eyes.

"I'm honored to have been able to help, Sister Lucia," Margaret replied. "How do you feel? Is your breathing any easier? Are you trying to eat?"

"Oh, yes, I'm eating more and my breathing is a lot better. But I do get tired."

Margaret got out her stethoscope and listened to Lucia's lungs front and back. She heard some rattling and wheezing, enough to make her wish she had more penicillin to give the still-sick nun. "You sound a lot better," she announced brightly. "However, I still want you to rest as much as possible for the next month, at the very least. Take small walks up and down the corridor a couple of times a day, but don't tire yourself out. And continue to cough up all the bad stuff in your lungs."

Margaret prepared the syringe of vitamins. "This injection will help you get better. It's more good English medicine."

After the injection, Margaret suggested Lucia return to her bed. The nun picked up a sheet of paper she had been working on and allowed Margaret to tuck her in.

"I'm going to leave you two alone so you can visit," Mother Superior said, then slipped out.

"This is a letter I've just written to the Holy Father," Lucia said. "It's something that has been on my mind for a while, but I had to get the words right. Would you please look and tell me if it reads properly? Sometimes my grammar and punctuation is not the best."

Margaret took the single page of lined paper and quickly read the several paragraphs, her eyes lingering on a sentence towards the bottom of the page.

Most Holy Father, Our Lord promises a special protection to our country in this war, due to the consecration of the nation, by the Portuguese prelates, to the Immaculate Heart of Mary; as proof of the graces that would have been granted to other nations, had they also consecrated themselves to her.

Tuy-12-2-1940

"I wouldn't recommend changing a thing. Thank you for sharing it with me." She glanced toward the desk and spotted an envelope addressed to Pope Pius XII. Already the germ of a plan began forming in her mind. She picked up the envelope and handed it to Lucia. "I will be meeting with Cardinal Cerejeira on another matter later this evening," she said, hoping her voice sounded matter-of-fact. "I'd be happy to give him your letter to forward to Rome."

Margaret could barely hide her excitement! This would be the perfect excuse to see the cardinal; far better than the one Commander Fleming had suggested which would have had the Cardinal know the letter from Lucia to Hitler was nothing more than a hoax created in England. This, though, was truly a godsend! She could now hand the cardinal two letters at the same time, and he would have no reason to doubt they were both coming from Lucia. She deliberately controlled her breathing. This was a miracle to rival any other, she allowed, realizing such thoughts bordered on the sacrilegious.

"You are most kind," Lucia said, then placed her letter inside the envelope and licked the flap shut. She handed it to Margaret who immediately placed it in her bag before Lucia could change her mind.

Margaret raised the small hand to her lips and kissed it. The two said their goodbyes, and the tears flowed freely.

The Mother Superior was waiting for her in the hall. "Before you go back to Lisbon, Doctor, could you spare a minute and take a look at another patient?"

Margaret was instantly alert, noting that the Mother Superior had not said another nun, another sister, but had used the word patient. This could be dicey, she thought, because she really knew nothing of illnesses and their treatments. She would have to be careful. "What seems to be wrong?"

"She suffers from stomach cramps and pains in her feet," the nun replied. "She saw a doctor a while ago, but I'm still worried. I would appreciate it if you could put her mind at ease. She knows little Portuguese or Spanish, but she does speak English."

The nun led the way along an overgrown path to a small grotto at the edge of the property where a woman was seated, reading from what appeared to be a breviary. Margaret immediately noticed that she was wearing a dark, ankle-length formless dress and not a nun's habit.

The woman rose, and as she did, Margaret saw her wince.

"Please, stay seated," she said holding out her hand. "I'm Margaret Smalling, an English doctor."

The woman enfolded the proffered hand into her own, before smothering it with her other hand. She held on tightly as they both lowered themselves onto the bench. "It's been so long since I've heard English! I thought I had forgotten the words."

"Where did you learn English?" Margaret asked, keeping her tone conversational and casual. "Your command of the language is excellent."

"Many years ago," the woman replied, "in Russia, where I was born."

My God, this is Anastasia! Margaret remained calm as she slowly withdrew her hand and studied the face before her. The woman appeared to be in her late thirties, early forties—her features fine, even slightly pinched. She was woefully thin, but her eyes were a wondrous shade of blue. "What is your name?" she asked.

The woman hesitated for a fraction of a second. "Catherine. I was named after two of my grandmothers from long ago. I also named my only child Catherine, but she died shortly after she was born." As she said this, she crossed herself from right to left in the Orthodox fashion.

The small lie about her true name was not untoward, Margaret had to admit. She really had not expected to hear the woman announce she was Anastasia, Grand Duchess of Russia. "Well, Catherine, Mother Superior tells me you've been having stomach cramps and some problems with your feet."

"My toes, yes, but I know that will not be cured other than with an operation. The pain comes and goes, but it does make walking difficult."

"And the stomach?"

Catherine shrugged. "Like my toes, it, too, hurts, sometimes very much. But I have had these problems since as far back as I can remember. It seems to be the will of God that I must suffer."

The resignation Margaret heard in the voice was real. "Is there anything you took in the past that stopped the stomach pains?"

"Milk," was the immediate reply, "but the good sisters are too poor to get much milk." Catherine smiled at Margaret. "Please don't say anything to Mother Superior about milk. That will only cause her to worry even more about me."

"I promise," Margaret replied. "Is there anything I can get or do to make you more comfortable?"

Catherine shook her head. "No, child. My ailments will not kill me, and one day after I leave this sanctuary I might find a cure. But until that day comes, I say my prayers and read my holy book." She held up the small, leather bound volume with faded Cyrillic script on the cover.

"Is that written in Russian?"

"Yes. My parents gave me this in remembrance of my first communion and Christmation—the sacrament you Roman Catholics call confirmation—and I have carried it with me ever since I learned to read. It brings me comfort." Catherine patted the cover, the gesture implying she didn't want to continue talking about it.

Margaret took hold of Catherine's hands and as she did, noted a too-large gold signet ring encircling the middle finger of the left hand. How odd, she thought. Obviously, the ring had once belonged to a man. "I hope one day soon you will be able to return to your home." What else could she say, knowing this daughter of Czar Nicholas II would never again see Russia.

"Thank you for visiting with me." Catherine withdrew her hands, and looked Margaret in the eye. "Every day I pray for the English to defeat the Germans. I know it will happen, because you have a good king and a good prime minister. God will not fail you."

* * * * *

Back at the embassy, she inquired if there was any news from either Olivia or London. There was none.

She initiated a call to Cardinal Cerejeira through the embassy's switchboard so that the patriarch would know she was not some foreign crank seeking an audience.

Cardinal Cerejeira graciously agreed to meet, his curiosity palpable when told she was carrying two letters from Sister Lucia at the convent in Tuy.

* * * * *

It was now eight o'clock. The streets of Lisbon were dark and wet, and even though the rain had stopped an hour earlier, there were no pedestrians about. The taxi driver had let her off by mistake on the south side of the cathedral, instead of the entrance to the cardinal's residence. She drew her purse protectively to her side, noting the street lamps were few and far apart. From out of nowhere, a pair of hands grabbed her coat and roughly yanked her into the shadows. The attacker slammed her against the rough stone façade of the Sé de Lisboa Cathedral.

"I told you we would meet again, Fräulein." The breath reeked of stale beer.

Willy, the German spy!

Ian A. O'Connor

"What do you want?" she stammered, only to be struck with an open hand on the side of her face.

"Shut up. If you so much as make a sound I'll slit your throat." This man was not the buffoon so easily dismissed by the ambassador. "We wait for my car, then you will tell me why you went to visit that Russian woman in the convent. And you will tell me what you two spoke about."

He knows about Anastasia, but not about Lucia! Thank God. "I will tell you nothing, you pig," she said, with a newfound adrenaline-induced courage. Then she spat in his face. An infuriated Willy grabbed a handful of hair and jerked her head back; with his other hand, he brought a stiletto's blade up to her throat.

This Nazi is going to slash my throat and leave me to die in the gutter!

"Franz!" The word rang out crisp and clear, like a rifle shot. "This is Dieter! Put that damn knife down. We want her alive you fool."

"Who's there? Who are you?" Willy called out in a low voice. "Show yourself. I don't know any Dieter."

"You do now." A man emerged from the shadows holding a German Walther PPK .380 outfitted with a custom British silencer. He took aim and shot Willy between the eyes. Willy was dead before surprise or shock could register on his face. His monocle sailed off into the night as his legs buckled, and his lifeless body crumpled to the pavement.

God in heaven, this can't be happening to me!

"Margaret, are you all right?"

Commander Fleming! She began to shake uncontrollably.

Fleming's gun disappeared inside his jacket, then he reached out and folded her into his arms. "It's OK. He's dead, Margaret," her protector whispered, while gently patting her back. "Willy can't hurt you."

She clung tightly to Fleming for several seconds, taking deep breaths, allowing herself time to relax, to regain her composure. She was safe. But how was it possible?

Fleming brushed strands of hair away from her face. "Margaret, there's no time for explanations, but I followed you here. Now gather yourself together, and go see the cardinal. You're so close to the end and you've got to finish the job. Churchill's counting on you; I'm counting on you; England's counting on you." He realized he was pouring it on, but he also felt it necessary. He couldn't afford to have her collapse; not this close to the finish line.

"Wh...wha...what...about...him?" she stammered, pointing at the dead Willy.

"I'll take care of him. Now go. I'll see you back in London." Fleming gave her a gentle nudge, setting her off in the direction of the cardinal's front door.

Only two minutes had passed from the moment Willy had first grabbed her.

* * * * *

"Good evening, Madam," Cardinal Cerejeira said in English as he entered the room, followed by the most beautiful Persian cat Margaret had ever seen.

"Good evening, Your Eminence," she replied in Portuguese, then bowed. "Thank you for allowing me a few moments of your time."

Cerejeira smiled, hoping to put the attractive Englishwoman at ease. "Ah, I see you speak Portuguese. Is that a Brazilian accent I detect?"

"Rio de Janeiro," Margaret said, "but I left there for England many years ago."

The cat jumped onto Cerejeira's lap and stared at her with the bluest of eyes, reminding Margaret of the woman she had met that afternoon at Tuy.

"This is Christopher Columbus," the cardinal said, looking down at his feline friend while running an affectionate hand through the animal's luxuriant fur. "He's every bit as adventuresome as the explorer with whom he shares a name."

"I don't know about the first Christopher Columbus," Margaret said, "but this one is gorgeous."

"And he knows it," Cerejeira added with a laugh. Then the prelate turned serious. "Did you say earlier that you've just come from the convent at Tuy where you were visiting with Sister Lucia?" His question was in no way confrontational, but one reflecting mild surprise.

"This was my second visit," Margaret replied, deciding not to stray too far from the truth. "I'm a doctor," she added, "and when I was in Lisbon a couple of weeks ago, a friend asked me to take a look at Sister Lucia because she was so sick. My friend is Miss Olivia de Gama. Perhaps you know her?"

"Indeed I do. Her family and my family are old friends. How is Olivia?"

"I don't know," she answered truthfully, "we have not had a chance to get together during this visit. I certainly hope to see her before I return home." With that, she opened her purse and took out the two letters. "These are from Sister Lucia," she said. "When she heard I was coming back to Lisbon she asked if I would deliver them to you. I said, of course."

The cardinal took the letters. He raised a questioning eyebrow at the one addressed to the Chancellor of Germany.

Margaret shrugged. "Sister Lucia said both letters were extremely important, that both refer to messages from the Virgin Mary. I said you would see they get to their destinations. All I can add, Your Eminence, is that Sister Lucia seemed troubled, and wanted both letters sent to their intended recipients with all dispatch."

Cerejeira absently tapped the envelopes on the arm of his chair as if he was pondering how best to accomplish this mission. Delivering the letter to Pope Pius XII would not be a problem, for he and the former Giovanni Cardinal Pacelli were old friends from way back. However, getting the second letter into the hands of the German chancellor was quite another matter. He would have to give that task some extra special thought. Of course, the easiest route would be to hand it over to the German ambassador in Lisbon, but reason cautioned against that. No, he concluded, it would have to involve either Adolf Cardinal Bertram, the Chairman of the Fulda Conference of Bishops, or maybe it would have to be channeled through the offices of the papal nuncio in Berlin.

He glanced once more at the envelope addressed to Adolf Hitler. What could Lucia, or the Virgin Mary for that matter, possibly have to say to the German dictator? In all of his years as a priest, this was the strangest request yet asked of him, stranger by far than the one to allow the Russian woman to hide in the convent at Tuy.

But Cardinal Cerejeira knew he would do Sister Lucia's bidding.

Ian A. O'Connor

CHAPTER 12
London. December 1940

The following morning brought terrible news to Margaret. Apparently, the police had discovered the body of a woman in one of the city's seedier neighborhoods the night before. Her throat had been cut, her purse was found beside her and she had been positively identified as Olivia de Gama.

Ambassador Gibbons, the bearer of the awful news, had more to say. He motioned for her to wait a moment longer. "It seems someone else we both know has also been killed. Willy, our German spy, was found floating in the Tagus River sporting a hole between his eyes. This town is beginning to show its tawdry side, Margaret. An awful shame, too, because I've always felt it to be one of the safer cities in Europe."

* * * * *

Before she left for England, Margaret again wrote a thank you note in the guest register, stating that her translation duties regarding Portugal's agricultural cork production had gone smoothly. As she was about to put her pen away, she decided to add a couple of sentences in Portuguese. It was an impulsive thing. She wanted some sort of record, no matter how oblique, of what she had accomplished, what she had done to help England with the war effort. She thought for a moment, smiled, and began to write. *Won't HWF and EBC be thrilled when I recount my successes; even grumpy old Alexander will surely be impressed! Not to mention the other dashing man with the same last name, I'm sure.*

* * * * *

Her debriefing with Commander Fleming felt somehow anticlimactic. And not because he didn't cover her visit to Tuy in great detail, as well as drawing out her impression of Cardinal Cerejeira and his promise to deliver the letter to Hitler. He was also interested in hearing whether she thought the mystery woman was in fact the Grand Duchess Anastasia, and why.

Fleming lit another cigarette, then spoke about Willy. "I wanted to draw Willy out, and he took the bait, which was you. He followed you to Tuy, and probably saw you meet with Anastasia in the garden. Willy almost did us in, but for all the wrong reasons. Anyway, he's no longer with us, our plan is going to work beautifully and it's all because of you."

Despite the kudos, Margaret felt a gnawing sense of letdown. A void was rapidly forming in her life. She had tasted excitement, the thrill of adventure and danger, and the prospect of returning to Oxford and the cocoon of the research team no longer seemed fulfilling.

Fleming noticed her anxiety. "What is it? You've done a bang-up job for us."

"But I'll never know the outcome, Ian," she replied, embarrassed at the hot tears forming.

"Not true," Fleming replied. "I'll keep you informed of any and all progress on that front. That's a promise, but remember this. If England is invaded come springtime, then we'll know nothing came of our plan."

Margaret wiped her eyes and looked squarely at Fleming. "I'd like to come and work for you fulltime, Commander. I now feel I have lots to offer, and what I don't know, I will learn."

"But what about the penicillin trials and the mass production?"

"It's no longer enough," she whispered, then paused to blow her nose. "You see," she continued, "I don't need to spend months and months working on the human trials. I know penicillin works! I saw it with my own eyes. What happened with Sister Lucia was not because of any heavenly intervention. The team will soon find the way to mass-produce the stuff and then the next step will be to synthesize it. Maybe the Americans will be asked to help, but it's no longer enough for me. I need to continue doing what I've been doing for the last few weeks. I can never go back to my old life as long as we are at war, I just can't!"

Fleming hung to Margaret's every word and, as he did, found himself having to admit he had truly enjoyed working with this bright and beautiful woman. In a word, Lt. Commander Ian Lancaster Fleming was smitten.

He came to a decision. "Tell you what. I'll bring it up with the admiral and get his OK." Fleming took Margaret's hand. "Go back to Oxford and prepare to leave." He frowned. "What about your husband…Michael, isn't it? What will he say?"

"Michael's the best husband in the world," Margaret replied without hesitation. "If this is what I must do to help win the war, then he'll stand with me all the way."

Fleming led her to the door. "Then let's say we'll meet again in two weeks, shall we?"

CHAPTER 13
Berlin. December 1940

*E*ighty-one-year-old Adolf Cardinal Bertram of Berlin alighted from his massive 1938 Mercedes-Benz 770K Grosser limousine and made his way slowly up the steps of the floodlit New Reich Chancellery at the *Wilhelmsplatz* entrance to a smattering of applause from well-wishers and fellow dignitaries. The date was December 20, 1940, the last day of fall, and the diplomatic corps was assembling this Friday night to pay their seasonal respects to Führer Adolf Hitler; Deputy Führer Rudolph Hess; Foreign Minister von Ribbentrop and a gathering of lesser luminaries of the Third Reich. The city, indeed all Germany, was in a festive mood this Yuletide; the war was going spectacularly well.

Accompanying Cardinal Bertram this clear, cold night was Archbishop Cesare Orsenigo, the Apostolic Nuncio and, in a rare display of ecumenicism, they were joined by a close friend of Hitler's, the Protestant Reich Bishop, Ludwig Müller.

The receiving line was scheduled to start at eight-thirty. Preening uniformed and tuxedoed diplomats, accompanied by wives or mistresses dressed in their finery were slowly moving towards assigned places while gaily chatting to longtime acquaintances and newfound friends. A military string quartet played favorites of the season, while liveried waiters glided back and forth offering canapés and flutes of champagne. A state dinner, scheduled for nine, was limited to a select few with special invitations.

The line began to move, and as Cardinal Bertram inched closer to the front, he could see the Führer was in a jovial mood. Hitler exchanged easy pleasantries with his guests and actually laughed aloud a couple of times. Several of the dignitaries presented him with small gifts, which he readily accepted, offered his thanks, then deftly passed them off to a military aide standing a pace behind and slightly to his left.

Ian A. O'Connor

"Ah, Cardinal Bertram, it's a pleasure to see you," the Führer said with a hint of a smile. "Let me extend my sincerest Christmas Greetings to all of the Church's faithful."

And the same to you, sir," Bertram replied, bowing slightly. He straightened and smoothly passed an envelope to Hitler. "If I may make a suggestion, Excellency. Keep this on your person," he said, then added under his breath, "I understand a similar letter has been delivered to the pope."

An expressionless Führer slid Lucia's envelope inside his double-breasted jacket.

* * * * *

One hundred guests dined on Polish goose, quaffed recently liberated French Champagne, danced to the music of Strauss and Schubert, and sang Christmas carols. Cardinal Bertram wandered among the tables, pausing here and there to shake a hand and then chat for a minute or two. At ten thirty, Hitler and his entourage left the large hall. At midnight, the band struck up Norbert Schultze's melancholy rendition of *"Lili Marleen,"* signaling an end to the evening's festivities. Cardinal Bertram found an army major appearing at his side.

"The Führer would like to see you in his office," the major said. "He often works until dawn; for him the day is still young."

Bertram followed the jackbooted aide down several marbled hallways to Hitler's private study deep within the bowels of this borderline obscene, oversized building. Hitler was standing next to a granite-topped table, wearing glasses and reading.

"Do you know the contents of the letter you gave me earlier, Cardinal?" Hitler asked, as he removed his glasses and began twirling them absently between thumb and forefinger. His unblinking eyes bore deeply into Bertram's, looking for the slightest sign of hesitation or fear.

"No, mein Führer, I was merely given a sealed envelope from the Patriarch of Lisbon and asked to make sure it arrived safely in your hands."

"And you mentioned earlier that a similar letter was also sent to Rome, hmm?" Hitler pressed, onyx eyes penetrating; unblinking and unnerving.

"Cardinal Cerejeira merely mentioned that a letter from the same source went to Rome at the same time. Alas, I was not privy to its contents either."

"Do you suppose Cardinal Cerejeira knows what's in this letter?"

Bertram slowly shook his head. "It's my understanding he does not." His own curiosity was now piqued. Bertram waited as Hitler put his glasses back on and slowly read the two-page letter again. Two minutes passed before he looked up. He allowed a brief smile to cross his face, as if a decision of some sort had been reached.

"I hope you enjoyed the evening, Cardinal, and I offer my best wishes for your continued good health." The meeting was over.

"Likewise, Excellency. Good night." Bertram could not bring himself to render the Nazi salute, so he just bowed and left. Very strange, indeed, he mused, as he followed the major back to the main entrance of the building that Albert Speer, master architect to the Reich, had designed solely to create feelings of awe in all who entered its portals.

* * * * *

Before summoning Cardinal Bertram, Hitler had asked Rudolf Hess' personal secretary, Martin Bormann, to find a military linguist on duty in the building who understood Portuguese, and bring him back.

Bormann had returned ten minutes later with a young sergeant in tow. The man took less than a half hour to translate then type a copy of the two-page letter into German for his Führer. Hitler dismissed the sergeant after warning him never to speak to anyone of what he had just read.

Adolf Hitler spent the rest of the night alone. As the first rays of dawn began to push aside the night through the huge, mullioned floor-to-ceiling bulletproof windows behind his desk, and with his mind hovering somewhere between heaven and earth, he vowed to learn all he could about this nun who had the power to influence popes. But already he knew he would obey the will of God. God's plans were his plans, and before him lay the proof that he had been destined by the Almighty to lead humanity into the world of tomorrow.

Then, as if in prayer, he began to mouth aloud Lucia words, starting with *ein,* the numeral one at the top of the first page.

1.

Sir; October 13, 1917 was the date of the last visit from the Virgin Mary at Cova da Iria, Fatima. She spoke to me and to my cousin Jacinta. As before, cousin Francisco Marto could not hear Our Lady's words.

"There shall spring forth from the land of Barbarossa, a king who will be blessed in heaven. He will obey my Son, Jesus, and banish forever from the earth the scourge which is the communist unbelievers of Russia. The day of their destruction ordained by Jesus shall begin on the twenty-second day of the sixth month of the second millennium and nine hundred and forty-one years after the birth of my only begotten Son. This German warrior shall reign triumphant in Moscow before the first snow falls upon the land; he will have dominion over all of Russia and his kingdom shall last for a thousand years. There shall follow a great peace on earth and joy in heaven."

These are the spoken words of the Blessed Virgin Mary of Fatima, and Mother of Christ.

Maria Lucia, Servant of God, Tuy, December 1, 1940.

2.

The Holy Mother appeared before me last night. She commanded I write these words.

"If the successor to Barbarossa chooses not to obey the holy will of God, then a great calamity shall fall upon Germany and disfavor shall be sown throughout the land as a warning of the coming of the end."

Then she said the following.

"Our Heavenly Father did create the firmament, the earth and all of its creatures and fishes in seven days. Now the Day of Judgment is at hand. The Father in His infinite wisdom shall allow the Archangel Lucifer, now the Prince of all Darkness, to smite the firmament, the earth and all of the creatures and

fishes, and do so in fourteen days, a doubling of the days of creation. And the first day of Lucifer's unholy toil leading to the Day of Judgment shall commence on the fifth day of the first month following the third year aforementioned in this decade of the second millennium after the birth of my only begotten Son. And the seven seals shall be broken. That is the will of the Heavenly Father."

These are the spoken words of the Virgin Mary of Fatima, and Mother of Christ.

Maria Lucia, Servant of God, Tuy, December 2, 1940.

Hitler glanced at the huge chronograph hanging on the marble wall next to the fireplace and studied its complex face. The time was 7:58. The date was December 21, 1940. This was the first day of winter and a half-moon graced the sky. More importantly, there was a stronger omen attached to this date in history, one he of all people could not ignore. On December 21, 1907, his beloved mother and protector, Klara, had died after a long and painful struggle with breast cancer.

He slapped an open hand against his thigh. The die had been cast. He walked over to a giant globe, placed a thumb squarely over Moscow and began to gloat.

Six months from now, and one day after the summer solstice, he would obey the will of God and unleash his forces to conquer Russia. The date would be June 22, 1941, one year to the day after the surrender of France.

Returning to his desk, he took out a sheet of paper and immortalized the day's date by writing boldly across the top of the page: Directive No. 21: *"Operation Barbarossa."* He paused to savor the words, then deliberately backdated the document to December 18 in honor of the birthday of the Archduke Franz Ferdinand, a fellow Austrian warrior whose assassination by a terrorist's bullet in Sarajevo not only marked the beginning of the Great War, but of his own purpose-driven vision of world conquest as well.

He was invincible.

Ian A. O'Connor

CHAPTER 14
London. January-June 1941

True to his word, Fleming recalled Margaret to London two weeks after the New Year. He met her at the front door of the Admiralty and escorted her to Godfrey's office.

"Wonderful to see you again, Margaret," Admiral Godfrey said, obviously pleased. "No last minute faintness of heart, young lady? You can change your mind you know, and neither Ian nor I will ever think any the less of you."

"Not a chance, sir. I'm ready to be put to work."

"Jolly good." Godfrey picked up a sheet of paper from his desk then cleared his throat. "What I am going to do now is commission you into the reserves of the Royal Navy as a sub-lieutenant. Please raise your right hand and repeat after me…"

It was all over in twenty seconds. Margaret Rivera Smalling was an officer in the King's navy.

"Congratulations, Lieutenant. These are your commissioning papers. Tuck them away in a safe place."

"Yes, Admiral, thank you, Admiral." She came to attention and rendered a salute.

Godfrey returned her salute and smiled. "First thing to remember, Margaret; you don't salute when you're not in uniform. Otherwise, not bad for your first attempt, and I'm honored to have been the one to receive it."

Margaret turned a deep shade of red at her gaffe, but silently vowed to have all of the military formalities down cold in no time. She had always been a fast learner.

* * * * *

Churchill had given some specific orders to Admiral Godfrey—who in turn had issued them to Fleming and Smalling. The moment anyone staffing the ULTRA desk at Bletchley Park heard the word *Barbarossa* mentioned on the ENIGMA radio traffic net, he was to be told at once, no matter the time, either day or night.

On the night of February 14, 1941, the phone awakened Margaret in her rented room. She jumped up and answered it on the second ring.

"Margaret, it's Ian. Get dressed. Pack a suitcase and be prepared for a stay of several days away from London. I'll pick you up in fifteen minutes."

Fifteen minutes later a staff car glided to the curb and she jumped in the back, dragging a small suitcase behind her.

"Good evening, Margaret."

It was Admiral Godfrey. "Good evening, sir." What was happening? Where were they going in the dead of night? She peered at the driver who had turned around to grin at her. It was Commander Fleming!

"We're off to Bletchley Park," Godfrey said, as Fleming eased the saloon away from the curb; the inside of the car so dark she could barely make out the admiral's face. "Seems that an hour ago the ULTRA folk began to pick up a rush of traffic with the word *Barbarossa* plastered about in several messages. They called me, and I phoned the PM. Mister Churchill instructed me to personally go up there and bring him back a full report. Before we discuss any of the particulars of what we'll be doing in the days to come, I want to offer you my congratulations, Margaret. The fact that we're in this car heading to Bletchley on such a cold night is the proof that Hitler has taken the bait. It would never, and I stress the word never, have happened without your courage, grit and determination. I'm sure Mister Churchill will want to meet with you again in the not too distant future to offer his heartfelt congratulations as well."

She didn't know what to say. God, how she wished she could tell Michael. Maybe one day that would be possible.

Fleming must have sensed her unease at being thrust into the limelight of center stage because he began talking in a loud voice, not daring to turn his head or take his eyes off the pitch-black road, even for a moment. "Margaret, I suggested to the admiral that you stay up at Bletchley for the next few days. It is my guess the ULTRA traffic regarding *Barbarossa* will increase dramatically, because the German High Command has a monumental task ahead of them. You see, they are now going to have to turn several huge armies away from facing

England and move them to the east, to a jumping off line for the invasion of Russia. No small task that. It involves the repositioning of at least a million and a half soldiers, all of their equipment and supplies, to say nothing of the massive numbers of fighters and bombers the Germans will have to dedicate to the task. And they've only got something like a hundred days left in which to do it, that is if the June twenty-second deadline means anything to good old Adolf."

"I've often wondered what was so special about that date," Margaret said, her composure now fully regained.

Godfrey let loose a hearty laugh. "That was all Ian's doing; and keenly clever, if I may say so myself. Why don't you do the honors, Commander?"

"Thank you, sir," Fleming replied, eyes glued to the road. "My reasoning was simple, Margaret. It is the day after the summer solstice, the longest day of the year. If we had picked a date in late April or even in May, the Hun could have easily been inside the walls of Moscow before the onset of winter. Then Jerry could have re-supplied his forces before the first snowfall. The rest of Russia would collapse, and a year or so later Hitler could well decide to take another stab at invading us. God forbid if that scenario plays out—and it's still a real possibility, mind you—because we would have done too good a job, and cooked our own goose in the process."

Margaret now understood. "But if the Germans get bogged down in the mud, the snow and freezing winter temperatures before taking Moscow…"

"…Then the chances are excellent Hitler's army will suffer the same fate as Napoleon's did in Eighteen Hundred and Twelve," Fleming said, completing her thought. "That elementary blunder cost France dearly," he added, eyes scanning the road ahead. "Napoleon abandoned his Grande Armée and returned to Paris with less than thirty thousand men out of an original force of over six hundred thousand. The Russians burned everything in sight, leaving nothing for the French to forage on during their fifteen hundred mile trek westward. Theirs must have been a nightmare of hellish proportions."

Admiral Godfrey took the opportunity to weigh in, adding his tuppence worth to the conversation. "Russian winters are giant killers,

Margaret. Always have been; always will be. Any army caught in the field in that godforsaken land without the proper winter clothing and supplies is a doomed army." Godfrey was silent for a long moment then asked, "I wonder if the field marshals have brought any such concerns to the attention of their Führer?"

"And tempt Herr Hitler to disobey the word of God?" Fleming asked in reply.

Godfrey smiled in the dark. "Your point's well taken." He turned to Margaret. "For our ruse to work, Hitler must launch *Operation Barbarossa* too late in the year. On June twenty-second, summer will be in full bloom and his troops will easily smash through any Russian resistance. The German army will be heady with success, and Hitler will be totally convinced Lucia's letter was indeed heaven-inspired. But here's my prediction. Hitler's army will have Moscow in its sights when the first snow falls. The Germans will come within a hair's breadth of victory, but they will fail."

"And England will be spared," Margaret added in a whisper.

"And England will be spared," Godfrey repeated. "That's our fervent hope, anyway, Lieutenant."

"What is it you want me to do when we get to Bletchley, Admiral?" Margaret was excited at the prospect of soon being in the thick of things again.

"I'll be needing you to closely monitor the situation," Godfrey said. "You'll be my eyes and ears. No one on the ULTRA team has a clue as to what we've done to instigate *Operation Barbarossa*, and I do not intend to tell any of them the details. I dare say it will be an interesting meeting I'll be conducting later this morning."

"Well, I, for one, can hardly wait," said Fleming, turning the car onto the long gravel road leading up to the military checkpoint at Bletchley Park Manor, often called Station X, a reference to the radio station built inside the mansion in 1939.

* * * * *

Immediately after breakfast, the three navy officers were briefed on what the ULTRA unit had deciphered about *Barbarossa*.

"To be honest, Admiral, none of us knows what to make of it," said Alan Turing, a twenty-eight-year-old mathematical whiz and head of the ULTRA team. "The word has popped up several times in the last eight hours, all in one-way traffic from Berlin. The recipients have been field marshals, but no naval flag officers other than your counterpart, Admiral Canaris. Bloody odd, what?" He immediately looked at Margaret and mumbled an apology for using the somewhat crude intensive word.

She nodded her forgiveness.

"Anyway, I've got the message flimsies right here from the interpreters for you to go over when you're ready."

Admiral Godfrey stood up, clasped his hands behind his back and took a moment to look each of the seven other people around the table squarely in the eye. It was pure theater; something he had picked up from studying his young protégé.

"Gentlemen," he said, ignoring the fact Margaret was present, "the word *Barbarossa* refers to a new German offensive they've codenamed, *Operation Barbarossa.* It is a name handpicked by Hitler himself, and it is the plan for the invasion of Russia. If everything goes as scheduled, that invasion will kick-off on June twenty-second, Nineteen Forty-one, which is exactly one hundred and twenty-seven days from today."

Alan Turing coughed loudly and tapped on the tabletop for attention. "Er, Admiral Godfrey, wi...with all due respect, s...sir," he stuttered, "nothing out of Berlin suggests anything of the sort about an invasion of Russia in the *Barbarossa* messages." He laughed a small, high-pitched, embarrassed laugh, then continued, "All the messages we've deciphered basically tell the recipients that as more information becomes available they will be told more; but until then, the word *Barbarossa* at the head of a signal means that what follows is an eyes-only, top-secret message for the recipient. That's it."

Godfrey didn't move. "What I've just told you about *Barbarossa*, Dr. Turing, is one hundred percent accurate..."

Alan Turing found the nerve to cut him off. "We're the code breakers, Admiral, which means all of the Germans intelligence radio traffic passes from us here at ULTRA to you, then from you to all others on a need to know basis..."

Godfrey face was sphinxlike as he faced down the Princeton educated Ph.D. The group around the table squirmed in their seats. Finally, he said, "I do have other intelligence sources, Doctor Turing, sources you know nothing about, and I'm telling you now exactly what *Barbarossa* is so that your intelligence people will have a heads up as to what is going on. I've just saved you lots of valuable time, possibly as much as several weeks."

"But…"

Godfrey waved an impatient hand for the civilian mathematician to be quiet. "Commander Fleming and I first briefed the prime minister about *Barbarossa* several months ago. It is a top priority with him. That is why I ordered you to listen for the word and to notify me immediately when you heard it. You did so last night. Now you will begin to capture everything transmitted about this plan so that the PM will know exactly what the Germans plan to throw against the Russians, right down to the last roll of toilet paper. Am I clear?"

"Yes, Admiral, and I apologize for my poor behavior…"

Godfrey immediately softened. "Alan, I don't want a yes-man running ULTRA. You were within bounds to question me, and I'm not so thin-skinned or pigheaded that I won't entertain dissenting opinions. The chief reason we'll beat the Hun in this World War just as we did in the first one is that unlike Hitler's admirals and generals, we British foster debate, thrash out our ideas and come to a consensus. And in the doing the loser doesn't have to worry about forfeiting his head."

"Thank you, sir."

"One last thing. Lieutenant Smalling will be staying behind for the next few days. She's my personal liaison. Vet everything through her; keep her informed on even the most trivial of details because she's going to be responsible for giving briefings to the PM on *Barbarossa*'s progress right up to the crack of dawn on June twenty-second." Godfrey looked down at his watch. "Right, then. If no one's got any questions, it's time to get back to work. Carry on."

Margaret Smalling remained seated long after everyone had left the room. She was rendered numb by the enormity of the challenge destiny had delivered to her doorstep. It was the stuff of fiction. As she slowly rose, she vowed to herself England would forever have reason to be proud of her!

* * * * *

Four weeks before the Germans stormed into Russia, Winston Churchill sent a message to Joseph Stalin warning him that such an invasion was coming.

Stalin harrumphed at the brazenness of the message, and dismissed the admonition out of hand. That crafty old English fox! Why, the plump Englishman was trying to goad him into breaking the Treaty of Non-Aggression that Foreign Minister Vladimir Molotov had inked with his German counterpart, Joachim von Ribbentrop on August 23, 1939, right here inside the walls of the Kremlin. Churchill wanted him to make a preemptive strike against the Third Reich and, in the doing, take the heat off the all-but-beaten British. Not a chance! Then Stalin laughed heartily in front of a roomful of terrified generals until he could laugh no more.

* * * * *

On the night of May 18, 1941, Winston Churchill dined at Number 10 along with his guests, Admiral John Godfrey, Lieutenant Commander Ian Fleming and Sub-Lieutenant Margaret Smalling. The four of them were in rare form, and the servants later remarked they had not seen the old man so thoroughly enjoy himself in a long, long time.

Margaret sat to the PM's right. He was the most solicitous host. Churchill openly fawned over her—much to the amusement of Godfrey and Fleming—making sure her wine goblet was topped; her plate full.

Margaret was the reason for this celebration. She had brought back some wonderful news from Bletchley Park to Admiralty Godfrey the day before. Intercepted ULTRA traffic had confirmed the official end of the Luftwaffe's saturation bombing campaign against England. All available German bombers were now being posted to the east for the upcoming invasion of Russia.

For the first time in a year, Winston Churchill felt that a great weight had been lifted from his weary shoulders. It was simple. He had won. England was spared. And only because of these three sharing his table this night. He looked at them all, beamed broadly, stood, and offered a toast. They, too, rose, accepted their prime minister's gracious words and replied with a toast to king and country, rendered by Fleming. The four friends drained their goblets.

It was a moment flash-frozen in time for one Margaret Rivera Smalling. She would treasure it until the day she died.

* * * * *

At 4:45 a.m. on the morning of June 22, 1941, and one day after the summer solstice, Adolf Hitler launched *Operation Barbarossa* with a force of 2.6 million men, confident he would reign triumphant in Moscow before the first snowfall.

It was the will of God.

The following day, the mysterious resident at the convent in Tuy known to the sisters as Catherine, vanished as quickly as she had arrived, leaving behind her few meager possessions, including a photograph of a painting depicting an old man praying by candlelight. That photograph would be discovered, quite by accident, in December 2009, tucked away in the corner of an attic in a convent in Paris.

Ian A. O'Connor

PART TWO
THE PRESENT
CHAPTER 15

Day 1. Rome. Monday afternoon

*V*ideotaped images of Justin Scott in action were captured on four security cameras strategically mounted atop both the Terminal C building and the parking area directly across the street at Rome's Leonardo da Vinci Airport. Six hours later, selected portions of the tapes detailing the early morning carnage were released to the clamoring media and, thanks to CNN International, the world was an eyewitness to the event. It was the last thing Justin had wanted.

He had spent several hours being debriefed by the Anti-Terrorism Police, telling only as much of the truth as he had deemed necessary. "I'm here to visit my friend, Cardinal Kettering, nothing more," he had said early in the session, later regretting admitting even that.

He had seen the tapes and had tried to persuade the technicians to at least digitally blur his face before releasing copies, and he had also asked to have the accompanying press release simply state an unknown passerby had managed to stop one of the terrorists. Both requests were vetted past the chief, and after some back and forth, all agreed not to identify Justin by name, but the video was released unedited. However, Justin knew this information would leak within a day, two at the most, leaving him scant time to prepare for the inevitable consequences. He had already decided what he had to do to level the playing field, what special protective device he needed to be sent to him immediately from Washington. War had been declared and he was not about to be caught carrying a knife to a gunfight.

Justin had whiled away the last three interminable hours in a sparsely furnished office with only two well-thumbed, borderline pornographic magazines for company. His bona fides were finally confirmed by Cardinal Kettering's office, and shortly after that, Washington acknowledged—after receiving his fingerprints via satellite—that, yes, Justin Scott was who he claimed to be—a retired FBI agent.

* * * * *

Detective Mario Castellanos plopped himself down in a plastic chair next to a standing Justin, fired up the Marlboro gripped between his teeth and took a deep drag. Squinting from behind a monstrous cloud of bluish gray smoke, he began a rapid-fire recitation of what the anti-terrorism unit had been able to piece together in the last few hours.

"First, *Joosteen,* the terrorist you shot is still alive, but only barely, hooked up to many machines." Castellanos flicked his ash into an empty soda can commandeered from underneath his chair. "As for her companions, they have vanished," he said with a wave of an arm, "along with their getaway van. But not before they left six dead and four badly injured members of a trade delegation from Ukraine. And let's not forget two of our police officers. Not a good day for us in Rome, *Joosteen.* In fact, it's been a very bad day."

Justin slouched against the doorjamb, saying nothing, but waiting to hear more.

Castellanos obliged. "It seems the doctors got a surprise when they started working on your lady friend. Care to guess what it was?"

Justin raised a questioning eyebrow.

"She's not an Asian," Castellanos announced as he stuffed his cigarette butt into the soda can and began shaking it. "Her eyes had been skillfully made-up to look Asian; her face was covered with fine rice powder and she wore an expensive wig of real Japanese or Chinese hair. And would you like to know why, Justin?" Castellanos didn't wait for an answer. "Because she was completely bald, that's why! Not bald like in shaved-bald, oh no, I mean, bocce ball bald!"

Castellanos jumped up and came face to face with Justin. "Then they got a second surprise, only this was a real doozy." He frowned. "Is that an English word?"

Again, Justin raised an eyebrow, but also nodded.

Castellanos arched high on his toes as if to get closer to Justin's ear. "When they cut off her clothes and she was lying naked in the emergency room, the doctors discovered this she was not a she but a he—at least from the waist down it was a he—but a he with fully matured female breasts. And this creature was also round in the way a woman is all round and curvy, you know?" His hands described the curves while his voice betrayed a genuine amazement at his tale. "And there wasn't a hair to be found anywhere else on the body, not even so much as an eyelash." He now waved both hands high in the air for added dramatic emphasis. "So, what does Justin Scott from the FBI think of all that, huh?"

Justin managed to keep his tone neutral. "Justin Scott thinks that maybe her three friends could have a similar problem."

Castellanos let loose a nervous giggle and lit another Marlboro. "Well, I had her—him—whatever—fingerprinted while she was being worked on by the ER staff and I sent the prints to Interpol and to Washington. I can only pray that one or the other will tell me who this freak might be." He stuck out his hand. "You are free to go. But please, keep me posted as to where you will be staying, and when you decide to leave the city, let me know that also, OK? *Addio.*"

* * * * *

Monday Evening

Justin checked into the Hotel Rome Cavalieri Hilton, phoned the Vatican protocol office to confirm his appointment for the following morning, grabbed a light meal in the coffee shop, then retreated to his room. It was now late afternoon. Exhausted, he set the bedside alarm and crawled under the duvet. He ached all over, and his left thigh was sporting a huge purple and black bruise from where he had first made contact with the pavement in his attempt to seek cover. He had begun to favor the leg more and more as the day wore on, but through a sleepy haze, he kept thinking this was definitely something he could use to advantage. He made a mental note to remember to act on an idea he had formed earlier, but it was something that could wait until morning.

I'm way too old for this Boy Scout stuff was his last coherent thought.

CHAPTER 16
Day 2. Rome. Tuesday morning

At ten o'clock the following morning Justin taxied onto the grounds of Vatican City, a hillside 110-acre walled enclave and the world's smallest sovereign nation. After a couple of false starts, he intercepted a civilian security guard who guided him to his destination, the Medieval Palace. A protocol officer ushered him into the secretary of state's suite where he was greeted by an expectant Francis Cardinal Kettering. Standing to Kettering's left was his special assistant and Justin's longtime friend, Monsignor Jack O'Bryan. Both clerics were dressed in black cassocks trimmed in the colored piping of their respective ecclesiastical ranks; Kettering in red, O'Bryan in the crimson of a monsignor, but more formally known as a Prelate of Honor to His Holiness. Each was girded in a magnificent silk sash, and both wore a small zucchetto, or skullcap. Theirs were the uniforms of power and prestige in this city-state at the heart of Christendom.

Kettering stepped forward, his pale, angular face beaming, and both hands outstretched. "As the head of government, may I say, welcome, Justin, and God bless you for coming on such short notice." He pumped Justin's hand. "Let me get a good look at you," he said, his face still reflecting the genuine pleasure he felt as he studied the tall, well-dressed, lean and handsome American before him. Justin had become a favorite, and not just because he had almost died in a shoot-out on one of the meanest streets of Washington some five months earlier. No, Kettering had grown to respect and admire the retired FBI agent, and he genuinely enjoyed being in this particular American's company." You are the proverbial breath of fresh air," he added.

Justin was embarrassed with the high praise. He tugged at the knot on his tie.

Anyone casually looking at Francis Cardinal Kettering would only see a rigid, Teutonic cleric, a man who took every aspect of life seriously. He was average in height, painfully thin, but blessed with a headful of snow-white hair. Cardinal Kettering presented an imposing, intimidating presence to the world, which often caused other members of the curia to refer to him as the 'Nazi' behind his back because of what they perceived as his unbending nature.

Justin now realized he was treading on foreign ground. He had no idea of the formalities to be followed, because no one had briefed him. He found himself wondering whether he should have kissed Kettering's ring as a sign of respect after the handshake—or was that a ritual reserved for the pope?

In a conscious effort to put his friend at ease, Kettering said, "Jack and I saw the TV coverage of that terrible massacre at the airport yesterday and, of course, we immediately recognized you on the security camera film. A short time later the police called wanting me to confirm I knew you and that you were expected here. Is it possible, those assassins were really after you?"

Justin shook his head. "Not a chance, Your Eminence. If that were the case, they could have whacked me in a heartbeat. In fact, for a moment or two I actually stood less than three feet away from them. No, my hunch says they got who they came for, namely those Ukrainians. The police still have no idea why, and according to the TV news reports this morning, no one has come forward to take responsibility."

"Let me add my two cents' worth of welcome, Justin," O'Bryan said, stepping forward. "It's great to see you again." He, too, was an admirer. As they shook hands, his thoughts harkened back to the summer before when he had recommended the Vatican hire Justin to investigate a murder apparently committed by Cardinal Kettering in Washington.

When asked by the now-deceased secretary of state, Raphael Cardinal Miglianico, to present the case to the pope for hiring Justin Scott, O'Bryan had told the pontiff, "Justin's a retired FBI agent, and we became friends while I was at Georgetown getting my doctorate. He taught a course in international terrorism. I also had the good fortune to see him in action firsthand. He helped the Church manage a delicate situation involving the kidnapping of a priest and three children. The kidnapper was captured and no one was harmed, thanks to Justin. He's simply the best at what he does."

O'Bryan asked, "Are you sure you're completely healed from last October's gunshot wounds? I thought I detected a limp."

Justin chuckled. "The limp's genuine, Jack, but it's more the result of yesterday's fracas than a flaring up of old wounds. I'm probably going to need to get a cane for a few days until the leg is better. I have one at home I'm quite fond of. I bought it last year while I was recuperating." He turned to Kettering. "Your Eminence, is there any chance you could have it sent over in the diplomatic pouch from your embassy in Washington?"

"Consider it done."

Kettering patted Justin's arm. "Please don't stand on formality when we three are alone. I would like you to call me Francis, as my friends do, few that they are," he added in a rare display of dry humor.

Kettering walked over to his massive antique oak desk, picked up a phone and gave muted instructions in rapid-fire Italian that he was not to be disturbed. His face took on a serious mien as he lowered himself into a brocade wing chair, part of an intimate seating group off to the side of the spacious office. He beckoned his guests do the same, and opened his hands in a gesture suggestive of inner torment and indecision. He shrugged his thin shoulders. "Where do I begin?" he asked, his penetrating blue eyes riveted on Justin's.

"How about with the letter you received from Russia, Eminence…I mean Francis," Justin said, "because you sure sounded worried when we spoke on the phone. That's why I dropped everything and came immediately."

"Yes, of course, I'll start with the letter, but before I do, I must ask you a question that will seem to be way off point but I assure you, it isn't." He waited a long moment then asked, "What do you remember of the miracle at Fatima?"

The question caught Justin by surprise. He shrugged, closed his eyes to better concentrate and tried to recall that snippet of history. A few moments later he opened one eye, then the other, and replied, "Like all good Catholic kids of my generation I learned in parochial school how the Virgin Mary appeared several times to three shepherd children in a town called Fatima, located in some godforsaken corner of Portugal. And, if my memory further serves me correctly, that was back in Nineteen Sixteen, or maybe it was Nineteen Seventeen. Anyway, there were three secrets, two had something to do with Russia—but I could be wrong on that—and the third was supposedly known only to the Holy Father. At least that's the way it was until a few years ago when he allowed it to be made known to the faithful and to the rest of the world. That long-anticipated event turned out to be one giant letdown for many folks at the time, including me. For decades, we had all been led to suspect it was something bad. In fact, Pope John the Twenty-third was supposed to have fainted when he learned of the secret back in the late fifties. Then there was the great hullabaloo in Nineteen Sixty, because the word had spread around the world that the secret would be revealed before year's end. Well, Nineteen Sixty came and went, and guess what? No secret. I remember how we Catholics always prayed for wayward Russian souls every Sunday for about an additional five minutes right after mass. I confess that as a kid wanting to skedaddle out of church and go play with my friends, I really came to resent those Ruskies and their heathen souls." He let loose a chuckle. "But several decades' worth of prayers from all of us children must have finally been answered because the Commies were tossed out of power and the Russians are once again pretending to be our pals."

"Very good," Cardinal Kettering said approvingly. "You've certainly retained the gist. But, I must correct you on one small item. There was really only one secret," he said, "a secret with three distinct parts; a secret which was divulged over many appearances by the Virgin. In the first part, the children were shown a vision of hell; a vivid display of agonized souls doomed to spend eternity in that terrible sea of fire. In the second part, the Holy Mother spoke to the devotion of the Immaculate Heart of Mary and told the children that if the peoples of the world faithfully prayed the rosary for the consecration of Russia, then God would listen and Russia would be freed from the tyranny of communism. But the Virgin also told the children that if the world failed to do as she instructed, then an even greater war would break out than the one that was ravaging Nineteen Seventeen Europe, and in that new conflict untold millions from many nations would perish." Kettering reflected on his words for a long moment, then added, "Quite an upsetting revelation for three small, uneducated peasant children to hear. Francisco Marto and his sister Jacinta died shortly after the visions ended—their demise having been foretold to Lucia by the Holy Mother—in the influenza pandemic, which swept across the world at the end of The Great War. Lucia lived out her last sixty years as a Carmelite nun, and died in Two Thousand and Five at the age of ninety-seven. You know, she was a special favorite of the late Pope John Paul the Second, and he always remembered her in his daily prayers."

Kettering continued without referring to any notes.

"Anyway, sometime in early August, Nineteen Forty-one, Lucia was persuaded by her bishop to commit to writing the first two parts of the secret as told to her by the Virgin. She did as instructed—reluctantly, we're told—but only after much soul-searching and meditation. And shortly thereafter, those two secrets were made public. Then for reasons never explained, she revisited the letter again in early December to either add or subtract something. She had been sick for most of that year and the preceding one, so maybe she had a premonition she was dying, even though during one of the visions the Blessed Mother had told her she would live a long life because she had much work ahead of her in spreading the word of Jesus. In October, Nineteen Forty-three, the Bishop of Leiria ordered her to write down the third and final secret, which she finally did in January, Nineteen Forty-four. She sealed the envelope and handed it over to him. It remained in Lisbon until Nineteen Fifty-seven, at which time it was transferred to the Vatican and given to Pope Pius the Twelfth with instructions—written on the outside of the envelope by Lucia herself— that it was not be made public under any circumstances before Nineteen Sixty. And it's important to know this: nothing was ever said by Lucia that the contents *had* to be made public. She said it would be entirely up to the reigning pope of the day. Pius we know read it, and died in Nineteen Fifty-eight. His successor, John the Twenty-third, read the letter in Nineteen Sixty but chose to let the date pass without comment. When asked why he remained silent on the issue, his reply was uncharacteristically terse for that gentle soul. 'It is not of my time,' was how he phrased it. His successor, Paul the Sixth, read the letter but did nothing, and the first John Paul we are told died before reading it.

"However, I must take a moment to tell you of an interesting rumor which floated around the Vatican at the time—that the letter was stolen from the secretariat's office sometime during the night of September twenty-seventh, Nineteen Seventy-eight, and the following morning Pope John Paul One was found dead in his bed. Some even went so far as to suggest he had been murdered. John Paul the Second, remained silent on the subject for the better part of two decades until he decided to have the letter read to the world by Cardinal Sodano while he was in Fatima for the canonization of Lucia's two young cousins. That was in Two Thousand. Of course, we know nothing was said publicly at the time of any impending doom, something, as you just pointed out, Justin, many of the faithful had expected would come with the unfolding of the new millennium. A week or so later a full explanation and interpretation of the third secret *was* released through the Vatican public affairs office by my good friend, Joseph Cardinal Ratzinger, and done so with the pope's blessing."

Kettering reached over to an end table on his right and picked up a parchment envelope. "Which brings me back to the Russian letter that arrived at our embassy in Warsaw two days ago. It was addressed to me here in Rome, so the nuncio faxed me a copy and forwarded the original in the diplomatic pouch which I received later that day. I can tell you, Justin, its contents have frightened me as I've never been frightened, and that includes the trying times I experienced in Washington last year. Jack and I suspect the letter's origin is Russian, so that's why we've taken to referring to it as the Russian letter. It is also of consequence to note that the author deliberately chose to communicate in a vulgate Latin from the fourth century. But that's almost secondary, because it's the enclosed one-page letter purportedly written by Sister Lucia regarding the third secret of Fatima that has caused us all such genuine alarm. I deliberately use the word, purportedly, because we're just not sure it's real, and that is the reason I have asked you to help. The letter is written in Portuguese, it seems genuinely old, and the writing appears to be in Lucia's hand."

Justin kept his eyes glued to Kettering's as the cardinal continued. "Jack and I have read both letters. In fact, we've read them many times and now, in accordance with the pope's wishes, I'm asking you to do the same. Then I will want to hear your thoughts."

Justin shook his head. "Don't count on me being much of a help, Francis. You say the cover letter is written in vulgate Latin? Well, my understanding of Latin, vulgate or classical, runs the gamut from slight to nonexistent. Let's just say studying that particular dead language wasn't one of my stronger subjects, either as an undergraduate at Notre Dame or during my law school days at Fordham." As he spoke, Justin found himself wondering what Kettering might have told the pope about him.

As if anticipating such a response, Kettering stretched far to his left, and from the opposing side table picked up an intricately tooled leather folder. He withdrew two envelopes and signaled to Monsignor O'Bryan with an almost imperceptible nod.

O'Bryan seized his cue and segued seamlessly into the conversation. "First off, Justin, let me echo Francis's choice of words: both letters are as frightening as he says and you'll soon see that for yourself. My understanding of Latin is good, yet I experienced more than a passing difficulty with certain parts of the letter. However, Francis came to my rescue and suggested the author in all likelihood was thinking in German then translating his thoughts into Latin. He thinks certain phrases, certain nuances in the structure of some of the sentences hinted at a Germanic mother tongue. I tend to agree. But, if it turns out our author isn't a Russian, or even German, then the mystery becomes that much more profound."

"Just so!" exclaimed Kettering. "I translated both letters into German and Italian, then Jack put the results into English. Now we had copies in four languages, all of which I gave to the Holy Father. He is now fraught with worry over what he has read."

Kettering handed Justin the English translations. "I'm not trying to scare you with that last statement, but I do want to prepare you for some terrible news. Take however long you need to digest what's been written, and after you've finished, we'll talk." He glanced at his watch.

"But not for too long, because we meet with the Holy Father in less than an hour."

"Will Caffarone be present when we meet with the pope?" Justin asked, eyes narrowing, jaw hardening.

Caffarone was Monsignor Ignacio Caffarone, the papal secretary, a man of considerable power and influence who counted among his myriad duties the scheduling of all who came before the pontiff. If a petitioner should find himself out of favor with Caffarone for either real or imagined slights, then the long-anticipated opening in the pope's schedule never materialized. Because of his high office, even members of the College of Cardinals saw Monsignor Caffarone as almost an equal and treated him with an undeserved deference. Few in the Curia actually liked him.

Justin did not trust the man. The secretary's bloated face had been spotted in photographs taken the prior summer and autumn in various European cities in the presence of men thought to have been responsible for the murder of one Maritha von Snellenberger in Washington. And even though Justin lacked hard proof of complicity against the secretary, he wanted nothing to do with Caffarone.

Kettering shook his head. "Jack and I have met with the pope twice within the last twenty-four hours on this matter and both times the Holy Father has excused his secretary. This meeting will be no different."

"Good," Justin said as he rose. "May I use your desk?"

"Of course."

"Can I take notes?"

"I'd rather you not," Kettering replied. "After you read the letters you'll understand." He made the sign of the cross and, with O'Bryan in tow, left the room.

Justin settled into the cardinal's oversized leather chair and began with the translation of the Latin letter. The unknown author opened with a claim of having come into possession of a letter written decades ago by a nun named Sister Lucia, who as a child had professed to seeing visions of the mother of Jesus near the small town of Fatima, in Portugal. After some further observations about Lucia, he turned his attention to an unfolding religious calamity he claimed was about to devolve into a violent and bloody clash for supremacy between the

Eastern and Western Rites. He named places and dates, then predicted that the Russian Church would be the lone survivor because it was willing to do the unthinkable and march to that place where even angels feared to tread.

Justin found himself acknowledging that such a fracas would indeed prove bad for all concerned, but he felt that if the right people stepped up to the plate in time, they could stop the madness before it had a chance to spin out of control. The unknown author ended with a promise of further signs to come, then added a sobering caveat. "My warnings and my promises might well come to naught, not from any lack of faith or good intention on my part, but because our Father in Heaven has other plans; plans which are being misread by some who claim they are only obeying 'the revealed word of God.'"

He then directed the reader's attention to the enclosed seventy-five-year-old letter from Sister Lucia and the third and final secret of Fatima. Lucia first described an avenging angel brandishing a fiery sword, and followed with a gruesome picture of tormented souls doomed to an eternity in hell. She then segued to speak of the death of a "Bishop dressed in White," which she said would be followed eight years later with the prophesy written in the last paragraph.

Justin's eyes flew to the bottom of the page, and within seconds his heart began pounding. This was definitely not what the now-dead Pope John Paul had relayed to the world at the turn of the millennium. Far from it. And in that moment, Justin realized that what he had in his hands was a document which spoke not to any fundamental change to history, but to its end. It was the blueprint for the Dies Irae.

>*"Our Heavenly Father did create the firmament, the earth and all of its creatures and fishes in seven days. Now the Day of Judgment is at hand. The Father in His infinite wisdom shall allow the Archangel Lucifer, now the Prince of all Darkness, to smite the firmament, the earth and all of the creatures and fishes, and do so in fourteen days, a doubling of the days of creation. And the first day of Lucifer's unholy toil leading to the Day of Judgment shall commence on the fifth day of the first month following the thirteenth year aforementioned in this second decade of the third millennium after the birth of my only*

begotten Son. And the seven seals shall be broken. That is the will of the Heavenly Father."

These are the spoken words of the Virgin Mary of Fatima, and Mother of Christ.

Maria Lucia, Servant of God, Tuy, December 2, 1940.

Justin drew in a ragged breath and let the page slide onto the desktop. Now he understood why Kettering and O'Bryan were so genuinely alarmed.

"What does the pope expect of me?" he whispered aloud. He looked at a calendar on the desk and began counting aloud. According to Sister Lucia, only twelve days remained until the world would come to its cataclysmic, pre-ordained end.

CHAPTER 17
Day 2. Rome. Tuesday afternoon

Kettering slipped silently to a spot a step behind Justin and O'Bryan in the Raphael Room of the Vatican's eighteen room Picture-Gallery. They were standing in front of *Foligno Madonna*, a magnificent painting created by *Raphael Santi*, the room's namesake.

"What are you two villains plotting?" he asked in a sinister voice, catching his American friends off guard. Rare was the day Kettering engaged in any form of levity; rarer still when so preoccupied as he was this day.

O'Bryan cut loose with a small laugh. "No plot, Eminence," he replied, his face creasing into a grin, "although these halls have been home to more Machiavellian schemes and shenanigans than the two of us could ever dream up. No, I was asking Justin for his reaction to our earlier meeting with the Holy Father."

Justin found himself uncharacteristically searching for the right words. "It was a meeting like none other," he finally offered, "and not just because of the frightful messages in both letters. I found myself truly in awe. I think you know me well enough by now, Francis, to agree when I say I'm one not easily overcome by people or events. That was not the case earlier today. This pope is simply the embodiment of everything good the Church stands for. His elevation to the throne of Peter was an inspired choice by the College of Cardinals."

"Nicely put," Kettering said, then led them across the intricately patterned floor to the opposite wall and to a spot in front of a sizeable painting hanging to the right of Raphael's *The Transfiguration.*

"This is Michelangelo's *Wedding Feast,*" he announced, squinting at a nameplate he knew by heart. "It is only hanging in this room temporarily," he added. "Now, do either of you notice anything special; anything that strikes you as familiar?"

Both men stepped closer and scrutinized the painting.

It took O'Bryan five seconds to come up with the answer. "I sure do," he said. "Those candlesticks," he added, pointing from one to the other, "they're identical to the pair Maritha and Freddy von Snellenberger gave you for your sixtieth birthday."

Kettering smiled a noticeably sad smile. "That's a keen eye you have, Jack. I agree with you; they most certainly appear to be mine, don't they?"

The three men soaked up the beauty of Michelangelo's masterpiece. On a banquet table laden to the point of overflowing, and guarding a sumptuous array of meats, fowl, vegetables and exotic fruits, the artist had painted two magnificent candlesticks, a near-photographic likeness of the pair owned by Kettering.

This canvas had graced the walls of the papal palace for over 450 years. The men stared back across the centuries at the two-dimensional candlesticks, knowing that one had been used to bludgeon to death a young Maritha von Snellenberger. Kettering's had been the only fingerprints the Washington police had recovered from the priceless murder weapon and that candlestick had been crucial in building a seemingly solid case of murder against him. However, thanks to the detective work of Justin Scott, the evidence had been proven wrong. While the world believed Cardinal Kettering had killed his young, pregnant mistress, Justin and O'Bryan were privy to a secret no one else knew. Maritha had not been Kettering's mistress, but rather, she was his daughter, conceived mere days before he had entered the seminary.

As if such a loss was not enough, his son-in-law, Manfred—Freddy to family and friends—had vanished inside the vastness of Russia, probably not knowing of his wife's tragic death. Now, several months later, there was still no word as to his whereabouts; Freddy had simply been swallowed-up inside the chaos of that disintegrated empire. The unspoken consensus among the several police agencies still halfheartedly looking for him was that he had been killed by the same people who had murdered his wife. Kettering now held the same opinion.

Noticing that Kettering had momentarily retreated to another place and time, Justin, too, willed his mind to hearken back to the autumn just past when he had outlined for Kettering how the Vatican Bank under the leadership of Archbishop Dominico Torrelli was complicit in the laundering of hundreds of millions of dollars for the Russian mob and the Italian Mafia.

Armed with this information, Kettering had bided his time. One of his first acts as secretary of state had been to convince the pope to relieve the corrupt archbishop of his duties, but it was a pyrrhic victory at best, for Torrelli was still free to cause mischief. The Holy See could ill afford to have Torrelli's crimes made public and still hope to weather the ensuing scandal that would surely follow.

However, the chicanery inside the Vatican and inside Russia did not stop with the removal of Torrelli. The criminal enterprise was too extensive, too lucrative, and had been dubbed the Russian Mafia. Those criminals forged unholy alliances with European and American organized crime syndicates, but it was the Italian Mafia which had become their pre-eminent partner. There were fortunes to be made in this lawless land and no shortage of players wanting into a game whose rules were ruthless in their simplicity. Death was the punishment for double-crossing and double-dealing, and there was no court of appeal. Therefore, it was common for a city the size of St. Petersburg to record as many as a half dozen such executions in any given week, the bodies of the condemned dumped onto the streets from fast-moving cars. Most of the police in Russia no longer kept up a pretense that they represented the demarcation between civilization and anarchy. Whole departments openly sold their services to the highest bidders—those services being protection and the promise of a turned blind eye.

Justin shook off his reverie and waited for Kettering to continue talking.

A couple of moments later Kettering turned from the picture. "Now I must show you both something else, but for that we must leave the Picture-Gallery. I am very aware that time is not a luxury we can squander, but this is important, and I'm hoping it's something that will help us find the solution to our problem—if indeed one is to be found this side of heaven."

He led them out of the Pintacoteca and down a dimly lit corridor to a timeworn door with a state-of-the-art digital lock and a brass plate etched with the words Staff only, in Italian, English and Braille. He hit several buttons in rapid sequence, the door swung open and Kettering ushered them into an anteroom. Moving quickly, he continued through two more similarly locked doors and on into a dark, cavernous area crammed with paintings and other treasures.

"We call this the infirmary," he explained, snapping on several lights in rapid succession as he made his way toward the far wall. "Here, teams of experts gather from all over the world to perform their miracles of repairing and restoring." He came to a stop in front of a compact wooden crate sitting next to an impressive reference book, both on a felt-covered workbench.

"This arrived yesterday from His Holiness Sergius the Second, Patriarch of Moscow and all Russia," Kettering said, gently prying off the lid. His hands vanished inside a mound of packing silk and emerged a moment later holding a gilt-framed painting the size of a sheet of legal paper. He blew away some stray strands and held the masterpiece aloft for both to see. "The patriarch took pains to explain in an enclosed handwritten letter that this painting is a gift from the faithful of both the Russian Orthodox Church and the Russian Orthodox Church Outside of Russia in celebration of my recent appointment as secretary of state. These two distinct and different Churches healed their longstanding schism back in Two Thousand and Seven, but their reunion only came after an eighty-year-long very nasty parting of the ways. The patriarch ended by expressing his hope that he and I would meet in the near future. His letter was written in Italian, something that struck me as a thoughtful gesture."

All three stood in silence and admired the painting.

"It's exquisite," Justin finally said, breaking the spell. "What do you know of it?"

"Well, for starters, it was painted by *Guido di Pietro,* a man better known to the world as *Fra Angelico,* and in all probability was finished close to the time of his death in Fourteen Fifty-five. It is entitled *Evening Prayers* and of all his known works—and there are many— this one stands alone for two reasons. First, it does not depict a Christian motif, and two, it's an oil on canvas and not a tempera on wood or a fresco on plaster which were the usual media of his day."

They continued to gaze at a weather-beaten and bearded Methuselah; an ancient wrapped in a threadbare *tallith* and seated in a cold, dank room, the likeness frozen on canvas by the artist at the exact moment of exhalation; his breath a hanging mist of the finest gossamer. The subject was praying—or reading—from a large scroll seemingly as old as time itself. A cone of yellowish light flickering from a lone candlestick perched on a couple of roughly hewn boards masquerading as a table illuminated the scroll and the words inscribed on it. The overriding message of the painting was evident: man in perfect harmony with his Creator. It was awe-inspiring in both its simplicity and beauty.

Kettering carefully laid the painting back down on the bench then picked up the sizeable book lying beside the crate. He opened it to a page he had marked earlier with a thin metal ruler and said without looking up, "A major benefit of working in the Vatican is having the world's greatest library at one's fingertips. Take this book for example. It's one of only three, published by a small house in Vienna that burned to the ground just last week. That makes me sad, because I remember the place from my days as a teenager." He began to read.

"Fra Angelico's magnificent painting entitled Evening Prayers had not been seen by the public for the better part of a century and was photographed only once, that being by Christie's in Paris for inclusion in a special sales catalogue in the spring of 1938. The painting was sold by a dealer from Lisbon. It was purchased by a wealthy Prague jeweler named Isaac Heppler for £100,000, a veritable fortune at the time. Heppler had managed to assemble one of the finest private art collections in Europe, but alas, all his masterpieces vanished soon after the Germans invaded the Czech Republic in 1939. Shortly thereafter, Heppler and his family suffered the same fate. It was believed Reichsmarschall Hermann Göring requisitioned this particular work for his own infamous and openly purloined collection. After the Red Army sacked Berlin in 1945, it was rumored Evening Prayers was taken back to Russia and hidden in the Hermitage at Leningrad, a city we once again call by its original name, St. Petersburg. The 1938 photograph which is reproduced at the bottom of the previous page was discovered quite by accident in a convent attic in Paris, in December, 2009."

Kettering looked up and held the book toward them for inspection. "And, now, these several years later, we have the painting here in the Vatican. Gentlemen, allow me to direct your attention to the photograph."

The two Americans peered at the photo, their heads almost touching. There wasn't any doubt; the image, although faded, was definitely *Fra Angelico's* painting.

"Now, it's no secret I'm known in some circles as something of an authority on *Fra Angelico*," Kettering continued. "An amateur, yes, I admit, but I do know the man and his work and I've had several articles published in obscure journals and art magazines over the years. I'm suspecting maybe one of them caught the eye of the Russian Patriarch which would explain my receiving such a gift."

"It's the same painting, all right," Justin said, straightening up and smiling at the cardinal. "Lucky you."

Kettering returned the smile, but shook his head. "Alas, not as lucky as you might think. You see, this painting is a forgery."

"Say that again!" Justin blurted out, his voice betraying a sense of spontaneous disbelief.

Kettering's response was to open a drawer on the bench, pluck out a sizable magnifying glass and hand it to Justin. "For starters, take a good look at the candlestick. Examine the one in the book's photograph first, and then do the same with the one in the painting. Compare them carefully and tell me what you see." He stepped back a pace, took his arms and secreted them inside the ample sleeves of his cassock, then waited in silence for them to render their verdicts.

When Justin was finished, he wordlessly handed the glass to O'Bryan.

"Well, I'll be!" O'Bryan exclaimed less than a minute later. "They're different, but ever so slightly, and because of the poor condition of the photograph it's sure something that's easy to miss. But now that you've pointed it out, I can see they're not the same."

"And that's not all," Justin chimed in, "because I think the candlestick in this painting of *Evening Prayers* is identical to the two candlesticks in Michelangelo's *The Wedding Feast*, which means it's also a dead ringer for the matched pair you own."

Kettering nodded his agreement and countered, "Yet *Evening Prayers* was already some twenty years old by the time Michelangelo was born in Fourteen Hundred and Seventy-five. The candlestick shown in the photograph proves that the painting I just received from the patriarch is a forgery because it does not have the same candlestick that we know was painted by *Fra Angelico*. So the question is this: why would the patriarch deliberately send me a forgery, knowing I was something of an expert on the work of *Fra Angelico*?"

"And why would the Russians go to such lengths to forge a painting only to change the candlestick?" O'Bryan added. "I mean, how could they have really been sure you would notice the difference, expert or not? Just look at it," he challenged. "The difference is so subtle it could easily have been missed altogether. It's like looking at a near perfect counterfeit of our latest one hundred dollar bill."

"I couldn't agree more," Kettering replied.

Justin, still studying the painting, remarked, "I have a hunch you suspect there's a message, or maybe a warning of some sort, hidden somewhere else in this painting, right?"

Kettering let loose a small sigh. "How perceptive of you to come to that conclusion, but yes, Justin, that's exactly what I suspect. However, I'm still left with a conundrum. Is that the correct word to use in a situation such as this?"

"That's a good word and, I agree, it certainly presents us with a difficult problem," Justin replied. "Not necessarily a riddle; but definitely a dilemma." He looked at Kettering's perplexed face then added, "There's something else that strikes you as odd with the painting, isn't there?"

Kettering tugged his lower lip with a long, delicate index finger and thumb before answering. "Well," he began slowly, "the work is painted on a canvas which appears to be from the right century, but I would need expert analysis to confirm that fact. However, just for argument's sake, let us agree that what I said is a true statement, which suggests a lesser piece was sacrificed in order to create this one. You see, to make such a scheme work, someone had to have first removed the paint from a very old canvas, then painstakingly reconstituted the colors using the same original sources of pigments to create this counterfeit *Evening Prayers*. That was no mean feat, I assure you. Several coats of varnish were then applied, layer by painstaking layer, and I have no doubt that they mimic exactly the chemical composition of varnishes used over the intervening centuries. They appear to be genuine, but I suspect they are not. Lastly, the writing which is visible on the scroll in this painting differs, but just barely, from the writing seen on the scroll in the photograph. The words are different, but it's tough to see without a careful examination because they take up exactly the same amount of space on both torahs. Both texts appear to be Hebrew, but I'm no expert, so I can't say for sure. In summary, someone went to great lengths to produce this counterfeit masterpiece, but the million dollar question is why?"

"Simon Chertoff could tell us about the writing," O'Bryan replied, not really answering the question as he peered at the painting.

"Who?" Kettering wore a bewildered look for a split second, then his eyes lit up and he clapped his hands in a rare demonstrative moment. "Yes, of course, Simon! Good thinking, young man."

Simon Chertoff was a scholar on loan to the Vatican Library from the University of Tel Aviv. An internationally acclaimed expert in his field, namely the translating of ancient Hebrew manuscripts and the authenticating of Middle Eastern antiquities, Chertoff had helped O'Bryan the summer before by solving a crucial part of the puzzle which had led to Kettering being exonerated of the crime of murdering the young woman in Washington. Simon was also one of a handful of scholars who had near unfettered access to the pope's private documents housed in the Vatican Secret Archives.

"I'll ask Simon to translate what he sees on both scrolls. It's my hunch someone is indeed trying to send me a message; maybe the Patriarch, maybe someone else." Kettering gave a quirky shrug of his thin shoulders. "Anyway, I thought you would both find all this most interesting."

"Do you think there's a connection to the Russian letter?" O'Bryan asked. "And if so, then where do we go from here?"

"Yes, I think there's a connection, but in my next breath I must confess I haven't a clue as to what it could be." Kettering stole a glance at his watch. "And to answer your second question, I suggest we go back to my office where I'm hoping Justin will tell us how to proceed before the Doomsday Clock strikes midnight."

He then took Justin's elbow and drew him close. "The unexpected arrival of this painting reinforces my belief I made the right decision when I asked you to come to Rome. And as the Holy Father observed during our meeting earlier, like it or not, we're a brotherhood of four frightened souls—a brotherhood which has been bestowed with the terrible misfortune of knowing the when, the where and the how of the Apocalypse, if the letter from Lucia proves to be genuine."

Justin and O'Bryan remained silent. Kettering's pronouncement spoke volumes.

Ian A. O'Connor

CHAPTER 18
Day 2. St. Petersburg, Russia. Tuesday morning

*I*nspector **Mykel Charin** sat hunched over an ancient manual Cyrillic alphabet typewriter striking each key with deliberation. Computers—even clumsy, old-fashioned word processors—were still reserved for the chosen few, and Mykel Charin had no illusions as to his status in this new Russian order. Because it was January and the building was without heat, he wore his parka and fur hat. A confiscated Marlboro hung from the corner of his mouth, its glowing tip dancing perilously close to his Cossack-styled cavalry mustache. Just as the possibility of self-immolation was about to become a reality, he extracted the filtered remnant from his mouth and tossed it into an overflowing ashtray fashioned from a Cuban coffee can. His eyes never left the page as he plucked the next cigarette from the box, placed it between his lips and lit it with a wooden match. He coughed once, then again, and smiled to himself. These American cigarettes were better than sex.

Charin had been a police officer for fifteen of his thirty-nine years, working his way up through the ranks until landing this assignment ten months earlier. Olga, his physicist wife, had been cynical when he had told her it was a promotion. "Funny," she had remarked to their identical twin twelve-year-old daughters with a heavy dollop of sarcasm, "I always believed a promotion meant more money. *Silly me!*" Both girls had giggled nervously.

Yuri Solotov, his partner, sat at a scarred and dented metal desk butted-up against Charin's own relic and stared at eight stacks of American bills covering the better part of both surfaces. He had counted the treasure trove twice. One hundred and sixty-five thousand dollars in new, one hundred dollar bills. It was all the money in the world—well, at least a good portion of it.

Charin looked up, squinting through the blue-gray haze at his friend's trance-like stare.

"Don't even think about it. Dream all you want, but that's as far as it goes. Stealing those hoodlums' cigarettes was bad enough!" He started to laugh except it turned into a choking cough and as he hacked, the Marlboro bobbed and weaved from one side of his mouth to the other.

Both men were detectives assigned to a division called the Corrupting Crimes Suppression Unit, a special branch that hadn't existed a scant few years ago. The reason was simple. Under the communists, there had been no corrupting crimes! Indeed, for eighty years Moscow had insisted there was no criminal class in the workers' paradise. Semantic nonsense elevated to the status of an art, an outspoken Charin told anyone who would listen. The only difference between then and now was a matter of openness and degree. Today, the citizens running the country were well-dressed thugs living lives of unchecked grandeur.

Now, before them lay all this American money. Theirs for the taking and no one would know. It could disappear inside their pockets and they could simply vanish. Few would care. That, too, Charin knew, was a sad reality.

He dragged the sheet from the typewriter carriage and scrawled his name across the bottom. It was a summary of an arrest made of three individuals two hours earlier.

For months, he, Solotov, and a half dozen other officers, had kept a ring of thieves under surveillance, a gang suspected of plundering and selling off the treasures of the Hermitage. Several priceless works had surfaced in the West starting about a year ago with two candlesticks crafted by Michelangelo. The story of the candlesticks had been widely reported throughout Europe, recounting how the new owner, Francis Cardinal Kettering had authenticated their Renaissance origins. He had been presented the pair on his sixtieth birthday, a gift from longtime friends, Mr. and Mrs. Manfred von Snellenberger, of Bern, Switzerland.

Although it was decided by the powers in Moscow to remain silent about the plundering, the latest incident became the catalyst for the authorities to focus attention on this new and lucrative business venture—stealing and selling the nation's treasures. Some had put the take at close to four hundred million U.S. dollars in that first year alone.

When a well-placed snitch had alerted Charin that a transfer of two Rembrandts and a Renoir from the Hermitage was about to take place, he found himself being led on a wild goose chase on the coldest night of the year. When he finally turned on his blue light and flagged down the new Mercedes S600 as it headed out of the city, he arrested the occupants on the only charge he could think of: car theft. He summoned a paddy wagon and tossed the three angry entrepreneurs into the back. A search of the Mercedes uncovered no stolen art treasures, but Charin seized a cache of automatic weapons, two bags stuffed with American one hundred dollar bills and a carton of Marlboros.

Once Charin got the three back to the station, he couldn't find a camera for taking the mug shots, or ink for the fingerprint kits. Thoroughly disgusted, he took his displeasure out on a frozen radiator by kicking it. The century-old building hadn't been heated for weeks; the phone system was a joke; and more often than not half of the duty shifts never bothered to show up for work at changeovers. Charin sadly admitted to himself that any pretense at even the most rudimentary maintenance was but a faded memory. His nose, too, now reminded him that the place smelled like a urine-filled pigsty.

Charin relieved the prisoners of their valuables and cell phones, marched them to the cellblock and locked them up. The trio laughed in his face, boasting they would be back on the street before he got off duty. He shrugged as he walked away.

He was about to say something to Solotov when the chief of police stormed into his second floor cubby hole excuse of an office.

"What the hell do you two buffoons think you're up to?" Colonel Boris Pritkin wanted to know, standing before them like an apparition. The man was dressed for a midnight stroll down the Champs-Elysées, his mohair coat draped over his shoulders in the French style, its inky luster set off by a dazzling white silk scarf.

This…this…dandy dares to call me the buffoon? Charin thought, trying, but failing, to mask his contempt.

Pritkin was a survivor and his influence had increased tenfold over the years. He had publicly renounced his party membership scant minutes after Boris Yeltsin had done so on national television in a bold, calculated step to change the course of Soviet history.

Pritkin was among the first to jump on board, and was rewarded handsomely for his decision. He was well on his way to acquiring real wealth in the present order, but it had come at a steep price. He was now just another hired gun doing the bidding of the new elite.

Both detectives remained at attention and faced their sovereign. Pritkin's porcine eyes narrowed in anger, then widened with greed as they fell upon the pile of American Federal Reserve notes. He strode over to Charin, snatched the single page from his hand and quickly read it.

With a look of utter disdain, he asked, "So, Detective Sherlock Holmes Charin, where are the priceless paintings you were going to confiscate? Where is the proof the businessmen in the lock-up downstairs do not own the car they were in? Show me that their armaments importation documents aren't in proper order." He tore the sheet in half, tossed the remnants onto the floor, stomped on them with both feet and yelled in disgust: *Show me you're not a couple of idiots!*"

Charin stubbed out the cigarette he had been holding at his side. As he opened his mouth, Pritkin held up a gloved hand. "Spare me. I don't want to hear it!" He turned towards the door. "Put that money back in the bags and meet me downstairs. Meanwhile, I'll try to repair the damage. I should remand you to traffic patrol, or better yet, to school crossing guards, because it's obvious neither of you are fit to be called detectives."

Five minutes later, Charin and Solotov appeared on the ground floor, each carrying a canvas bag. As they plodded toward the holding cells, Charin noted that the booking camera was now busily snapping digital photos of several handcuffed prisoners while an officer had mysteriously found ink for the fingerprint kits and was collecting prints from the same group. Maybe Pritkin's right, he thought dejectedly. Maybe Solotov and I are the only fools left in this city. Maybe everyone else knows he has a new boss except us!

They met up with Pritkin and the three just-released men. Pritkin began passing them their belongings from large brown envelopes while apologizing for the boorish conduct of his detectives. Charin realized that one of the bandits had obviously managed to call Pritkin on his cell phone before it had been confiscated.

"Ah, think nothing of it, Colonel," the oldest said with a dazzling smile, displaying the best bridgework money could buy. "I'm sure it was an honest mistake, but our Italian guest must think we're a nation of barbarians." The gangster affixed a Rolex Presidential to his wrist with a satisfying snap. "Now we are very late for our appointment."

The other two hastily slipped on similar watches, then secreted bulging alligator wallets and other sundry items inside expensively tailored suit jackets. The two Russians reached out and liberated the bags of money from Charin and Solotov, hefting them a couple of times as if checking their weight.

Five minutes later, their stately German car sat purring by the curb. And parked behind it, an impressive Bentley Mulsanne.

Charin took in the scene, surmising the accompanying car belonged to a friend of the three just-released prisoners. Two of its four occupants were standing outside. The three "businessmen" came down the steps of the station house escorted by a still-fawning Pritkin. Charin ignored the gangsters as Pritkin shook hands all round, instead allowing his eyes to settle on the non-smoker standing beside the Bentley. The man was immaculately dressed, mid-thirties, trimmed beard, strong features, but wearing a look of either inner torment or exhaustion. At that moment, the man glanced up and locked eyes with Charin. Then he did a strange thing. He gave an almost imperceptible shake of his head as if to ask: Please, don't say anything.

I know that face, Charin thought as he continued to study the man. But where have I seen it before? His memory refused to cooperate.

"Shall we get back inside, sir? It looks like we're ready to leave," the smoker said with deference, flicking his butt onto the snow, then holding open the door for his companion. Within a heartbeat both men disappeared into the sanctuary of the car and were immediately hidden from further view behind heavily curtained, film-covered windows. Moments later the caravan crunched slowly across sizable piles of dirty snow and slush, broke out effortlessly onto the open street, gathered speed and disappeared around the corner.

Charin remained transfixed, staring after the vanished cars. He was concentrating, committing to memory the license plate on the English luxury sedan.

Pritkin was halfway up the steps of the station when the large horn mounted on the front of the building began to bellow. The raucous sound was a command for all personnel in the immediate vicinity to report inside at once. The assembled staff stood at attention while their shift commander, Major Andropov, read them a fax regarding an incident that had taken place in Moscow several hours earlier. The Patriarch of Moscow and two priests had been shot dead on the steps of the Epiphany Cathedral at Elokhovo. Citizens in the capital had formed into mobs. Orders were now coming from the Ministry of Internal Affairs placing all police forces in Russia on Condition Red, the highest state of alert.

Pritkin then shouted to Andropov over the heads of the assembled officers. "I want you to get all the members of your command back here on the double, and I also want everybody to get into their uniforms and to fan out on the streets until further notice. Initiate procedures for containing massive demonstrations. Call the other stations and relay those orders on my authority. *And somebody turn off that bloody horn!"* Pritkin yelled the last command over his shoulder as he headed for the front door, struggling to get his arms inside flapping coat sleeves as he ran.

Charin trudged off to his locker. As he changed into his uniform, his thoughts returned to the man in the Bentley. Where have I seen him before? Damn! And I'm supposed to be a whiz at remembering faces! But most puzzling had been how the fellow's companion had addressed him. He had used the words, Your High Excellency, a title first introduced by Peter the Great in 1722 in his Table of Ranks. It was a form of address reserved for august members of the nobility.

Twenty minutes later, while driving as fast as he dared on a slippery Maly Prospect—and just as he was passing the Smolenskoe Cemetery—the answer came to him. Of course! That face had been on several flyers sent from Interpol late last summer. It was the face of a man who had disappeared in Russia while on a business trip; a Swiss banker whose wife had been murdered in the capital of the United

States. *"Yes,"* Charin yelled aloud, *"you are Manfred von Snellenberger!"* He thumped a gloved hand on the steering wheel in a show of delight and a regained pride in his ability to come up with not only the face, but the name as well. Then he frowned. What in the hell was von Snellenberger doing in St. Petersburg? Didn't the man realize that half the world was looking for him? And why had he seemed so defeated? Then he remembered something else. This was the man who had given the Michelangelo candlesticks to that cardinal accused of murdering von Snellenberger's wife. And one of those candlesticks had been used to kill her, candlesticks which had alerted Charin to the dirty secret that the nation's treasures were being stolen with impunity.

"Is this not enough of a riddle for you, Inspector Charin?" he asked aloud. "Does any of it make sense?" Not at the moment it didn't, he had to admit.

Charin slowed the car as he approached a hastily erected checkpoint. The man peered inside and gave a quizzical look that said, where's your driver? Charin shrugged and drove on.

You'll just have to put aside this mystery for later, he now said to himself, because something tells me it's going to prove important. But for the moment, Mykel, you've got to stop the good people of St. Petersburg from storming the Winter Palace for the second time in less than a hundred years.

CHAPTER 19
Day 2. Rome. Tuesday evening

Kettering accepted an invitation to join the pope for supper. Throughout the simple meal, he could see that his longtime friend was distracted. The pontiff picked at his food. Finally, he looked at Kettering and managed a weak smile. "I can see why you have such confidence in Mister Scott. The man exudes a calming sense of stability, and I appreciated his candor when he gave his opinion about the letters. I like him, and I'm glad he is with us." The pope paused for a second then continued.

"There was something I wanted to mention during our meeting with Mister Scott, but I decided at the last minute to keep my silence. This afternoon I prayed for guidance and came to the realization your American friend will need all the help I can render if he is to have any chance of stopping the upheaval we believe is about to befall us. And I fully understand just how pitifully small the odds for success seem to be. Should Sister Lucia's prophesy comes to pass, then the fate of all of creation will rest in God's hands anyway, but I still have a duty as Christ's vicar on earth to protect His Church until my last breath is drawn. Therefore, I've decided to make a full disclosure to Mister Scott about what John Paul the Second heard during his meeting with Lucia back in Nineteen Ninety-one, so I now release you to tell him and Monsignor O'Bryan about that conversation."

"Thank you, Holy Father. I think you've made the right decision."

"One last thing, Francis. In light of the gravity of these unfolding events, I've decided to summon all of my cardinals to Rome for a consistory. Monsignor Caffarone has already sent emails directing them to come with all dispatch."

Kettering's face reflected alarm. "Have you told Monsignor Caffarone about the letters?"

The pope shook his head. "No, Ignacio asked if there was something troubling me, something that required consultation with my collegial advisors. When I admitted as much, he suggested convening the College. I saw the wisdom in his thinking and agreed."

"I see." What was done was done. Kettering knew he should have feelings of grave misgivings over this turn of events, except he could find no flaw in the logic behind Caffarone's reasoning. Still, he must remember to inform Justin.

* * * * *

At eight o'clock that evening, Simon Chertoff rushed over to Kettering's office and delivered his two translations.

"An interesting challenge, Eminence," he said, as he handed Kettering the painting and the reference book. "And, thank God for computers."

Chertoff spent the next several minutes explaining certain irrefutable facts he had discovered during his examination of the painting and photograph. Finished, he stole a peek at his watch. "Good thing you got me when you did, because I'm leaving for Tel Aviv in the morning. Anyway, I hope I've helped solve your problem without creating any new ones."

 Kettering offered his hand. "You've done a splendid job, Simon. Have a safe journey, but please, say nothing of this to anyone."

* * * * *

When the two Americans arrived at Kettering's office a half hour later, they found him seated at the conference table fussily arranging a pile of papers. He then picked up a sheet embossed with the papal coat of arms.

"The Holy Father and I shared supper and during the meal he confessed to something that has troubled him all afternoon, something, he admits he should have told you both earlier."

The two sat silent, wondering what new problem had arisen.

"When Pope John Paul the Second asked Cardinal Sodano to read that radio broadcast to the entire world on the Third Secret of Fatima back in Two Thousand," Kettering began, his blue eyes squarely on Justin's, "he deliberately chose to withhold from his friend and confidant the information you read today in Sister Lucia's Russian letter. Of course, I'm referring specifically to that last paragraph regarding the *Dies Irae*. The Holy Father assures me those frightful words were not found anywhere in Lucia's Nineteen Forty-four letter, which, as you remember, had come to the Vatican from Lisbon in

Nineteen Fifty-seven. Lucia only spoke of that terrible scenario to Pope John Paul the Second during a private audience in Nineteen Ninety-one.

"John Paul rushed back to Rome and wrote down everything he could remember, and after his death, those private notes passed into the hands of his successor, and the current pontiff. He confirmed this evening that what John Paul recollected hearing from Lucia that day seems to be word for word what we have all read in her Russian letter."

O'Bryan wore a troubled frown. "So why didn't Lucia write about the coming Apocalypse in her Nineteen Forty-four letter to her bishop?"

"A fair question Jack, and one John Paul asked Lucia when they met that day. Her answer was astonishingly simple. She said that she had not been specifically directed by the Virgin Mary to put to paper the part of her vision dealing with the end of creation, so she chose not to."

Both Americans traded glances.

Kettering held the page closer. "Here's what John Paul the Second wrote of that meeting. *It was at this point in our conversation that Sister Lucia became agitated. She seemed to be inwardly struggling for many minutes, all the while exhibiting signs of terrible torment. Then she slipped into a trance and began to speak in Portuguese, a language I know, but not well. Her words came slowly, each syllable an utterance of unbearable agony, and she began to weep as she foretold how all of God's magnificent creation would end.*"

Kettering's now shaking index finger had reached the bottom of the page. He allowed a moment to pass in order to regain his composure. He continued. "Pope John Paul the Second ended with this striking observation. *It was as though Sister Lucia had long ago committed those dire words to memory, words which had apparently been dictated to her by a very saddened Virgin Mary. Yet despite her distress, I sensed Sister Lucia was now relieved to have finally shared this secret with another human being, especially with the Bishop of Rome.* John Paul the Second signed and dated his memo, then as an afterthought, penned a postscript in Latin. *This meeting and the message from Our Lady has affected me greatly.*"

"I'll just bet it did," Justin said after a long moment.

As if anxious now to press on to other matters, Kettering lifted the top folder from the neat stack before him.

"Simon Chertoff delivered this report a few minutes ago. He also said he needed a lot of computer help to solve our mystery."

Justin and O'Bryan sat up straighter.

"Here's what Simon writes. 'The words found on the scroll seen in the photograph of *Evening Prayers* are written in ancient Hebrew and are the opening lines of the book of Genesis.

In the beginning, God created the heavens and the earth; the earth was waste and void; darkness covered the abyss, and the spirit of God was stirring above the waters.'"

Kettering laid the top page aside and continued to read Simon Chertoff's words. "'*Fra Angelico* had faithfully copied them from a *Torah*. Nothing mysterious in that. But here is what's written on the scroll in the painting you received from the Patriarch of Moscow.

"And there fell from the heaven a great star, burning like a torch."

"The Apocalypse, chapter eight," O'Bryan murmured, a frown forming on his brow. "So why does the scroll in *Fra Angelico's* original painting speak to the beginning of creation, while the scroll in the forgery speaks to its end?"

Kettering held up a cautionary hand. "Wait, there's more. It was here that Simon told me he was having quite a bit of difficulty translating the last sentence found on the scroll in my painting until it finally dawned on him that what he was seeing was from neither the Old nor the New Testaments."

Kettering cleared his throat. *"Now I am become Death, the shatterer of worlds."*

"But that's the Bhagavad-Gita, a part of the Hindu sacred scriptures," exclaimed a thoroughly puzzled O'Bryan. "So why would a Russian artist place a passage from the Hindu scriptures on what is obviously an ancient Torah?"

"Or better yet, why would that same painter include a passage from the New Testament on any torah?" Kettering wanted to know. "That's what I'd call a mistake of biblical proportions." He turned to Justin. "What do you make of it all?"

"I haven't a clue."

Kettering's face crumbled. He had hoped for a miraculous explanation.

Justin correctly read the cardinal's pained expression. "That was clumsy on my part, Francis" he allowed, "because what I should have said was: I haven't a clue, yet! Look, if we can agree that I might be able to help the Holy Father—and I'm not sure at this point that I can—well, I don't want to go off halfcocked. Thirty years of FBI training has taught me to piece every puzzle together in a methodical fashion, and that's what I intend to do here. Which means I'm going to need a lot of help from the both of you."

"But we don't have much time," O'Bryan reminded his friend.

"You're right, but I have to dig deeper into all of this," Justin replied, pointing to the pile in front of Kettering. "I'll have to go over the Russian painting inch by inch, and then I'll need to study the mysterious Russian's letter, then Lucia's letter and all of your translations. And I'm going to need some good reference books regarding the secret of Fatima and the life of Lucia. Maybe I'll uncover something others have overlooked."

Kettering found himself suddenly rejuvenated. "And I know just the book for you," he said. "*A Life of Devotion*. It's chock full of facts. It was published by an American nun in Two Thousand and Eleven and has an excellent index, which makes it easy for any reader to zero in on important dates, places and events. That one feature alone will save you a lot of time."

Justin nodded his approval and continued. "I'll need a computer, plus copies of all the correspondence Lucia might have produced over her lifetime, no matter how insignificant."

Kettering allowed a smile to cross his face. "Justin, if you insist on reading everything Lucia ever wrote, then I'm afraid you'll be here well into the next century. The good sister was quite the prolific writer over her long life, and that includes the publishing of two inspirational books. No, I recommend you save her writings for another day and concentrate on what we have available here."

"Thanks for the warning," Justin replied, removing his jacket.

Kettering felt relieved. This was the Justin Scott from those trying days in Washington. "You shall have everything you've asked for, and

I'm going to set you up in an office next to mine. Are there any other requests while I'm still in a generous mood?"

"Just one. Can you spare our Jesuit friend here to come work with me fulltime until either this crisis is averted or we discover Lucia's letter is legitimate and we all end up meeting our Maker? I need Jack to help explain the sophisticated Church Dogma, and from what I'm hearing, he's quite the hotshot on such matters. And I'll probably need his skills in greasing wheels and opening doors when we have to hit the road."

Justin turned to O'Bryan. "You up to the challenge, sonny?" he asked, a false scowl covering his face. "I'm talking long hours, little pay, poor food, and no sleep."

Both priests laughed. The Justin Scott of old was back, and with a vengeance.

"Done," Kettering replied, and as he did, a red light on the telephone console began winking, a silent demand for his immediate attention.

Kettering picked up the receiver and listened for thirty seconds. His face drained as he slowly replaced the instrument and turned toward the expectant Americans.

"That was the nuncio's office in Moscow. Less than fifteen minutes ago, the Patriarch of Moscow and two priests were gunned down on the steps of Elokhovo Cathedral. They were shot from the back of a slow moving truck, and the initial report says all three were killed instantly. A witness said he thought the attackers looked Asian, possibly Japanese."

"Asian? Japanese?" Justin repeated, wondering if Kettering had misheard.

"That's what the witness said." Kettering rose and signaled O'Bryan. "Come, we have work to do, but first I must inform the pope." He turned to Justin. "I need Jack more than you do right now. The Russian letter prophesized the patriarch would be gunned down within the next few days. Well, the author has just been proven right." He stopped at the door. "Please find us the answer, Mister Scott, because time is fast running out for either the Church and perhaps for all of mankind."

CHAPTER 20
Day 3. Rome. Wednesday morning

The next morning the three men awoke after little sleep to news that rioting had broken out overnight in several Russian cities. All the international news organizations were being denied visas for additional reporters and TV crews to enter the country and, in frustration, began heaping open invectives upon the Russian government in their broadcasts. All characterized the denial of visas as proof of the Kremlin's backsliding into the heavy-handed days of the past. A few managed to get limited footage out via an English satellite in the early hours, but they were soon rounded up and their equipment confiscated. The last Sky Television Network package was successfully down linked to London moments before that plug had been pulled, and the correspondent had filed a report that the Patriarch of Ukraine had been attacked in his residence overnight and left for dead. The announcer said that in less than three hours the unrest was already spilling into the neighboring republics. He suggested that agitators seemed to be in place, just waiting for the command to arouse the populace.

Justin placed a tab-laden green folder on the table, hooked his thumbs inside bright red suspenders and waited. His one self-admitted weakness was clothes.

"What do you have for us?" Kettering asked.

"I don't think you're going to like it, Eminence," Justin began, deliberately not addressing the cardinal by his given name, "but I have to call it the way I see it. Anyway, keep this thought in mind; there is nothing that says I'm right, but my conclusions are based on my interpretation of the facts and not on wishful thinking. So let me be blunt. It is my professional opinion the information in the Russian Vulgate Latin letter will prove to be accurate, but Lucia's letter will in the end up prove to be bogus."

Kettering sprang to his feet. He was having none of it. *"No, Mister Scott, I insist on stopping you right now because you are wrong!* The information in Lucia's letter is legitimate, a fact, I must remind you, that's been confirmed by the Holy Father. Have you deliberately chosen to forget what Lucia told John Paul the Second during their face-to-face, private meeting her convent in Nineteen Ninety-one?"

"Please, let me finish," Justin replied in an even voice. "I said I could be wrong; but I don't think so. What I do believe is that something highly unusual and highly suspect is at play here, and I'll also grant you this: whatever it is, it is fiendishly clever and it's being flawlessly executed."

Kettering was now leaning against the table for support, his thin frame trembling with suppressed anger. *"That, statement, sir, is not only impossible, it smacks of heresy and blasphemy! I'll hear no more."*

Justin shook his head, unfazed. "Eminence, you asked me to drop everything and come to Rome. I did, so now, hear me out. According to what the pope told you yesterday, Lucia's Russian letter contains the same information that is in the Vatican's letter, but it also includes that all-important terrifying last paragraph about the impending Apocalypse." Justin paused several moments then said in a deliberately lowered voice, "I could also be persuaded to believe it's remotely possible there could be an entirely different explanation, which is that Lucia's Russian letter is legitimate, and the one the popes have been guarding here in Vatican City since Nineteen Fifty-seven is nothing more than a masterful forgery."

Kettering shook his head but offered Justin an avenue of escape. "Then tell me this. Let's suppose for a moment that the Vatican never had in its possession the real letter from Lucia. And let's also suppose that Lucia's Russian letter is—bogus— the word you used a minute ago—then where is the one true letter which we all know Lucia wrote? Because she most assuredly wrote such a letter. And if my memory serves me correctly, she verified her own handwriting when shown a photocopy of that letter at the pope's behest in Two Thousand, *and* she reaffirmed that the text was indeed the third part of the secret, just as she had written it in January, Nineteen Forty-four."

"Ah, now we're finally getting to the crux of the problem," Justin replied. "You see, I believe our Russian writer discovered something none of the popes since Pius the Twelfth have known since fifty-seven and that is, the part dealing with the Apocalypse is probably false. The Patriarch of Moscow ingeniously found a way to send you a warning which was; don't believe Lucia's letter; look for the truth elsewhere! His message was not just to a fellow prelate, Francis, but it was a message to one who has the ear of the pope. I also believe there are others inside Russia who read this purported letter from Lucia and they believe it's legitimate."

"And just how did the Patriarch of Moscow manage to do all that, pray tell?" asked a still-angry and openly skeptical Kettering. "I read the same letter you did and I don't remember seeing anything like that, either between the lines or otherwise. No, you've got to come up with something a lot better because we have very little time left." He looked at his watch. "What will you say when you meet your Maker, Mister Scott? 'I thought the message from the Virgin Mary was a bluff?'"

Justin leaned closer, eyes level with Kettering's. He ignored the cardinal's angry face. "The warning isn't in the Russian Latin letter nor is it in Lucia's letter," he said, "because it's going to be found in the painting instead. I'm guessing the patriarch was praying that you would spot the painting as a forgery and, by golly, you did. He, or someone else, was hoping you would examine the painting closely, declare it a fake and turn to a careful re-examination of both letters. And once it dawned on you that the last paragraph of Lucia's letter about the end of the world was not in fact legitimate, you'd be forced to conclude you were in possession of a false message from a false prophet."

Kettering wordlessly turned to O'Bryan, and arched a questioning eyebrow.

"Wait, I have more," Justin said. "For argument's sake, let's say I'm right so far, OK? Then let me suggest the following. Do we know for sure whether or not Lucia spoke to any of the other popes about her vision of the Apocalypse? Unfortunately, they're all dead and so is Lucia, which means we're left having to find the truth for ourselves."

"How do we go about doing that?" O'Bryan asked.

Ian A. O'Connor

"Follow along with me for a little while longer because I think someone did manage to get a message out of Russia on that skillfully doctored canvas. And I think it is something a lot bigger than an oddly placed snippet from Saint John's gospel and a single sentence from the Hindu scriptures. No, those passages were chosen with the utmost of care, hinting there's another message hidden somewhere deep inside that painting just begging to be discovered by us. Something to do with the candlestick would be my guess, something that will lead us to the one true letter written by Lucia and her legitimate Third Secret of Fatima. And, maybe, just maybe, that secret speaks to a far different future than the one we think the world is now facing. However, if on the other hand I am wrong and it is God's will to end creation ten days from now, then think about this. Does the pope have a moral obligation to share that knowledge with all the peoples of the world so that they have time to make peace with their Creator? Or does he keep his silence to prevent the biggest panic on earth since the waters began rising past everyone's chins a few thousand years back? You gentlemen are the theologians, so you tell me. How would Saint Augustine or Saint Thomas Aquinas solve this ethical dilemma?" He waited a long moment then added in a subdued voice, "Because I sure don't have the answer."

Justin could see it in their faces. He had just posed a question neither had thought through to its conclusion, and, he suspected, neither had the pope. He pushed himself away from Kettering's chair and began to pace. It was time to press on.

"Francis, let's, not dwell over this particular moral dilemma any longer," he said. "I was stumped for hours last night that the painting included that quote from the Bhagavad-Gita. It didn't make a lick of sense other than that holy verse also speaks to the destruction of the world. Then I had thought. Forget the Bhagavad-Gita, I told myself. Think, man, where else have you seen those words? Then it came to me. The physicist Robert Oppenheimer muttered that verse as he witnessed the first atomic explosion in the New Mexico desert in the pre-dawn hours of July sixteenth, Nineteen Forty-five. *'Now I am become Death, the shatterer of worlds.'* And in that moment, I found my answer. Our Russian friend is telling us where to focus our efforts. Look to that historic event from Nineteen Forty-five. That is his message to you."

Justin returned to his seat. "Francis, I believe the Patriarch of Moscow was murdered not just because of those letters, but mainly because of your painting. I think he stumbled across—or maybe he only heard rumors about—the letter from Lucia, but there were some really bad actors determined to stop him at any cost from revealing what he knew or suspected. I'm saying these are Russians with a far different agenda than the one we've been duped into believing is a message from the Mother of Jesus. We know for a fact from the Russian Latin letter that there is going to be a do-or-die, no-holds-barred struggle for supremacy between the Roman Church and the Russian Rite, and only one Church will survive. But, the writer warns, if it should be the Russian Church, then the Apocalypse will surely follow, because he speaks convincingly of a renegade faction within the Russian Rite with access to weapons 'which shall rain fire upon an evil earth' to quote his exact words. And he assures us, they will not hesitate to use them." Justin let loose a mirthless, cynical laugh. "Let's face it, there's no more frightening an enemy than a zealot; especially one on a religious crusade. We need look no further than to the Muslim fanatics and the havoc they've wrought in Allah's name for the past forty-plus years from the Sunni Moslem Brotherhood, to al-Qaeda, to ISIS, and to those Shiites in Iranian hell-bent on acquiring the bomb."

Kettering cradled his face in both hands. His steadfastness was beginning to waver. What was he supposed to do? What was he going to tell the Holy Father? How could any pope counter this? What army, what arsenal, could he call upon to offer up as a counterbalance to such terror? And what if such men actually wrested control of the Russian Church? Then what? He was overwhelmed by the myriad possibilities.

"But that's the down side," Justin was saying in a voice suddenly and deliberately upbeat, "because I think I've come up with a plan to avert the inevitable disaster we've all been telling ourselves is the irreversible will of God. And if I'm wrong, well, so what? The world will end according to God's timetable and it won't matter a whit what any of us does during these next few days. But, if the deadline comes and goes and we're all still alive, then we might well have missed a narrow window of opportunity to stop a Russian quest to destroy the Roman Church simply because we chose to believe the wrong message."

Kettering looked up. "If you are right, then I pray you've come up with a plan to overcome the impossible," Kettering said, allowing a hint of relief to creep into his voice. "What are you proposing to do?"

"What I'm proposing is that Jack and I go back in time some seventy-plus years, and we do that by first visiting Portugal as it was in the nineteen forties. Because that's where I believe this convoluted paper trail got its start."

"I'm not sure what you mean," Kettering replied, "but have you forgotten that Sister Lucia was living in a convent in Tuy, Spain, during the thirties and forties? The woman didn't join the Carmelite order of nuns in Coimbra, Portugal, until Nineteen Forty-eight."

"No, I haven't forgotten. I also haven't forgotten that Sister Scholastica wrote how Lucia was often sick and rested at a nunnery closer to her home in Portugal in Nineteen Forty-one. Sister Scholastica also wrote how Lucia confided that she had initially written down the third secret in a separate, never revealed letter in April, Nineteen Forty-one, four months before she penned the first and second secret in August, at the behest of her bishop. Then she says Lucia destroyed her April letter it in late Nineteen Forty-two without showing it to anyone. My question is: now why did Lucia do that?"

Kettering allowed a ghost of a smile to cross his face. "I should have remembered. You are the detective, and a good one. And I'm impressed how you have managed to remember all of those dates, and kept them in their right order." Kettering gave a slight bow of homage as he spoke. "I leave the decision as to what must be done next in your capable hands."

"Thank you for those kind words, Francis, but let me leave you both with one last tidbit of information to gnaw on. Remember, the real *Evening Prayers* painting by Fra Angelico surfaced in Portugal, of all places, and did so after disappearing for more than a hundred years."

"And…?" said a quizzical O'Bryan.

"I think that was by design and not by accident, Jack."

Ian A. O'Connor

CHAPTER 21
Day 3. Rome. Wednesday afternoon

"Tired?" O'Bryan asked late the following afternoon as he led Justin out of the biting wind swirling in bursts around the *Piazza San Pietro.* He had noticed his friend favoring his still-healing leg.

"Yeah, I'm tired, I'm old and I'm cold," Justin replied with a laugh. "Also, it's after five o'clock somewhere in the world, and methinks I'm in need of a wee dram and a sturdy chair to rest these weary bones. Any suggestions?"

"Dozens," O'Bryan replied."

"Then lead on, McDuff, and surprise me, only make it somewhere close because I've got some ideas I want to bounce off you."

Ten minutes later they were seated in *Armando,* a popular blue-collar *trattoria* at *Borgio Vittorio*, nestled in the long wintry shadows of Vatican City.

Justin settled into his seat, downed a handsome swallow of the single malt scotch presented by their young waiter, then released a long contented sigh. "Elixir of life, lad," he said, allowing a satisfied glow to spread across his tired face. "You should try it sometime."

O'Bryan smiled, and held aloft his cola. "I'll stick with this. What gives?"

Justin rubbed a hand over his cheeks and chin as he gathered his thoughts. "Remember the book Francis brought me, the definitive one by the American nun about Sister Lucia's life after the visions?"

"A Life of Devotion, by Sister Scholastica Osborne, OSB," O'Bryan replied somewhat formally. "Why do you ask?"

"Because something's been bugging me about what the good sister wrote concerning Lucia's several illnesses in the late nineteen thirties and early forties. Specifically, she wrote how the illnesses became more frequent and more severe and how the woman was on death's doorstep on more than one occasion. Remember?"

"Of course I remember. Chronic pleurisy, bronchitis and pneumonia, but so what? I mean, the woman got sick, she was treated by a doctor and she got better. Look at where she lived. In a convent in Tuy, Spain. Those nuns were—and still are—the poorest of the poor. The convent probably had no electricity and no heat during the winter months, so the place would have been perpetually cold, damp and downright miserable. A veritable breeding ground for respiratory infections, I'd say. No big mystery there, my friend."

Justin took another pull on his drink, swirled the amber fluid around in his mouth then swallowed. He leaned closer in an attempt to triumph over the din without having to resort to shouting. "Well, I think you're wrong, sport. Something big did go down, possibly during her bout with pneumonia in fall of Nineteen Forty, the one where she was administered extreme unction, or, as it's more commonly called today, the last rites. Sister Scholastica writes how an English doctor who was visiting a relative at the time was summoned to treat her, and everyone thought it was the end for our Lucia. At one point she says the rest of the nuns didn't think Lucia would make it through the night."

"But we know she did. She was relatively young and she pulled through. It doesn't have to mean there was a miracle."

"I'm not suggesting there was. I'm thinking more along the lines of an intervention from a more earthly kingdom; namely one called Great Britain."

That got O'Bryan's attention. He sat up straighter. "Go on."

"My theory is that during this period someone deliberately got to our Lucia and discovered the third part of the secret, and I mean *in toto*. I also believe the good sister really was on death's doorstep—probably delirious most of the time—and under those circumstances, she talked."

O'Bryan seemed curious to see where Justin was headed. "All right, for argument's sake I'll go along and agree that she talked. But how does that explain away the fact she says she wrote down the third secret, supposedly for the first time, in April, Nineteen Forty-one, then had a change of heart and destroyed what she had written in Nineteen Forty-two? And then two years later, in Nineteen Forty-four, she started the same letter again from scratch as commanded by her bishop? Then she sealed it in an envelope, gave it to the bishop, and he finally had it delivered to Pope Pius some thirteen years later?"

O'Bryan rushed to answer his own questions. "What it means, Justin, is that it's about one hundred percent certain the pope has the contents of the real letter and the real Third Secret, except for that last paragraph." He rushed on to complete his thought before Justin could interrupt. "I'm suggesting that somehow the Russians got a hold of a letter written by Lucia with the exact same information back in Nineteen Forty-one, or maybe it was as late as Nineteen Forty-four. But the real kicker is that her Russian letter in fact *contained that awful last paragraph about the Apocalypse, and the pope's letter didn't.* Which could explain how these many years later someone inside Russia can cite chapter and verse what's in the pope's letter in Vatican City, and which could easily lead a rational soul to conclude *both letters are indeed genuine.* Ergo, the pope has every reason to be worried about what the Russians seem to know."

Justin slowly shook his head. "I'll come back to punch holes in that scenario," he said, "but let's concentrate on Lucia herself for the moment." He took a last swallow of scotch and continued. "Sister Scholastica wrote that the dying Lucia was treated by a visiting British doctor and that she rallied unexpectedly to a full recovery. That is a fact which cannot be overlooked or ignored, and I'm betting it's the key to solving our mystery."

"Ah, Justin, we've been over all that," O'Bryan patiently reminded his friend. "The author painstakingly explained in a footnote that because no one could resurrect the name of the English physician, and because she had been told the story by a very old, and forgetful nun— namely the ninety-three-year-old Lucia herself—she rightly decided to include the information in Lucia's biography but with a great big red flag of a caveat—*maybe true, maybe not.* The doctor seems to have simply done his job then disappeared. Sister Scholastica was meticulous with her scholarship. She did not have a corroborating source, no second witness if you will, so she chose not to include that information in the body of the work, but only as a footnote. Anyway, it wasn't a watershed event."

"That's where you're wrong, Jack! It *was* a watershed event, and I intend to follow up on that missing bit of information. I'm going to track down the good Sister Scholastica and speak with her. Shouldn't be difficult; the book was published just a few years ago, and with the aid of the Internet and Google, it should be a snap."

O'Bryan shook his head. "That's not going to happen. Sister Scholastica died earlier this year. I was cross-referencing other works regarding Fatima on the Internet yesterday and I came across that bit of information. I thought it was not important, so I didn't mention it. Such a shame, she was only thirty-nine-years-old."

Justin stiffened. "How did she die?"

"Relax," the priest chided gently, "she was on vacation with her family in the Florida Keys and was hit by a power boat while riding a jet ski. It was an accident. No sinister forces did her in."

"Damn!"

"So where does this leave us? Does it blow away your plan?"

"No, just changes it a bit, that's all." Justin leaned in closer. "Here's the drill. You and I are going to Portugal tomorrow. In and out, we'll be home by late afternoon. As I said before, Lisbon is where we have to begin our search. We're going to track down that doctor, because he's the key to how this whole thing got started. Call it being obstinate, but that's my read on the situation, so humor me, OK?"

O'Bryan held up both hands in an exaggerated display of mock submission. "So we'll march off to Portugal and try to trace an unknown doctor who treated a patient over seventy years ago. Piece of cake. Just one question, though. Why not Spain? That's where Lucia was living at the time."

"We might have to go to Madrid later," Justin conceded, "but I'm hoping not. Lucia was Portuguese; the Spanish town of Tuy is just across the border, so in all likelihood any English doctor visiting the region was in Portugal and not Spain."

"Can't find fault with your reasoning," O'Bryan admitted.

"Good," Justin replied, looking around for their waiter, "so let's forget about our problems for a while and eat, because I'm starved."

Neither had paid any attention to the laborer who had followed them into the restaurant and had sat at the next table nursing a beer. After the Americans had paid and left, he waited a full five minutes before shuffling off. Outside, and with his back hugging the façade of the building as protection from the biting wind, he began talking into his cell phone in a strange Yiddish-sounding dialect.

Ian A. O'Connor

CHAPTER 22
Day 4. Lisbon, Portugal. Thursday morning

In the taxi en route to da Vinci Airport early the following morning O'Bryan asked Justin about his new walking stick.

"Bought it yesterday evening in the hotel gift shop," Justin explained. "My leg's still acting up, so this should suffice until I get the one I asked Francis to have shipped over in the diplomatic pouch. I'm guessing he wouldn't have approved had he known about all of the nasty little secret toys it hides. Let's just say I'm leveling the playing field and leave it at that." He then changed the subject for the rest of the 21-mile ride.

* * * * *

Upon deplaning at Lisbon's Portela Airport, they were ushered through customs without fanfare. Because Portugal was the poorest of the Western democracies, it welcomed all visitors with open arms and a minimum of inconvenience. Travelers delighted in not finding themselves subjected to the indignities of a bloated, self-perpetuating customs bureaucracy whether arriving from other EU member states or not.

Kettering had had photographs taken of both men the afternoon before, and diplomatic passports prepared overnight. Upon being given the documents by a staffer just before leaving for the airport, O'Bryan examined them and voiced his approval. He turned to Justin and handed him his document. "You should feel honored. There are less than six hundred of these things in existence, and even though I've been working here for a few years, I never rated one until now."

They presented their U.S. passports upon arrival, but still, it was comforting to know they could fall back on Vatican credentials should the need ever arise.

Justin flagged down a taxi and directed the driver to the British Embassy.

"This was quite the town throughout the war years," Justin remarked as his eyes and ears took in the sights and sounds. "Lisbon was a full-blown Mecca for spies from both sides, a fact I'm counting on for answers. Plus everyone knows the Brits keep extraordinarily good records. Adolf Hitler didn't label them a nation of shopkeepers for nothing."

"I don't think he quite meant it as a compliment," O'Bryan replied, turning on the narrow seat to better face his friend. "So, is that your roundabout way of telling me this has something to do with the war?"

"Padre, don't you find it more than a bit strange that this English doctor appeared like some bolt out of the blue, treated a dying nun and then vanished as quickly and as mysteriously as he came? And this at a time when the British were marshaling every available resource to protect the homeland from the invasion across the English Channel from Occupied France, an invasion they knew was inevitable? Think back to those times, Jack." He began ticking off points on his fingertips as he made them. "The British army had been soundly routed in France, Belgium, and Holland by the Germans, and had to be evacuated from the beaches of Dunkirk by a fleet of fishing boats, pleasure craft, and anything else that could float. To add to that humiliation, they had to abandon all of their equipment on the wrong side of the channel while Göring's Luftwaffe was spooling up to pound what Hitler called 'that island of shopkeepers' into a bloody pulp. So, given all of this to contend with, why would a British doctor suddenly show up in Lisbon? Had to have been for a damned good reason," he concluded. "Anyway, just follow my lead when we get to the embassy. We're going to keep it light, but let me do the talking because I intend to tell some little white lies and, if need be, a real whopper or two."

Once inside the legation, Justin flashed a thousand megawatt smile at a junior female staffer as he introduced himself and O'Bryan. In a relaxed, aw-shucks manner, he explained the purpose of his visit. "I wonder if it would be possible to see the embassy guest logs for the years Nineteen Forty and Nineteen Forty-one? I think my uncle stayed here for a week or two during that time," he rambled on. "Uncle George was an unabashed Anglophile, and he loved to wangle protracted stays in British embassies all over the world. Oftentimes he would drop the names of royals he had never laid eyes on to kind of help cement the idea he was someone important. Darn if his ruse didn't work! So, over the years when I'm visiting various capitals I take a moment to look and see if Uncle George got there before me. And guess what? More often than not, he did! George was a great one for writing home and boasting of his exploits, and from those letters I know he was in and out of Lisbon a couple of times during the early war years. He wrote in one letter, which I read years later, that the diplomatic relationship enjoyed between England and Portugal was the world's longest standing alliance, apparently dating back to Thirteen Hundred and Seventy-three. For some reason, I never forgot that nugget." Justin laughed heartily at the memory of his quixotic, nonexistent relative.

The staffer pondered this urbane American's amusing request. "You certainly seem to know your history about us, Mister Scott. But you're not wanting to take a peek at the official day-to-day working logs of the embassy, are you? Because if that were the case, then your request would have to be vetted and approved at the Foreign Office HQ level in London. Parts of those logs are still protected under the Official Secrets Act and that could take ages and ages."

"No, no, my dear, I'm just interested in a peek at the everyday guest book."

"Well, I don't see any harm in that. Mind you, it will take me a few minutes to find. That is, if it hasn't been tossed into the rubbish bin years ago!"

The few minutes stretched to twenty, then to thirty, and just as both were starting to worry, the young woman entered the sitting room cradling a leather-bound ledger reminiscent of the type found in most of the world's posh hotels of the period. "I think you're in luck! This is the one for late Nineteen Thirty-nine to early Nineteen Forty-two," she explained brightly, laying it on the coffee table before the two men. "Look all you want, but please, just don't tear out any of the pages," she added with a nervous smile.

"OK, Uncle George, come out, come out, wherever you are," Justin stage whispered, then began working his way through the heavy vellum pages of a tome which was as much a social register of the day as it was a guest log.

The entries reflected an almost party like atmosphere at this legation during the period that had since been dubbed by historians as 'The Phony War.' Most of the guests wrote a paragraph or two before departing, many adding a phrase in Portuguese, some in Spanish, each seemingly trying to one-better some earlier commentary with witty sayings interspersed among flowery prose and effusive thanks to their hosts.

The embassy was a busy place during the fall and winter of 1940-41. They scanned page after page of drivel; some of the names recognizable, most not; some entries were written in fine copperplate, others in the maniacal scrawl of gin-besotted minds.

They studied the pages for almost an hour and came up with nothing. They returned to the beginning and started again. Same result. As they readied for a third assault, Justin asked O'Bryan to direct the table lamp toward the book and to begin turning the pages on his command. He then began snapping away with a high-speed digital camera masquerading as a wristwatch.

Finished with his task, Justin signaled O'Bryan to close the book. "Well, Padre, there's no evidence of good old Uncle George passing this way," he said in a loud voice, "so let's say our goodbyes to the nice lady and scram."

The staffer took the book from O'Bryan. "I mentioned to one of my chums what you gentlemen were about, and she told me that a man had inquired about those same logs sometime last fall when I was on home leave. He was here for the better part of a whole day and a real charmer he was, too," she said. "Now isn't that a coincidence?"

"Wonder if that was my brother, Alan?" Justin asked of no one in particular. "Alan was in Europe last fall."

The woman shook her head and laughed. "I wouldn't think so. According to Bea, the gent wasn't an American. Japanese maybe, but definitely not an American."

* * * * *

Ten minutes later, they were in a taxi and on their way back to Portela Airport.

"The answer's got to be somewhere in that book," Justin said, "I can feel it in my bones, especially now that we know someone else has been sniffing around as well. We're going back to the Vatican and we're going to go over those pages till our eyes pop." He sat back and let his gaze follow a group of cyclists gathering by the roadside.

"Let's hope we haven't copied the wrong book simply because we got the year wrong," said an equally worried O'Bryan.

"Don't even go there," replied Justin.

* * * * *

Rome. Thursday afternoon.

At five o'clock, the Vatican press office delivered three large manila envelopes of photographic blow-ups to O'Bryan in Cardinal Kettering's office.

The quality of the photographs was excellent. Each was as readable as the original page.

"We're going to be looking for repeaters," Justin said. "I'm beginning to think that maybe our mystery doctor didn't announce he was a physician when he checked in at the embassy. There's no entry with the letters M.D. and we know how doctors love to let the world know of their presence."

O'Bryan shook his head. "There wouldn't be any such entry in this instance. The English use a different designation. Their medical degree is an M.B.,Ch.B."

Justin sat back and stared a long moment at the priest. Finally, he asked, "Now how in the world would you know that?"

"Because I'm one smart Jesuit, that's how. Also, think about this quirky little fact to throw into the mix. If our man happened to be a surgeon instead of a physician, then he would be called mister and not doctor, and he would sign his name as Mister. It's been that way in the British Isles for a couple of hundred years. Now, get to work, you ignorant lout," O'Bryan added, reveling in Justin's baffled look.

No luck. There were only two entries attesting to multiple visits for the entire year of 1940. The first was for a Lord and Lady Alfred Chauncey Darlington, landed gentry from the Oxfordshire Cotswolds who were spending much of their fiftieth wedding anniversary year touring neutral Spain and neutral Portugal. The second posting was for a single woman, a Margaret R. Smalling, who had been candid in her narrative about being sent from London to translate into English some

Portuguese agricultural manuals about the care and cultivation of cork trees for the wine and port industry back home. Both times she had gushed on, thanking the ambassador and the staff for making her time there feel like she was on holiday. Her enthusiasm was to a point of inducing nausea.

"Talk about sucking up to the boss," O'Bryan added as he finished reading her last entry aloud. "Probably some lonely old spinster and these two visits to Lisbon were the high points in her dreary life." The entries showed that Smalling had made near back-to-back trips during November and early December 1940.

Although neither could read Portuguese, the woman had added a couple of sentences in that language at the end of her final entry, a pathetic gesture made to impress those who came behind her with her total grasp of the language. It was really quite sad, Justin thought with a twinge of guilt to be mocking a woman long dead.

"Well, so much for the theory of looking for people making multiple visits," O'Bryan announced with a hint of defeat in his voice an hour later.

Justin refused to toss in the towel, so they soldiered on.

Kettering stopped by just before dinner and Justin explained in terse sentences what they had done and what they had hoped to find. "Francis, there's just no evidence of an English doctor being at the embassy in Lisbon at any time during Nineteen Forty."

While Justin was speaking, Kettering began an idle perusal of the photographic pages covering entries for November and December. Something caught his eye. Slowly, he extracted a small notepad from beneath his cassock and scribbled a few words. Then he turned on his computer, and, after a couple of minutes, produced a translation of the Portuguese in Margaret Smalling's last three sentences.

Won't HWF and EBC be thrilled when I recount my successes; even grumpy old Alexander will surely be impressed! So, too, that other dashing man with the same last name, I'm sure.

Kettering tapped the edge of the screen with a fingernail. "I asked Google to take those two sets of initials and join them to the name Alexander. This interesting gem came back."

Ian A. O'Connor

[HWF], Sir Howard Walter Florey [EBC], Sir Ernst Boris Chain: British biochemists. Conducted the initial clinical trial of the antibiotic penicillin which was first isolated from the Penicillium mold by [Alexander] Sir Alexander Fleming in 1928.

"While you were bemoaning the fact there was no record of a doctor ever being at the embassy," Kettering said, "it suddenly dawned on me that just maybe, to borrow from a well-worn cliché, you weren't seeing the forest for the trees. First off, I thought in all probability the doctor you were looking for would be a woman and, secondly, it made eminent sense she would also be fluent in Portuguese. I saw both these characteristics as most likely to be found in the secretary, Miss Margaret Smalling. It just seemed right. The nuns would certainly be more apt to trust a female physician, and in order to communicate with the patient, the doctor would have needed to be conversant in Lucia's native tongue. Lucia spoke Portuguese, maybe some Spanish, so Miss Smalling was the obvious choice."

"Simple as that, huh?" Justin asked.

Kettering nodded, thoroughly enjoying his newfound position at center stage. "Simple as that," he replied.

Justin began to extrapolate. "So that's what it was all about," he said. "Penicillin! The year is Nineteen Forty," he continued, taking them back in time, "and there's only enough penicillin in the world to fill a couple of thimbles. The stuff was worth a king's ransom, yet someone had just maybe made a decision to send a portion of that meager supply to Portugal to be injected into a dying nun. Now, who possibly had enough clout to order such a momentous undertaking? Only Winston Spencer Churchill, that's who," he said, answering his own question. "But why?"

Confirmation soon followed from another Google search. The two Americans crowded behind Kettering's chair and read over his shoulders.

(Dame, DBE) Margaret Rivera Smalling, 1917-
Widow of (Sir, KBE) Michael Smalling, 1912-1999
Born: Margaret Rivera. Rio de Janeiro, Brazil. Educated in Scotland. B.Sc., University of Edinburgh, 1936; M.Sc., University of Leeds, 1937; Ph.D., University of Leeds, 1939; MB.ChB., Glasgow

University, 1948. Employed by Sir William Dunn School of Pathology, University of Oxford 1939-1940 to work on the development of a promising new antibiotic, penicillin. Vetted to Naval Intelligence: 1940-1944.

Then there was a second page devoted to her many accomplishments, including the notation that she and her husband had been jointly honored by the queen who had named them to the Order of the British Empire with the rank of Dame Commander and Knight Commander respectively on the 1968 New Year's Honors list. The biography noted she was still an active member of the Royal College of Physicians of Edinburgh, (Chartered 1681) but was retired and living in Edinburgh, Scotland. There were two children, both listed as still living.

"Why, this makes her well over ninety," O'Bryan remarked, his voice full of awe.

"And it shows she didn't earn her medical degree until after the war," added Kettering as he continued to study the screen. "I think you gentlemen need to pay the doctor a visit, and I mean as early as tomorrow morning."

"Agreed," said Justin walking back to his chair. "I wonder who she was referring to when she alluded to that other 'dashing' man with the same last name as Alexander. Did Fleming have a brother who also worked with him?"

Kettering and O'Bryan both shrugged.

As Kettering was powering down the computer, the phone rang. O'Bryan picked up and identified himself. A moment later, his face broke out in a grin.

"Monsignor Allenby! No, no, it's Jack O'Bryan." A momentary pause, then, "Of course I remember the last time we met." He laughed at something the other man said, then replied, "I've forgiven you long ago; so has Justin. Look, hold on, Justin's right here, so is Cardinal Kettering. I'm putting you on the speakerphone." A second later he asked, "Can you hear me, Monsignor?"

"I can indeed. Are you there, Your Eminence, Mister Scott?"

"We are," Justin replied for all of them. "Are you on a secure line, Monsignor?"

A pause, then: "No, I don't think so. I guess I don't really know. I'm on a cell phone. But I saw something a few minutes ago that was so startling, so absolutely extraordinary that I knew I had to contact Cardinal Kettering or Monsignor O'Bryan immediately. I'm glad you're there, too, Mister Scott."

"What have you got?"

"I'm in Lausanne and I've just seen a ghost. I was driving by *Credit Lausanne* a few minutes ago, and guess who I saw step out of a car right in front of the building?"

"I have no idea."

"Count Laufenburg!"

Justin allowed an involuntary shake of his head while O'Bryan drew in a sharp breath. "That's impossible, Monsignor," he replied. "The whole world knows the count was murdered in broad daylight last summer in downtown Bern. It made headlines all over Europe, remember?"

"Of course I remember. His photo was in every edition of the papers for days afterwards; so was his partner's, Mister Klaus Furlan."

"Which means there's got to be some mistake…"

"I know what I saw," Allenby said, cutting him short. "Klaus Furlan greeted Count Laufenburg along with one other gentleman on the front steps. Believe me, it was Laufenburg. He's grown a beard since last September, but I'm telling you, the man's alive! I don't know what it all means, but I thought it important enough to relay the information to someone in Rome right away."

"I believe you, and you did the right thing in calling," Justin said. "Please say nothing about this to anyone. I'll be getting back to you shortly. In fact, you might be getting a visit from Jack and me. *Ciao*."

O'Bryan broke the connection and waited for Justin to speak.

"Well, well," Justin began, a cynical smile crossing his face, "so the pompous Count Laufenburg didn't croak last year after all. What a perfect way to take oneself out of the picture, and do so in such a way as to guarantee no one would ever come looking for you. I don't know how he managed it, but my hat is off to the rascal all the same. That stunt must have cost him a small fortune. But why? And where has he been hiding? And does it have any connection to our problem?"

Neither priest could think of an answer. Like Justin, they were still trying to digest Allenby's impossible revelation.

CHAPTER 23
Day 4. Rome. Thursday evening

Arrangements were finalized in record time for Justin and O'Bryan to fly to Edinburgh. With the help of one of Justin's friends at London's Metropolitan Police Service, Dr. Margaret Smalling had been traced to her son's home in that capital city. Dr. Edward Smalling was the dean of the city's medical school, a pathologist by specialty, and when reached by phone had replied to Justin's question regarding his mother's whereabouts with a chuckle. "Hold on, surrr," he replied in a wonderful Scottish brogue, "you can ask her yourself. The old girl's a wee bit hard of hearing, so you'll have to speak up!"

Justin introduced himself, spoke with Margaret Smalling for a couple of minutes, then arranged to meet with her the following morning. She gave him directions to the apartment in New Town, and reminded him to wear his woolies. "Edinburgh's cold this time of year," she had cautioned before hanging up. Not once did she ask—or even express—any hint of curiosity as to why an American FBI agent working at the Vatican wanted to come to Scotland to speak with her. It was as though such goings-on were an everyday occurrence.

Cardinal Kettering had left for Moscow, accompanied only by his secretary, Father Luis Dellapina. They would be the pope's official representatives at the funeral for the Patriarch of Moscow. Relations between both Churches remained strained despite the fresh breezes that had been created by the advent of glasnost. The latest contretemps had been fueled by Rome, which was being accused of trying to convert Russian Rite believers.

Justin had laid on some last minute advice. "Stay sharp, Francis. Don't trust anyone, and don't be lured off to any secret meetings. Most of all, don't give even a hint of being worried about anything. Sad and subdued is fine; worried isn't. Any questions?"

Kettering had expressed strong misgivings about leaving Rome at this troubling time, but both the pope and Justin had thought he should go.

* * * * *

A secretary tapped on the door, entered, curtsied and handed Justin an index card. "Mister Scott, the gentleman asked that you call him within the next few minutes. He said it was important.

Justin scanned the handwritten message. It was from a Russian named Inspector Charin with the St. Petersburg Police Department. He frowned and read it again. Then he picked up the phone and dialed the number. It was answered on the fourth ring.

"Charin."

"This is Justin Scott, Inspector," he replied, surprised at the clarity of the signal.

"Ah, Mister Scott, you're a hard man to find." Charin's command of English was excellent. "I was able to speak with your secretary, Paula Bateman, who gave me this number. And then I discover it's in the secretary of state's office at the Vatican."

"What can I do for you, Mister Charin?" Justin made sure his voice was polite but cold.

The American's frosty tone was not lost on the Russian. "I apologize for taking up your time, sir, but I'm calling on official police business. It is a matter which I think is of some importance to you. Has Mister Manfred von Snellenberger returned home yet?"

"Not to my knowledge," Justin managed in a calm voice. "Why do you ask?"

"I saw the gentleman yesterday morning...no, correction, it was Tuesday morning, but because of our recent difficulties this was the first opportunity I've had to follow-up. Your name was prominent in the Interpol narrative which noted you are a retired FBI agent."

"I see. Why didn't you contact Interpol?"

"In all likelihood I will. However, the man is not wanted in any jurisdiction I am aware of. The record only notes that Interpol has been looking for him strictly as a courtesy, and solely to inform him of his wife's death. A humanitarian gesture, it says on the card, and only because of his prominence in the Swiss banking community. However, the record also makes a reference to the interest you had in the case, or maybe still have, due to the fact it was a cardinal who had been accused of murdering the man's wife. It also says you had been hired by the

Vatican to look into the matter. That is how I got the telephone number of your office in Washington."

Justin's mind was now racing. First Count Rudolph Laufenburg, now Manfred von Snellenberger! And both resurrected within twenty-four hours of each other. "You say you spoke to von Snellenberger?"

"No, I didn't say that," Charin politely corrected the American. "I said I saw him. He was in the company of some unsavory characters who have made it their life's work to steal the art treasures from our Hermitage Museum and sell them in the West. And from the limited information I have at my disposal, it all seems to have started with Mister von Snellenberger giving some priceless candlesticks to Cardinal Kettering. However, I repeat; Mister von Snellenberger is not wanted in any jurisdiction, including mine. He has been accused of no wrongdoing. Yet."

"Mister Charin, is there a possibility you and I could meet? Could you come to Rome?"

"That's out of the question. There's no money in my department for such a trip, and, frankly, I can see no reason for me to go to Italy, much as I would love to spend a few days in the sunshine. Anyway, I'm too busy."

Justin thought fast. "I appreciate the fact you're a busy man. Let me suggest this. Could we meet in Helsinki? That should be less than an hour's flight from Saint Petersburg. I can arrange your plane ticket through *Finnair,* and have it waiting for you at their counter at Saint Petersburg's airport. I will cover your expenses. We could meet for an hour, talk, and you could be home the same day."

The suggestion was greeted with a long silence. Finally, "I could do it four days from now, that would be Monday. That's the only time I could squeeze in."

Four days? That was not what Justin wanted to hear, but something told him not to push too hard. "Is there just the one airport in Saint Petersburg?" he asked.

"Just one that handles international flights and that's Pulkovo."

"I understand. I'll make the arrangements immediately, and try and get you into Helsinki by ten o'clock Monday. I'll meet you at the arrivals gate. Thank you for your time, and I appreciate this call. Goodbye."

"Wait, wait. How will I recognize you?"

Justin eased up a bit and laughed in genuine relief. "That'll be easy. I'll be the old man standing at the gate with a walking stick to hold me up."

"One last thing," Charin said. "This number is to my wife's office, not mine. Olga is a physicist and her telephone line does not go through a switchboard. Call me here if you need me. I can get to her office quickly. I don't think I need elaborate any further."

"I'll remember that."

O'Bryan had been able to decipher the gist of the back-and-forth conversation. "Do you think the guy's on the level?" he now asked.

"The question did cross my mind," Justin conceded. "Maybe it's a shakedown by some backwater cop who knows jack-all but figures to squeeze some greenbacks from a rich, stupid American gumshoe. Nevertheless, I have to admit, the man threw me for a loop. First, Count Laufenburg is suddenly and mysteriously resurrected, and now he tells me Manfred von Snellenberger is also still alive. And I always thought Lazarus's' coming back from the dead was a one-time event. So tell me, could I afford to give him the brush off? Our Inspector sounds on the level, but then again, who knows?"

As O'Bryan was about to reply, someone knocked, paused a moment, then entered. It was the same secretary, only this time she directed her attention to O'Bryan. "Monsignor Caffarone called to say he would like to meet you and Mister Scott, here, at four-thirty."

O'Bryan shook his head. "Please convey my regrets to the papal secretary. Tell the monsignor that won't be possible, that Mister Scott and I will be unavailable for any meetings for the next few days."

When she was safely out of earshot, O'Bryan let loose with a blast. "That slimy little twerp is so desperate to find out what's happening that he's decided to try dividing and conquering while Kettering's away. Or maybe his handlers have started to put the squeeze on him to find out what's going down. Well, I have no intention of even giving him the time of day!"

"Bravo," said Justin, allowing his face to crease into a huge grin, "You took the words right out of my mouth, Padre. My sentiments exactly!"

CHAPTER 24
Day 5. Edinburgh, Scotland. Friday morning

Scotland welcomed Justin and O'Bryan from beneath a thick, swirling mantle of fog and with temperatures creeping towards 4° Celsius. Although past nine o'clock, the sun was invisible and all the city's lights were still on. Winter in these latitudes made for short days and long nights, Justin remembered, as he settled back in the cold taxi for the seven-mile ride into the city.

O'Bryan said, "I wonder how much Dr. Margaret Smalling will be able to tell us without divulging stuff still covered by the British Official Secrets Act? Could turn out to be a fine line the lady might be straddling."

"I suspect she has a good idea what she can and can't say," Justin replied, feeling upbeat and confident.

The going was slow due to the wretched visibility, and Justin marveled at how the driver was managing to find his way under near whiteout conditions.

"I say, what's this?" the man asked a few minutes later, more to himself than to his passengers. They had just turned into Dame Smalling's street, and through the mist could barely see the cluster of rotating blue beacons and piercing red and white strobes. Multiple police cars were stopping all traffic from entering the street from either direction. A constable appeared out of the gloom.

"Sorry, sir," the officer announced, "this road's now closed to all but police traffic until further notice. There's been an accident, don't you know."

"Automobile accident?" the cabbie asked, craning his neck and squinting into the nothingness beyond his windshield.

"No, the murder of an elderly lady, sir."

"Not Dame Smalling, I hope?" Justin asked, his spirits sinking.

The policeman stepped back a pace and shined his torch in Justin's face. "And who might you be, sir?" Still polite and proper, but suddenly on his guard.

"An American FBI agent," Justin replied. "I had a ten o'clock appointment with Dame Smalling."

The officer seemed to ponder Justin's last remark. "Please pull over to the pavement, if you don't mind," he instructed the driver." And to Justin, "I'd like you to step out of the car and follow me, if you would, sir. I think my inspector would like a word."

Justin grabbed his cane and followed the man to the yellow ribbon of plastic tape encircling the lower floor of an upscale apartment building. He made a pretense of studying the imprinted words he had seen at countless crime scenes *'Police Line—Do Not Cross'* repeated *ad infinitum.* The officer spoke rapidly with his superior who then made his way over to Justin. The man gave a two-fingered salute then held out his hand.

"Good morning, sir. I'm Inspector Angus Whittle. My constable tells me you're an FBI agent. May I ask the nature of your business with Dame Smalling?"

"Is she the victim, Inspector?"

"Please answer my question, if you would, sir. Also, would it be too much trouble to show me some identification?"

Justin dug out a leather folder from his suit jacket pocket, flipped it open and handed it to Whittle.

Whittle held the case at arm's length, the telltale sign of a man too proud to wear glasses for close-up work. "Says here you're a retired FBI agent," his jaw tightening as he uttered the word retired with deliberate emphasis. He tapped a finger against the laminated identification card in an involuntary expression of annoyance, yet kept his tone civil. He lowered his eyes and looked long and hard at Justin's cane. "Again, I must ask, what is the purpose of your visit to Dame Smalling?"

Justin noted that Whittle spoke of Dame Smalling in the present tense, a timeworn practice used by police the world over to keep a potential suspect off guard. Before he could reply, a police Daimler drew up and a visibly upset man jumped out. "I say, who's in charge here?" the newcomer wanted to know.

"And just who might you be?" Whittle asked, unsure if the man was an officer.

"Doctor Smalling. I'm told there's been an accident involving my mother. Is she all right?" He ducked under the tape and started towards the front steps.

"Please, Doctor, hold up." Justin was momentarily forgotten as Whittle scrambled to grab the doctor's sleeve. "Get back here! Yes, there's been an accident involving your mother. I'm sorry to have to be the one tell you, but she's passed away."

Smalling froze, his face reflecting utter disbelief. *"Dead?"* He shook his head. "You're mistaken. I had breakfast with her less than two hours ago. She was fine. She was going to be meeting with an American investigator at ten, and she was excited at the prospect." His demeanor said the conversation was closed. "No, you obviously have the wrong flat, Inspector." He broke free and started forward once more.

"Stop!" The word ricocheted off the building like the sound from a rifle shot. There was no mistaking who was in charge. "Stand fast, sir."

Justin stepped between them. "I'm Justin Scott, Doctor. I'm the American your mother was waiting for."

"Mister Scott, do not interfere." Angus Whittle was furious. He saw himself fast losing control and was not about to let that happen. "If you say another word, I'll have you arrested on a charge of obstruction of justice and interference with an officer in the course of his duty. Do I make myself clear?"

Justin exhaled into the mist. "Perfectly."

Apparently Smalling had reached his limit as well. He dug a cell phone from his coat pocket and dialed a number. "I'm calling my friend, Sir Guy Nedelman, Commissioner of the Metropolitan Police Service at New Scotland Yard," he announced to no one in particular. "I've had more than enough bloody nonsense for one morning."

Whittle reacted immediately. "That won't be necessary, sir, I assure you. Please cancel the call to MPS. I'll personally escort you upstairs. You can make the identification if indeed the woman is your mother. I hope I'm wrong; I pray there's been a terrible mistake on our part." He lifted the tape barricade, and turned to Justin. "Come along. I don't need to tell you not to touch anything. Clear?"

"Clear." Justin scrambled to catch up.

The apartment was a shambles. A photographer was moving from room to room, his shoes encased in paper booties, videotaping behind a blinding spotlight. Immediately in front of the men was an upturned recliner, its stuffing peeking through several slashes in the seat and backrest. The same treatment had been afforded to the rest of the furniture in what had been a once-elegant sitting room. They made their way to the rear of the apartment.

Dame Smalling was slumped over the kitchen table, her head resting sideways on her arms, her eyes fully closed. Justin thought she looked as if she had fallen asleep. She was dressed in a pale pink wool suit, and it was evident her hair had been freshly done. He saw no sign of a struggle, no evidence of violence; it was as though the woman had suffered a heart attack, possibly brought on by fright, yet from what he could see of her face there was no distortion to her features. Whatever had caused her death, it had been mercifully quick.

The son walked to his mother's side and gently placed two fingers on the carotid artery. He withdrew his hand, eyes clouding.

"I'm so sorry, sir," Whittle said in a muted voice. "I really didn't want you to have to see this." He looked to Justin for support.

"Doctor, did your mother tell you anything about the purpose of my visit?" Justin asked in a quiet, respectful voice. He had already forgotten Whittle's admonition to remain silent, and the inspector chose not to raise an objection.

"She mentioned something about Lisbon, something from many years ago. She told me yesterday she had called the Vatican to confirm you were indeed working for the papal secretary of state. She was satisfied with their explanation as to who you were." Tears splashed onto the floor as he stared down at the small, huddled figure.

That bit of news made Whittle look at Justin with a newfound respect. He waited for the American to further explain.

Justin sidled next to the body and looked down at the single sheet of paper lying partially hidden under Dame Smalling's crossed arms. He read what appeared to be a hurriedly penciled message on the crinkled page. The first word, *'eiir,'* was definitely not English he decided, and it was followed by three letters, *'ken'*...the word, the sentence or the message never to be completed. The rest of the sheet was blank. Justin looked around. "Where's the pencil?" he wondered, aloud. There was none in sight. He looked to the floor in case it might have rolled off the table. Nothing. The detectives would find it; most likely under the fridge, he thought. He glanced at Inspector Whittle who nodded that he understood.

At that moment, the coroner stepped into the small kitchen and Whittle motioned for the two to follow him out.

* * * * *

Justin was able to find a few minutes alone with Smalling, but the encounter proved disappointing. The son was unable to tell much of his mother's wartime sojourn into Portugal, yet he admitted his mother had spoken many times of her travels to Lisbon in late 1940. Nevertheless, he said that she had never divulged any particulars. "Mother painted the time as an adventure for a young girl on a lark, nothing more. Remember, this all happened before I was born," he reminded Justin.

Justin replied that he understood, then changed the subject. "Does the word, or partial word with the letters *e, i, i, r,* meant anything to you?"

Smalling had also seen the paper under his mother's arm. "I've thought about it, and finally came to the conclusion she was trying to tell me something. However, I don't know what it could have been. Maybe she started to write a warning in Portuguese," he volunteered, not sounding convinced, "but since I don't speak the language, that's only a guess. Even so, I'm surprised that whoever caused my mother's death left that paper for me or the police to find. It's as if they didn't care."

Justin could not find fault with Smalling's reasoning, and when it came his turn to answer questions by the son, he chose his words carefully, revealing nothing as to the true purpose for his futile visit. "I was hired by the Vatican to tie up some loose ends from a minor happening from long ago, that's all. It was nothing of consequence in the great scheme of things, certainly nothing to cause anyone to want your mother dead." Justin was uncomfortable having to lie, but he knew he had to say something. "Most likely the two events are entirely unrelated, and in all probability it was nothing more than a tragically botched burglary by amateurs."

Smalling looked him in the eye. "You don't believe that, and neither do I. My mother didn't die of fright in the throes of some botched burglary, to use your words. The woman was a physician. She knew at that moment she was dying, and that's why she tried so desperately to communicate. She learned something dreadful from whoever was in my flat earlier, and I intend to find what that something was, with or without your help. I hope you don't take that as any kind of a threat, because it's not meant to be."

"I understand. I promise if I find anything that provides an answer to what happened this morning, I will inform you."

* * * * *

Angus Whittle offered to drive Justin and O'Bryan to the airport. "I took the liberty of making some inquiries, gentlemen," Whittle began, as the Daimler saloon cruised effortlessly towards its destination. "I should have put your names together earlier, but I'm afraid I wasn't at my best." A wintry smile creased his face. It was obvious to Justin that it took considerable effort for the man to admit to any shortcoming. Now he segued nicely into a complimentary mode. "I must say, I followed that murder case involving your cardinal last year with all the fervor of a schoolboy watching his favorite television serial. I remember well the role both of you played in its outcome, and how severely injured you were at the finale, so to speak, Mister Scott. Anyway, I'm here to offer my support, and if I can be of any help, please don't hesitate to call me." With his eyes held firmly on the road, he handed Justin his card. "If you would like a copy of the police findings and the autopsy report, I'll make sure you get both. In turn, should you happen to remember anything, no matter how insignificant, but anything at all which you feel will help me find whoever did this, I would ask you to contact me right away."

Justin took the card and slipped it into his pocket. "Fair enough. Now I have a question for you. How did the police know to go to Dr. Smalling's apartment? Did a neighbor call?"

"Someone rang nine, nine, nine, using a public phone box around the corner. We automatically retrieved the number and I listened to the recording. An odd one, it was. A woman made the call. She sounded Eastern European, but the accent could have been a ruse."

"What did she say?"

Whittle cleared his throat as if preparing to deliver a recital on stage. "Repeat these words to the man who will come from Rome: 'That which has been ordained by God cannot be undone by man.'"

"That's it?" Justin asked. He repeated the phrase under his breath then fell silent, causing Whittle to realize the American had no intention of telling him what it meant.

* * * * *

Rome. Friday evening

Back in Rome, Justin reflected it had been a wasted trip. He was beginning to have some serious doubts about any continued success. He then set to work assembling the contents of a package that had been put in his room earlier that afternoon by the concierge. An accompanying note said it had been delivered from the Vatican, but he knew it was really from the Industrial Management Consulting Group, a company that dealt in counterespionage assignments on a contract basis for both the FBI and the CIA. The 'consultants' were all ex-government officers: FBI, DEA, CIA, and in the company's London office, retired MI5 and MI6 officers. Their toys were the stuff of fantasy; items oftentimes found in the pages of popular spy novels.

Justin was impressed as he admired the artisanship of this seemingly innocuous walking stick. What he now held in his hands was one of four, and each had cost twenty thousand dollars to create. He spent the next hour perfecting the use of its several components, and then he paced around the room with it tethered to his right wrist by a leather thong until the walking stick became a comfortable extension. He was confident this particular cane would pass muster at any airport security checkpoint using scanners looking for narcotics, weapons or explosives.

After a shower and a light meal, Justin set to the task of outlining his options, then committing each to paper for objective analysis. Forty-five minutes later, he had found fault with them all and, in a fit of exasperation, tore his work into small strips and flushed the remnants down the toilet. He admitted to being stumped and it rankled; maybe he had lost his touch. Maybe, for the first time in his career, he was out of his league.

* * * * *

It took Justin a moment to realize the noise was not coming from inside his head. He peered at the luminous face of his watch. 2:15 a.m. The rapping sound continued. It was insistent, demanding. He jumped out of bed, picked up his cane and tiptoed to the door. Then he heard a distinct, exasperated whisper. *"Dammit, Justin, wake up!"* Another round of handle rattling followed.

O'Bryan barged in as Justin fumbled for the lights. "Get dressed," he commanded, "there's a car waiting for us downstairs."

"Whoa, there, Jack," Justin replied, slightly miffed. "How about slowly telling me what's got your knickers all bunched in a knot."

"I'll tell you," O'Bryan replied, mimicking Justin's angry tone. "Cardinal Kettering's disappeared, that's what's got my knickers in a knot. The man's vanished; gone; disappeared, vamoosed! He never arrived back at our legation in Moscow after the funeral mass. Father Dellapina, the limo driver and the two-man security detail are also missing. The car's gone, too. The Vatican was informed just over an hour ago and the Holy Father sent a messenger to get us. We're to go to his private apartment as quickly as possible."

Justin had never seen his friend so agitated.

"Will you please get dressed? Just do it! And be prepared to advise the pope what his next step should be, because I've got a real uneasy feeling that he now sees you as his only hope."

Justin found himself at a loss for words as he struggled into his pants.

* * * * *

Six miles to the north, two men and one woman studied several short videos of Justin, including one taken with the newest model iPhone a few hours earlier in Edinburgh.

"He's obviously been hurt," the woman said in an unusual dialect as she studied the images. "Mister Scott took a nasty tumble at the airport last Monday. I was there; I saw it. I'm now betting he's re-injured that same leg or maybe he's even re-opened a bullet wound from last fall's gun battle in Washington. My advice to the both of you is to stay a good arm's length away from him and his walking stick."

"An injured Justin Scott is still a dangerous Justin Scott," the older man agreed. I'm going to inform Tel Aviv that we think what happened in Edinburgh will not put an end to Mister Scott's mission, so all of us must remain alert and expect the unexpected."

"And what might that be?" the woman asked.

"I'm working on something, Kirsten. I'll tell you more tomorrow. Good night."

CHAPTER 25
Day 6. Rome. Saturday morning

"*Holy, Father, we* must assume Cardinal Kettering has been kidnapped, which means the information must be shared with as few a number of people as possible. I know that's easier said than done," Justin conceded, speaking slowly so as not to be misunderstood. "Now having said that, I'll immediately go against my own advice and recommend you have the deputy secretary of state inform Cardinal Kettering's counterparts in the U.S. and Great Britain. But only those two. Both of their governments have the resources and the intelligence gathering capabilities to ferret out what is really going on inside Russia at the moment."

"And you, Mister Scott, do you have contacts inside Russia? Men you can trust; men who can help us?" The pope's face was drawn and his hands trembled.

"I do, and as soon as I leave here I intend to contact one person in particular." Justin's thoughts had turned to Detective Charin, a man he had never met, a man he had no idea he could even trust.

Back in O'Bryan's office, Justin agreed with his friend that contacting Charin was a long shot, but there was simply no one else to approach. He had no idea what time Charin's wife would get to the physics lab to start her day, but he remembered the Russian detective had mentioned she had access to a secure phone line, so he dialed the number the moment a distant clock chimed seven, two hours earlier than St. Petersburg. He couldn't wait any longer.

"Doctor Olga Charin speaking. How may I be of service?" Her words were in Russian, but Justin understood the gist.

This is one austere sounding woman, Justin thought as he introduced himself in English and said that her husband had given him this number. "I need to speak with him as soon as possible, Doctor."

"Mykel has mentioned your name, Mister Scott. I am familiar with who you are. I will have him here in one hour. Does that agree with you?"

Justin told her that it did.

He agonized for the eternity it took the large hand on his watch to circle its face. At eight on the dot, he picked up the phone and dialed the same number in St. Petersburg. Charin answered on the first ring.

"Mister Charin, I need your help. The Vatican's secretary of state, Cardinal Kettering, has been kidnapped in Moscow. So was his assistant. It happened several hours ago but there's been no ransom demand—yet."

"Do you think there will be?" the Russian asked.

Justin was taken aback with the question. Kidnapping for ransom was a growth industry inside lawless Russia. Where had this guy been hiding for the past few years? Maybe it wasn't such a great idea calling this policeman after all.

"Is he not the same cardinal who was in Washington last year?" Charin asked.

"Yes he is, and, yes I fully expect to get a ransom demand," Justin replied with a slight edge creeping into his voice.

"In light of what's happened to the Patriarch of Moscow and the Patriarch of Ukraine, I'm not sure I share your optimism. Of course, I hope I'm wrong."

Justin's mind snapped into overdrive. This Russian detective has only just learned in the last few seconds what has transpired and already he's tracking me in his thinking. This man is no fool, Justin realized. "You're right. I didn't think of that," he said, fudging the truth, hoping the Russian wouldn't call his bluff and question him on something so obvious. Justin rushed ahead. "Look, is there any possibility I can come to directly to you in Russia?"

"You will need a visa to do that and there's not enough time. No, I will go to Helsinki tomorrow morning. I'll worry about my superiors when I get back."

Justin was elated. "I'll be there, and, I will have cash to reimburse you for all your expenses. Euros or dollars, it's your call."

"Dollars would be good. Bring with you a completed application for a visa to enter my country. I will have the visa approved in Saint Petersburg and get it back to you within a day. That way you will be able to fly into Russia should the need arise."

* * * * *

Somewhere in Russia. Saturday afternoon

"You say would like unleavened bread and some wine to celebrate a Roman Rite mass?"

Kettering's request had clearly taken the man by surprise.

"Then by all means you shall have it. We are not an uncouth people, Your Excellency." He bowed and backed out of the room.

"Well, that's a start," Kettering said in a loud voice. "At least we'll be able to celebrate the Eucharist."

Father Dellapina studied his boss for a long moment. "Unless we figure out what we can do to help ourselves," he said in a low voice, "then we might well be soon celebrating our own requiem masses."

Kettering allowed a weak smile to appear and vanish. Then he began to whisper. "If I caught you off guard with that request, then I pray I've done the same with our captors." With hands held close to his chest, he pointed with his right index finger to the ceiling and the walls then mimed someone listening to a conversation.

Dellapina nodded imperceptibly that he understood.

"I want them to see us only as priests, just a couple of clerics incapable of causing trouble. Maybe they'll get careless."

Dellapina barely shook his head. "We're prisoners inside a country whose name has become synonymous with the word lawless. I fear we are now very much on our own."

"You sound remarkably like Mister Scott," Kettering murmured in reply.

"Well, from what you've told me about him, I sure wish that particular American was with us right now," Dellapina said.

CHAPTER 26
Day 7. Helsinki. Sunday morning

Standing shoeless at the security checkpoint in Rome's Leonardo da Vinci Airport, Justin deliberately paid scant attention as his walking stick underwent a perfunctory examination. The officer handed back his cane and waved him though the metal detector.

The flight from Rome with a stopover in Berlin was uneventful. Justin was the last passenger off the new *Finnair* Boeing 787 Dreamliner at Helsinki-Vantaa Airport, and as he entered the International Terminal, he spied a lone man wearing an expectant look and an impressive Cossack-styled mustache.

Charin's handshake was firm, his eyes clear and unwavering. Salt of the earth, Justin concluded, immediately liking what he saw.

Ten minutes later, they sat in a back booth of a fast-food restaurant nursing mugs of steaming hot chocolate.

"Have you heard from your cardinal or any possible kidnappers?"

Justin shook his head as he blew into the mug. He took a short sip, then another. "I'm hoping to hear something soon."

Charin daubed his mustache with a paper napkin. "When you do, please let me know. You must not expect much more than empty promises from the authorities in Moscow. If it turns out a gang of hoodlums is behind the abduction, then we must assume most of the police officers in the capital are on their payroll. But, the problem becomes ten times worse if we learn that Chechnya rebels are behind the crime, because then I would truly fear for your cardinal's life."

"You're right, Chechnyans would be bad." Justin decided he should open up just a little more. "Have you recently come across any Asian gangs operating in the Moscow and Saint Petersburg areas?"

Charin answered with an observation of his own. "So you have heard that a witness to the shooting of the patriarch in Moscow said he saw Japanese men at the scene of the crime?"

"That plus the fact the gang who massacred the Ukrainians at the airport in Rome were also thought to be Asians," Justin countered, staying mum about the one he had shot.

Ian A. O'Connor

"Ah, now that is something not shared by the police in Rome," Charin said, a dark look crossing his face. "I wonder why not? Or was it only Russian police that were not told of this?"

"Tell me about seeing Manfred Von Snellenberger," Justin asked, changing the subject. "You say it took place in Saint Petersburg?"

"Yes, and under the most unusual of circumstances." Charin revisited the night and early morning in question, painting a vivid word picture for Justin. He spoke of the three thugs he had arrested; dryly told of Colonel Pritkin's heavy-handed intervention on their behalf, and finished with a solid description of Manfred Von Snellenberger who he said was now wearing a beard and mustache. "It's uncanny how much he looks like the photographs of our last czar."

Charin continued. "He could see that I found his face familiar because he did a strange thing. He gave me a slight shake of his head as if to say: don't ask me anything, I beg you."

Charin dug a piece of paper out of his pants pocket and handed it to Justin. "The Bentley they were in is registered to a Latvian citizen from Riga, a man named Alexander Panov. He owns a fancy home in the best section of St. Petersburg. Panov is from an old, very wealthy family that fled Russia shortly after the end of our participation in the Great War but sometime before the Bolsheviks stormed the Winter Palace in October, Nineteen Seventeen. They absconded with a huge fortune, most of it the property of depositors of the bank they owned. Rumor has it the money eventually found its way into a bank in Lucerne, Switzerland run by two Russian ex-patriots, but who really knows? That was a long, long time ago and it's none of my business now. Probably most of those whose money was stolen were members of the bourgeois and purged by Stalin, so it is now nothing more than a footnote found buried in a chapter from our tragic Russian past. I have no reason to arrest the man or even bring him in for questioning. Panov has broken no laws, although I have deep suspicions about him."

Justin slid the paper into his own pocket. "I will have some friends follow up on this. Could be nothing, or it could be a lot, we'll have to wait and see."

Charin's eyes found Justin's. "Do you think von Snellenberger's sudden appearance could somehow be related to the disappearance of your Cardinal Kettering?"

"The thought has crossed my mind." He was not about to drop the bombshell that Cardinal Kettering was Manfred von Snellenberger's father-in-law. Less than a handful were privy to that secret. He made a decision. It was time to ask a favor.

"Do you have the manpower to put Panov's house under surveillance for the next few days? I'm hoping it could prove important and productive."

Charin's response was immediate. "I can. There are still a couple of men I trust, good men not on the take."

Justin slipped an envelope across the table. "Here's ten thousand American dollars to cover your additional expenses. If you need to use some of the money for bribes, then do it. And if you need more, just ask."

"What if I should come across Mister von Snellenberger again? Do you have any message for him?"

The question caught Justin off guard. Now why hadn't he thought of that? "Yes," he replied immediately, "tell him you were sent by Cardinal Kettering. Ask him if he's in danger; ask if he needs help. I have confidence in your judgment. Thanks for even thinking about it." He gave Charin his cell phone number. "Use it day or night."

Charin rose and held out his hand. "I pray all will end well, but I harbor a nagging fear events are conspiring against us. And here's the frustrating thing: I have no idea why any of this is happening, none at all." He shook Justin's hand. "My instinct tells me that you, my friend, do know. I only hope you decide to share whatever it is with me before it's too late. Goodbye, and I'll remain in touch. I'm going to take a quick turn outside in the fresh air to enjoy a Marlboro cigarette before my flight back to Saint Petersburg."

Justin settled the bill and walked out into the main terminal. He had less than an hour to kill before his flight, so he limped off in search of a magazine stand.

* * * * *

"Paging Finnair passenger, Justin Scott. Please pick up any white courtesy telephone for a message."

"Justin Scott," he announced, fully expecting to hear O'Bryan's voice.

"Ah, Mister Scott," a plummy voiced female replied, "could you tell me where you are in the terminal?"

Justin described the magazine shop and the luggage boutique.

"Please go to room one hundred and fourteen which you'll find about twenty meters down the hallway on your right. Our Mister Matilla with airport security would like a word with you. It should only take a moment."

Justin turned the handle of Room 114 and the door swung inward. He was immediately grabbed by a pair of strong hands and shoved headlong into the room. A second man slammed the door and turned the lock. Justin stumbled but managed to keep his balance, thanks in large measure to the support offered by the walking stick tethered to his right wrist.

Strong Hands punched Justin hard on the side of his head and tossed him unceremoniously into a metal chair, which slid against the concrete wall in a bone-jarring bang. With ears still ringing, he watched as the second man took up a stance directly in front of him, his legs wide apart. He studied Justin as one would a maggot under a magnifying glass.

Justin sized up the situation. This would be the inquisitor, the good cop.

"Why were you meeting with that Russian police officer, and what did he want?"

Justin shook his head as if to clear it, disgusted at being snookered like some rookie fresh out of the FBI Academy. He hoped his face reflected the right amount of fright as he tightened his two-handed grip on the walking stick. "I'm afraid there's been some mistake..." he began in a trembling voice...

Strong Hands cut him off by raising a huge right arm and drawing it back in a menacing manner.

"Don't waste my time, you old cripple," the Inquisitor said. "I'll ask you once again, and if you don't tell me what I want to hear, then I'll let my friend do with you as he will." The man leaned over. "Now answer my question." A wafting of sour breath crossed the narrow divide.

Justin replied by letting loose a fearsome roar. He simultaneously thrust his cane upward, propelling it deep into the man's crotch. Before either shock or disbelief could register on the Inquisitor's face, Justin leapt from his chair, spun around and swung the stick like a baseball bat, catching an equally startled Strong Hands with a solid blow to his left ear.

With all of his muscles infused by a huge jolt of epinephrine, Justin spun back to confront the Inquisitor. He deftly drove his cane into the man's solar plexus. The Inquisitor stared helplessly at Justin before shooting an arching shower of vomit onto the floor, then collapsing inside a pool of his own mess.

Strong Hands roared behind Justin, reached out and managed to hook a fingertip into a belt loop on his overcoat.

Don't allow this psychopath to wrap you into a bear hug! Justin pivoted on the balls of his feet and moved willingly in the direction he was being pulled, making sure to keep his arms up high and away from his body, the tethered cane held aloft.

The sudden and unexpected lack of resistance caused Strong Hands to falter for a moment, creating the advantage Justin had hoped for. Nose-to-nose with Strong Hands, he drove the knuckles of both middle fingers squarely into the man's eyes, dug deep, then rotated each knuckle in opposing directions.

Strong Hands howled in pain, rage, and confusion as he clawed at his ravaged orbits. Justin lined up for the kill. Lashing out with a spinning kick, he guided a heavy shoe squarely to the side of man's left kneecap. He heard an ugly snapping sound and Strong Hands dropped to the linoleum. For good measure, Justin struck a solid blow to the head with his cane. Strong Hands lay still. Eight seconds had passed from the moment he had first attacked the Inquisitor.

"Never let your guards down, even for a moment, but especially when facing an old cripple, you worthless turds," he said to unhearing ears.

Justin bent down and relieved both men of their wallets and a Kahr K40 secured to Strong Hands' belt. He begrudgingly approved the man's choice of weapon; it was light, compact and deadly. He ejected the round in the chamber then expertly removed the magazine and scattered its .40 caliber bullets around the room. Then, with the heel of his right shoe, ground the empty pistol into the Inquisitor's pile of vomit to remove his fingerprints. He cleaned his shoe by passing it back and forth across the back of Strong Hands' head.

Justin was sending a message neither would soon forget.

Before limping off to his gate, he called security from a courtesy phone and warned of two suspicious looking characters that he had seen breaking into Room 114.

CHAPTER 27
Day 7. Rome. Sunday evening

It was past suppertime and still no word about Kettering. Heeding Justin's advice, the pope had directed the assistant secretary of state to notify Kettering's counterparts at the U.S. State Department and the British Foreign & Commonwealth Office. Hints were dropped that the Holy See believed the cardinal was likely being held for ransom by criminal elements somewhere inside the Russian capital. It was the one scenario that would make the most sense to any foreign government.

* * * * *

Justin donned a pair of cotton gloves and began emptying the wallets he had liberated from his Helsinki tormentors. There were no credit cards and little cash, all euros. Each held a Finnish driver license, both probably illegitimate. It was doubtful either man could have deplaned in Helsinki because Strong Hands had been armed.

However, Justin was at a loss to explain how they could have known of his meeting with Charin. Then an idea hit home. He dug out his cell phone and speed dialed his friend Steve Mannix at Industrial Management in New York. When Mannix came on the line, Justin explained what he had on the two John Does.

"Steve, I'll have their wallets sent over in the diplomatic pouch to the Vatican's United Nations mission there in Manhattan, which means you should get them sometime tomorrow. I'm hoping you'll get lucky and recover some fingerprints. I kind of need answers like yesterday, so track me down as soon as your people get something. Best bet is to call me on my cell."

"Roger that, but remember, if you need the cavalry, just holler. I don't know what you're working on, but also keep this in mind: I can get a team from my London office over to you at the drop of a dime. In fact, I'll be in London myself within a few hours, so you can also get me on my cell."

"Good deal, pal, now before I forget, many thanks for the new walking stick. I broke it in on the two clowns I just mentioned, but they didn't get to experience all of its bells and whistles. You'll be pleased to know it passed through security at two airports with nary a challenge."

* * * * *

The call from his secretary, Paula Bateman, took Justin by surprise. It was four in the morning in Rome, six hours earlier in Washington.

"Justin, why haven't you been checking your email?" she began without preamble. "There's a message for you from Cardinal Kettering's kidnappers. It's been parked in your in-box for almost four hours."

"Thanks for the heads up. I'll call you back later with a 'to do' list." Justin pocketed his phone, powered up the laptop on loan from Kettering and opened his email. It was easier for him to read on the bigger screen. There were thirty messages. He scanned the list until his eyes came to one marked *KardinalKetteringKeep* at Izvestia dot org.

"We will only contact you via the email system. Do not attempt to trace our messages. Each will be sent once, and the sending site will be permanently shut down after that transmittal. Each message will direct you to a different return address which will remain active for only ten minutes. If you go to the police, Kettering will die; if we see you trying to trace any message, Kettering will die. This is your only warning. Our next message will be sent at noon, GMT."

Before he could react, his cell phone rang.

"Justin Scott."

Silence. He could tell the line was open. Someone was listening.

"Justin Scott," he repeated.

"I see you've finally opened your mail. Good. Be ready for our next message, and don't be late answering. You will always open your mail on time, because if you ever miss doing so by as little as three minutes, Kettering will die." The muted click told him the line had been severed.

The number was immediately blocked, but Justin had managed to record the voice. It sounded metallic, as if it had been filtered through a synthesizer, making it impossible to know whether the caller was a man or a woman, American or European. After playing it for a second time, he decided he had been listening to a recording and not a live person. Someone had thought through this kidnapping very carefully and wanted him tethered to a short leash.

"Bad move," Justin whispered into the night, "because I'm coming after you. That's not just a promise; it's a vow."

Ian A. O'Connor

CHAPTER 28
Day 8. Rome. Monday morning

Justin met O'Bryan for breakfast, and between bites and sips, brought his friend up to speed, including a brief retelling of his encounter with Strong Hands and the Inquisitor.

O'Bryan was visibly impressed. "You took them *both* out?"

Justin chuckled. "It wasn't as bad as it sounds. Anyway, I sent their wallets to Industrial Management in New York. I'm hoping to get a handle on who they might be."

O'Bryan drove them to the Vatican. The weather had returned to near normal; clear skies, negligible winds and a temperature predicted to reach a high of 14° Celsius. A perfect day for sightseeing, Justin thought as they inched their way amidst ten thousand impatient drivers and an equal number of arm-waving, traffic-weaving hellions on colorful scooters.

In the waiting room to Kettering's suite of offices, Justin spotted a man staring out the window. He turned as they approached. It was Edward Smalling.

Smalling's handshake was firm, but his tired eyes betrayed a sense of worry. "My mother and Inspector Angus Whittle, that's what brings me here, Mister Scott," he said in reply to the unasked question.

O'Bryan ordered two pots of coffee and the three men drank it strong and black as Smalling told his story.

"It's my sad duty to report Inspector Whittle was run over by a lorry late yesterday afternoon. Chances are he never knew what hit him." Smalling's voice was devoid of emotion. He could have been conducting an autopsy in front of a theater packed with medical students. "The lorry was found abandoned ten minutes later and the police are still searching for the driver. I got that bit of information off Sky News at the airport. But what didn't come from the reader was this. I was the last person to speak with Angus Whittle. He called me and said it was urgent we meet as soon as possible. He even volunteered to come to the hospital."

Smalling bit on the inside of his cheek, waited for a couple of beats, then continued in a quiet voice. "When he confided in me, I realized my mother's death was not the result of some random act of violence but was rooted in something of the utmost national importance. These were Whittle's exact words: 'Doctor Smalling, why didn't you tell me your mother and the queen had an enduring relationship going back to the days shortly after World War Two?'"

Justin and O'Bryan were visibly caught off guard by the remark.

"Now, how on earth would Inspector Whittle know something like that about the queen and your mother?" Justin asked. "I mean, did you?"

"Yes," Smalling replied in a voice dropping to a near whisper, "I did, but it was something my mother and I discussed just once, and that was the evening prior to your arrival in Edinburgh. Mother took an uncommon delight in fencing with me that night. Having said that, I must also say my mother always spoke warmly of the queen—they had met only twice that I was aware of—but I did not know of any special relationship, such as one Angus Whittle seemed to be implying."

"Please go on," Justin said.

"My mother was giddy with excitement when she learned you were coming. She was transformed right before my eyes. I was looking at a woman again in her twenties and not the nonagenarian who was living under my roof." He hesitated and smiled weakly. "Well, maybe I exaggerate a wee bit, but I think you get the picture."

* * * * *

Edinburgh, Scotland. Last Thursday evening

Dame Margaret Smalling replaced the receiver in its cradle, gave it an absent pat then turned to her son. Was that an enigmatic smile he saw?

"Laddie, I've waited more than sixty years for that telephone call and never once dreamt it would come from an American. I always thought it would be a German, or maybe even a Russian, who would make the first contact, but not an American."

Laddie? She hadn't called him that since he was ten! "I don't understand..."

"No, son, of course you don't." She eased herself into a straight-backed chair and drew a tartan cashmere throw around her lap. That smile was back.

"Are you going to tell me what it's all about?" Edward asked.

"That American, Mister Scott, he said he's clearing up some small matter for the Vatican and that he'd like to speak to me. Well, I know that's not altogether true. In fact, I daresay something serious is now unfolding because that small matter began when I was a newlywed and the world was at war. More than that I cannot say, but after I've had my meeting with Mister Scott, I'm sure I'll be able to tell you more."

"Mom, I'm sixty years old, for God's sake! I'm sure you can tell me your wee secret from so long ago. Maybe you want to confess you took a wartime lover and that Mister Scott is my illegitimate big brother."

Margaret Smalling laughed heartily at the idea, but shook her head. "Och, don't be daft! No, lad, it's nothing of the sort. My 'wee secret' as you dismissively call it is something that changed the course of history. And it's still covered by the Official Secrets Act, even after all these years."

"Oh, go on with you!"

Margaret Smalling would not be swayed. "You'll just have to wait until my American visitor leaves. And, Eddie, I'm going to ask that you not be home when he comes. You see, I know he's going to need to speak freely, which means he must know we will be alone. Did he tell you he was an FBI agent when you answered the phone?"

"No, but how do you know he's telling the truth?"

"Believe me, I've never been so sure of anything in my life. And I can say this much. The queen is privy to my secret. I had to meet with her because of it. The first time was literally hours before Winston Churchill died in January, Nineteen Sixty-five, now more than that I'm not saying, even if you threaten to tear your old mom's fingernails out. And unless you have to dash over to the hospital, why don't you make us each a nice warm cuppa."

* * * * *

Rome. Monday morning, continued

Justin absently stirred his coffee as he wondered how Dame Smalling could have known about the Russian letter? Or, for that matter, anything covered by the Official Secrets Act. Also, what was that about Winston Churchill and the queen?

"Before I forget," Smalling was saying, "this was among my mother's effects which were returned to me from the morgue." He handed Justin a mechanical pencil. "Seems it rolled off of the kitchen table and got lodged in her skirt's waistband. You remember, in the kitchen…when mother started to write something..."

Justin nodded then studied the pencil. It was quite heavy, obviously expensive. Gold, he confirmed, spying the 18k marque stamped on the head of the clasp. He turned the pencil around and studied it further.

"It's part of a set," Doctor Smalling was now saying, "a fountain pen and a propelling pencil, given as a gift from the queen at mother's honors list investiture in Nineteen Sixty-eight. She was oh so proud of that set. Horribly expensive, I must say, but she used them both every day."

"Propelling pencil?"

Smalling shrugged. "Americans call it a mechanical pencil."

"Do you know where the fountain pen might be?"

"Mother kept them both in a tooled leather box on her desk. I'm sure the pen is still there. She would never take them out of the house at the same time. She said she'd die if she ever lost them both."

It was then Justin spied an inscription. It was a simple two lines of delicate lettering engraved on the barrel. He had to hold the pencil at just the right angle, and needed to squint in order to read the words. *To: Dame Margaret Smalling, Jan. 1968. From: Elizabeth II Regina.*

"The inscription on the pen is identical," Smalling said. "My father was honored the same day, yet he didn't receive a similar gift. Mother would often tease him about it, suggesting he wasn't a favorite of the Crown and that he'd better toe the line or she'd have the queen chop his head off." He managed a fleeting smile at the remembrance.

Justin said, "Doctor, I would like you to try and remember your last conversation with Inspector Whittle. Would you say he sounded excited? Upset? Happy? Anything like that pop into your mind?"

Smalling frowned as he tried to replay that exchange with Angus Whittle, but he finally had to shake his head. "The inspector was a man of few words. He was adamant that we meet quickly, but he was also polite while being forceful. Sorry."

"Do you remember the words your mother had started to write on the paper we found in your kitchen that morning?"

"Of course. The first word wasn't English," Smalling replied. "*E-i-i-r*, if memory serves me correctly. Maybe it was the first few letters of a Portuguese word. I've even thought maybe she was trying to write the word *Eire*, you know, a variant for the Irish Republic."

Justin held out the pencil for Smalling. "Take a look at the inscription."

"Yes, Mister Scott, I've read it a thousand times," Smalling replied with a hint of irritation in his voice. *"To: Dame Margaret Smalling, January Nineteen Sixty-eight. From: Elizabeth II Regina.* Then his face lit up. "My word, would you look at that*! Elizabeth, Two, Regina. E-I-I-R."*

"Yes, and do remember the next word your mother wrote on the paper?"

"Ken. She wrote the word ken," Smalling said in a voice rising with excitement.

"Which is Scottish for *knows,* is it not? As in, *the Queen knows?"*

Justin could see by the look on Smalling's face that this possibility now opened up a completely new dimension regarding his mother's life and the secrets she had apparently harbored from a time long ago.

"When will the autopsy results be available?" Justin asked in quiet voice.

Smalling shook his head. "Not for another week and that would be the earliest."

"Please see if you can speed up the process," Justin said. "And I also need you to do two more things for me. First, find the matching pen, and second, help me pave the way for a meeting with the queen within the next twenty-four hours."

"Are you daft?" Smalling actually laughed aloud at the preposterous request. "That's utterly impossible!"

"Nothing's impossible, Doctor. I will be approaching the pope within the hour to make the same request directly to Buckingham Palace. He will be doing so as the head of the Catholic Church wanting to approach his counterpart, the queen, in her capacity as the Supreme Governor of the Church of England. He will also have to notify the prime minister's office simply because the PM is the head of the British government, but I assure you, I will move heaven and earth to make such a meeting a reality. And, yes, I'm sure nothing like this has happened before, but there's always a first time for everything."

Smalling was speechless. Then seeing that Justin was waiting for an answer, he threw up his hands. "I'll be home this afternoon and I'll go find the pen. Then I will contact Number Ten Downing Street to see if the PM has received any communication from the Vatican regarding your request."

Justin softened his tone. "Let me help put your mind at rest because I can tell you this much. Your mother was privy to information shared by only a handful of people. It dates back to the early days of World War Two; but now, some seventy plus years later, there are people wanting to put a very harmful agenda into play. And time is now very much our enemy," he added, his voice somber.

There was a rap on the door. A beanpole monsignor wearing high-water pants and a too-short cassock entered and beckoned to O'Bryan.

"This is my friend Monsignor Salvatore Manzini. He's the assistant secretary of state," O'Bryan said, by way of introduction. "Monsignor, please meet Justin Scott. And this is Doctor Smalling from Great Britain."

Monsignor Manzini scrutinized Smalling. "Then I can assume Doctor Smalling has already told you the news about the Archbishop of Canterbury's disappearance?"

Seeing the three men's looks of genuine astonishment, Manzini continued. "From what little we know, the archbishop received an urgent message asking him to go to Moscow to help prevent further bloodshed amongst the hierarchy inside the Russian Church. He was considered a trusted mediator. The request was vetted through Number Ten Downing Street, and I'm told the British prime minister placed a Royal Air Force executive jet at the archbishop's disposal. He arrived at Moscow's airport where he was met by a Kremlin protocol officer. The archbishop got into a ZIV limousine, and that's the last anyone has seen or heard from him. The British received word an hour ago that he's being held by a group affiliated with the Church of Constantinople."

Justin wasted no time deciding what needed to be done. "Monsignor, I suggest that you immediately inform all of the leaders of the major Christian denominations in Europe and the Americas to be vigilant against possible kidnapping attempts until further notice."

"I concur, Sal," O'Bryan quickly added. "But first you must tell the Holy Father what's happened to the archbishop. Hurry, and God help us all."

CHAPTER 29
Day 8. St. Petersburg. Monday morning

The old woman shifted her weight from one foot to another. Every so often, she would beat gloved hands against her chest to ward off the numbing cold. She had just finished setting up a makeshift flower stall on the sidewalk, an incongruous splash of multi-colored beauty in sharp contrast to a monochromatic St. Petersburg buried in winter snow.

The staged scene in the city's most fashionable neighborhood was meant to convey the reality of nature's expected rebirth that would surely come with the advent of spring.

The old peddler's eyes followed every car. She was very much the grandmother she appeared to be, but she was also a police officer.

She had sold three bunches of flowers in less than fifteen minutes when the front doors of the mansion across the street opened and two men stepped out. They probed their way down snow-laden steps and onto a sidewalk still buried under half a meter of hardening powder. One halted, hunched over and lit a cigarette, while his companion turned his head skyward and inhaled the pristine winter air. He was taller than average, immaculately dressed, and wore a stylish beard.

What a handsome man, the old peddler thought, as she boldly waved both arms in an attempt to get his attention. "Buy some of my beautiful flowers for your wife—or for your lover," she called out. "Better yet, buy them each a bouquet."

The man approached. The peddler felt her heart begin to race.

"He's coming," she said for Charin's benefit, bending her head down toward the microphone hidden under her collar.

"What have we here?" the gentleman asked, as he stood and admired her offerings.

She answered in a low voice. "Do not be alarmed, Mister von Snellenberger. I am a police officer, and I'm here to help you, that is, if you want to be helped. Please, continue to look at my flowers and act as if you cannot make up your mind."

The surprised look on the bearded man's face was real. "Who sent you, Grandmother? How did they know where to find me?"

"Cardinal Kettering sent me. He needs to know if you're being held against your will."

A worried look settled on the man's face. He paused for several beats before answering. "Yes," he finally whispered.

"Do you want the police to rescue you? We can do that, you know."

"No…yes…yes, I do." The voice was a tad stronger, but the vacillation was there, lurking below the surface.

The police officer knew she had to press on. "How many men are in the house?" As she said this, she pointed toward one particularly colorful bouquet, nodded and smiled brightly as if they were agreeing to something said.

"Four, but at times there can be as many as six."

"Any women or children?"

"No. There is a tall, beautiful blonde woman who shows up once in a while, but not in the past fortnight."

"Any guard dogs?"

"No."

"Are the men armed?"

"Yes," von Snellenberger replied, as he picked two bunches off the makeshift stand and handed them to her.

The woman wrapped the flowers in red tissue paper and beamed up at her benefactor. "That will be eighty-five Rubles," she announced in a loud voice, "and may God bless you for your kindness to this old widow." She lowered her voice. "We will come for you at nine o'clock tonight. The moment you hear the first loud bang, get down on the floor and stay there."

Manfred von Snellenberger pressed some crisp notes into her hand. "Yes. Nine o'clock. I'll be ready." He rejoined his companion and the two men started down the street on a brisk stroll.

The police officer opened her clenched fist and looked. One, two, no, three, old American fifty dollar bills! She pocketed her windfall and waited five minutes. Then from behind a scarf pulled over her mouth and nose and announced, "OK, Mykel, it's time for a big bad policeman to come and arrest me for loitering. My fingers and toes are ready to fall off."

* * * * *

Rome. Monday afternoon

His cell phone's ringing caught Justin by surprise. It was Charin calling to say they had made contact with the subject who said he was being held against his will. He continued, saying von Snellenberger would be in his protective custody at 1700 GMT. "Do you have any instructions as to what you want me to do with him after that?"

That was all Justin needed to hear. "As soon as you have him in protective custody, drive straight to Pulkovo. There'll be a private jet waiting. I'll have to call you back with further instructions, but I want him out of Russian airspace well before midnight."

"I'll be waiting."

Justin speed dialed Steve Mannix's cell, hoping to find him at the Industrial Management's London office. When he reached his friend, he asked for a plane to be on the tarmac at Pulkovo Airport shortly before ten o'clock that evening. "Manfred von Snellenberger will be the lone passenger," he finished up.

Mannix let loose a low whistle. "*The* Manfred von Snellenberger?"

"In the flesh."

"Not a problem. I'll have a plane fly into Saint Petersburg from Helsinki. Those two airports trade traffic with each other around the clock, so a late night private flight coming or going won't look unusual or raise any red flags. Tell your man to have your friend delivered to the Pulkovo Airlines ramp. I've used their services several times. They're good, so you're in luck. Where do you want the plane to go?"

"I don't care. I just want my man out of Russia. Any suggestions?"

"Well, if I use our Gulfstream Six Fifty, I can deliver von Snellenberger to any airport in Europe without refueling, or even to the U.S. East Coast if need be. But how about to Rome? I can have the necessary documents on board to get him through customs at Fiumicino."

"Now why hadn't I thought of that?" Justin replied. "Rome it is. And, Steve, if for any reason I'm not there to meet you, tuck him away somewhere safe, because there are going to be some pissed-off folks wanting to do him some heavy duty harm."

Ian A. O'Connor

CHAPTER 30
Day 8. Israel. Monday morning

Simon Chertoff walked out of *Greenwald's Pastry Shoppe* with eyes cast downward and into the bagful of jelly and crème doughnuts, salivating in anticipation of the epicurean delight soon to follow. As he stepped into the street, he found himself lifted off the ground and thrown into the back of a car. One captor fell heavily on top of him while the other jumped into the front passenger's side and yelled at the driver to go, go, go! The dust-covered Mercedes with no license plates shot forward, peeling rubber. The only evidence left of Simon Chertoff''s presence from moments ago were the dozen doughnuts scattered in the gutter oozing their sweet, sticky innards to a score of flies which had swarmed seemingly out of nowhere.

Two Arab women standing at a bus stop a few yards away witnessed the abduction. The older whispered, "Didn't those men look foreign, like maybe Japanese?" They shrugged in unison. This was definitely none of their business.

* * * * *

Rome. Monday afternoon

Justin opened his email and began to read.

The pope must come to Moscow immediately. To refuse means Kettering will die. Do not reply, as this address site is already defunct. I will send a message in one hour from a new address, at which time you will respond by telling me I should expect to see the Holy Father in Moscow by midnight.

Justin decided to throw them a curveball. He would raise the ante.

When the new message arrived, he wrote, Prove Kettering is still alive. If you refuse, I will not bother to reply because I'll know Kettering is dead. But if you agree, say so, and await further instructions. This warning will not be repeated.

Justin called Paula and quickly told her what he had done. He heard her quick intake of breath. He was raising the ante to a level wholly meant to catch the kidnappers off guard. They would no longer be in control of the situation, and that's exactly what he wanted. Turn the tables on them; play for time. He had honed his skills while heading up the anti-terrorist unit at the FBI, and had passed his knowledge on to eager students through courses he had taught at the FBI Academy and at Georgetown University's Graduate School of International Studies where he was still an adjunct professor.

"I can only pray you're right about this, Justin." After a momentary pause, Paula asked, "If they agree to your terms, what do you want me to do?"

He looked at his watch. 2:40 p.m. "Tell them they have to reactivate the *KardinalKetteringKeep* email address at Izvestia dot com at midnight, Rome time, for a message from me. When they do, you will instruct them to send a picture of Kettering holding the front page of today's edition of *Izvestia* in his left hand and a photo of the pope in his right. Let them know I'll be enlarging the picture, so they had better make damn sure I can read the headlines and the date. That should keep them busy for a while. Is there anything else while I have you on the line?"

"No," Paula replied, "but I wish I knew more about what's really going on."

"I understand, but I just can't say any more at the moment. My communications link here is not secure, and the Vatican walls have ears. Trust me on this. I'll talk to you soon."

Justin was hopeful of one thing. While Kettering's kidnappers were being kept busy complying with his orders, he would at least free von Snellenberger from the clutches of what was beginning to look like the same group of terrorists.

Ian A. O'Connor

CHAPTER 31
Day 8. Rome. Monday afternoon

Justin and O'Bryan had eaten a late lunch in the office to save time. Trekking to one of the many restaurants outside the mixed medieval and Renaissance walls of the Lilliputian sovereign nation would have burned up two hours they could ill afford to squander.

O'Bryan had spent thirty minutes with the pope in the late morning, asking the pontiff to clear the way for a meeting with the Queen of England. The Holy Father had been shocked to learn of the Archbishop of Canterbury's abduction, but after hearing that Justin thought a meeting with the British monarch was vital, he assured O'Bryan he would do all in his power to make it a reality.

They were now reexamining the letters from the unknown Russian author and Sister Lucia for the umpteenth time.

Justin drummed an impatient index finger on the polished wood. "Dammit, we're missing something."

"Care to give me a hint?"

Justin picked up the English translation. "Lucia begins her narrative with a description of the Virgin Mary and of an avenging angel brandishing a flaming sword. They are the exact words the world heard in Two Thousand. However, it's in this particular letter that she segues into her last frightening paragraph where the Virgin warns her of the world coming to its end."

O'Bryan took the letter from Justin. "We must remember that she wrote in August Nineteen Forty-one that she would only commit the first two parts of the secret to paper, and not the third. When later questioned why not the third part, she replied without hesitation that she had not been given permission to do so by the Holy Mother. Yet if we are to believe this Russian letter, then we have irrefutable evidence that's not altogether true because here it is in her own handwriting, a direct contradiction of what she had so often repeated before her death in Two Thousand and five."

"Which could well explain why she destroyed her original letter regarding that third secret in Nineteen Forty-two," Justin said. "You sound like you're beginning to lean a lot closer toward my contention that this purported Russian letter from Lucia is shaping up to be a fraud." He glanced at the Portuguese original and shook his head. "Jack, I sure wish we had the original envelope her letter came in."

"Why?"

"Because we need answers to three questions. How did Lucia's letter find its way into Russia in the first place? Where did the letter come from? And when was it sent?"

"All valid questions," O'Bryan replied, "but right now I'm finding myself a lot more worried about the contents of the accompanying vulgate Latin Russian letter. Whoever authored it is predicting an overthrow of the Church hierarchy beginning with the pope. Then he speaks of creating a new order of a Russian Rite Church and a Russian who will reign over a single, unified Christendom."

"Sounds like someone's planning on starting a new line of popes," Justin said.

That caught O'Bryan by surprise. Finally he said, "You know, I never thought about it from that angle, but you could be right. There was the Great Schism from Thirteen Hundred and Seventy-eight to Fourteen Hundred and Fourteen where an imposter pope in Avignon, France, claimed he was the true pope, while the real pontiff reigned in Rome. However, it was a lot more complicated than just having some upstart up one day and lay claim to Peter's throne. You see, the papacy had indeed moved to Avignon for a seventy-year period beginning in Thirteen Hundred and Nine, but when Pope Gregory the Eleventh moved his entire court back to Italy, some of the folk left behind didn't like that idea so they set the Bishop of Avignon up as a sort of a parallel pope. The ensuing fracas was really all about political issues and not theological ones, but it was still one whale of a big deal at the time. It was finally resolved in Rome's favor in Fourteen Hundred and Seventeen."

Justin thought about that bit of history for a long moment, then said, "So here we are six hundred years later and there are people now hell-bent on relocating the center of this new ecclesiastical universe to Russia, and they're willing to move heaven and earth to make it happen."

"It would appear so."

"Let me go back to the letter from our unknown Russian author for a moment. He writes that if anyone gets in the way he will be killed for opposing the revealed word of God. But tell me this. Where is this supposed 'revealed word of God' to be found? I sure didn't read where Sister Lucia made any such claim."

O'Bryan put down the letter. "You're right, she didn't, which brings us back to the painting *Evening Prayers*. You believe there's a message hidden in there, don't you?"

"More now than ever," Justin replied as the high-tech phone on Kettering's desk began to chime.

"Justin Scott, here."

"You're a hard man to track down. I thought maybe you had left Rome without saying goodbye."

The voice sounded familiar, but Justin was unable to put a face to it. "Who is this?" he asked, sounding slightly peeved at the intrusion.

"Joosteen, It's Mario Castellanos, you know, the police officer..."

"As you can see, Mario, I'm still in Rome. What can I do for you?"

"Joosteen, I am in the hospital with our he-she friend from the massacre at the airport. The doctors say she will live, but her recovery will take a long time."

"Thanks for the information..."

"Wait! I thought you would want to know what else I found out." Castellanos said, then rushed on. "I was allowed to speak to her for a few minutes. At first, she refused to talk, so I told her that as soon as the doctors released her I was going to move her into the men's prison to await her trial for murder. I explained how there were many deviants in residence there who would love to have her around to while away their boring days and lonely nights. That got her attention. She begged me to kill her first, but I told her the choice was hers."

"So did she talk?"

Castellanos chuckled. "I couldn't shut her up! Here's what she told me. The four of them were sent to the airport to make sure the delegation from the Patriarch of Ukraine never reached the Vatican. I replied that she had her facts wrong, that it was a trade delegation they attacked. No, she insisted, I was the one who had it wrong, that it was some sort of a secret delegation going to the Vatican." Castellanos hesitated for a couple of beats then said, "And there's something else. She said the other three that were with her at the airport are normal, if you know what I mean, but when I asked what she was doing with Japanese terrorists, she said they were not Japanese, but North Koreans."

Justin frowned. This was an unexpected wrinkle. "You think she was telling the truth?" He was well aware of the link between Japanese terrorists and factions of the Italian Red Brigade going back to the early 1970s, but this was the first time he had heard of the North Koreans getting involved in such a high stakes game. What could possibly be in it for them?

"Oh, she was telling the truth all right," Castellanos replied. "Now, I need you to answer a question for me. Why did you not tell me those Ukrainians were coming to meet with high officials at the Vatican?"

"Mario, you must believe me when I tell you I'm hearing this for the first time. I guarantee you, no one I have visited with in the Vatican has any knowledge of what you're telling me, and I include the Holy Father." What Justin didn't give voice to, was his suspicion that maybe the delegation had been coming to meet in secret with the papal secretary, Monsignor Caffarone.

A long silence followed, until finally, "That is your word as a fellow policeman?"

"It is. I promise I'll follow up on what you've just told me and I'll get back to you."

"Thank you, *Joosteen*." Another pause, then, "Why are all of the world's cardinals descending on Rome? Usually the Vatican informs the Rome police well in advance of such comings, yet I only found out less than an hour ago."

This was something Justin did not care to discuss. However, he knew the man would not buy an outright denial of any such knowledge on his part.

"I only heard about it a few hours ago myself and I'm just as puzzled as you. When I know more, you'll know more, OK?"

"OK. *Ciao*."

CHAPTER 32
Day 8. Rome. Monday afternoon

The pope invited Justin and O'Bryan to a four o'clock meeting. With him was Monsignor Manzini. He beckoned the two Americans forward. Justin found he was still treading on unfamiliar ground in matters pertaining to Vatican protocol, so he took his cue from O'Bryan and let his friend lead the way.

"Monsignor Manzini and I have just hung up from talking with the British prime minister," the Holy Father began. "My English is not that good so the monsignor was gracious enough to translate."

Manzini told Justin that the British prime minister was aware of the two missing Catholic clerics as well as the Archbishop of Canterbury. "It seems the queen already knew of Mrs. Smalling's murder," he continued, "so when she was contacted by her prime minister, she immediately offered to meet with envoys from the Holy See. The prime minister has suggested meeting at ten o'clock tonight at Ten Downing Street and not at Buckingham Palace. You both have diplomatic passports, so clearing English customs will not be a problem. And I have asked for an Alitalia corporate jet to stand-by to fly you out of Ciampino Airport."

Justin was impressed. "The fact the queen is willing to meet with us tells me there's a lot more going on than any of us dared imagine. My guess is that she knows whatever it was Dame Smalling knew, and I'm hoping the meeting will also help us solve the problem posed by the two letters."

"And show us a way to get Cardinal Kettering and the Archbishop of Canterbury freed," added O'Bryan.

While Justin and O'Bryan were talking, the pope had taken a single sheet of heavy linen stationery from inside his desk. He began writing. Finished, he lit a wooden match, and then picked up a stick of red sealing wax. With flame held to wax, the tip quickly melted, causing a couple of large drops to plop onto the paper. The pope blew out the match, placed the charred remnant into a cut glass bowl, slipped off his papal signet ring and pressed it into the already congealing mass. He then held the paper up to his lips and blew on it. Satisfied with the results, he placed the page inside a parchment envelope, penned the address and repeated the process to seal the envelope.

Justin had found himself thoroughly captivated by the entire scene. He had never before witnessed anyone using sealing wax. It was a ritual from another time.

The pontiff handed the envelope to O'Bryan. "Please give this to the Queen," he said. "It is a communiqué from one Head of Church to another. In it I have informed Her Majesty that you and Mister Scott speak for me in all matters pertaining to the letters in question, and that the rendering of any assistance by the Crown will be most appreciated by the Holy See." The pope closed his eyes, offered up a silent prayer, then made the sign of the cross over their heads.

CHAPTER 33
Day 8. St. Petersburg. Monday evening

Mykel Charin went over the plan in his mind for the hundredth time. He had handpicked his 12-man team and had told each the operation they were about to execute had been ordered from Moscow. No one else in the precinct was to know until afterwards.

Standing at the end of the darkened street with Yuri Solotov, he scanned the area through night vision glasses. The roadway had been blocked off, and Svetlana Podgorney was in his car ready to leave for the airport on his signal. Solotov's mission was to make sure the prisoners were whisked away, each to different jails.

Charin was proud of his men. All looked appropriately menacing as they stood in full military-styled battledress uniforms and armor, not unlike their American SWAT counterparts he had seen in many popular television shows and movies. The last thing each man would do before engaging the enemy would be to pull down a knitted mask over his face for protection against identification and possible later retribution.

8:55 p.m. It was time. "Everybody move out," he said in a low voice. "My team, follow me; Yuri's team, you'll be going in through the rear."

At 9:00 p.m., all the lights in the house went out as the main power line was cut, the signal for Charin's battering ram-wielding duo to spring into action.

The heavy doors flew open under the assault, and the officer directly behind lobbed a flash-bang grenade into the darkness. Everyone crouched low, closed their eyes and cupped their ears. The flash was blinding, the noise deafening. Charin's team jumped up and poured into the house, as did Yuri's squad from the rear.

"Manfred von Snellenberger, get down and stay down," Charin yelled at the top of his lungs in English, then switched back to Russian. "This is the police! Everyone stand up and place your hands on top of your heads. Do as you're told and no one will get hurt."

Three officers thundered up the broad staircase, all holding semi-automatics at the ready while shouting for people to come out with their hands up. It was a tactic meant to frighten confused and dazed men into submission.

Charin heard two shots ring out on the first floor followed by a high-pitched scream, "Don't shoot, I give up!"

"Drop your weapons and come out. I want to see lots of hands, people!"

It was an anticlimactic ending. Four thoroughly chastened men were led outside. Charin looked them over carefully. The mansion's owner was nowhere to be seen. In all likelihood he was probably back in Riga.

Charin went back inside and climbed halfway up the staircase. He stopped and called out in English. "Mister von Snellenberger, where are you? You can show yourself now. This is Inspector Mykel Charin of the Saint Petersburg police. Cardinal Kettering sent me to rescue you."

"I'm coming out," a muffled voice replied.

Charin cocked his head. That's strange. The words were coming from beneath his feet. He heard a creaking noise and suddenly a figure came into view from under the stairway. He pulled out a flashlight and trained it on the man's face.

"I'm Manfred von Snellenberger," the man said, holding his spread-fingered hands aloft to show he held no weapon. "I hid myself in a closet under the stairs about five minutes before you arrived." He began to smile. "My ears are still ringing even though I plugged them with candle wax."

"Are you hurt?"

Von Snellenberger shook his head. "I'm fine." He slowly lowered his hands.

Charin secured his weapon, took the stairs down two at a time and gave him an intimate thump on his back. "Then let's get you out of here. Follow me."

Once on the street Charin waved his left arm high above his head then spoke into his radio. "Svetlana, get the car started." He took in the scene before him. The four prisoners were seated on the sidewalk, hands cuffed behind their backs with plastic restraints. Cotton hoods covered their heads. One started to complain in a loud voice, but was immediately silenced with a slap on the side of his head.

"I don't want to hear a peep out of anyone, understood?" Charin heard Yuri say in a loud voice. He gave a thumbs up sign to his partner still hidden behind a mask, but identifiable nonetheless by the band of reflective tape on the upper arms of his camouflaged jacket. Yuri returned the gesture.

As Charin started up the street with von Snellenberger in tow, two dark, hulking, American SUVs roared up to where Svetlana was waiting and skidded to a stop, one abreast the other. Eight doors flew open and a score of men poured out.

"Throw down your guns," a voice roared through a bullhorn. "This is Colonel Pritkin. You men are all under arrest."

One of the prisoners began to laugh under his hood but his glee was short-lived. Someone in Pritkin's group let loose a burst of fire from a Kalasnakov AKSU74 submachine gun.

"Fire at will," Charin commanded, then returned a burst on Pritkin's men from his own Kalasnakov. He saw Svetlana drop to the ground and roll under the rear bumper of his car.

It was obvious to Charin that neither Pritkin nor his men had expected such a response. They were caught off guard, all bunched together. A withering fusillade erupted from Charin's professional force, and screams were heard as the 7.62 mm bullets found their marks within Pritkin's ranks. Other rounds tore into both of the vehicles, shattering the windshields and chewing up the wide-open doors.

"Withdraw!" Pritkin yelled to his men above the din, and then led the retreat by scrambling into the driver's seat of the SUV he had only moments before leapt from like some conquering Caesar. With doors still ajar, he slammed the big, four-wheel drive van into reverse and floored the gas pedal. All four tires spun in unison with none finding traction in the mud and snow and slush. They began to pour smoke. Pritkin slammed the transmission into drive and stomped even harder on the accelerator. The huge van lumbered off sideways like a deranged crab and careened into its neighbor, pinning a screaming officer between both cars.

"You miserable coward, Pritkin," Charin shouted into the night.

Pritkin had switched back into reverse gear and was now turning the steering wheel hard left. The tires finally grabbed and he was able to back up. Two of his men jumped in and slammed the doors shut as he continued picking up speed until he rounded the corner and disappeared.

"This is Inspector Charin. You men throw your weapons onto the ground and get your hands up. You've got two seconds to obey or you'll all be shot!"

The defeated group obeyed. Guns clattered to the pavement. A voice called out. "Inspector Charin, this is Lieutenant Kaminsky. Pritkin told us you guys were a bunch of terrorists who had taken several police officers hostage. We thought we were coming to free you."

"Pritkin lied," Charin shouted back. "He intended for you to kill us. We have four prisoners of our own; all of them wanted felons and friends of Pritkin's, the same coward who has just managed to save his own ass while leaving you to face the music." He turned to his partner. "Get this mess under control. Call for some ambulances and then get these prisoners out of here." He grabbed von Snellenberger by the arm. "Let's go before something else goes wrong."

The two dashed toward the waiting car and jumped in the back. Svetlana put the car in gear and inched forward.

"Do you want to drive, boss?" she called over her right shoulder.

"You're doing fine," Charin replied as he peeled off his woolen balaclava mask and began to un-strap his armor. He turned to von Snellenberger and flashed a grin. "I'm Inspector Mykel Charin, and I was sent to get you by an American FBI agent named Justin Scott, who is working for Cardinal Kettering. We are on our way to the airport where you will be met by a private jet and flown out of Russia. I don't know where it will land, but if you don't want to go, tell me now."

Von Snellenberger took in a deep breath then exhaled loudly. Even in the dim light Charin could make out his companion's confused look.

"Things are happening so fast," von Snellenberger said. "For many months, I believed people were trying to kill me and that if it had not been for the intervention of some patriotic Russians, I would have been dead long ago. In fact, I have been led to believe Cardinal Kettering killed my wife last summer in Washington. And I had been told that the order to do so had come from the highest levels in the Vatican."

"I really don't know the particulars of any of this," Charin replied as he wiped his face with a handkerchief, "other than to assure you that what you have been told is not true. Cardinal Kettering had nothing to do with your wife's death." He studied the grime on the handkerchief. "However, I do know that your being with Panov has something to do with the terrible events that are unfolding inside Russia. Something evil is taking place, something that has to do with pitting the Church of Rome against the Russian Church. People are rioting and clashing with the authorities throughout Russia and Ukraine over several brutal attacks on the leaders of our Church."

Suddenly, von Snellenberger's face lit up. "I remember now where I've seen you before. It was outside the police station a couple of days ago! I immediately suspected you had recognized me. However, I was not sure who you might be."

"We've got company, boss," Svetlana interrupted, her eyes darting back and forth from the road to the rearview mirror. "They've been with us for the past five minutes. It's a big American SUV, very much like the one Colonel Pritkin was in. But it's staying a ways back, letting cars get between him and us."

Charin peered into the darkness to get his bearings. A road sign flashed by. They had already covered more than half of the sixteen kilometers to Pulkovo, putting them ahead of schedule. "Slow down," he ordered, "and let's see what they're up to."

Svetlana moved to the inside lane. Oncoming traffic was light. Two cars overtook them at high speed, the drivers seemingly unconcerned to be challenging a marked police car. Then a huge tour bus thundered past, spraying gallons of slush and muck over the side windows and windshield.

Svetlana cursed aloud and slowed even more. She turned on the wipers and immediately the windshield turned opaque. She was now driving blind. "Shit!" she yelled to no one in particular.

"Turn on your blue flashing light and stop," Charin said, as he looked to the side of the road. There was enough room to pull over safely.

An air horn from a metal behemoth sounded behind them. The driver flashed his high beams in rapid succession then thundered past, mere millimeters away. The vortex created by its wake buffeted them violently.

"Holy God," von Snellenberger yelled out in fear.

"Svetlana, steer hard right, get off the road right now and kill the engine!"

The moment the car stopped, Charin flung open his door and jumped out. The SUV was pulling up behind him, close enough for him to see two men inside. He raised his weapon.

"Get out, and keep your hands where I can see them," he yelled.

Svetlana jumped out of the car, took up a position behind her open door and trained her sidearm on the van.

The driver rolled down his window. "Inspector Charin, don't shoot. It's Federenko and Tallas. Yuri ordered us to follow you to make sure nothing happened. Please, don't shoot! We're coming out with our hands up."

Within thirty seconds, the world was back to normal and Charin made a command decision. They would all travel in style to the airport in this big, warm SUV, and he would send someone for his car in the morning.

At ten o'clock, Charin escorted von Snellenberger onto a Gulfstream G650 parked at the Pulkovo Airlines ramp. He tried hard not to reveal his childlike awe upon seeing the indescribable opulence of the plane's interior. The military-looking pilot-in-command shook his hand then von Snellenberger's, and announced they were cleared for an immediate departure.

Charin turned to von Snellenberger. "You're safe now, sir. Please give my regards to Mister Scott when you meet. He is quite an impressive man, but you'll soon see that for yourself. I only hope one day you will return to my Russia and really get to enjoy our hospitality. But until that day comes, good luck to you."

Charin remained standing on the tarmac until the jet was airborne and climbing westward out over the Gulf of Finland. He finally trudged his way inside, but only after he could no longer see the flashing white anti-collision beacon on its tail.

CHAPTER 34
Day 8. London, England. Monday evening

The midnight blue Cadillac limousine purred its way through the large black steel gates at the entrance to the street, made its way to the edge of the pavement and stopped in front of the black brick house with the black front door. The building sat on a narrow street in the heart of Westminster, itself nestled inside the confines of Greater Metropolitan London. The small street was named after Sir George Downing, a developer who had built both the street and his home there in the 1680s. One of two bobbies on duty stepped forward and opened the car's rear door, allowing O'Bryan to step out, followed by Justin.

The second bobby discretely called inside the building on his walkie-talkie to announce the visitors. A protocol officer appeared at the gleaming black single front door adorned with two simple brass numerals; a one and a zero, an imposing lion's head knocker, and a letterbox inscribed with the words 'First Lord of the Treasury.'

Justin immediately felt the power of the place, and remembered reading somewhere that there were two identical doors for this home; the one in use while its twin was being repaired or re-painted. And it had been this way since sixteen years before the American Revolution.

The lone lamp hanging above fan-shaped glass panes shone brightly, its glow spreading to illuminate a swath of the home's black brick façade. What had been thought by all to be a rare black brick used in the construction of the house was found quite by accident to be something else entirely by a surprised cleaning crew in the 1950s. They had discovered that two centuries worth of soot and grime had managed to hide the walls' true color: a pleasant shade of yellow. However, a strong sense of history and a desire for the familiar won over the day, and the yellow bricks were painted black to match the door. England heaved a huge sigh of relief. All was right with the universe once more. The house at 10 Downing Street and its famous black front door was once again the most recognized residence in the Western World.

"Monsignor O'Bryan, Mister Scott, welcome." The protocol officer made a slight gesture with his right hand. "And if you would care to follow me…"

Justin remained a step behind O'Bryan who was now adorned in his 'official threads' as he had put it to Justin after having made the change of clothes during the flight. For the occasion, Justin had chosen a conservative dark wool pinstripe, a white shirt with French cuffs, a maroon tie and a white silk cravat peeking discretely from his breast pocket. He had to admit as he shot a hand to his tie's knot, that he felt just a tad nervous at the prospect of meeting the Queen of England and her prime minister. He stole a quick glance at his watch. One minute to ten. He strode forward, no sign of a limp. He had deliberately left his cane on the jet, telling O'Bryan he had no desire to be caught armed while in the company of the queen.

The English prime minister smiled a big, genuine toothy smile as he met them at the entrance to the formal White Room and warmly shook both their hands. "Thank you for coming. Please, gentlemen, let me introduce you to my monarch and the foreign secretary."

Both Americans approached the queen who was dressed in a pale pink suit, her favorite color Justin seemed to remember hearing or reading somewhere.

"Here are my *bona fides*, Your Majesty, and a personal message from the Holy Father," O'Bryan said, after gently shaking the queen's proffered gloved hand. Justin took note of his friend's slight bow. He found himself half expecting to see a crown—or at least a tiara—resting among the snowy waves of her perm. It was hard to believe the woman was in her late eighties. The queen in turn introduced him to the foreign secretary, a man Justin had seen many times on television.

She quickly got down to business. Resting in front of her on the heirloom quality conference table was a vermillion colored folder marked Top Secret: For Her Majesty's Eyes Only.

Justin was ready. "Your Majesty, he began, "I'm pretty sure Dame Smalling was murdered because of events from a time long ago, events which had their roots in wartime Lisbon. You see, during the course of an investigation on behalf of the Vatican into the matter at hand, namely the abductions of the Archbishop of Canterbury and Cardinal

Kettering, I came across items of interest which in turn led me to Winston Churchill, several British spies, Alexander Fleming and, finally, a nun known as Sister Lucia of Fatima." He slipped a hand into his jacket pocket and extracted an envelope. "In here are copies of the two letters from Russia that the pope told you about earlier today. I think what's in these letters is the reason the Archbishop of Canterbury and Cardinal Kettering were both kidnapped by persons still unknown in Moscow."

The queen responded by opening the folder and extracting two sheets of paper. She handed the top page to Justin. It took him a few moments to realize that what he had in his hands was an exact copy of Lucia's Russian letter. Startled, he studied the Portuguese writing closely. *This is no copy. Look at the ink. It's an original. But how is that possible?*

The queen allowed a hint of a smile to crease her lips. "I am now the last person still alive who knows the full story. Before tonight, this folder has not left Buckingham Palace since the day it arrived in January, Nineteen Sixty-five, delivered to me by an emissary from Prime Minister Churchill just days before his death on January twenty-fourth. Shortly after, I asked Dr. Margaret Smalling to come to London and tell me in her own words exactly what had happened those many years earlier." The queen paused, as if for dramatic effect. "What I'm about to say to all of you will sound like fiction, but I assure you, it is not. And, to add a strange touch of irony to this evening's events, I realized only a few moments ago that today is the anniversary of that date in January, Nineteen Sixty-five, when I was given this folder for safekeeping by Winston Churchill."

The Queen of England and Monarch of sixteen other Commonwealth Realms began in a firm voice. "To properly set the stage, gentlemen, I must take you all back to the dark days of November, Nineteen Forty..."

CHAPTER 35
Day 8. London. Monday evening

"*That*, **gentlemen, is** a summary of events in Nineteen Forty and Nineteen Forty-one leading up to the eve of the German invasion of Russia." The queen took a sip of water from a crystal glass and continued. "History records Hitler did indeed launch *Operation Barbarossa*, and in the doing spared England, yet you gentlemen look doubtful." Her words were directed to her prime minister and secretary. "I can assure you that Mister Churchill himself warned me about that very issue just before my coronation. He said that there would be those who would claim proof that the country had been saved by the Almighty. 'Rubbish!' he said. 'The intervention was caused by deeds of this earth and not of heaven.'" The queen tapped a clear-polished nail on the folder before her. "Of course I hadn't the faintest idea what he was talking about and I put it out of my mind. Then twelve years later, in January, Nineteen Sixty-five, this information was delivered to me just hours before his death."

Justin decided to weigh in. "Your Majesty, did you and Dame Smalling ever speak of these events after that meeting in Nineteen Sixty-five?"

The queen nodded. "We touched briefly on the subject during the reception following Dame Margaret's investiture, but we never corresponded on the matter. We both felt some fields were better left lying fallow, and this was one."

"How about Ian Fleming, Ma'am?" O'Bryan asked. "Do you know if he ever said anything public about *Operation Barbarossa*?"

The queen shook her head. "The Official Secrets Act would have prevented his talking to anyone, Monsignor. I never met the man, but of course I've read all of his James Bond books beginning with *Casino Royale*." As soon as the words were spoken, her face clouded and her brow furrowed.

"What is it, Your Majesty?" The PM prompted.

"I just remembered something. Margaret believed the Russians might have had a hand in Ian Fleming's sudden and premature death in

August, Nineteen Sixty-four. It was said to have been some sort of a heart attack, if I remember rightly, a rare condition causing him to bleed to death internally. You see, Commander Fleming had just come from Jamaica to bury his mother and he was already quite ill. Margaret thought the Russians had poisoned him with something, maybe an anticoagulant, and not because they had finally uncovered the truth about *Operation Barbarossa*, but rather due to the worldwide, non-stop bad press they were getting as a result of his James Bond books and movies." The queen shrugged. "You know, she could very well have been right on that score."

Justin was the first to respond. "The autopsy results on Dame Smalling have not yet come back, Your Majesty. However, we do know she was murdered. And the Russians are known to carry long grudges. It could be the Kremlin is sending us a warning because they've finally discovered that Margaret Smalling had helped Ian Fleming sic the Germans on them during war."

The queen nodded. "But England was saved while Russia paid a terrible price."

CHAPTER 36
Day 9. Rome. Tuesday morning

"*The lion's share* of the credit has got to go to Ian Fleming though," O'Bryan said, using the plane ride back to Rome to review the staggering facts uncovered during their meeting. "And to think he did it start to finish in less than thirty days. Now that's a plot worthy of one of his James Bond novels!"

"The man was a brilliant rascal, all right," Justin said, his admiration genuine, "but he's sure left us with one hell of a mess to clean up several decades later." As he spoke, he turned on his laptop. "We now need to put our heads together, write down what we know so far, and plan our next moves."

Twenty minutes later, they had agreed on seven points. Justin cut and pasted them into a priority order.

1. Who wrote the letter in Latin to Kettering?

(a.) Did its author see the entire two-page letter Ian Fleming sent to Hitler in 1940?

(b.) Where is the first page of the original letter Hitler received?

(c.) Where is the top half of the second page?

(d.) Does the original envelope still exist?

(e.) Will clues still-hidden in the fake painting of *Evening Prayers* provide answers?

2. Evil people are using the doomsday message to paralyze the curia.

(a.) Why?

(b.) What will they gain? Can they do so without starting a full-scale war?

3. Is Anastasia involved?

4. Why were Kettering, the Archbishop of Canterbury, and von Snellenberger kidnapped?

5. Who killed Dame Smalling?

6. Is there an Asian connection, or is that just a coincidence?

7. Which all leads to this: How much time do we really have?

After Justin read the seven points aloud, both agreed the last was the most important. Justin moved it to the top of the list.

They reread the items, committed them to memory, then Justin hit the delete key and shut down the computer. He yawned and moved his oversized leather seat into a reclining mode. "Don't know about you, sonny, but I'm going to catch a couple of winks. Getting old sucks, as you will one day discover."

* * * * *

Because the Dassault Falcon 50 executive jet was too small to use the airport's regular jetway system, they deplaned onto the concrete ramp and set out for the arrivals building two hundred yards away. It was just after three a.m., and the night air was brisk, the sky starless. The Italian pilot had announced minutes before touchdown that Approach Control was reporting fast moving thundershowers in the area. Luckily, the rain hadn't reached this corner of the sprawling airport—yet.

Justin was a step behind O'Bryan when something caught his eye. It was a red dot, which had suddenly landed on the back of O'Bryan's coat. The dot did not linger. It jumped off O'Bryan, landed on Justin's right arm for a brief moment, then flew back to O'Bryan.

Someone was aiming at them with a laser-scoped long gun!

Justin heard the unmistakable whine of a high velocity bullet as it passed within an inch of his ear and thudded into a metal luggage container.

"Run, Jack!" he yelled, pushing O'Bryan off in the opposite direction. The two of them cut in behind an Emirates double-decker Airbus A380-800 that had begun backing away from a gate under its own power. The mind-numbing, bone-rattling noise from the four GP7200 engines hanging below its fenced-tipped wings was deafening.

Suddenly, O'Bryan stumbled, lost his balance, and fell directly into the path of the ganged landing gear assembly under the left wing of the 600-ton aluminum and composite behemoth.

"Jack, roll to your right!" Justin cried out, his words swallowed up inside a sea of indescribable noise. As he dashed diagonally across the plane's backward path, a blast of hot deflected exhaust swept him off his feet and threw him down onto the tarmac. He managed to look up

in time to see that he, too, was now in danger of being squashed by the monster's right landing gear assembly situated under the fuselage. A bullet loosed a shower of concrete chips into his face, followed immediately by another. Either the plane or the sniper would finish him off, he thought. He rolled into the narrow pathway that had opened up between both the main gear assemblies, and once the plane had trundled on, he jumped up and staggered towards a clearing and out of harm's way. He looked around. O'Bryan was nowhere to be seen.

"Jaaaaccckkk!" He screamed in one long, agonized, atavistic cry, knowing it was for naught.

With the huge airliner behind him, he continued to look around wildly. *What was that?* He could just make out the shape of something shadowy lying on the ground; something outside the path of the plane's wheels. Then the shadowy something stirred. It was O'Bryan!

O'Bryan looked up, his eyes filled with fright as Justin sprinted over. "I just knew I was a goner!"

"Hallelujah, you're not!" Justin yelled back, then placed his hands under O'Bryan's armpits and helped him to his feet.

O'Bryan began to laugh heartily, a sure sign his body was relieving itself of pent-up stress, Justin realized. "You've still got your cane, I see. How did you manage that?"

"Because it's strapped to my wrist, that's why," Justin said. "Can you walk?"

"I...I think so." O'Bryan took a couple of tentative steps. "Yeah...I'm OK."

"Good. Then let's scram before the cops show up and start asking us a bunch of questions we don't want to answer."

"Or the shooter decides to have another go at us," added O'Bryan.

* * * * *

After a detour into a deserted washroom to clean up, they presented their Vatican passports to a yawning customs agent who stamped the books and waved them through.

Once inside the main terminal, Justin spotted a dozen cardinals and their retinues even though it was still a couple of hours before first light.

One hundred and twenty-six princes of the church were pouring into Rome from all over the world. These particular men were called Cardinal Priests, and they were flocking to join the forty-one Cardinal Bishops and Cardinal Deacons who were among the select few permanent residents of the Holy City.

Not a one had a clue why he had been summoned to Rome by the Holy Father.

* * * * *

Justin and O'Bryan met with the pope at nine o'clock. Again, Monsignor Ignacio Caffarone was unable to hide his hostility as he ushered them before the pontiff. He nodded curtly to the pope and took his leave. The pope said nothing. Justin was the first to speak. "I think it's safe to say with ninety-nine percent certainty, Holy Father, that Lucia's Russian letter is a clever fake."

"But how is that possible?" the pontiff asked. "Especially knowing John Paul the Second was told exactly the same thing when he met with Sister Lucia in Nineteen Ninety-one."

O'Bryan said, "What we're saying is that the words did not come from the Virgin Mary and Sister Lucia. They came instead from the minds of Winston Churchill and a young British naval officer named Ian Fleming. That last paragraph we all read was the finale of a British forgery that had been sent to Adolf Hitler via the Patriarch of Lisbon commanding Hitler in God's name to attack Russia and not England. The queen showed us an exact copy of that letter. It seems Mister Churchill had expressed his worry to a young Queen Elizabeth in Nineteen Sixty-five that Ian Fleming's forged Lucia letter to Hitler would one day surface, and would come to cause the world untold grief."

"And you both saw this letter?"

"We did, Holy Father," O'Bryan said, as he reached into a pocket and drew out an envelope. "Her Majesty had a photocopy made for you as we were leaving the prime minister's residence." He handed the pages to the pope. "Of course, it's in Portuguese, but you'll see it appears identical to the one we received."

The pope quickly scanned the letter. It seemed right. He looked up. "Then where is the rest of Lucia's Russian letter? Someone still has to have held onto this first page where God directed Hitler to invade Russia. But the more important question is: how did they manage to get their hands on it in the first place?"

"As you can see by comparing the copy with the one Cardinal Kettering received," Justin chimed in, "it's not only the first page that is missing, Holy Father. "We're also missing the top half of the second page, which suggests to me that the Russia letter was a forged copy of the original British letter hand-delivered to Hitler by a cardinal in Nineteen Forty. Hitler was snookered into believing it came from Sister Lucia, and we know its message worked, because a few months later he invaded Russia and not England."

Justin could tell the pope was having difficulty following the conversation, but he pressed on. "Somebody, or a group of somebodies, inside Russia went to great lengths to get this false message into your hands," he said, now speaking slowly. "At the same time, they couldn't have you seeing the entire letter, so they made an exact copy of just the one section of Lucia's phony letter they wanted you to see, and that was the part dealing with the Apocalypse." He suddenly lowered his voice, "But here's something that's just crossed my mind. The Russians were counting on the fact you would compare it content with John Paul Second's written account of his startling meeting with Sister Lucia in Nineteen Ninety-one, and they were banking that you would be forced to conclude it was indeed a genuine letter written by Sister Lucia."

"Which is precisely what I thought," the pope said, his voice now close to a whisper. "But how was this even possible?"

"Maybe because there's a traitor here inside the Vatican," Justin replied. "Someone who was close to your predecessors; someone now close to you. Someone like Monsignor Ignacio Caffarone, perhaps?" There, he had said it.

"I will dismiss the man at once," the pope said," his face blanched with horror. "I should have done so long ago, but I felt John Paul and Benedict still trusted Ignacio despite what you uncovered last fall. Now I see that my indecision has caused irreparable, harm to the Church."

Justin shook his head. "Maybe you should stick with the enemy you know instead of replacing him with one you don't. My recommendation is that you allow the monsignor to stay, at least for the moment. But don't let on you suspect him of treachery. That way he might become complacent, lower his guard and make a mistake that we can turn to our advantage."

"I'll make sure Ignacio hears nothing from me," the pope finally said to both men, then turned to face Justin. "We must now redouble our efforts to discover what the Russians are really up to, and then find the way to stop them."

"I agree," Justin replied. "There's not the specter of an Apocalypse in our immediate futures, Holy Father, but I still haven't been able to figure out what the ultimate goal is. What grand prize awaits that has them willing to turn the world asunder?"

The pope changed the subject. "Have you heard anything new about Cardinal Kettering or the English archbishop? Do we even know if they are still alive?"

"They're alive," Justin replied without hesitation. "And even though I don't know the endgame yet, instinct tells me both prelates are of value only as long as they remain alive."

"You sound confident there will be a favorable outcome, Mister Scott. I wish I could fully share in your optimism. However, I am grateful that you continue to help us, and I don't know anyone who could be doing a better job."

Justin saw that as a signal to end the meeting. He stood up. "It will end soon, and it will end favorably," he promised.

But despite his assurances, Justin Scott knew the hourglass was fast running out of sand.

CHAPTER 37
Day 9. Rome. Tuesday morning

Back in Kettering's office, Justin saw he had two phone messages. He punched up the first.

"This is Mannix. I tried your cell, but you must have turned it off. Your package has arrived. Call me ASAP because I need final delivery instructions." Justin was pleased. Von Snellenberger was safe. He pulled his cellular from his pocket and turned it on. The screen failed to light up.

"Your cell phone working, Jack?"

O'Bryan fished out his phone. It looked OK. He scrolled down the menu, dialed a number at random and as it started to ring, abandoned the call. "Seems to be."

Justin shoved his phone back into his pocket. "Of all the times for mine to go on the fritz! I can't even transfer my stored numbers to a new phone!"

"Then send an email to Paula and have her shoot back a list of your must-have numbers, and we'll store them in mine. No big deal."

"Good thinking." He typed a quick message to Paula in Washington on O'Bryan's phone. He knew Mannix's number by heart so he could call him back after hearing the second stored message.

"This is Mykel Charin." The Russian sounded tired. "First off, your friend is safe. I saw his plane depart, so I speak with confidence. However, my contacts tell me Cardinal Kettering has been moved from Moscow and that he is now being held here in Saint Petersburg. Rumor has it there is an English archbishop with him. Also, during the night, a dozen Orthodox bishops in several countries have mysteriously disappeared. The newspapers and TV reporters will be all over that story by this afternoon. Also, my boss, Colonel Pritkin, tried to kill me last night but, as you can see, I'm still here, whereas he is now nowhere to be found."

Charin hesitated, as if deciding whether to say something more. He pressed ahead. "Justin, something big is about to go down in St. Petersburg, something having to do with the Saints Peter and Paul

Cathedral. However, I don't think that the..." Click. The machine went dead.

He was about to punch up Mannix's phone number on the landline when his cell phone began ringing in his pocket. Even O'Bryan was startled by the sound of the suddenly working-again phone.

"Doctor Edward Smalling, here, Mister Scott."

Justin hadn't expected to hear from him so soon. "Good morning, Doctor. What have you got for me?"

"Two things. First, by a process of elimination, preliminary pathology on my mother's blood and lungs seems to be leaning toward a very nasty nerve agent as the cause of death. A newer and more deadly form of Sarin. I'm a practicing pathologist, so I have some understanding of how it works. Sarin can be delivered either in liquid form or by aerosol. Either would cause paralysis and unconsciousness within moments, and death would follow less than thirty seconds later. I really don't believe my mother had time to grasp fully the enormity of what was happening to her. It was over very fast, and I thank God for that." Silence followed.

Justin allowed a long moment to pass then asked, "Who would make this stuff?"

"The Russians and the North Koreans would be my chief suspects. The Germans invented Sarin back in Nineteen Thirty-eight. The West produced it for a while, but destroyed its stockpiles long ago because Sarin is just too deadly, too unstable. The last time Sarin was used as a weapon was in an attack on a subway train in Tokyo in Nineteen Ninety-five. A dozen or so passengers were killed outright, and a thousand more were injured. Conjecture at the time favored the theory that the radical Japanese faction got its supply from the North Koreans."

Justin immediately harkened back to Detective Castellanos and his interview with the wounded terrorist after the airport shootout. She had distinctly told him her three companions were not Japanese, but North Koreans. Here now was more evidence of a possible North Korean connection. "Doctor, could those Japanese terrorists have possibly made the Sarin themselves back in Nineteen Ninety-five?"

"Not a chance. The process for manufacturing Sarin is devilishly complex. It involves the chemical bonding of a fluorinated molecule with phosphorus, and if you know anything about chemistry you'll understand when I say that the mere mention of playing around with that mixture sends shivers up and down the spines of every chemist I know."

Justin couldn't imagine. This was scary, scary stuff. "And the delivery of Sarin against a victim: Is it difficult?"

"Whoever administered it to my mother knew what they were doing. Had to, or they too, would have died alongside her."

Hearing this made Justin suddenly very nervous because it reinforced what he already knew. His enemy was extremely sophisticated and they had done their homework. "So you're saying there's no antidote?" he pressed.

"Practically speaking, no, there isn't," Smalling replied. "But if someone was anticipating a Sarin attack—and had enough auto-injectors on hand loaded with oxime and atropine—then it's possible they could cheat death. However, with this new form of Sarin, it's tough to say with any degree of certitude that a person could be saved. And if it were a large group that found itself exposed, well, the effort to save them would have to be one of heroic proportions indeed."

Justin told himself this was important information he was hearing and that he needed to store it in his memory. "Anything else?"

"My mother's pen is missing."

"You've looked everywhere?"

"Everywhere," Smalling replied. A pause, then, "What do you make of it?"

"I honestly don't know. Do me a favor, look some more."

"I will."

"Doctor, I'm so sorry about your mother. I was in London last night, and she was very much at the center of a remarkable conversation. My one regret is that I didn't get the chance to meet her that morning. Dame Margaret Smalling was beyond special."

"Thank you for those kind words, sir, they do bring a measure of comfort. Of course I will look further for the pen, and when I get more information from the pathology report I will call you, if you'd like."

"I would be most grateful. Goodbye."

Justin recounted for O'Bryan what Edward Smalling had just said, ending with the information that some new version of Sarin was suspected as being the cause of Margaret Smalling's death.

"I heard you mention Japan and North Korea."

"You did. But Doctor Smalling told me the stuff probably came from either Russia or North Korea, which adds credence to the possibility there's an Asian connection to this mix." He looked down in amazement at his now-working cell phone. "You believe in miracles, Padre?"

O'Bryan laughed. "I do now," he said, as the phone rang again.

"Justin Scott."

"Mannix, here. Tried you earlier; no answer. Calling to let you know I have von Snellenberger tucked safely away. Any instructions?"

"Is he with you now?"

"Yes."

"Could you put him on?"

"Manfred von Snellenberger speaking," said a voice a moment later. "Mister Mannix has told me about the disappearance of Cardinal Kettering." He paused a moment then added in a saddened voice, "and he told me about the truth behind the death of my lovely Maritha. I had heard about it from the Russians, but what I was told by them was far different from what Mister Mannix has said. For months, I believed Cardinal Kettering was complicit in Maritha's murder; that Mister Panov was my friend, but I now know I've been terribly wrong on both counts. I will do anything I can to help you find her murderer."

"Please tell Steve everything you can remember about your stay in Russia. Where you were held, what your captors wanted, who they are, and what they told you, if anything, of events that are unfolding right now inside that country."

Justin also gave Mannix permission to be as candid as he wanted with von Snellenberger. "I have a gut feeling he holds the key to things I haven't had time to tell you."

"I'll get started with the debriefing right away. Do you want to know where I've got him stashed? I'm less than twenty minutes from the Vatican," Mannix added.

"Not for the moment," Justin replied. "If something should happen to me, then I can't tell anyone what I don't know. By the way, my cell's been acting up. It seems to be OK now, but here's O'Bryan's number just in case."

* * * * *

Rome. Tuesday afternoon

Paula called at two o'clock to tell him she had emailed all the numbers in his cell. He didn't bother wasting time telling her the problem seemed to have fixed itself.

Paula continued. "I've heard nothing from the kidnappers. I'm not sure what it means."

That surprised Justin. He had expected some communication, even if it was only a wheedling for more time. Maybe he had misread these people. If that were the case, then he well might have already caused Kettering's execution with his calculated bluff. On the other hand, he found himself thinking, maybe the man had already been murdered before he called their hand and the captors knew the game was over. Whatever the truth, this was not good news.

"Continue monitoring my email," he instructed. "Maybe they've been trying to contact me but can't because an Internet server is down. Russian computer technology still sucks."

He heard her sigh. "I hope you're right."

While Justin had been talking, O'Bryan had been studying Ian Fleming's letter to Adolf Hitler. He could see that his friend was perplexed. Something in the text was obviously bothering him.

"What is it, Jack?"

O'Bryan shook his head. "Something about this letter is causing alarm bells to go off in my head."

"Could be nothing more than a false alarm," Justin said, not meaning to be flippant.

O'Bryan continued to shake his head. "I don't think so. There's something that's trying to grab my attention, but I just can't seem to wrap my mind around it. Getting tired, I guess."

"Well, we both could use some shuteye," Justin replied.

* * * * *

Lausanne, Switzerland. Tuesday afternoon

Ian A. O'Connor

The man seated behind the mahogany desk tilted back in his swivel Moroccan leather executive chair and studied the two erstwhile trusted agents standing before him. He was disgusted and angry, and toyed absently with a bejeweled dagger. Both men sported multiple bruises and lacerations about their heads, and the bigger of the two was leaning on a crutch, his left leg wrapped in a soft cast.

"We will have Justin Scott bawling like a frightened little girl when we're through with him," the seated man said, throwing back the words spoken some forty-eight hours earlier by the Interrogator from the Helsinki Airport. However, the colorless eyes flashing from behind rimless glasses were far from amused. "And we will get you everything you want to know."

In a display of disgust, the man threw the dagger which doubled as an envelope opener onto the desk's intricately tooled leather surface. It bounced off a Baccarat crystal paper-clip holder, its point nicking the leather.

"Well, that particular old American won't be so lucky next time..." Strong Hands began, before being cut off with a slashing motion from an angry hand.

"There won't be a next time, at least not for you," the man shouted. "I needed the information yesterday. Mister Scott now has both of your identification cards and because of that, the Finnish police already have your mug shots plastered over every law enforcement computer on the continent. Your services are no longer of any value to me," he said with a dismissive wave of a hand. The meeting was over.

Klaus Furlan, Managing Director of *Ibel and Laufenburg*, a private investigation service specializing in matters for the moneyed elite, and also in charge of *Credit Lausanne*, a private bank in Lausanne, Switzerland, now found himself still seething as he tried to concentrate on a letter he had plucked at random from a folder on his desk. How could two professionals have botched the job in Helsinki so badly? If Justin Scott could somehow appear before him this instant, he would reach out and throttle the arrogant American with his own bare hands! Boastful unspoken words that he knew rang hollow. The long drawn out sigh that followed spoke of defeat, for deep down, Klaus Furlan knew he was no match—physically or mentally—for this particular American or his friend, Monsignor O'Bryan.

Klaus Furlan had crossed swords with those two in the opening days of the autumn just past, and in this very building no less. They had come to Lausanne sniffing about like a couple of bloodhounds, looking for information regarding the murder of a woman who had been a client for but a brief moment in time, namely one Maritha von Snellenberger, wife of a prominent Swiss banker. Count Rudolph Laufenberg, the senior member of *Ibel and Laufenburg* at the time had intervened, and in the doing had deftly diffused a situation which could have easily blossomed into a scandal of international import. Laufenburg had also fallen madly in love with the beautiful Maritha von Snellenberger. In the end, though, Justin Scott and Monsignor O'Bryan were forced to take their investigation elsewhere, and the identity of the 'twelve apostles', those twelve families who were the only clients of the private banking concern housed under this same roof still remained secret.

Furlan sat back and allowed his mind to dwell on the clients, all of them descendants of Russian nobility. Their forebears had left Russia with fortunes intact, doing so mere months before the storming of the Winter Palace and the start of the Russian Revolution back in 1917. Throughout the intervening years—and thanks to astute investing— their assets with *Credit Lausanne* were in excess of twenty billion euros. And, he, Klaus Furlan, was the man in charge.

You must stay focused, he told himself, because the biggest prize in all of Christendom is only hours away, and you will soon be rich beyond imagination. Furlan reached for his phone and punched up an extension. A minute later, a willowy, elegant blonde entered his office without knocking. She glided to his side, slipped an arm around his neck and kissed his cheek. "I warned them back in Rome about Mister Scott's capabilities," she murmured into his ear, her warm breath causing stirrings quite unbecoming of the staid Swiss banker. "They're lucky he didn't kill them both."

The woman was Kirsten Havel, granddaughter of a long-dead Jewish-Hungarian forger named Szűrös Havel who had worked for Winston Churchill and Commander Ian Fleming in London during the

World War, and her throaty words were uttered in a peculiar Yiddish dialect rarely heard or spoken.

Furlan sighed. "You're right again, my dear, as always," he replied in the same tongue, his eyes filled with adoration.

CHAPTER 38
Day 9. St. Petersburg. Tuesday afternoon

Colonel Boris Pritkin stood at attention like a novice cadet, despite the fact he was not in uniform or in the presence of a superior officer, but rather an old man.

"You're telling me that Manfred von Snellenberger has been taken away by one of your own officers?" the ragged voice said, filled with disbelief.

"A renegade detective by the name of Mykel Charin, Excellency," Pritkin answered. "I have a team searching for him with orders to shoot him on sight."

The old man erupted. "If Charin dies, then so do you! If your goons kill him, any chance I might have of getting von Snellenberger back will be lost. Do you honestly believe that the millions of euros I have spent on this endeavor will all be for naught because of your incompetence?" The old man heaved himself up from his chair. "I have waited a lifetime for this moment in our country's history. So have eleven other families. Our window of opportunity will soon slam closed forever." He brought both his hands together, creating a sharp cracking sound. *"Like that!"* he screamed. *"Do you understand? There will never again be a possibility like this for saving Russia."*

The old man stumbled and would have fallen had it not been for his bodyguard. Powerful hands reached out, steadied him, then guided him back to his chair. The old man slumped down and seethed. He then muttered a prayer of thanks that he had not been in the house last evening, or he, too, would now be sitting in a jail cell. That would have definitely ended the plan he had worked on so diligently for the past seven years. A shudder passed through his body.

He finally looked up at Pritkin with eyes still filled with rage. "You had better get the word to this Mykel Charin that I want to see him. Tell him I will personally guarantee his safety, but I want him here before sundown. If he is not at the police station then turn Saint Petersburg upside down, but find him." He pointed a gnarled finger toward the door. "Now get out of my sight and find that son of a bitch!" He turned to his bodyguard. "Have my car brought around to the front. We're going to the Peter and Paul Cathedral."

* * * * *

The old man seated in the back of the Bentley Mulsanne rushing toward the Peter and Paul Cathedral had not always been old, but he had always been rich. He was Alexander Panov, born in Riga, Latvia, in 1925 to a family of Russian expatriates. His grandparents and his father had left St. Petersburg in 1916, sensing change was in the air. The Panovs quietly moved their fortune into a bank in Lausanne, Switzerland, but planted roots in Riga, a city whose architecture reminded them of St. Petersburg—a city of culture; a city steeped in the Art Nouveau style.

The Panovs and eleven other expatriate families were tied to each other through their bank, *Credit Lausanne*, itself founded by Russians émigrés Messrs. Ibel and Laufenburg in 1909. Over the decades, the immensely wealthy families came to be known within the walls of the bank as the twelve apostles and, as the generations passed, intermarriage further strengthened their bonds. Their many friends left behind in St. Petersburg and Moscow had publicly scoffed at their leaving, only to discover too late in the fall of 1917 that escape from Russia was now impossible. They had stayed too long at the dance. Entire families vanished alongside countless millions of their fellow citizens, all swallowed into the vastness of Siberia while their magnificent estates were sized by the new government. Czar Nicholas II and his family were murdered in 1918, thus ending rule in Russia by a family that could trace its beginnings back to the first czar, Ivan the Terrible, who had placed himself upon the throne in 1547 at the tender age of sixteen.

In January 1938, the Panovs realized that Latvia was no longer the place to be. With war clouds hanging on the horizon, they liquidated their holdings in Riga and sold most of their heirlooms, including a masterpiece by *Fra Angelico* entitled *Evening Prayers*, a painting that had been in the family for over a hundred years and was the particular favorite of the young Alexander. *Evening Prayers* was consigned to an art dealer friend in Lisbon to be sold at the special Christie's auction scheduled to take place in Paris that spring. The cash received from the liquidation of assets was turned into bullion and stored in the bank at Lausanne, a city where the family also settled.

Alexander missed his home and friends, and vowed to one-day return. He had to wait more than fifty years to fulfill that vow, but on October 25, 1997, he moved into a baronial home on the banks of the Daugava. There was a huge significance in that date. It was eighty years to the day after the storming of the Winter Palace, and his long-dead parents had gone to their graves grieving the end of the House of Romanov.

Early in November 2011, Panov decided the time had come to right this terrible wrong. As patriarch of the twelve apostles, Panov sent word to the other heads of families that he thought they should meet and, on December 20, 2011, they all gathered at *Credit Lausanne*. Two days later, a consensus was reached. The twelve agreed to invest whatever sums necessary to first find, verify, then crown a Romanov descendant to once more sit upon the Imperial Throne of Russia. That terrible wrong of October 25, 1917, would be righted and, in the doing, they would restore to greatness that which was once called the Holy Russian Empire, a land mass encompassing one-sixth of the earth's surface. They also agreed that with the coronation of the new czar, the Russian Rite and the Roman Rite should become enjoined; bringing an end to the Great Schism that had separated Christ's Church since 1054. Any lingering vestiges of that social failure called communism would finally be purged from the nation's psyche.

The apostles gave themselves five years to accomplish their task. They would be going home, a dream fulfilled.

How had Panov come to such a bold, visionary decision? What was it that had compelled him to undertake such a gargantuan task in the twilight of his days?

He had discovered a letter which had changed the course of history; a letter which had been delivered to Adolf Hitler on December 20, 1940.

It was a letter from Sister Lucia of Fatima.

* * * * *

Alexander Panov stepped out of the car unassisted and gazed up at the 404-foot spire of the Cathedral of Peter and Paul, built inside the walls of the Peter and Paul Fortress. Atop its spire stood an angel holding a cross, which over the centuries had become an important and enduring symbol—as well as a focal point—for the city's inhabitants.

Panov never tired of visiting this church. To him it represented the greatness of Russia. Here was the final resting place of all the czars from Peter the Great to Nicholas II; the latter being interred in 1998 in the small Chapel of St. Catherine, along with his czarina and three of their children. Still missing was daughter Anastasia, and the only son, Alexei.

Inside the cathedral scores of workers representing many of the artisan trades were busy scraping, painting, repairing, replacing, polishing, smoothing, sanding and adding the finishing touches to the delicate 24-carat gold leaf on the gilded ceiling. The work had been ongoing for months, but today was the last. By tomorrow morning, the building would be ready for its greatest moment since the first cornerstone was laid in 1712 and its consecration on April 1, 1733.

Panov was pleased. Here, the next czar of Russia would be crowned in ninety-six hours and a pope twelve hours after that. But first he had to find Detective Mykel Charin, because the fate of Russia and Christendom now rested in the hands of this one man.

CHAPTER 39
Day 9. St. Petersburg. Tuesday, late afternoon

The afternoon had turned bitterly cold, the wind having shifted from the north.

The unrest across the country of the last few days had subsided, but tensions were still running high. It was as if the people were just waiting for their next command to demonstrate—or worse. To Charin, the feeling was downright eerie. And adding to the already surreal situation was the fact the Kremlin had suddenly turned uncommunicative.

Riding in Charin's marked car, he and Yuri Solotov were crossing the Fontanka River on the Anichkov Bridge on their way to a meeting with Lieutenant Kaminsky, a trusted deputy. Charin had no idea where Pritkin had vanished to but had told Solotov he would arrest him on sight, or shoot him on the spot if he tried to make a run for it.

Solotov changed the subject. "What do you make of those bishops disappearing in Europe and the Middle East, eh, Mykel? First, we had that cardinal being kidnapped, then the Archbishop of Canterbury, and now these other religious leaders."

"The bigger question is why?" Charin replied, shaking his head as he kept his eyes on the road. The wind swirled around the car in sudden bursts, blowing snow up from the surface and often reducing visibility to zero. He knew he had to stay alert or they'd end up in a ditch, or worse. "I've never seen quite anything like it, and I don't think it's going to end well." As he spoke, a loud burst of static from the police radio hanging under the dashboard announced an incoming call.

"Firefox One, do you copy? This is Colonel Pritkin. Come in Firefox One." The reception was as clear as if Pritkin was sitting in the back seat.

Solotov scooped up the mike. "This is Firefox One, I copy."

"Where in the hell are you, Charin?" Colonel Pritkin asked, sounding more relieved than angry. His tone was not lost on either detective.

"What do you want, Pritkin? You've got a giant pair of stones to even be on this net."

"That's not Charin," Pritkin said, as if addressing someone else. He paused and came back with an unexpectedly polite plea. "Would you put Inspector Detective Mykel Charin on the line?" A heartbeat later, the mollified voice added a word neither man had ever heard pass from Pritkin's lips in the years they had known him. "Please."

Both men traded glances that spoke volumes.

"Mykel, please listen and don't hang up," he said. "This is important. I'm asking you to go to the place you were last night for a meeting with the owner. He unconditionally guarantees your safety. In fact, if anything should happen to you, I will forfeit my life. It's that serious."

"How do I know you're not setting a trap so that you can finish what you started last night?"

"On my mother's grave, I swear there is no trap. This whole affair has escalated into something far bigger than either of us; in fact, the future of Russia now hangs in the balance. I'm begging you, Mykel. Please."

Something in the sound of the man's voice told Charin this was legitimate. He made his decision. "Kingpin," he replied in a formal, professional manner and using Pritkin's official call sign, "Firefox One is moving. I'll be at the destination in ten."

CHAPTER 40
Day 9. St. Petersburg. Tuesday evening

The first thing Charin noticed as he and Solotov mounted the mansion's steps was the front doors. There was no sign of last night's battering ram damage. Both doors had been repaired and repainted. He looked closer. Not repaired, *replaced!*

Before Charin could ring the bell, the doors opened and a giant appeared.

"Give me your guns," the Goliath demanded as he held out one huge hand, palm up, and wagged a sausage-sized index finger.

Charin laughed. "Tell your boss the police don't take orders from thugs. At least these cops don't. Let him know he's just used up his one chance," He turned to Solotov. "Let's go," he said, and started back down the steps.

"Wait," the giant called out, "don't leave."

Just then, Colonel Pritkin appeared, his face white with fright. "Mykel, of course you don't have to give up your gun. Come, Mister Panov is waiting."

As Pritkin led them toward the back of the house, Charin saw no sign of last night's raid. Everything apparently was the way it had been at one minute before nine.

They entered the sitting room and the two-legged leviathan wordlessly walked over to Panov's oversized leather armchair and took up station behind his master.

"Forgive me for not getting up," Panov, said, sounding cordial, then waved them closer. He peered at Solotov but directed his question to Charin. "And who is he?"

"My partner. And before you even ask the question, the answer is no. He stays."

Panov's eyes flashed in momentary anger, but he held himself in check. "Very well, he stays." Panov held a blue-veined, parchment colored hand aloft with the fingers open in an expectant manner. His eyes never left Charin's. The giant wordlessly scooped up a bottle of water from a silver ice bucket beside his feet, removed the cap and placed it into the claw. The old man took a couple of sips and handed it back.

"Mister Charin," he began in a strong voice, "what I have to say will not take long. Also, it will not be open to discussion or debate."

Charin voiced neither agreement nor disagreement. He raised an eyebrow that said I'm listening.

"First, you will release my men. Second, you will return Manfred von Snellenberger from Rome within twenty-four hours. Third, you will never interfere with me ever again."

"And if I tell you my answer to all three of your demands is no?"

"Then I will present you with the body of the Archbishop of Canterbury before the clock strikes eight. And one hour after that, I will tell you where you can find the body of Cardinal Kettering."

"And if I still say no?" Charin said, passing a thumb and forefinger in a slow, deliberate downward stroking motion over his Cossack-styled mustache. He shot a withering glance toward Pritkin in time to see the man's eyes widen in disbelief.

Panov shook his head. It was a sad gesture. "After both of those priests are dead, I will no longer care what you do or don't do because you will no longer be of any value to me."

"So you'll have me shot?"

Panov feigned a look of shock and again shook his head. "No, you will not be shot. Indeed, I will pray you live a long life so that you will have ample time to reflect on your stupidity. Instead, you will forfeit the lives of your wife and daughters. And you can be sure their deaths will be particularly unpleasant."

Charin took a step forward, his face contorted in anger. "You son of…"

Panov raised an ancient hand and the mountain stepped out from behind the master's chair and stood towering over the detective.

Pritkin jumped back; Solotov stood his ground.

"Did I just hear you say yes to all three of my demands?"

Charin's heart pounded inside his chest. This monster will kill Olga and the twins, but not before they beg to be put out of their misery. What in God's name would anyone else do facing such an impossible choice? He answered in a hoarse voice. "If I agree to all of your demands, how do I know you will keep your word?"

"Because it is in my best interest to do so," Panov said, visibly relieved. "I want everybody to live, simply because they would be of no value to me dead. And that includes your family of pretty women." He motioned impatiently for the giant to step aside. "I shall explain why you will willingly want to follow my instructions. You see, there is something taking shape which is greater than either of us, something that will determine a glorious future for our beloved Russia."

Determine the future of Russia? He had no idea how such a thing could be possible.

Panov continued. "Before this week is out Russia will have a new czar. A man who is a direct descendant of the Romanovs, and his coronation will return Russia to a state of imperial greatness. Then twenty-four hours after that, a new pope will be crowed in the Saints Peter and Paul Cathedral, a pontiff elected by bishops from all of the major Christian denominations. The new czar and the new pope will reign side by side from this holy city of Saint Petersburg." He smiled up at Charin as one would to a child. "And you will be instrumental in making it all a reality."

The name of this new czar exploded into Charin's consciousness. *"Manfred von Snellenberger,"* he blurted out. *"He's to be your new czar!"*

"Correct. He is a direct descendant of the Imperial Family, and let me tell you how I know this is true." Panov sat up straighter, his eyes on fire. "In Nineteen Ninety-one, the Russian government wanted to confirm that bodies recovered from a sealed pit a dozen miles from the town of Yekaterinburg were those of our beloved Nicholas and his family. They approached some English scientists for help. The Englishmen compared samples of what is called mitochondrial DNA— generously provided by Prince Philip of England—to those found in bone fragments identified as belonging to the Czarina Alexandria. Two years later the English experts came back with a perfect match." Panov reverently crossed himself in a subconscious show of respect for those royals, all canonized saints on August 14, 2000.

"Does von Snellenberger know any of this?"

"He knows," Panov answered, truthfully. "There were times during these last few months that I thought he suspected, but I wasn't certain. However, as of a week ago, he knows for sure, even though he still might want to say no. But to answer your first question, it is an indisputable fact that von Snellenberger is a Romanov because his blood also tells me so. And DNA never lies."

"What about the president and the prime minister?" Charin asked. "How do you suppose Tweedledum and Tweedledee will take to the idea of a czar returning to rule over Russia? Even the new masters in the Kremlin are loathe to share power, and everyone knows Russia is a democracy in name only."

"Mister Charin, I will say no more other than even our president and prime minister have come to realize Russia needs a titular head of state, someone the people will rally behind, just as the British have done for centuries. Today, we are a Third World nation that happens to possess nuclear weapons, but with a strong secular leader and a strong spiritual leader, Russia will become the pre-eminent nation on earth within a generation, and all this will happen if for no other reason than it has been so ordained in heaven. You see, God has revealed to me the hour and the day of this happening, and that time is at hand."

The comment caught an already reeling Charin completely by surprise. *This man is insane!* He's a religious zealot of the worst kind, which makes him doubly dangerous. Realizing this did not provide Charin with any sense of comfort. "I will have Mister von Snellenberger brought back," he said in a resigned voice, "but first I must have your promise nothing will happen to the cardinal, the archbishop or my family."

"You have my word. Now hurry. Bring our next czar home. You have less than twenty-four hours, because after that, it will be too late. No matter what else happens, our czar must be as far away as possible from Rome before dawn on Thursday."

CHAPTER 41
Day 9. Rome. Tuesday evening

Justin fielded the call from Mannix shortly after six. "I need you here," Mannix said without preamble. "What I'm getting from Mister von Snellenberger is right out of a thriller novel." Justin took down the address and within ten minutes, he and O'Bryan were in the Fiat. Mannix's directions took them over the Tiber at the *Vittorio Emanuele II Bridge*, then east-southeast along the *Corso Vittorio Emanuele II* until they were forced by the bumper-to-bumper traffic onto the side roads. They were no better, and Justin could see O'Bryan's frustration. Finally, the priest let loose a mild expletive under his breath and shot a glance into his rearview mirror. Without warning, he floored the gas pedal and bolted into a narrow, dimly lit cobblestone alley.

O'Bryan worked his way around several haphazardly parked trucks, most with motors idling while their drivers dropped off wares to shopkeepers readying their stores for the next day. Halfway up the dingy lane, the delivery truck they were following stopped, blocking them from going further. O'Bryan inched closer and leaned on the horn. The driver jumped out of his cab, grinned and shot them a finger. Then he sprinted to the back of his truck, grabbed a dolly and disappeared into a clothing store on the right. *"Son of a bitch!"* O'Bryan yelled, thumping angrily on the steering wheel.

An equally enraged Justin began to open his door. "I'm going to drive the damn thing up to the end of the alley," he announced. "Get ready to follow." As he was about to step onto the cobblestones, a Vespa scooter pulled up alongside, and halted mere inches from his door. The driver was dressed in black from head to toe and his nose and mouth were covered with a large, dark handkerchief. Out of the corner of his eye, Justin spotted a second scooter pulling up on O'Bryan's side.

Justin swung the door open with all his might. The edge struck the rider with such force that the impact sent him and his bike sailing into the rear of the idling truck.

"Back up, Jack, and get out of here!" Justin yelled.

He didn't wait for a reply. Justin dashed around the front of the Fiat and body-slammed the second driver who had just dismounted his metal and plastic steed. However, the man had anticipated Justin's running attack. He skillfully deflected the full force of the hit by presenting a padded shoulder, then smartly sidestepped out of harm's way. As he did, he lashed out at Justin's head with the heel of an open left hand. The man was small and compact, but moved with the fluid motion of a well-trained athlete.

"Voi nessun buon bastardo Americano. You no good American bastard," he spat at Justin. The man then spun in a full circle, and as he and Justin again came face to face, Justin saw he was now holding a small caliber Berretta. He pointed it at Justin's chest and squeezed the trigger. Nothing. He squeezed again. It was jammed. A confused look appeared in his eyes. He looked down at his weapon.

Justin did not wait for a third attempt on his life. He filled the air with a horrific scream and swung his cane.

The assailant nimbly danced to his right, managed a derisive laugh, then raised his gun hand once more, readying for a third attempt. He expertly activated the Beretta's slide with his left hand, the first step in bringing a fresh bullet into position while ejecting the one jamming the chamber.

Justin jumped back and toggled a recessed button on the top of his tethered cane. With eyes trained on the man's neck, he raised the stick and mashed it with his thumb. Two ultra-thin wires propelled by compressed nitrogen and armed with barbed tips shot out and buried themselves in the assailant's neck. A microsecond later, the man fell to the ground writhing in agony as three hundred kV coursed through his body from the cane's hidden Taser.

A couple of beats passed, then O'Bryan roared by, heading for the second rider who was now standing with a gun drawn and his face fully uncovered. He caught the man with the side of the Fiat's passenger-side fender. The would-be assassin cried out as he fired ineffectually into the air while cartwheeling into the brick wall on his right. As he fell hard onto the cobblestones his gun went sailing. It hit the ground, bounced once, then clattered off into the night.

O'Bryan slammed the car into reverse and backed up several feet, peeling rubber. He then dropped the transmission into first gear, turned the steering wheel hard to his left and took aim at the Vespa still parked in the middle of the alley. He floored the gas pedal. The impact turned the scooter into a plastic and metal pretzel.

Justin glanced at the unconscious figure half-seated by the wall then did a double take. *The man was Asian!* He climbed into the truck cab and roared off toward the head of the alley. Leaning on the horn as he approached the street, he manhandled the huge rig into the stream of traffic without stropping. Horns started blaring; people began cursing.

Justin steered his commandeered truck to the side of the road, jumped out and flung the ignition key far up the busy street. Serve that damn inconsiderate delivery driver right! He sprinted to where O'Bryan had pulled over and yanked open the passenger door. "Get us the hell out of here," he yelled.

O'Bryan sped off. Within five minutes he had turned so many corners and had run so many red lights that he found himself lost. And through it all, he hadn't uttered a single word.

Justin finally turned to his friend. "Got to tell you," he said with a grin, "you've become quite the nasty little street fighter, Monsignor O'Bryan."

* * * * *

Justin's first impression on meeting Manfred von Snellenberger was that he reminded him of someone else. Must be the beard, he concluded, because he had not worn one the year before. He had seen the Swiss banker in several photographs taken last spring and summer, and had marveled at the time how much he had complemented his beautiful wife, Maritha. The von Snellenbergers were indeed a head-turning couple.

Manfred von Snellenberger took a long drink of ice water then brushed the back of a hand against his lips. "I told Mister Mannix that something is happening inside Russia, something that will soon cause massive shockwaves throughout the world." He seemed embarrassed by his remark and shrugged his shoulders as if to say, "I know that sounds like the ravings of a crank."

Justin decided on candor, but only up to a point. "I know Steve has already told you what really happened to your wife last summer in Washington," he began in a low voice. "Maritha was murdered, but not by Cardinal Kettering as the world was led to believe at first, but by men with a nefarious agenda. What's happening now in Russia is in all likelihood related to her murder."

Von Snellenberger replied by saying that he had been in St. Petersburg that whole time except for a quick trip into Switzerland just the week before.

"To the offices of *Credit Lausanne*, by chance?" Justin asked.

Von Snellenberger showed genuine surprise. "Yes, and I was accompanied by a man named Alexander Panov."

"The same Alexander Panov who owns the home in Saint Petersburg where you were being held. And you met with a Mister Klaus Furlan," Justin continued, his tone suggesting he already knew the answer. "Were there any others present?"

"Several, and all were clients of the bank."

"And at any time during your visit did you hear the words 'twelve apostles' spoken?"

Again, von Snellenberger showed surprise, and nodded.

"And what language was the meeting conducted in?" Justin asked.

"Russian for the most part, sometimes German, but every once in a while there were three older folks in the group who would break out in an unfamiliar tongue. It sounded a bit like Yiddish. Anyway, that only happened when the three of them became excited. One was Alexander Panov. I also felt that Mister Furlan understood, even though he never joined in those particular conversations."

"And how did they treat you during this meeting?"

Manfred von Snellenberger reddened. It was obvious he was uncomfortable, causing Justin to wonder why as he waited for an answer.

Finally, "I know this will sound silly, but they treated me with the utmost respect. In fact, deferential is a word that comes to mind. Within minutes of my arrival, several remarked how much I looked like the last Russian Czar."

That's exactly who he looks like! Czar Nicholas II. Justin suddenly realized that he could have easily been mistaken for Nicholas' younger brother if the year was 1918. He now remembered how Charin had also remarked about the similarity.

O'Bryan spoke up while studying the banker. "Justin, I believe Mister von Snellenberger is the person Monsignor Allenby saw going into *Credit Lausanne* last week when he telephoned us to report he had seen a ghost. It wasn't Count Laufenburg that he had spotted. Allenby had never met either man and had only seen photos of them in the papers. Obviously he became confused and thought it was the dead Count Laufenberg he had just seen, because of the beard."

"I think you're right," Justin agreed. "The moment our friend here said how his only trip outside of Russia had been to Lausanne, I, too, remembered how Allenby told us Laufenburg was still alive and now wearing a beard. It was a case of mistaken identity, but at least it answers the question that hadn't made any sense at all."

Von Snellenberger shot a confused look from one to the other then continued with his tale. "One very old man, older than Panov, asked if I had ever heard of my grandmother spending time in Spain or Portugal. When I said no, he turned and spoke rapid fire in that strange language to a woman seated beside him. And he repeated the name Anastasia three times." Von Snellenberger let loose a nervous laugh, then rushed on as if wanting to set the record straight. "No, Mister Scott, I didn't think for a moment they were talking about that Anastasia...well...at least not then I didn't." He frowned. "I do know my Grandmother Catherine—that's what I always called her—was several years older than grandfather and that she had been married before, sometime between the World Wars, I think. There were whisperings in certain family circles that she had given birth to a daughter who had died in infancy, but again, it was nothing more than an unsubstantiated rumor. And Grandmother Catherine herself certainly never spoke of such things to me."

"You actually met her?" asked a surprised Justin.

"Grandmother Catherine? Of course! There was one time I remember vividly. It was on my fifth birthday and she had come to visit for a few days. She was quite old by then and coughed a lot. She had to sit most of the time because her feet were sore. She was also woefully thin and could only eat small amounts due to stomach problems, but I also recall that she had the bluest of eyes which could look right into your soul. But not in a scary way, mind you."

"And what made you remember this particular visit?"

"Because of the present she gave me. She said it had belonged to her father and that she knew he would have wanted me to have it before she died. She then told a story about how as a young girl she had carried it sewn inside the hem of her dress along with several precious jewels. The jewels were long gone, she said, sold over time to keep her alive, but this one item she had kept, along with a prayer book her parents had given for her first communion. Grandmother carried that book everywhere and read from it all the time."

"And what was the present she wanted you to have?"

"A gold signet ring with a carved crest of the double-headed Imperial Eagle of St. George. When grandmother gave it to me she was crying, which upset me, so I began to cry, too. She had taken it from her middle finger, drew me close and kissed me, and whispered that I must never, ever lose it, and that I had to pass it on to my son when it was time for me to go to heaven."

The three Americans remained silent for a long moment. The ring Manfred von Snellenberger had just described had indeed been worn by the last Czar of Russia.

Justin and O'Bryan traded knowing glances. So the female spy from Lisbon all those years ago had been right after all! The mysterious woman residing in the convent at Tuy when Margaret Smalling went there to treat Sister Lucia in 1940 was in fact the Grand Duchess Anastasia, the sole survivor of the ruling Romanovs.

"Mister von Snellenberger, I also believe your grandmother Catherine was in fact the Grand Duchess Anastasia," Justin said, "and I say so with confidence because it fits with other information I have come to know."

Von Snellenberger shook his head, but slowly, as if trying to reconcile some inner torment. Finally, he said, "Let me be the devil's advocate for a moment. I don't think so, and here's why. If I remember my history, Anastasia was seventeen when she was murdered by the Bolsheviks along with the rest of the royals. That was in Nineteen Eighteen, which means if she were my grandmother she would have been in her early forties when her daughter, my mother, was born. Both biology and time were no longer her allies by then. However, my mother's conception would only have been possible if Anastasia had escaped the Bolsheviks' bullets; something we all know in spite of the many rumors to the contrary was highly unlikely."

"You could be right, of course, but I don't think so," Justin said, in a matter-of-fact voice, then added, "or let's just say there are people a lot more knowledgeable than us who also think you're wrong, including the twelve apostles."

O'Bryan spoke up. "Did Panov have your blood drawn while you were in Saint Petersburg?"

"He did," von Snellenberger said. "I was placed under a doctor's care shortly after I arrived. You see, I had lost a lot of weight and was badly dehydrated. The doctor diagnosed dysentery, so drawing blood under such circumstances would be expected, would it not?"

"Indeed," O'Bryan quickly agreed, "but it's also possible Panov wanted to compare your DNA with that of the Czar and the rest of the family. We know their bodies had been found and exhumed on orders from the Kremlin back in the nineteen nineties, and that the government had hired English forensic experts to run several sophisticated DNA tests using blood samples from Prince Philip for their control. They were particularly interested in Philip's mitochondrial DNA; that's the genetic material that is passed by the mother from one generation to the next. Nuclear DNA which all of us carry is passed by both parents. But what the English scientists found was quite revealing. Prince Philip's mitochondrial DNA was a perfect match with that of the Czarina Alexandra, the younger sister of Philip's grandmother, Victoria. Of course, both women were the granddaughters of England's Queen Victoria, which makes Prince Phillip the great nephew of the last czarina."

"I'm impressed you know so much of Russia's recent history, Monsignor," von Snellenberger said, his admiration genuine. "I, too, had read how the bodies had been discovered in a pit somewhere in

Russia a decade or so earlier, and how the government had wanted to confirm for once and for all they were the czar and his family."

"Then you'll also remember Anastasia's body wasn't found at the time and neither was her brother's," O'Bryan added.

Von Snellenberger shrugged. "Maybe yes, maybe no. But I also recall some news stories back in Two Thousand and Seven and Two Thousand and Eight saying how the bones of the son, Prince Alexei, had supposedly been found and identified, along with those of his missing sister. In fact, some Russian scientists even claimed the bones were in fact Maria's and not Anastasia's."

Justin weighed in "And all those claims have been summarily dismissed by European and American geneticists as nothing more than sensational nonsense created by Russians with an agenda," Justin said. "It seems the powers in Moscow wanted closure to this story, so they unilaterally pronounced the entire Romanov clan to be now dead and buried."

"Which really means...?" von Snellenberger said, raising a questioning eyebrow.

"Which really means, like it or not, you are a direct descendant of Anastasia," O'Bryan answered. "And that fact was of the utmost importance to the twelve apostles."

"Mister von Snellenberger, let me ask a question, if I may," Mannix said, joining into the conversation for the first time. "Are your parents still alive?"

A sad look passed over von Snellenberger's face. "No, both died along with my only brother in the crash of TWA Flight Eight Hundred off the coast of Long Island in July, Nineteen Ninety-six. Their deaths were very hard for me to accept, but I've always thanked God for bringing me Maritha when He did." His eyes then turned to somewhere far away.

After a decent interval Justin asked, "Were their bodies ever recovered?"

"Only father's."

"Did your parents ever tell you other things about your grandmother, I mean, after she had died and you were a bit older?" Mannix asked.

Manfred von Snellenberger shook his head. "Only that Grandmother Catherine was born in Dresden."

"And where is she buried?" Justin asked.

Suddenly von Snellenberger seemed to realize where this line of questioning was leading. Again he shook his head. "Grandmother Catherine died in Nineteen Eighty-eight. She was cremated along with her prayer book because that was her wish. Her ashes are interred in the family mausoleum in Bern."

"Of course it's impossible to recover DNA from ashes," O'Bryan murmured.

"And Dresden was thoroughly destroyed by Allied bombers in February Nineteen Forty-five, which means birth records and baptism records are long gone, as well," Justin said to no one in particular. "Now how's that for a convenient way of making sure any trail would turn forever cold for anyone trying to discover Catherine's true origins?"

His statement was met with a protracted silence. It really does add up, Justin told himself as he studied Manfred von Snellenberger's face. This has to be the last direct descendant of Nicholas II, which means he's more precious than gold to Alexander Panov and his friends. Justin had only a couple more questions.

"How did your meeting at *Credit Lausanne* end?"

"It was late at night when the group finally made their intentions known. They asked if I would accept the throne of Russia if it were offered. Well, I was shocked into silence by that, I assure you. I couldn't speak for at least a minute, but I finally was able to stammer that I didn't think so, that I already had a life in Switzerland and that I needed to get back to my bank. It was then that things turned strange. Mister Furlan began speaking to me as if the others weren't present. Looking back on it now, I must say, it wasn't only strange, it was downright eerie."

The three Americans were fully absorbed in what they were hearing.

"First," von Snellenberger continued, "he assured me my bank had gotten past its recent setbacks and was once again thriving. His words were a tremendous relief for me to hear, because I had been worried for months about my employees. He then said he had been authorized by the apostles to turn over to me the sum of two hundred million Euros immediately upon my being crowned czar. That money would come without strings, he said, but suggested it should be used to offset expenses, which he suggested would be formidable. He went on to explain that the apostles did not think the Russian government would be eager to financially support a new czar, at least not until an heir was born, and maybe not even then."

"Permit me to be the one to play the devil's advocate this time," Justin finally said. "Becoming Czar of Imperial Russia would be a life-altering event to say the least. Maybe you would end up as nothing more than a pawn, a foreigner in a foreign land whose citizens never embrace you. Your life would spiral downward into a very lonely existence, and you could end your days as the proverbial bird in a gilded cage."

Manfred von Snellenberger nodded his agreement. "Believe me, that thought, or one similar, crossed my mind many times this past week." He looked first to Justin, then to O'Bryan and finally to Mannix. "The truthful answer, gentlemen, is that I just don't know what I will do."

"That's good enough for us," Justin answered. "Whatever you decide, you can rest assured the three of us will back you all the way."

"Thank you. Now, is there anything I can do for Cardinal Kettering? He was always a wonderful friend to Maritha and her mother."

While the four were talking in the kitchen, the TV in the living room was tuned to the International CNN nightly news. The reader was ending with an item from New Delhi about a private Russian consortium having just launched a satellite atop an Indian-built rocket from the Satish Dhawan Space Centre at Sriharikota.

"No one has yet revealed what its mission will be," she said, *"but a scientist familiar with the two hundred-pound satellite said it's being called Genesis-Omega. He tells CNN that Genesis-Omega is a communications platform and will be placed in a geostationary orbit thirty-five thousand four hundred kilometers above the earth."*

Justin found himself listening to the unfolding story with only one ear. He filtered it through his subconscious for any relevance, found none, then thought nothing more about it.

What the newsreader had failed to mention in her beautifully accented English was that the satellite named *Genesis-Omega* was now poised directly over Rome.

CHAPTER 42
Day 9. Rome. Tuesday evening

Justin's cell phone rang. It was Charin and he sounded worried. When Justin began to repeat von Snellenberger's tale, the Russian cut him short. "I know all about it, and that's why I'm calling. Mister von Snellenberger is supposed to be crowned the next czar of Russia, either tomorrow or the next day, and that's why he must be flown back to Saint Petersburg immediately."

"Mykel, listen, we..."

Charin would not be interrupted. "If he isn't back before the sun rises, then your Cardinal Kettering will die, as will the Archbishop of Canterbury along with other Eastern and Roman Rite bishops from around the world who have also been taken hostage. There is one unbelievable crisis unfolding here, Justin, and I don't know why. The man who told me this is a very dangerous individual."

"Alexander Panov," Justin said.

"Alexander Panov," Charin parroted, then allowed his voice to drop to a whisper. "If von Snellenberger does not return to Saint Petersburg immediately, Panov will execute my wife and my daughters." Charin stifled a sob. "His coronation will be held in our Peter and Paul Cathedral, and Panov is implying that the Kremlin has given its full approval, though God only knows why. The bribes must have been in the millions."

"Mykel, stand by. I'll get back to you within five minutes."

Manfred von Snellenberger listened to Justin's synopsis of Charin's plight. His hard-won freedom had lasted less than twenty-four hours. At that moment, Justin's phone rang again. He took note of the caller's ID. It was Paula.

"What's up? I'm kind of in the middle of something..."

"Justin, open your email," she replied, her voice breaking.

His heart plummeted. "Kettering's dead, isn't he?" As he asked the dreaded question, he turned to Mannix. "Steve, do you have a computer here? I need to get into my email and I don't trust my phone."

Mannix answered by reaching into his pocket and taking out a BlackBerry®. "Get it from here. Tell me your server and password and I'll open it for you." Justin rattled off the two words and returned to Paula.

"Justin, it's not Kettering," she said. "It's Doctor Smalling, and, yes, he's dead. There are several photos online, none pretty. Take a look. I'll wait."

Thirty seconds later Justin began studying the photos of Edward Smalling. There were a total of six. Someone had photographed him using a cell phone, and the shots showed him hanging from the understructure of a bridge. Justin could make out some sort of a note pinned to his chest, but the image on the BlackBerry's screen was too small for him to read the words. The last picture was a wide-angle shot of the bridge. Justin was shocked into silence as he forced himself to look again at the gruesome stills. Then he went into action.

"Paula, I want you to look up the name and number for the chief of police in Edinburgh. Tell him—or his assistant—who you are, then forward these pictures. If they have not already discovered the body, they'll need to know where to go to retrieve it. They should recognize the bridge from the last snapshot." Justin was beyond anger. "And remind whoever you talk to that I was working with Inspector Angus Whittle on the Dame Smalling killing and ask if he could let us know the cause of death for the son just as quickly as possible. Things are ratcheting up here, so don't become alarmed if I'm incommunicado for a stretch. I'm safe, so is Jack, and so is Steve Mannix who's also joined us. And lastly, Freddy von Snellenberger is with us and he's also OK."

He heard the sharp intake of breath. "How is that possible?"

"No time to explain. Got to run."

As soon as Justin broke the connection, von Snellenberger asked, "That man who was murdered. Was he somehow connected to this Russian thing?"

"I'm afraid so." Justin then looked to O'Bryan. "Want to bet we learn the doctor was murdered with Sarin, just like his mother?"

Manfred von Snellenberger rose. "That's it. I'm going back. I will not allow any more people to die because of me." He held up his right hand, ready to parry the expected protest. "It is my decision alone to make, Mister Scott, and I'm going." He turned to Mannix. "Can you fly me back to St. Petersburg?"

Mannix shot a questioning look at Justin who nodded his approval.

Mannix heaved himself up. "I can have the plane ready to roll within the hour. Justin, I'm going, too. I have a valid visa, so I can team up with your Russian inspector friend and be on the ground for added backup when and if you have to follow." Mannix's tone told Justin that this, too, was not a subject open for discussion.

Justin, as usual, had a piece of advice. "When you get to Saint Petersburg, listen to Mykel Charin. I'm going to call him now. He's one hell of a cop so see him as a powerful and trustworthy ally."

As Mannix and von Snellenberger prepared to enter the lion's den, Justin and O'Bryan grabbed a couple of hours of much needed sleep.

CHAPTER 43
Day 10. Rome. Wednesday Morning

At six thirty the next morning, O'Bryan learned from the Vatican homepage that all but three of the world's 120 elector-eligible cardinals were now in Vatican City. They were housed in the 105 suites and twenty-six single-rooms of St. Martha's House, a hotel-residence built during the reign of Pope John Paul II expressly to accommodate cardinals coming to Rome on business, ordinations, or for a conclave to elect a new pope.

O'Bryan then raced through his messages. The last was from the pope and had been written five minutes earlier. He leaned closer and began to read.

Monsignor O'Bryan; I have asked my cardinals to gather in the Sistine Chapel at 8:00 a.m., where I will tell them of the two Russian letters. I would like you to be there, with Mister Scott, if he is available. I cannot remain silent on this matter any longer. I will also tell them what has happened to their brothers in Christ, Cardinal Kettering and the Archbishop of Canterbury. The time has come for me to seek their counsel.

O'Bryan had Justin read the message. His face hardened. "It's not what I would have advised the Holy Father to do, but then again, I'm not the pope. Unfortunately, I suspect the particulars of the meeting will leak to the media within an hour of its ending and the world will believe the Apocalypse is less than seventy-two hours away. And you can bet the farm that the message will fracture into as many different versions as there are cardinals, which means there will be worldwide chaos by noon."

O'Bryan conceded that his friend was probably right. "But the Holy Father is still plagued with the possibility that the letter really *is* from Lucia and the message *is* from the Virgin Mary. We told him we were ninety-nine percent sure the letter was a hoax, but the pope has to deal with that one percent."

Justin nodded. "Unfortunately, this is going to play right into Panov's hands. He's banking on the fact people everywhere will fall to their knees and begin praying for forgiveness. And while the world is distracted, Panov will install Freddy as the new czar. Then he'll use the following days to consolidate his position of power, which I'm damn sure has something to do with the pope and the College of Cardinals, and none of it good. Speaking of the cardinals, I'm real uneasy knowing they're all now gathered in the Vatican because they're just too tempting a target."

O'Bryan sighed. "I agree. Remember, it was that slimy Judas named Ignacio Caffarone who made the suggestion to the pope to summon them to Rome."

"How could I have forgotten? Well, here's another something for you to chew on, Jack. When word of this morning's meeting leaks out, and it will, that could well cause some of the world's more unstable leaders to decide the time has come to settle old scores. They could lash out at neighbors in one last display of frenzied hatred. I'm thinking specifically of certain rogue nuclear states which could easily trigger the fiery Armageddon mentioned in Lucia's Russian letter. Talk about a self-fulfilling prophesy." He sat down heavily. "How bloody ironic to think that Ian Fleming and Winston Churchill could be responsible for bringing the world to its end, all because of a well-intentioned gamble to save England from the Nazis several decades ago."

CHAPTER 44
Day 10. Rome. Wednesday morning

"*Mister Scott, Dr. Smalling* here." Both men froze upon hearing the message from a dead man on Cardinal Kettering's answering machine. "I've found my mother's pen and you were right, it does have the most devilishly clever...I say, who let you into my home?" Smalling's voice was both surprised and scared. *"Get back, oh, God! There's two Korean, aaahhhhh..."* then silence. A wintry voice finally took up the phone.

"You next die, Justin Scott. You been much trouble so I make sure you beg me kill you quick." Then the line went dead.

"My God," O'Bryan whispered as he placed a steadying hand on the desk.

Justin's features turned to granite. "This is all the more reason we can't afford to fail. We owe it to both of the Smallings."

"And Inspector Angus Whittle," O'Bryan added.

* * * * *

One hundred and thirty-seven cardinals made their way into the world's most magnificent chapel and spent the next ten minutes shuffling about, some shaking hands with old friends then trading gossip; others were visibly subdued, even withdrawn.

Justin and O'Bryan found seats two rows behind the cardinals amongst a smattering of archbishops, bishops, monsignors and priests. They had entered the chapel fifteen minutes earlier and O'Bryan had taken Justin on a spur-of-the-moment tour where he had found himself openly marveling at Michelangelo's freshly restored frescoes on the barrel-vaulted ceiling. The beautifully rendered depictions told of the nine stories of Creation from the Book of Genesis. Justin shook his head in silent wonder. No photograph, no television special could do justice to the panorama before him.

He next studied the north wall, adorned with paintings of long-dead popes and saints, rendered by such Renaissance luminaries as Botticelli, Signorrelli, Pinturrichio and Ghirlandaio. And on the opposing south wall, were pictorials of Moses along with a gathering of popes and several lesser saints. And above all this beauty was Michelangelo's *The Forefathers of Christ.* Justin allowed his gaze to drop to the panorama of the lower sidewalls, both of which were bedecked in drapes of two-dimensional fabric, painted to suggest descending folds of expensive golden cloth.

As they returned to their seats, Justin noticed a newly erected scaffold on the east wall, slightly off to the side of Hendrick van den Broeck's *The Resurrection of Christ.* Beneath the temporary platform lay several stacks of neatly folded workers' overalls, rubber boots, rolls of masking tape, toolboxes, and even respirators. He told himself that the artisans working on such priceless surfaces needed to be as free of contaminants as possible, including the means to trap even the moisture from their breaths. Obviously, some new restoration work was about to begin, although he had to admit that even to his untrained eye the Dutchman's masterpiece looked perfect.

Settled now in their chairs, O'Bryan murmured, "If the reason for today's gathering was to choose a new pope, then only those cardinals aged eighty or younger would be allowed to cast votes. Under canon law, the election of a pope must take place on the grounds of Vatican City, and these Princes of the Church would be completely cut-off from the outside world until the successor was chosen. And in all likelihood he would come from within their ranks, even though canon law only says a pope needs to be a baptized male who is neither a schismatic nor a heretic."

O'Bryan paused, allowing a smile to flit across his face at the very thought of such a thing. "Yet even on this issue," he continued, "there seems to be disagreement. For example, some theologians interpret canon law on the subject to mean one needs only be a male who is willing to be baptized and ordained; but not necessarily both, which could suggest that the pope theoretically might spring from the ranks of the laity." He looked Justin squarely in the eye and grinned. "That could even include you!"

"Fat chance," Justin murmured back, then chuckled aloud at the preposterous thought.

O'Bryan continued. "Ballots must be cast in secret and they're burned immediately after each vote is taken. Campaigning for the office is verboten, and no one is allowed to vote for himself. Anyway, the process has been known to drag on for weeks, even months in centuries past, but John Paul the Second changed all of that by streamlining how the conclave works. However, his successor changed the rules in Two Thousand and Seven back to the way it was before John-Paul and, once again, a two-thirds majority of the cardinals in the conclave must agree on the choice for a new pope. Anyway, as soon as white smoke starts wafting from the chimney, that's the signal the Church has elected a new spiritual leader, and a couple of hundred thousand of the faithful who have been waiting silently or in prayer in St. Peter's Square, break out in cheers and clapping. It's quite the sight to behold."

While O'Bryan was speaking, Justin was studying the backs of the heads of the assembled prelates and saw only targets. He allowed his eyes to sweep the interior of the chapel, taking comfort in the several pairs of Swiss Guards stationed at all the doors, as well as a scattering of Italian plainclothes men along the walls. He spotted Monsignor Caffarone seated at the end of a row of bishops, head down and reading.

You no good traitor, Justin thought, a righteous anger percolating to the surface at the mere sight of the Judas.

At exactly eight o'clock, the pope entered the chapel from the adjoining Medieval Palace, made his way to a portable altar and genuflected beneath the imposing backdrop of Michelangelo's heroic painting, *The Last Judgment.*

How fitting, Justin thought, especially in light of what was about to be revealed.

With shaking hands, the pontiff gestured for the assembled to sit.

"Salvete, meus fratres in Christus," he began in Latin, the official language of the Church since the time of Peter. "Good morning, my bothers in Christ. After much prayer, I find myself in need of your wise counsel." He paused, looked up, then scanned the chapel. "Would the Swiss Guard please withdraw," he said in German, then repeated the request in Italian for the benefit of the civilian security detail. He waited until the doors were again closed.

"Ten days ago, Cardinal Kettering received two letters, both sent by an unknown source from somewhere inside Russia...," and for the next fifteen minutes the pope told the prelates the how, the what, the when, and the why. He ended with an acknowledgment that he personally harbored doubts that the second letter was indeed from Sister Lucia written many decades ago.

"But what if I'm wrong, my brothers?" he asked, assuming the mantle of the devil's advocate, an ecclesiastical office since abolished by Pope John Paul II in 1983.

It was a question on every lip.

The chapel broke out with the hum of a hundred possible answers as clerics from around the globe began debating the issue.

The senior cardinal present, prefect of the powerful Congregation for the Doctrine of the Faith, stood, leaned heavily on his cane and waited for silence.

"Holy Father, let me say on behalf of the conclave you did the right thing in summoning us. I admit I now tremble before God at the news you bring, for if it indeed is our time, then it is our time. The peoples of the world have a God-given right to be told, for this message from the Blessed Virgin is meant for all to hear and heed, and not just the few. I personally believe it is indeed the word of God as foretold to John the Divine. The right to salvation is a universal right, guaranteed by the Creator, and so the word must go forth from this place. And if it should come to pass that we are spared at this moment in time, then mankind must bow and give thanks to that ever-loving and benevolent Creator."

A black cardinal from sub-Sahara Africa rose and asked in a booming voice, "Who among us would dare suggest the letter from Lucia was not the word of the Virgin Mary? Who would be the apostate lurking within our ranks, tempting the Holy Father to ignore the warning from God and, in a fit of blasphemy, ascribe the truth that has come to us from the lips of the Holy Mother to be turned into something that was birthed in the bowels of Protestant England? To suggest as much is to do the work of Lucifer."

A cardinal from Latin America was next. "Remember, my brothers, only a small part of the supposed letter from Mister Churchill to Adolf

Hitler—a letter whose existence the Holy Father only learned about from a source in London mere hours ago—was delivered to the Holy See by an unknown Russian. So I ask: why did he not send the entire letter?" The cardinal answered with his next breath. "It wasn't sent, because it doesn't exist! No, this message before us is in fact a message from Mary, Mother of God, and she has spoken in words none of us should ignore. The time is now to prepare mankind for the *Dies Irae*."

And so it went. For an hour. Finally, the pope rose and once more addressed his prelates. "While we've been here," he began, "I have had delivered to your rooms packets containing copies and translations of the letters. I now ask you to adjourn, read them then pray for guidance from the Holy Spirit. We will all meet back here at one o'clock."

The pope then blessed his assembled clergy and walked slowly out of the Sistine Chapel, the weight of the world pressing downwards upon his frail shoulders.

* * * * *

Justin and O'Bryan left the chapel after taking special note that Monsignor Caffarone had darted out moments after the pope. They agreed the man was up to no good.

It was just after nine o'clock, and the day was shaping up to be more like March than January. Many of the cardinals were walking in small groups back to St. Martha's House.

The pope had chosen not to say anything of the role played by either Justin or O'Bryan. Justin thought the Holy Father must have decided his cardinals would not have been pleased to learn that a layman, least of all a retired American FBI agent, had sway over the pope in such important matters of faith.

Stepping into the small Square of the Furnace, they were forced to stop and wait while three men in sparkling white coveralls carefully rolled a huge metal container off a flatbed truck. On its sides were painted giant 3M™ logos, each showing a cascade of multi-color prints flying out of a state-of the-art, digital color copier.

"Well what do you know," O'Bryan remarked, his face lighting up, "a brand new color copier. It's about time, and would you look at the sheer size of it," he marveled. "Bet that rascal cost a ton!"

One of the men heard his comment, looked over and smiled. He yanked a bill of lading from a hip pocket and held it toward O'Bryan. "Father, we have instructions to set this machine up in the Apostolic Library," he said in heavily accented English. "Are we going in the right direction?"

"You're doing fine," O'Bryan replied, pointing toward the Hall of Ligorio. "Go down this corridor and turn right at the first cross-hallway. That will take you to the Sixtus the Fifth Library. Someone at the entrance can direct you from there."

"Thanks," the technician replied, then placed two protective hands onto the side of the huge box to help steer the dolly and its expensive cargo off in the right direction.

"You've just done your good deed for the day," Justin remarked as he followed O'Bryan through a veritable maze back to Kettering's office.

CHAPTER 45
Day 10. St. Petersburg. Wednesday morning

Charin was waiting on the tarmac by Pulkovo Airlines to greet the two disembarking passengers. He said hello to von Snellenberger and introduced himself to Mannix.

Within minutes, the trio was packed inside Charin's police car and heading toward the city. Mannix briefed the Russian, and ended by saying that a couple of minutes before landing he had given von Snellenberger a homing device to swallow.

"It looks like a slightly bigger version of a cold capsule," he said, "and should still be transmitting forty-eight hours from now." Mannix handed Charin a BlackBerry phone, had him spell out M-Y-K-E-L on the keypad. They all heard a distinctive chirp. "That signal is coming from inside Mister von Snellenberger and can be intercepted up to a mile away."

"Very impressive," Charin murmured and slipped the device into his pants pocket. He then asked, "Do you speak Russian?"

"*Niet*," Mannix replied sheepishly. "That and *da* are the only words I know."

Charin gave Mannix an introductory letter that proclaimed he was an honored guest of the St. Petersburg Police Department.

"Good thinking," Mannix replied, placing the envelope into his windbreaker's zippered breast pocket. "My passport and visa says I'm an Interpol officer with business in Saint Petersburg, and that cover should hold water if challenged. But your letter will definitely win over anyone who might have doubts, so thanks."

Von Snellenberger wondered aloud what would happen to him.

"You will be treated as royalty, Mister von Snellenberger," Charin answered, making eye contact with the banker in his rearview mirror.

Von Snellenberger shrugged. "If I am crowned czar and the Russian people choose to reject me, I will end up like Nicholas—shot in the head and my body thrown into a pit of quicklime."

"I think you will be accepted by the people, Excellency," Charin said. "I believe Russia is ready for the return of a czar, especially one who has studied the mistakes of the past rulers and promises to work for the betterment of all of his subjects."

Charin pulled up to Panov's mansion and shut off the engine.

"And if I had a say in the matter, I'd vote for you, too," Mannix said as he reached for the door handle. "OK, Mykel, it's time for me to meet your pal, Panov. Won't he be surprised to see you arriving so early, and dragging along a Pooh-Bah from Interpol to boot."

"Is that what you intend to tell him? That you're with Interpol?"

"Of course. Mister von Snellenberger still has an open Interpol file. I've been sent here to find out where he's been for the last several months and why Panov didn't report his whereabouts. Just another bureaucrat doing his job." He swung open the door, grinned, then added, "In America we like to say the best defense is a good offense so I'm going on the offensive. It's never failed me yet to put the opposition at an immediate disadvantage."

"Whoa, not so fast, hold up for a second. Are you armed?" Charin asked.

"Of course I'm armed," Mannix replied, pretending to be shocked at the question. "You think I'm crazy?" He unzipped his windbreaker enough to reveal a shoulder holster. "That's a Glock G-seventeen, nine millimeter pistol. Standard issue for all of us Interpol gumshoes."

"So silly of me to ask," Charin muttered with a pretend sigh.

* * * * *

"Ah, Mister von Snellenberger, I'm glad to see you back, and apparently no worse for the wear. Please sit." Alexander Panov was the perfect host. He turned to Charin and Mannix. "Sit," he commanded. Gone was the civility shown to von Snellenberger.

"Did I hear the magic word coffee somewhere in what you were just saying?" Mannix asked in an exaggerated British accent.

"And who might you be?" Panov asked in Russian, his eyes burrowing deep into those of the stranger.

"He is Chief Inspector Steven Mannix, an English member of the Executive Committee at Interpol's headquarters in Lyon," Charin lied. "The European police forces want to know where Mister von Snellenberger disappeared to for the last few months. They're suggesting you kidnapped him, and they're none too happy."

Panov stared at the American imposter. "You are welcome in my home, Mister Mannix. I don't know what this man has told you," he said, nodding toward Charin, "but I assure you, Mister von Snellenberger has not been held here against his will. To the contrary, he has been my honored guest."

Mannix quickly threw the ball back to Panov, asking only for one full day of his time, well, maybe two at the most, he fudged, to get all of the particulars written down for a full report to take back to Paris. "Maybe we can start right after breakfast, hmm?"

Panov refused to be baited. "I have much to do and I'm already behind on my tight schedule, so I'm going to ask you to leave. Make an appointment with my secretary for sometime next week," he said dismissively, then turned to von Snellenberger. "Could you give me a few moments of your time, sir?"

Panov didn't wait for an answer. He shuffled out of the room supported by a heavy cane and his huge bodyguard.

Mannix and Charin prepared to leave, but would remain within hailing distance of von Snellenberger's transmitter.

Ian A. O'Connor

CHAPTER 46
Day 10. Rome. Wednesday morning

"*M*ister Scott, this is Detective Mario Castellanos with the Anti-Terrorism Police." No, 'Hi, *Joosteen*, my old friend, how great to be talking to you. I wonder if you could help me with a small problem?' Castellanos was all business this morning, his voice as hard as diamonds.

Justin took his cue from Castellanos. "How can I help you, Detective?"

"You told me that as soon as you found out why all of the cardinals were in Rome you would call. You lied. I had to find this out from another source."

"And what exactly is it that you have found out?"

"That the pope is telling everybody the end of the world is at hand, *that's what I found out!*" Castellanos screamed the last at the top of his lungs.

"And just who told you this?" Justin wanted to know, his maddeningly calm voice only serving to further infuriate the Italian police officer.

"None of your damn business," Castellanos yelled back, forcing Justin to hold the receiver away from his ear. "I think it's time I bring you in for further questioning regarding that woman you shot at our airport. We don't like American cowboys coming to Italy."

"Who told you this?" Justin repeated.

"That's it! I'm getting a warrant right now for your arrest."

"Shut up and listen to me," Justin snapped back in a voice one would use on a recalcitrant child. "I hold a Vatican diplomatic passport so your threats of arrest don't mean jackshit, *capisca?*"

Castellanos was blindsided. What the hell was going on over there at the Vatican? He came to the only logical conclusion. The rumor had to be true!

"If you don't answer my question, Detective Castellanos, I'm going to hang up, because I'm too damn busy to waste any more time with you. So for the last time, who told you?"

"Archbishop Torrelli. He called about five minutes ago."

That good-for-nothing, thieving troublemaker, Justin thought, as he heard the name of the ousted director of the Vatican Bank. He then tried to remember if he had seen Torrelli in the Sistine Chapel earlier. He couldn't say.

Justin decided to level with the angry detective. "First off, the world isn't coming to an end any time soon. Archbishop Torrelli has it all wrong, but the man is nothing more than a common criminal. Second. Yes, I admit there's a crisis unfolding inside the Vatican, but it's a crisis that will be resolved within the next day or two. However, I'm glad you called, because I'm going to need your help. That is, if you're willing to believe what I'm telling you is the truth."

"Is Archbishop Torrelli really a crook, *Joosteen*?"

Ah, so he was *Joosteen* again. Good. All was forgiven.

"He is, but that's not important at the moment. What is important though is this: can I count on you to help me?"

"Of course you can, and I'm sorry I was so angry. Please forgive me."

"It's already forgiven and forgotten. Now here's what I need. Could you come over to the secretary of state's office, say at twelve thirty? Ask for Monsignor O'Bryan and you'll be directed to the right place."

"OK, I'll see you at twelve thirty."

"One last question, Mario. Are you allowed to carry a gun when you come to Vatican City?"

"If I'm going there on official business then the answer is yes."

"I'll have Monsignor O'Bryan call the security office right now to confirm your status. And, Mario, do me a favor. Bring along a second gun."

That request was met with a long pause, then, "Things have turned serious, haven't they?"

"Things have turned very serious," Justin replied, and hung up.

CHAPTER 47
Day 10. Rome. Wednesday afternoon

The time was one o'clock, and the Holy Father was in the Sistine Chapel, facing a sea of red birettas worn by his College of Cardinals. Behind them sat scores of bishops, monsignors and priests, most ready to record for their superiors what the pope was about to say. All were still numbed by what they had been told in the morning session. Again, the Swiss Guard and the civilian security men were dismissed. Justin and O'Bryan had decided to skip the meeting. They had too much else to do.

Detective Castellanos had arrived on time, and Justin had spent the last twenty minutes briefing him. He spoke of the Russian letter, but not of Lucia's; he talked of the abductions of Kettering and the Archbishop of Canterbury, and explained how groups of Asians had been seen at the various crime scenes in several different countries, all involving victims with connections to the Vatican. He ended by suggesting the Russians could be installing a new czar within the next few hours. As an afterthought, he mentioned last night's altercation in the alley.

Castellanos jerked upright. "You were responsible for that?" he asked, incredulity spilling over into his voice. "News of that escapade spread last night like lightning throughout all the police departments. Are you suggesting there's a connection between the Asians who attacked the Ukrainians at the airport and what's happening inside Russia?"

"I am, but I haven't figured out exactly what it is. All I know is they have access to a new strain of Sarin and they've shown they're not afraid to use it."

Castellanos paled. He was well aware of Sarin and the havoc it could wreak. Indeed, his department practiced every few months for terrorist attacks on the city with just such a chemical agent—or something similar. The written consensus in every classified after-action report was that such an attack would panic the population to the extent any semblance of law and order would fast fall apart. Rome would turn into an every-man-for-himself battleground as the terrified population stampeded toward the city's gates. There would be anarchy in the streets. The biggest challenge facing the *Carabinieri* and the *Polizia Municipale* would come from the rapid spread of misinformation since everyone now carried cell phones. Some commanders had even suggested disabling the cell phone transmission towers so the citizens couldn't communicate with each other—or with the outside world. What that would accomplish, no one could say.

As Justin was about to speak, O'Bryan's cell phone came to life.

"Monsignor O'Bryan," he said, while activating the speakerphone.

"Jack, it's Sal Manzini," announced Kettering's deputy secretary of state, the panic in his voice evident for all three to hear. "I'm in the Sistine Chapel. About a half dozen armed men dressed as clergy have just taken over the place," he said, talking rapidly in heavily accented English. "They've shot two priests and a bishop. At least two of the attackers appear to be Asians and they've just announced that all cell phones must be turned in. Anyone caught using one will be shot immediately."

The three were riveted to Manzini's small electronic lifeline.

"I don't know what they want," he continued in a low voice, "but the first thing they did was whisk the pope away. You've got to contact the authorities at once." A momentary pause, then, "Jack, listen carefully to what I'm about to say. I think…"

The sentence was interrupted by the sounds of a struggle. Manzini grunted loudly, and they could tell the phone had just been wrested from his hand. In one, last, desperate attempt to communicate with O'Bryan, he managed to cry out, "Tell Mister Scott they all have gas masks on their…"

Manzini's words were cut off by the sound of a single pistol shot.

"Sal!" O'Bryan yelled into the phone while looking wildly at Justin.

A cold voice came on the line. "Mister Scott I know you there. Tell police if they interfere, everyone here die. And I do mean everyone." The line went dead.

"Those sons of bitches have Sarin," Justin said, his face suffused with anger. "Dammit, how could I have been so stupid? I should have foreseen something like this happening. Now the entire hierarchy of the Catholic Church can be wiped out in less than five minutes!" He looked from one to the other. "I'm talking the pope and every cardinal, as well as the majority of the world's archbishops! And all because of that bastard, Caffarone. May he burn in hell!"

O'Bryan grabbed ahold of the side of the desk. "Justin, do you realize such a scenario would mean the end the Catholic Church?" Looking as though he was about to throw up, he sank heavily into a chair. "If there are no cardinals left alive to elect a new pope..." He couldn't find the words to finish his sentence.

"Then why couldn't the surviving bishops step up to the plate and do the job?" Justin asked, his mind trying to focus on more pressing matters. "What would be so difficult about that? You're just not thinking straight, Jack."

O'Bryan was already shaking his head. "Because before Pope John Paul the Second died he reiterated that as a matter of Church law only the College of Cardinals can elect the papal successor. It's been that way for centuries and, as of today, the rules haven't been changed by this pope."

"Well, that's not good, is it?" Justin replied in the understatement of the year.

"Maybe the letter is from Lucia after all," O'Bryan whispered, resignation and defeat leaking out with his every word. "Maybe we've all been taken-in by a terribly cruel hoax. Maybe the Holy Father is already dead and the other prelates in the chapel will follow shortly."

Justin, too, found himself unsteady as he contemplated the enormity of the problem O'Bryan had just outlined, but he knew he could ill afford to collapse into a state of paralysis.

He reached over and grabbed O'Bryan's shoulder. "Jack, snap out of it! Call the head of the Swiss Guard and tell him what's happening inside the chapel. Impress upon him there can be no sirens and that none of his guards or plainclothesmen begin running helter-skelter all over the place. And especially tell him no Italian cops! Instruct him to clear the buildings and the grounds of all tourists and non-essential personnel. Have him say it's an exercise, or to make up something else. Just tell him to get everyone out of here."

"He's called the commandant," O'Bryan said in a faraway voice.

"I don't give a damn what he's called, just get a hold of him," Justin replied.

"Should I call my department?" Castellanos asked, his cell phone at the ready.

Justin shook his head. "They said no police, and they mean it. I've got to figure out how to open up a channel of communication with the captors. They will have a demand for something; everyone does in these kinds of situations."

"To think we were just talking about Sarin," O'Bryan said, his voice so low it was as if he was muttering to himself. "May God have mercy on us all."

"Dammit, Jack, I said snap out of it!" Justin squeezed O'Bryan's shoulder all the tighter. "Now call the Swiss Guard commandant. *Move!* There are lives are depending on you!"

A nagging question filled Justin's mind: Where had he heard that terrorist's voice on Monsignor Manzini's cell phone before?

Ian A. O'Connor

CHAPTER 48
Day 10. Rome. Wednesday afternoon

It **took less** than two minutes for Justin to hear the first of the sirens. They started out faint, but as the minutes passed, they kept getting louder and more distinct, telling him that many police cars were converging on the Vatican. *Damn them all!*

"Mario, get out there, find who's in charge, and bring him to me."

"He won't listen to me—or to you. I'm sorry, but you carry no weight here. The Vatican and Italy have a long-standing treaty stating that the police departments from Rome will help protect the Holy City if the Swiss Guard becomes overwhelmed."

Justin was in no mood to back down. "Listen to me. Tell whoever is in charge that if he sends his officers onto these grounds then the pope and all of the cardinals will be killed. It's that simple. But if still he insists, then I guarantee you, the people of Rome could well turn on the police and string them all up on lampposts when they hear their pope is dead. It will be a replay of what the citizens of Milan did with Mussolini and his whore back in Nineteen Forty-five! You tell him that from me, you hear?"

Castellanos tore at his hair. "Justin..." he began, his face twisted in torment. That was as far as he got. O'Bryan's cell phone sounded its familiar reveille.

Justin snapped his fingers, signaling O'Bryan to hand it to him.

"Justin Scott," he said as he activated both the speakerphone and record functions. "Who am I speaking with?"

"Mister Scott, this is Cardinal Sincero," the voice replied in heavily accented English. "I have been chosen to speak to you by the men holding us captives."

Justin was having none of it. "How do I know this is really Cardinal Sincero?" he replied in his most reasonable voice.

"Is Monsignor O'Bryan there?" the man asked.

"He's standing right beside me and he can hear you."

The man began speaking rapidly in Latin. O'Bryan listened intently for about ten seconds. He then looked at Justin and nodded. It was Sincero.

"Thank you, Cardinal. Now, what is it they want you to tell me?"

"Mister Scott, the leader says he will only speak with you, through me, and no one else. If anyone should interfere, he has instructed his men to kill us all. He says you have already figured out how he will do this, and that you know he is serious."

"I understand, Cardinal. Please put him on."

"He will not speak to you just yet, Mister Scott. He will tell me what to say."

"OK, what does he want me to do?"

There was a faint murmuring, an exchange between Sincero and at least two others. Justin couldn't make out what they were saying, or even what language they were speaking.

Cardinal Sincero came back. "The pope has told the leader he wants you to be the person in charge and not the Swiss Guard commandant or Rome's police department. The Holy Father insists that only you have an understanding of the gravity of the situation and that it would take too long to educate someone else. Anyway, this man says he will call you back in one half hour, at which time he wants you to assure him the police will not surround the Sistine Chapel and then break down the doors and storm in here like a bunch of hooligans. His words, not mine, Mister Scott."

"I will tell the police exactly what you have just told me, Cardinal. We will speak again in a half hour. Goodbye."

He looked at O'Bryan. "What did Sincero say to you in Latin?"

O'Bryan's face was pale and drawn. "The situation is not good. Sincero thinks they are going to kill the pope regardless, but before they do, they want him to do something. After that, they intend to move all the voting members of the College of Cardinals to another country, but plan to kill the other clergy in the chapel before they leave. That's all the time he had before they cut him off."

Justin's shocked expression mirrored O'Bryan's. This was shaping up to be something way beyond his worst nightmare. But the pope had said he specifically wanted him to remain in charge which meant he had to keeps his wits about him.

"OK, here's what we're going to do. The three of us are going out to Saint Peter's Square right now and meet with whoever is in command of the city cops. I'll play him Cardinal Sincero's recording, then Mario will further convince the guy to stay off the property, that is if he needs any more convincing. We'll pick up the Swiss Guard commandant on our way."

"Wait, Justin," Castellanos said, bending over and pulling up his pants leg. He unfastened an ankle holster. "I'm sorry it's only a twenty-five caliber, I couldn't get anything bigger on such short notice."

"This will do fine," Justin replied, knowing it was anything but. As he strapped the holster to his left leg, he decided to hold onto his cane for a while longer.

* * * * *

Justin stood behind the camera operator in the Vatican's security center and studied the color images from inside the Sistine Chapel. Six strategically mounted cameras made it easy for him to pick out the faces of all of the prisoners. He could not identify the captors, however, because they were also dressed as clergy. He turned to the chief of security, one of only four officers attached to the small, but elite, one hundred-man military force.

"Lieutenant, start pulling down individual face shots of everyone in the chapel. Compare those pictures with the databank file photos of the cardinals and all of the other clergy members being held. This will give us an accurate head count, and by a process of elimination we can ferret out the captors."

The lieutenant appeared to do some quick math, and after surveying the cameras closely, replied, "I can have your answer within the hour. We use several facial recognition computer programs, similar to those gambling casinos use to catch card cheats. It will not be difficult. I'm guessing I have maybe two hundred, possibly two hundred and twenty faces to shoot and match. I will call you."

"Good," Justin said. He had other equally pressing matters to take care of.

* * * * *

The *Polizia Municipale* established a perimeter around the exterior walls of Vatican City, the officers further backed up with motorized roving patrols. All tourists and employees leaving the city-state would be funneled through one checkpoint where they could be photographed and questioned. No one would slip away unseen.

Returning to the control center, Justin sought out Castellanos. "Mario, do you think you could get me a thousand auto-injectors of atropine? You know, those special syringes that hold the antidote for Sarin poisoning. The kidnappers will use Sarin if the police insist on storming the chapel, and they'll set it off in an aerosol form. I'm just hoping that with auto-injectors already on hand we could rush in and save twenty, possibly thirty people."

"Those are terrible odds," Castellanos said, "but, yes, I will get the injectors. I'll make the call right now."

A few minutes later Justin noticed the tourists were beginning to stream from the buildings. Because of the unusually warm day, there were far more people milling about than he wanted to see. Yet despite the inconvenience of being asked to leave early, they made their way in good-natured groups and clusters—and in an orderly fashion—to the lone checkpoint at the front of St. Peter's Square.

Justin and Castellanos joined O'Bryan in his office. A couple of minutes later he realized O'Bryan was being uncommonly quiet.

"Something you want to share, Jack?"

"I'm thinking about the worst case scenario and what will happen to the Church if the pope and all the cardinals are killed."

"Well, for starters, you said earlier it would effectively end the Catholic Church as we know it because canon law says only a conclave of cardinals under the age of eighty—and not to exceed one hundred and twenty in number—must gather on Vatican soil and vote to elect a new pope. But if they've all been killed…"

"But they wouldn't all be dead," O'Bryan replied in hushed voice.

Justin looked at O'Bryan in surprise. "I'm not following. Are you suggesting we might be able to rush in there and just concentrate on trying save only the younger cardinals with the auto injectors? That scenario presents me with a huge ethical dilemma, because that would be asking us to consciously choose who will live and who will die. To be forced to make such a draconian decision on the hallowed grounds of the Vatican itself, well, that would turn out to be the biggest irony of all time."

O'Bryan was already shaking his head. "No, no, I'm talking about all of them dying; I'm saying we couldn't even save one."

Then you've lost me."

"Justin, all of the cardinals under age eighty aren't in Rome! Two are still en route and a third is in a hospital in Chicago for prostate surgery." O'Bryan then rattled off their names.

Justin immediately grasped where O'Bryan was heading with this revelation. The logic was inspired. His friend had just posited the question of the century, one that had most assuredly never been thought of before. Not even by the Holy Father. Because what O'Bryan was now suggesting was that those three absent cardinals had the power to choose from within their own diminutive ranks the next pope. A two-thirds majority would be reached under Canon Law with two cardinals agreeing to elect the third.

Justin was awestruck. "I think you might be onto something," he whispered.

"Ah, but there are four cardinals, not three," Castellanos added. "Cardinal Kettering, he's also still alive, is he not?"

"Son of a gun!" Justin's face creased into a hint of a smile. He grabbed his cell phone and speed dialed Industrial Management's headquarters in New York. The connection was seamlessly made, and he was patched through to Mannix's deputy, a retired FBI agent and old friend named Charles Conrad.

"Charles, it's Justin Scott." He had no time for pleasantries. "I need you to do something for me, and I need it done yesterday. I'm sorry, but there's no time to vet this through the boss."

"Fire away."

"There are two cardinals en route to Rome; Cardinal Dougherty of Australia and Cardinal Kimbuturi of South Africa. There's also a third, Cardinal Pritchard of Chicago, but he's in a hospital somewhere in the Windy City being treated for prostate cancer. I need your agents to find the two travelers and put them under the tightest security possible.

I mean so tight that no one gets to them; no bishop, no priest, no nun. Not even the police. You must make them disappear until I personally give the all clear. Same goes for Prichard. Move him to a secure medical facility. They all have been targeted for immediate assassination, and should they be killed, then the Roman Catholic Church will cease to exist. I don't have time to explain, just do it, OK?"

"I'm moving on it right now. I'll call as soon as I have info on all three."

"No, Charles, call me with the conformation as it comes in on each one. It's that important." Justin hung up and nodded to O'Bryan. This was the first bit of good news in hours. He crossed his fingers then pumped his fist in a sign of victory. He didn't know a whole lot when it came to canon law, but O'Bryan sure did, and the look on his face told Justin that his friend was feeling a whole lot better than he had a scant couple of minutes earlier.

* * * * *

Forty-minutes later, Justin was called to the security center. The lieutenant motioned him to come and look at the bank of monitors.

"They're smashing the cameras."

Two had already been destroyed, and three frustrated terrorists dressed as priests were seen heaving objects at three of the four remaining. It would only be a matter of time until they, too, would cease transmitting.

The sixth camera, mounted high in the ceiling and toward the front was not panning, but broadcasting a picture looking down the length of the chapel. The lieutenant toggled a joystick and the camera zoomed in on the men gathered below. "Not the best angle," he conceded, "but better than nothing." As he spoke, the fourth camera winked once and went off the air.

"We've positively identified all of the clerics though. These are your bad guys." He tapped his keyboard and five faces appeared. The images were crisp. Justin carefully studied each one, then zeroed in on the third man. That was a face he had definitely seen before. *Yes, you're the son of a bitch from the airport!* The one who had made the gesture of slitting his throat as the getaway van had roared off, leaving a wounded colleague on the pavement to die.

Justin tapped the image on the glass screen. "This one, lieutenant, I recognize this dirtbag." Justin's Asian assassin was dressed as a bishop. "And the others are all dressed as priests?"

"Yes, which tells me your man is their leader."

Justin had a distinct feeling that events were now ever so slowly beginning to turn in his favor. Nevertheless, he had been bothered by something for hours; something he had not been able to put a finger on. Try as he might, his mind would not release the hidden nugget.

CHAPTER 49
Day 10. Rome. Wednesday evening

Justin decided to make his command post the inside of the Swiss Guard security center because it boasted a state-of-the-art communications net. The commandant reported that only essential personnel were now inside the walls of the Vatican. "The tourists and employees were cooperative, thank God," he was saying, "and we only had to finally shoo away some workmen from the Apostolic Library who were installing a new color copier."

It was now six thirty. Darkness had overtaken the city. "I'm wondering about food and drink. It's been several hours, and most of the prisoners are old men," said the lieutenant.

Justin had larger worries—the kidnappers demands. He changed the subject. "Until I know their demands, I can't begin to consider launching a rescue attempt. Twice I've asked Cardinal Sincero to have the leader tell me what he wants, but his only answer is, not yet."

* * * * *

Justin suddenly remembered the nagging question that had been bothering him for hours. He went over to the bank of monitors and asked the officer if it was possible to bring up file imagery taken earlier in the morning, before anyone had entered the chapel.

The man tapped rapidly on his keyboard and all six monitors sprang to life. The images were crisp, and the date-time clocks in the lower right hand corners of each panel read 6:45:05 a.m. The screens blinked in unison as their clocks changed to 6:45:10 a.m.

Justin pulled up a chair, sat down and closed his eyes. He needed a moment to think. Finally, he said, "See if you can pick up an image on the entrance wall. Specifically, I'm looking for video of the scaffolding."

The man's fingers flew across the keys and within moments, Justin had his scaffolding displayed from different angles on two of the six screens.

"Yes," Justin whispered, edging his chair closer. "Now, can you enlarge the pictures? I need to see what's under the scaffold, because if

I remember right, there were clothes and other stuff stashed down there."

Five seconds later he was intently studying pictures of several stacks of overalls, boots, respirators, rolls of tape and toolboxes.

"Zoom in some more if you can."

Bingo! Justin felt as though he could have reached into the screens and touched the items on display. He began to count the respirators. One, two, three, four, five. He next counted the pairs of boots. Again, five. Coveralls—five. He peered at the metal toolboxes—only three and all appeared padlocked. He sat back and stared at the screens. He now knew what was inside those locked boxes. *Sarin.*

Justin rubbed his face and tried to think. There would be no negotiating with these men because their diabolical plan called for everyone inside the Sistine Chapel to die, and die quickly. Yet if that was the case, then how did they plan to escape? Something didn't make sense. A thought came to him. He sat up straighter.

"Can you maneuver the one remaining camera to see if it can pick up a picture of the stuff under the scaffold right now?"

The operator frowned, but finally he had captured an image, albeit one none too clear.

Justin craned for a better look. "Down, down, down a skosh more," he coaxed. His heart missed a beat. Everything under the scaffolding was now gone, including the toolboxes.

"What does it mean?" the Swiss commandant asked.

"It means the five terrorists are now either dressed, or getting dressed, for handling Sarin," Justin said, his voice suddenly hoarse and whispery. He stared at the empty space beneath the scaffolding. "That stuff is so toxic they have to be covered from head to toe with rubber-lined coveralls, and all of the openings at their necks, hands, and boots must be taped so that no air gets in. It also means they've been planning to kill everyone inside the chapel from the gitgo."

"You can't be serious," the commander whispered back.

Justin continued to stare at the screen, one word driving all others from his brain.

Checkmate. He violently shook his head as if to exorcise a demon. No, dammit, it's not checkmate! He turned to the officer at the controls. "Is there any way for you to find out if two specific clergymen are among the prisoners? I'm looking for an archbishop and a monsignor."

"Yes, sir, just give me their names and the computer will match them with the faces we recorded earlier."

"Archbishop Torrelli and Monsignor Caffarone."

After a flurry of fast taps, there they were! Justin studied three shots of Torrelli standing alone, then two with him next to Caffarone. Both were in deep conversation. On the last picture Justin thought he could see a worried look on Caffarone's face.

"Well, well," he said, not taking his eyes off the screens, "I wonder if those two bastards have figured it out yet?"

"Figured what out?" O'Bryan asked.

Justin turned in his chair. "Figured out there are five respirators for the terrorists and none for them. I bet it has finally dawned on those two weasels they have just outlived their usefulness and that they're slated to die along with the men they've sold out. What a fitting end for a couple of despicable Judases!"

"I think you're right," O'Bryan said. "Yeah, I do believe they realize what's coming and there's not a thing they can do to stop it. Poetic justice."

"Then again, maybe not," Justin finally said. "Maybe what we're seeing is the two of them scheming to somehow turn on their captors in a last desperate attempt to save their own miserable hides."

* * * * *

Rome and St. Petersburg. Wednesday evening

A discreet cough from the Swiss Guard commandant caused Justin to wake with a start. He had been napping. He instinctively reached for his ankle holster but stopped when he recognized his visitor.

"Mister Scott, I have two thousand auto-injectors outside. What do you want me to do with them?"

Justin thought for a moment. Two thousand! That was more than he had dared hope for.

"First off, I want your men to carry two injectors apiece. They all have radios, so if the word comes down for them to inject themselves, I want to know that they will do it immediately. There can be no wasting time calling back to the command post for confirmation because if they hesitate they'll be dead inside of a minute. Understood?"

"Yes, sir."

Justin took a swig from a bottle of warm water then slipped into his shoes. "How many chemical warfare suits do you have?"

"Maybe a half dozen; I'm really not sure. Even though my men have been trained with the gear back home, it's not a scenario we practice for here."

"Have six of your best men standby to jump into those suits if I give the word. They will form the vanguard if we have to storm the Sistine Chapel. Their job will be to inject as many folks as fast as they can. The only person I would concede they should try to inject first would be the pope, but they must be told to start treating the clerics closest to them. They cannot attempt to save cardinals over bishops, monsignors instead of priests. Everyone in that chapel must be afforded the same chance at life. Also, make sure all are wearing body armor. They might have to go in behind the local police who will be using flash-bang concussion grenades against five heavily armed terrorists."

"I'll get on it right away."

In the communications room the duty lieutenant reported that the leader still wouldn't let them deliver any food. Justin looked at the lone picture feeding down on the number six screen. All cameras in the other buildings throughout Vatican City had been turned off. Justin did not want any distractions in the control room. Camera six's digital clock kept changing, a clear indication it was working. Justin could make out shadowy forms stretched out on chairs drawn tightly together, while others were lying on the cold floor. Then something caught his eye. Movement. He looked closer. It was three men coming together. He turned to the operator. "Can you switch from still to full motion?"

Without waiting to be told, the operator zoomed in on the three. All were terrorists, and gone were their clerical clothes. They were now wearing hazardous materials-handling suits, hoods and boots, and all carried gas masks slung over their shoulders. He knew that at the first sign of a forced entry into the chapel they would whip on their masks and start tossing canisters of Sarin in all directions. A man in the center of the small group pulled out a cell phone and begin dialing. He put it up to his ear and stared into the camera. A moment later O'Bryan's phone sounded reveille. Justin counted to three and opened the connection as the camera operator zoomed in on the caller. There was no doubt in Justin's mind; he was the assassin from the airport.

"Are you looking at me, Mister Scott?"

So he knows about the camera. "I am," Justin replied in a matter-of-fact voice. He leaned closer to the monitor. The cleric standing beside the ringleader was Archbishop Torrelli, who had obviously told the man about the lone operating camera.

"Here's my demand. You will tell the person who answers the phone at the number I'm going to give you to have five buses brought to the Sistine Chapel at six in the morning. If the police should interfere in any way, all of the prisoners will die, starting with the pope. And, yes, it will be with Sarin."

The last thing Justin felt he could allow to happen was for the prisoners to be hauled away on buses where he could no longer control events. What if some trigger-happy cop took matters into his own hands and opened fire? The ensuing gun battle would bring disaster. No way was he going to allow the prisoners to be moved. Easier said than done, he admitted to himself, now realizing he had to stall, play for time and come up with a plan.

"What's your name?" he suddenly asked the terrorist in a reasonable voice.

The man answered immediately. "Mister Scott, you're wasting my time. Here is the phone number. You will place the call within the next five minutes." He rattled off a twelve-digit number starting with 397.

"Until you tell me your name, I have no intention of carrying on with this conversation. You see, I never talk with people who don't have a name. And if you threaten to harm another hostage, then I will make sure you never see a single bus."

Justin hung up before the man had a chance to reply. He did not leave the rest of the group hanging. "I intend to call him back in five minutes," he explained, "and when I do, I will again ask him his name. He will still be furious, but he'll tell me. Then I will say I must talk to Cardinal Sincero, and that I'll ring him back in ten minutes to do so. I

Ian A. O'Connor

want him to feel that he is not quite as in charge as he thought he was. I intend to buy us time. The Olympic Village scenario in Munich in Nineteen Seventy-two when all of those Israeli athletes were killed will not be repeated on my watch. And for your information, gentlemen, the third digit in the phone number that he rattled off was a seven, which tells me his call is going to Russia."

"I sure hope you know what you're doing," O'Bryan said, the nervousness in his voice evident for all to hear.

"I do," Justin replied with confidence, then remarked, "Jack, did you notice how the assassin now speaks perfect English; no more pidgin like before."

"Now that you mention it..." That was as far as O'Bryan got before being interrupted by Justin's cell phone. Both men showed surprise that it was still working.

"Justin, it's Steve Mannix. Charin and I have just left Panov's house and he told us something that has my hair standing on end. It involves your situation there in Rome. Panov says a bomb has been placed somewhere inside the Vatican and that it's set to detonate at noon on Saturday. He then mumbled something about it being the fulfillment of the letter from Sister Lucia, and how in that instant the Church of Rome will cease to exist. He was actually gloating when he told us, and he said that if anyone tried to either move or disarm the device it would be triggered automatically by an electronic signal and detonate immediately. He said his bomb was tamperproof. Justin, that lunatic took an uncommon delight in saying that when it explodes it will render the Vatican uninhabitable to all but Lucifer and his minions for the next twenty-four thousand years. He added that in case we had forgotten our physics, that particular number represents the half-life for the plutonium isotope two thirty-nine. He laughed in our faces then booted us out of his home for the second time."

Justin felt his chest constrict. And just when he had thought the situation couldn't get any worse, he was now being told the stakes had been raised a thousandfold—no, make that twenty-four times a thousandfold.

"Steve, I'll call you back. I need a moment to think." Justin severed the connection with St. Petersburg. He took a few deep breaths. The pounding in his chest lessened and the noise in his ears subsided. He began to marshal his wits. What had to be done first? What before everything else? *Come on, man, think!*

Then it came to him. With this latest bit of bad news he now had no choice. He had to alert the authorities to be prepared to evacuate the entire city of Rome because it was the morally right thing to do.

He turned to the Swiss lieutenant. "Please ask you commandant to come here, then get the police commander at the Saint Peter's Square checkpoint on the phone."

While he waited for the commandant, Justin made sure O'Bryan understood the gravity of this new, more terrifying threat. "Jack, I want you to speak in Italian to the police commander. You must make him understand that he has to be ready to evacuate Rome if I give the word there's an atomic bomb here we cannot disarm. Tell him we're thinking along the lines of something about the size of the one dropped on Hiroshima, which means the entire population will need to be evacuated out to a distance of about thirty miles from ground zero."

* * * * *

Five minutes later the Swiss commandant arrived and Justin explained what he had learned from Mannix about a possible nuclear weapon being hidden on the grounds. He suggested assembling the entire force of 100 soldiers. "I need your men to begin a building search. Tell them to look for anything suspicious and have them radio their reports into the control center as they go."

* * * * *

Justin fretted over this new worry. Supposing the terrorists holding the pope and his entire College of Cardinals hostage had no idea there was a bomb in the Vatican? What if Alexander Panov had hatched a truly evil plan, a plan which called for everyone in the Sistine Chapel to die alongside much of the population of Rome? Supposing the terrorists holed up in the chapel had also been deemed expendable by Panov. He had to see if he was right. He flipped open O'Bryan's phone and dialed into the chapel.

"Mister Scott," the leader said, walking into full view, "could it be you actually want the pope to die?"

Justin ignored the taunt. "Are you ready to tell me your name?"

"My name is Agamemnon," the man lashed out in anger.

"Now that wasn't so hard, was it?" Justin said, then with all the inner fortitude he could muster, forced himself to laugh. He knew he had to sound relaxed and fully in control. "I must admit though, you don't look like any Greek I've ever met."

"Mister Scott, I am going to delight in killing you, but until then, I will ask you once more: have you telephoned for my buses?"

It was at that moment Justin realized where he had heard that voice before. *On the answering machine in Dr. Smalling's apartment.* The voice that had told him he would be the next to die!

"Well, that's the reason I'm calling," Justin said. "There's been a change of plans on this end, which means your buses won't be arriving at six, or at seven, or ever. It's now impossible to find a driver who will come within a hundred miles of the Vatican."

Justin decided to show a hole card. He rushed on. "It seems your Russian pal has double-crossed you, Agamemnon. He's telling me that he's hidden a nuclear bomb somewhere in one of the buildings and that it's set to go off if anyone so much as breathes wrong." Justin allowed a few moments for this news to sink in. "You know, Aggie, the damn thing could be hidden right there inside the Sistine Chapel."

Agamemnon began to laugh. His was not the hysterical laugher of a frightened man, but a deep belly laugh from one truly amused. "Mister Scott, that is rich. A nuclear bomb, no less, and it's going to go boom right here and blow us all up. Oh, my!"

Justin willed his voice to remain calm. "Why don't you call Alexander Panov? I bet the old boy is just dying to hear from you. I'll ring you back in ten minutes."

Agamemnon reacted as if he had been shot. His body went rigid. "How do you know about Panov?"

Instead of answering, Justin severed the connection. He turned to the technician. "Disable the Vatican cell phone tower right now," he commanded, "I want that terrorist thoroughly rattled."

Justin thought about this new wrinkle for a couple of seconds, then added, "We'll re-activate the tower whenever we need it ourselves." Then he had a follow-on thought. "Is there a landline into the Sistine Chapel?"

"There are two, sir."

"Disable them. Have one of your men cut the lines."

A doable plan of action to rescue the prisoners was beginning to coalesce in his mind, but to make the scheme work he had to first find, then neutralize, Panov's bomb.

Justin picked up a landline phone on the desk and dialed Mannix who grasped the idea right away.

"You want me to tell Panov you've found his bomb and that you've disabled it. You want me to taunt him. You want him to become so pissed off he'll say something that will help you find it."

CHAPTER 50
Day 10-11. Rome. Wednesday night, Thursday morning

*W*hen **Mannix called** back an hour later Justin could hear the electricity in his voice.

"I swallowed a micro-transmitter before entering Panov's house and had Charin record everything from his car. The old fart has learned to speak damn good English since I last saw him."

"...All I can say is the bomb your Mister Scott claims to have defused doesn't belong to me," came the faraway voice of Alexander Panov. "You see, my people are monitoring it as we sit having this chat, and I assure you, my bomb is still armed and active. In fact, it speaks to me continuously by way of the newest star in the heavens."

Panov might be insane but he isn't stupid, Justin thought. But what did that reference to the newest star in the heavens mean? Was he speaking in riddles?

"Panov finally opened up," Mannix was saying. "I'm guessing he had to show me just how brilliant he is. He said that the recently deceased Patriarch of Moscow gave you an excellent clue for finding the bomb. In fact, he openly admitted to personally ordering the patriarch be executed after learning the man had sent Cardinal Kettering a painting with a warning message." Mannix paused. "I hope that makes sense to you, because it means nothing to me."

Justin's mind flew back to *Evening Prayers*.

"It does," Justin said. "Now play the rest of the recording for me."

"...I was going to make Patriarch Sergius the Second the leader of all Christianity," Panov was saying, "but he chose to turn his back on me and warn the pope. And to think the traitor almost succeeded." Justin heard a muffled sigh. "You can inform your friend Mister Scott there will be no poisoning of the pope and his cardinals with Sarin as I'm sure my man in Rome is now threatening to do," Panov said. "And there will be no atomic bomb blast in the Vatican, at least not from any bomb of mine. However, the pope and his cardinals will die nonetheless, and their bodies will be left to rot in that magnificent chapel because no one will dare retrieve them. My five men inside will likewise perish because they have now outlived their usefulness. The leader and two others are North Koreans, as I'm sure Mister Scott now knows" Panov was saying, "but it was the leader who secured the Sarin and the plutonium for me. That man turned my lifelong dream into a reality. But, Koreans can never be trusted which means I cannot allow them to live. You see, eventually they would turn on me, too."

Panov paused for a few seconds, but when he continued his voice was stronger. "Enough about all that. Before the sun sets today, there will be only one Church and that will be the Holy Church of Russia. The Patriarch of Saint Petersburg will sit upon the throne once occupied by Saint Peter, and our new Russian Church will reign supreme over Christendom uninterrupted until the end of days. And that will be the fulfillment of what the Blessed Mother promised many years ago in a vision to a simple peasant girl in Fatima when she spoke of the consecration of Russia. But I suspect you know nothing of that."

Mannix's voice fairly boomed in comparison to Panov's. "You're right, I haven't a clue what you're talking about, but I do know this. In spite of what you think, your terrorist friends plan on packing their prisoners onto buses and whisking them away at six o'clock this morning. That's about four hours from now, and they have already warned Mister Scott that if anyone tries to interfere they will kill them all with Sarin."

"No, they won't," Panov said in a voice filled with confidence, "because the stuff doesn't work. You see, I was the one who arranged for it to be brought into the Sistine Chapel along with the chemical suits and respirators and gas masks, which by the way, are also defective. I switched out the real Sarin canisters with ones filled with air. Those five men will be dead well before that six o'clock deadline, as will everyone else on Vatican soil."

"You're quite mad," Mannix replied. "You'll never get away with this."

Panov's abrupt laugh sounded like a bark. "Mad? Possibly I am, but I assure you I will get away with this. Of course, if you should decide to tell anyone your preposterous story, I will simply deny it. That is why I took your cell phone when you barged in here. To make sure there would be no recording of this little chat. It's your word against mine. No one will believe you and, frankly, by then no one will care, least of all me." Panov began to cough and Justin waited impatiently for the old man to catch his breath.

"I really must thank Adolf Hitler for making my dream a reality," Panov finally said. "To think that the Führer lost his Third Reich because of a mysterious letter he received at Christmastime in Nineteen Forty. That very special letter disappeared at the time of Germany's surrender in Nineteen Forty-five to the Allies, but it fell into my hands quite by accident some sixty-plus years later. It had been hidden behind a beautiful painting liberated by the Red Army and taken to the Hermitage. I suspect Hitler himself placed the envelope there, suggesting he probably commandeered the picture from Reichsmarschall Göring. Regardless, that painting lay undisturbed in a crate, the envelope barely peeking out from a slight opening in the backside of the frame when I spotted it. The envelope was addressed in Portuguese to *Sr. Adolf Hitler, Chanceler de Germany*, so I had the letter translated. What a letter it turned out to be! It was from Sister Lucia of Fatima, and she boldly told Hitler it was the will of God that he destroy communist Russia. Apparently, he had to commence his attack on the day following the summer solstice in Nineteen Forty-one. However, God also warned that if Hitler did not obey, then a great calamity would befall Germany and the end of the world would follow shortly thereafter. In the last paragraph Sister Lucia told Hitler of the day and the hour when creation would end. Well, that day has come and long gone, and nothing happened. The world still survives. But her warning to Hitler gave me an idea. I would use her letter as a basis to produce one of my own. Mine was the perfect plan! I would have my art restorers duplicate Sister Lucia's handwriting and put her words onto a piece of paper identical to what she used in her Christmas message to Hitler. I would faithfully copy her last paragraph, except I would substitute the words *third millennium* for *second millennium* along with using *thirteenth year aforementioned* to replace *third year* aforementioned, and, lastly, I inserted the word *second* in front of the words *this decade* which would now show Lucia's date for the ending of creation to be this coming Saturday.

"Once I was committed to this course of action, there could be no turning back. The date I had chosen with such care was now cast in stone. My letter was sent to Cardinal Kettering along with a second letter written in vulgate Latin, and both have accomplished their intended effect. The pope really believes what he has read or, at the very least, is confused and uncertain. But you know the only thing I found truly puzzling is that God chose not to keep his promise to Adolf Hitler. Was it because the Führer failed to destroy Russia, or was it for an entirely different reason. But we'll never know that now, will we?"

Justin heard a loud sigh of finality. Panov continued. "So, you and I find ourselves here on this cold winter's night because of the fateful coming together of a letter sent to Adolf Hitler from a simple Portuguese nun who saw visions of the Holy Mother, with an exquisite masterpiece painted more than five hundred years earlier. I like to believe it was divine intervention. By the way, do you know the painting I'm speaking of and who painted it?"

"I haven't a clue."

"It's called *Evening Prayers* and was painted by *Fra Angelico* around the year Fourteen Fifty. It hangs in my bedroom and that glorious masterpiece is the last thing I see before going to sleep every night and the first thing I see when I awaken each morning. I never tire of looking at it. But what I find to be a true mystery is that although the subject matter is so obviously Jewish, for some inexplicable reason Herr Hitler saw past that and seized this particular work for himself. However, I see it as a gift to me from the Creator, but you wouldn't understand that either."

"Thank you for the history lesson."

"Now you will leave, Mister Mannix. My man will give you back your cell phone at the front door. Don't ever come back. The same goes for Detective Charin. If you should dare to ignore my warning, I will have you killed."

"I sure hope that helps, Justin," Mannix said in summary.

"It does," Justin said, his heart pounding as he hung up. *Panov had just confirmed what he had suspected all along: Lucia's Russian letter was a fake!* He had minimally altered the dates he had seen on Fleming's Portuguese letter to Hitler, and in the confusion of the moment no one had compared the two documents painstakingly word by word by word! Everyone had assumed they were identical because they had just looked identical, as had both paintings of *Evening Prayers*.

Justin shook his head to clear his mind. He had more pressing problems to solve. Now knew the bomb was set to explode at three this morning, and not on Saturday. He took little comfort knowing there would not be a nuclear blast, but in its stead a conventional explosion which would still kill everyone inside the chapel before spewing a cloud of deadly weapons-grade plutonium throughout Vatican City. That cloud would effectively doom everyone else within a few minutes, although some unfortunates would languish in agony for a week or more. Nevertheless, the Holy City would be rendered off limits to all living creatures for a millennium, and all of the priceless treasures of Western Civilization inside its palaces would also be lost forever—to say nothing of the hierarchy of the Holy Roman Church.

That was if Panov was telling the truth, and Justin had no reason to doubt him.

* * * * *

O'Bryan had also heard Mannix's recorded conservation, but now was hard at work on the laptop. "What's the newest star in the heavens?" he asked Justin without looking up.

"Haven't a clue, I'm not into astronomy."

"Me neither," O'Bryan replied. "But I suspected Panov was talking about a satellite, so I went to the Johnson Space Center website. Listen to what NASA writes in a blog."

A Russian satellite was launched several hours ago atop an Indian rocket at the Satish Dhawan Space Centre in Sriharikota, India, and is now in a geostationary orbit over Rome. At 8:00 p.m. last evening, Rome time, the satellite began transmitting what appears to be a nonstop stream of random numbers using a mechanical voice.

NASA suggests it's an orbiting numbers station. However, after querying their Russian counterparts at the Baikonur Cosmodrome, the Russians say they have also been monitoring the signal and are unsure what it means because it's not their satellite and are insisting they are very unhappy about this situation.

The Russians confirm it was put into orbit by a private concern, but admit the signal is being illegally beamed to their GLONASS system. They say that if they can't determine its purpose, they will start jamming the signal at noon tomorrow, (GMT time) which will render the satellite useless.

Justin suddenly recalled the snatches of the newscast he had heard a few hours earlier on the TV at the safe house. He sprang into action.

"Jack, call the Jet Propulsion Lab in Pasadena, California, and ask any scientist there what he can tell us about this satellite. If he cannot, or will not say, then phone NORAD Headquarters at Peterson Air Force Base in Colorado and tell them you're calling from the Vatican. Let them know it's urgent and that many lives are at risk. First thing they'll do is trace your call and see you're legit."

"What exactly are you looking for?"

"I need to know if this satellite is transmitting its signal directly to a receiver inside Vatican City. If it is, then we can triangulate using the Russian GLONASS system and pinpoint where Panov's bomb is hidden. Now hurry!"

Within five minutes O'Bryan had someone in Pasadena on the landline speakerphone. She introduced herself as Judith Baum, and in a pleasant voice admitted to holding a Ph.D. in acoustical physics and telemetry.

O'Bryan asked her about the satellite above Rome.

"We don't know what to make of it," Baum began. "It's transmitting on a frequency found on the high precision L-Two band which is reserved for the Russian military. This particular frequency has never been used in any day-to-day working mode by a Russian satellite, and the information seems to be a non-stop spewing out of random numbers. Think of it as something akin to the first stream of data that was sent over the Internet from one computer to another in October, Nineteen Sixty-nine. The content then was pure rubbish. However, someone here thought he detected a pattern, like the sequence of numbers following the decimal point for pi. You know, three point one four one five nine *etcetera, ad infinitum*, but that idea was quickly nixed. We do know the signal is being beamed down to a location in Rome, which in turn just sends it back up to the Russian

GLONASS Twenty-four satellite system—that's what their GPS is called—in a streaming process. It doesn't make any sense. There is nothing of value in this for anyone, so my guess is somebody has lots of money to waste on spectacular nonsense."

"Dr. Baum, this is Justin Scott. I wonder if I could ask a favor?"

"Of course."

"Would you please remain on the line? I have feeling I will need to speak with you again shortly. Meanwhile, I'm going to see if I can pinpoint the location of the object here on the ground."

"Well why didn't you say so? Let me give you a hand."

The small group of men gathered in the Vatican's communication center could hear her rapid tapping on a computer keyboard nine time zones to the west.

"Ah, here it is. Now let me zoom in like this," she said, speaking aloud but to herself. "There, found you," she announced triumphantly. "The item you're looking for is located on the grounds of the Vatican and my map is telling me it is in the Apostolic Library."

O'Bryan suddenly yelled out, startling everyone. "Justin, I know exactly what we're looking for! It's the new color copier! The one delivered to the library. I even gave the deliverymen directions. That's your bomb!"

Justin wheeled to face the Swiss commandant. "Stay on the line with Doctor Baum." He then directed the communications technician to activate the Vatican cell tower and grabbed O'Bryan by the arm. "Show me, Jack."

Justin tore out of the communications center and, with O'Bryan beside him, sprinted toward the Apostolic Library. The dimly lit streets were eerily empty at 2:15 in the morning. The ancient palaces crowded onto the hilly terrain were dark and foreboding, with only a faint smattering of lights showing in windows few and far apart.

O'Bryan led Justin into the unlocked and hastily abandoned library, home to the world's most priceless collection of books, manuscripts and artifacts.

"Where the hell is it?" Justin fumed.

"There, by the Head Librarian's desk. It's the one at the end!"

The giant color copier was plugged into a wall socket, its high-tech screen lit up by blue light emitting diodes. Justin crouched down beside it, his heart hammering. How was he supposed to disarm the thing? One wrong move and Panov had said it would explode.

He spotted what appeared to be two small antennae on the back. So that's how it communicates. Sweat began to trickle freely. He dialed the communications center on O'Bryan's cell and was patched through to a waiting Dr. Baum.

"What I have in front of me is a bomb inside a color copier that is set to go off at three o'clock," he said, "and when it does, half of the buildings in Vatican City will be leveled and the grounds covered with a fine dusting of weapons-grade plutonium. That stuff will kill anyone still alive after the blast and this place will be off limits to all of humanity for a thousand years. I need you to tell me how to disarm this thing."

"I know nothing about bombs, so I'm afraid I can't help you."

"Yes, you can," Justin insisted. "You told me those numbers being transmitted via the satellite are random numbers, which means this machine isn't trying to make sense out of what it's receiving. It only knows that if the transmission stops for any reason, then it will activate a firing mechanism—probably a fulminate of mercury switch—which in turn will set off several hundred pounds of C-Four explosive or even Semtex. So let's both take a big deep breath and think this problem through, Doctor Baum."

"I'll do what I can," Baum promised, then took the suggested deep breath. "First off, the downlink side is the key," she began. "If that communication link is interrupted, even for a second, then your bomb will explode."

"Why not the uplink side?"

"No," Baum replied firmly. "All that does is tell anyone listening in on the frequency that everything is working fine. Think of it as a passively monitored fire alarm or burglar alarm system hooked into your home telephone line. It chirps every fifteen seconds or so. The noise is annoying, but it lets you know the system is functioning. Well, that is the same thing here. I'm guessing it's what we call a housekeeping frequency; one of a very few obfuscated HP signals the

Russian military would use to do maintenance, or to possibly conduct secret tests on their recently upgraded GLONASS system. Which means the downlink side is the signal you do not want to interrupt. Are you following all this, Mister Scott?"

"I think I do. So how do we work around that?"

"Easy. You record the downlink signal for about fifteen minutes, maybe less, and then you transmit it back to the bomb on the same frequency, using a local transmitter to replace the one coming from the geostationary satellite. However, you must make sure the new signal is broadcast on a continuous loop, that way it will keep sending an uninterrupted stream of mindless numbers to the bomb. You will then have rendered it safe. It will not explode. Of course, when the people regulating the signal from the satellite shut it off, thus hoping to trigger the explosion at three o'clock, they will know within moments that they no longer have control over their weapon. You can then call in your experts to disarm it. I can tell you the frequency it's using." Justin heard more tapping. "Your frequency is one twenty-five nine point nine one zero megahertz which is right at the top of the HP L-Two band."

This woman's an angel sent by heaven! Justin was truly impressed.

"Mister Scott, I'm hearing all of this," said the Swiss technician in the communications center. "I can have a looped recording made and the proper transmitter in your hands within ten minutes. I know how to wire it into the machine so there will be no interruption of the signal, then I can unhook the downlink as Dr. Baum suggests. Your bomb will be rendered harmless in less than a half hour, I guarantee it."

Justin looked at his watch and whispered, "Jack, there is a God!"

"I've always known that," O'Bryan whispered back.

CHAPTER 51
Day 11. Rome. Thursday Morning

Justin and O'Bryan returned to the communications center where Justin commandeered Castellanos' walkie-talkie to ask the Italian police commander and his deputies to come join them. He had decided on a plan to free the hostages and needed a bullhorn to make it possible.

Ten minutes later, he had finished briefing the group. They whispered amongst themselves then came to an agreement: this should work.

Justin took O'Bryan aside and the two of them spent the next several minutes taking turns typing on the laptop. They finally looked at each other and nodded. It was showtime.

At exactly 3:30 a.m., a SWAT team quietly moved up to the main doors of the Sistine Chapel while two other teams were doing the same on the opposite side of the building. Justin had changed into in a black suit and a Roman collar. Just another priest.

O'Bryan picked up the bullhorn and began to plainsong in Latin in the fashion of the hauntingly beautiful Gregorian chanting which dated back to the reign of Charlemagne.

"Listen well, my brothers," he sang, "for you are about to be rescued. I will speak three sentences. You will answer with the *Kyrie eleison* at the end of the first sentence to signal you understand. *Christe eleison* will be your reply for the second, then *Kyrie eleison* again for the third. Then I will end with a great amen. You will chant the great amen in reply, and immediately drop to the floor and stay there, because the last note of your amen will be the signal to the police to break into the chapel. The terrorists must be made to think you are singing the solemn of the mass. Make sure Torrelli and Caffarone do not speak to any of them because both men are traitors. Please answer now with *Kyrie eleison* to let me know you understand."

Two hundred voices filled the night air in chant with the requested response.

"Kyrie eleison."

The ethereal refrain sent shivers up the spines of the officers outside the building. Several instinctively blessed themselves.

Again, O'Bryan began to chant. "Stay away from the doors and do not rise up from the floor until you hear the all clear from me. *Christe eleison.*"

"*Christe eleison.*"

"There might be shooting, so you must all stay down until you hear my voice," he repeated, more for the sake of the older men who were hard of hearing and those well into their dotage. "*Kyrie eleison.*"

"*Kyrie eleison.*"

"This is my last sentence. Aahhmen."

"*AHHHMMMEEENNN,*" came the drawn out, thunderous reply from inside the Sistine Chapel.

Justin raised his right hand for the command element to see, then dropped it.

Three teams with battering rams smashed open the three sets of doors in unison, allowing scores of officers to pour into the chapel and immediately fan out. All wore armor and night vision glasses. Justin followed behind the first wave, without helmet, goggles or armor. The terrorists would see him as one more cleric in a sea of clergy.

He had also made a conscious decision to go in without the small caliber gun in hand, reasoning he didn't want to be shot by an adrenaline-wired special tactical unit police officer mistaking him for a terrorist dressed as a priest. He had but one goal in mind—taking out Agamemnon.

In the dim light he could see that the handful of men still standing were all terrorists. Everyone else was down on the mosaic floor amid scattered and upturned chairs. He ran past the gilt barrier and into the nave of the chapel.

A gunshot rang out from a handgun somewhere to his left, down toward the front, close to the altar. It was immediately answered with a burst from an automatic weapon. Someone screamed while another let loose with a torrent of high-pitched pleadings off to his right, but was quickly silenced by an audible thud.

Justin's eyes swept the chapel. Agamemnon was standing in full view, his back to the altar, handgun drawn, and looking down at a group of clerics lying several inches from his feet. The Korean suddenly dashed forward, grabbed a prostrate figure by the back of his cassock and began pulling the man to his feet. Agamemnon was intending to escape with a hostage in tow!

"Agamemnon," Justin roared at the top of his lungs then started towards his nemesis.

Agamemnon looked up. "Today you die, Justin Scott," he screamed, and began firing. He fired once, twice, and then the gun jammed.

Justin kept coming.

Agamemnon threw down his useless weapon and dashed toward the back of the altar.

Justin vaulted over a group of clerics and followed the fleeing Agamemnon through a side door and out of the chapel. He sprinted down a narrow hallway and into a gloomy room. He slammed the door shut with a swift kick, locking himself in with the terrorist.

Agamemnon had heard him coming. He wheeled, his face contorted in anger while his eyes darted around the darkened space. They came to rest on a bronze statue of a knight, a larger than life figure dressed in the coat of mail of a medieval Crusader. This was the last creation of Gianlorenzo Bernini, the greatest of all the Baroque sculptors. It had been cast in 1678, just two years before the maestro's death at age eighty, commissioned by a Florentine duke to stand eternal guard over his family tomb. That burial vault had long since been abandoned, and the knight's home for the past century was now this solitary niche in a wall tucked away in an obscure corner of a room behind the world's most beautiful chapel.

Agamemnon closed the divide with a mad dash. Bernini's knight was armed with a broadsword worthy of Goliath. Agamemnon pulled on the enormous blade with all of his might. Nothing. Roaring in frustration at the top of his lungs, he gave a second, more powerful, adrenaline-laced wrench at the recalcitrant weapon. The statue shuddered once then begrudgingly surrendered his fearsome oversized blade.

Without a word of warning, the Korean rotated the sword in a two-fisted full circle above his head and lunged.

Justin jumped back as the blade whistled past his head, the strong draft ruffling his hair in its wake.

"Now it's just you and me, Justin Scott," Agamemnon crowed, as he began circling his prey, the room lit by a lone dim bulb. "My greatest pleasure will be the moment I sever your head."

Justin spotted a copper urn on the stone floor some six feet to his left. He feigned a quick movement to his right.

Agamemnon jumped to the spot where he anticipated Justin would land. Instead, Justin took two short steps to his left, grabbed the urn's handle and heaved the fifteen-pound vessel with all the strength he could muster directly at Agamemnon's chest. It caught him just below the sternum, the momentum causing the terrorist to stumble then fall heavily onto one knee. The momentary advantage became Justin's, and he seized his opening by dashing toward the back wall where a dozen fourteenth century halberds stood like so many soldiers. He grabbed the closest nine-foot, two-handed deadly pole-weapon fashioned with both a spear and axe at its head, and turned to face Agamemnon who was staggering to his feet. Justin knew he had to press his advantage immediately. Holding the metal-sheathed spear in both hands, he lunged at the Korean.

Agamemnon tried to parry the deadly thrust with his sword, but Justin followed through by landing a back-sided strike squarely on the terrorist's left arm. Agamemnon gasped in agony. Justin knew the hit had to have caused some serious damage. Somewhere beyond the closed door he heard O'Bryan sound the all clear in Latin on his bullhorn. Justin swung his flagstaff with a renewed vigor. Agamemnon was breathing heavily.

Justin heard the crash of a battering ram. The ancient door shuddered but held. Then the ram slammed into the wood for a second time. The huge iron hinges groaned and buckled under the attack causing the locking hasp to bend upward at an impossible angle. But still the door held. Agamemnon seemed to realize the end was near, because with one last, supernova-like burst of energy, he flung the huge broadsword at Justin, catching him diagonally across the chest.

Justin roared in pain as he fell hard onto the flagstone floor. His vision began to tunnel and the world was turning to black.

Agamemnon, with a look of impending triumph in his eyes, reached behind his back, drew a stiletto from a scabbard and without a sound leaped toward his fallen prey.

Somehow, Justin was able to raise his spear.

A terrible scream told him that Agamemnon had landed on its tip. The sharpened steel point had passed completely through his neck, impaling him.

The door shook violently and flew open, smashing against the granite wall. Four officers rushed in and stopped, stunned by the horrific scene. The dying terrorist writhed on the floor, a bloodied metal pole protruding from both sides of his neck.

Justin managed to roll onto his side and stare into Agamemnon's dimming eyes.

The terrorist was in his death throes. His body was bent like a bow, but still he searched out Justin's eyes. He struggled to purse his lips, hoping to find enough strength with his dying breath to spit upon his enemy. The effort proved too much. Agamemnon went limp, and his eyes dimmed. The body shuddered one last time then lay still.

Two of the soldiers hurriedly blessed themselves, and then all four reached down and helped Justin to his feet.

"Are you all right, sir? Do you need a doctor?"

"I'm…I'm OK," Justin managed, although the act of drawing a breath sent searing pains shooting through his lungs. "How is the Holy Father?" he gasped. "How are the cardinals and the rest of the prisoners?" The effort to speak was exhausting.

"The Holy Father is fine, thank God, and so are the cardinals. Archbishop Torrelli and Monsignor Caffarone were killed in the attack. I'm sure they will be given martyrs' funerals," one said.

Justin began to laugh at that remark, although his pain was beyond excruciating.

Four pairs of caring hands tried to ease him to the floor, but Justin feebly brushed them aside.

"I'm going to walk out of here under my own steam," he said, then lurched out of the room without giving the dead terrorist so much as a backward glance.

EPILOGUE
Rome. One week later

One week later, Justin's body had healed considerably. No ribs had been broken, but his chest sported a huge multi-colored bruise.

It was time to go. A waiting taxi whisked him to the Vatican and he was ushered into Kettering's office as a clock somewhere in the distance struck nine.

"Ah, Justin, come in, come in," Cardinal Kettering said warmly, standing with his back to the window and holding a framed painting up to the bright morning north light. O'Bryan stood beside him.

Justin did not need to be told which painting. It was a masterpiece by *Fra Angelico* entitled *Evening Prayers*. It had arrived two days ago from the Patriarch of St. Petersburg.

Justin walked over to Kettering's desk and held aloft the forgery received three weeks earlier. "You must admit, this bogus painting the Patriarch of Moscow sent is a dead ringer for the real one," he marveled. To all appearances, the two were identical, but to their now-knowing eyes, the differences seemed vast.

"I believe by the time the Patriarch sent you his counterfeit he already suspected the worst," O'Bryan said. "It's my guess he had learned some months earlier of Panov's plan to destroy the Church of Rome and decided then and there that he wanted no part of it. The Patriarch hoped you would spot the work for the forgery it was, then by following its clues find a way to save the Roman Church."

"And I pray daily for the repose of his immortal soul," Kettering said.

Justin put down the copy and signaled for Kettering to hand him the original. "There's something I gave a lot of thought to last night, and I finally came up with an idea." He flipped the painting over and studied the back of the frame, paying particular attention to its sturdy protective dust cover of specially treated heavy brown paper. Then he began to feel his way slowly around the paper backing.

Both prelates followed Justin's hands in silence. *What was he looking for?*

Justin began to knead something. They all heard a rustling sound.

"Francis, do you have a letter opener?"

Kettering wordlessly retrieved one from his desk.

Justin made a careful slit in the protective backing and gingerly worked the hidden object loose. It was an envelope! All three craned to read the words on once-white paper that had long ago turned to the color of old parchment. The dark blue ink, though faded, was still legible.

Sr. Adolf Hitler, Chanceler de Germany.

The three men stared at the envelope in silence.

Justin was the first to regain his voice. "Well, I'll be...it's Ian Fleming's letter to Adolf Hitler."

The flap was not gummed shut so he was able to remove the two pages inside with relative ease and held them up for his friends to see. They were identical to the two pages he and O'Bryan had seen in London. And the last paragraph spoke to the end of creation, the fourteen day countdown starting on the fifth of January 1943, should Hitler fail to obey the will of God.

"Incredible," was all O'Bryan could manage to whisper as he examined the letter.

"Whatever possessed you to think of looking there?" Kettering finally asked.

Justin shrugged. "Panov told Steve Mannix how he had discovered a letter hidden behind the frame of *Evening Prayers*. This painting was his talisman. He kept it in his bedroom so he could admire it day and night. He said the painting was a gift from God and that he was going to succeed where Hitler had failed. Alexander Panov was going to rule the world through a czar of his making and a pope of his choosing. So he kept the letter tucked safely away behind the painting as a reminder of where his dream was supposed to take him."

"But in the end that dream failed him, just as it did Hitler."

"Yes it did, and when Mykel Charin went to arrest Panov for the murder of the Patriarch of Moscow, the man shot himself in his bedroom. But the last thing he saw before meeting his Maker was *Evening Prayers*."

Ian A. O'Connor

"Have you been able to figure out the meaning of the clues the patriarch had painted into the counterfeit masterpiece that he sent me?" Kettering asked.

"I think so," Justin said. "As best as I can cipher, the scroll in the painting spoke to the enriched plutonium dust Panov had placed inside the color copier to explode on his signal from the satellite, which means this plan had been carefully thought out as far back as a year ago, possibly longer. That particular clue was telling us the painting was a near-perfect duplicate of the original.

"Next, I really think Panov started out believing the letter delivered to Hitler in Nineteen Forty was indeed the word of God as told to Lucia, and that it truly spoke to of the end of creation. But once Panov realized that date had come and gone several decades earlier and that creation was still intact, he brilliantly decided to change a couple of key words to suit his evil purposes. And on what more fitting of a stage than the Sistine Chapel in which to orchestrate the end of the Roman Catholic Church? To have the pope and his cardinals all die underneath two of Michelangelo's most famous paintings, namely *Creation*, and the *Last Judgment.*"

"Which were represented to perfection in the messages written on both painted scrolls found in *Evening Prayers*. The real painting which spoke of the creation of the universe as written in Genesis, and the other scroll in the phony painting telling of creation's fiery end," Kettering replied. "And to think he came within a hairsbreadth of succeeding with his dastardly plan." Kettering shuddered as he gazed at the two paintings for a long moment then changed the subject. "Justin, you said yesterday that those people in Switzerland—the twelve apostles, I believe you called them— knew nothing of Panov's plans to control both the Church of Russia and Russia itself?"

"That's correct," Justin said. "They freely admitted to having worked long and hard to place a legitimate heir onto the Russian throne, but insisted they knew nothing of Panov's plan to destroy the Western Rite Church along with the Vatican. I believe them. And I'm also hearing from Mykel Charin that the Russian president and his prime minister are claiming to be equally shocked that such a thing was being contemplated, and are now distancing themselves from Panov just as fast as they can."

"What do you think will happen to Freddy?" Kettering asked.

"The twelve apostles still want him to consider their offer," Justin replied. "He told Mannix he favors the idea of letting the Russian people decide if they want the throne restored. Freddy said he would consider putting his life on hold for eighteen months while the Russians debate its merits before voting yes or no in a national referendum."

Kettering nodded his approval. He had liked Manfred von Snellenberger from the moment he had been introduced by Maritha. He made his way back to his desk. "There is one good thing that came out of this frightening affair and it's this," Kettering said, picking up a folder and opening it. "Here is a copy of the message the pope sent to the leaders of all the Christian denominations. It's an invitation to an ecumenical gathering for the purpose of celebrating all that binds us together while de-emphasizing our differences. The Holy Father envisions a convocation of Roman, Orthodox, and Protestant clergies, the likes of which have not been seen since the Council of Basle some six hundred years ago. He suggests it be held in Saint Petersburg, and the response from around the world so far has been overwhelming. In fact, the first reply came from the Archbishop of Canterbury who sees it as a further building on the public outreach the last pope made to Anglicans and Episcopalians in late Two Thousand and Nine."

"You know, with all that's been going on, I forgot to ask you something," Justin said. "Were you and the archbishop held prisoners together in Moscow and then in Saint Petersburg?"

"No," Kettering said. "I was only with Father Dellapina the whole time. In fact, I didn't hear of the archbishop's abduction until it was over and we had been freed." He shrugged his thin shoulders. "It seems Mister Panov's plan called for the two of us to be seated side by side in the Saints Peter and Paul Cathedral where we would bear witness first to the crowning of the new Russian czar, then to the coronation of the Patriarch of Saint Petersburg as the first leader of a new universal Catholic Church. Of course, the Holy Father would have been dead at this point, as would all of the cardinals, so in effect, the center of gravity for Christianity would shift from Rome to Russia because of Panov's rendering the Vatican uninhabitable for centuries to come. Our presence in the cathedral was supposed to signal our approval to Christians everywhere. Needless to say, the Patriarch of Saint Petersburg is still aghast at the thought of how he was duped; he knew nothing whatsoever of what was planned."

"Panov may have been clinically insane, but he was also a genius," Justin said. "There should be a lesson hidden in there for all of us to learn from, except for the life of me I haven't been able to figure out what it could possibly be."

"Time will tell you, I'm confident it will," Kettering said.

"Well, it sounds like there's still hope for us all," O'Bryan said, weighing into the discussion, "and just maybe Ian Fleming and Winston Churchill will end up having the last say. They started out with the best of intentions when they penned Lucia's phony letter to Hitler, but instead of just saving England, maybe those two will end up saving Christianity from itself these many decades later. Mister Churchill would most assuredly revel in the irony of that outcome."

Justin glanced at his watch. It was time to be going.

Kettering noticed the gesture. "Once more I find myself rendering a heartfelt thanks to you, Justin. You have been a godsend, and the Holy Father asked me to come up with a special gift to remind you of what you have accomplished."

"The six figure check you gave me yesterday is more than enough, Francis. In fact, I'm still embarrassed by the generosity of the Church."

Kettering was having none of it. He dismissed Justin's statement with a gentle wave of a hand. "Without you and your steadfastness under such terrible pressure there might not now be a Catholic Church—at least not one most of us would recognize. No, the pope would be offended if you did not accept the money. And so would I. Do not see it as charity, you earned every penny."

Thank you, Eminence, I mean Francis," Justin said, his face reddening. He tugged at his tie knot.

Kettering held out a veined hand and Justin gently enfolded it in both of his own.

"In keeping with the further wishes of the Holy Father, I would like you to accept the copy of *Evening Prayers* as a special token of our esteem and appreciation. Fake or not, it is still a beautiful painting. I will have it sent in the diplomatic pouch to you in Washington."

He then removed his hand from Justin's and plucked an item off the desk. "Here is your Vatican passport. I want you to keep it. As you know, there are only a few, so whenever you see it, hopefully you will think of us with fond memories."

Justin slipped the document into his suit jacket pocket. He almost could not trust his voice. He willed the lump in his throat to subside.

"Instead of saying goodbye, Francis, let me just say take good care of yourself, and I'll see you again soon."

He turned to O'Bryan. "You ready to take an old duffer to the airport, Padre? This broken down warhorse is anxious to get home."

O'Bryan laughed. "I just hope the old duffer doesn't fall asleep in the departure lounge and miss his flight."

Kettering smiled at his American friend. "Godspeed and God bless, Justin."

# # #

Ian A. O'Connor

About the author

Ian A. O'Connor is a retired USAF colonel who has held several senior military leadership positions in the field of national security management. In this page-turning thriller, *The Barbarossa Covenant*, featuring returning retired FBI agent Justin Scott, the author's expertise in neutralizing nuclear, biological, and chemical warfare threats against the United States provides the backdrop for the story's compelling reality and electrifying sense of urgency.

He is also the author of *The Twilight of The Day,* first published by Writers Club Press. This debut novel garnered high praise in a lengthy review in the *Military Times* for its realism and chilling story line. This was soon followed with the publication of *The Seventh Seal,* by Winterwolf Publishing Company, a thriller that introduced readers to retired FBI agent Justin Scott.

Ian also co-authored *SCRAPPY: A Memoir of a U.S. Fighter Pilot* published by McFarland & Company. He is a member of Mystery Writers of America, and lives in South Florida with his wife, Candice, where he is hard at work writing the next Justin Scott thriller, *The Masada Option.*

Contact Ian at: ianaoconnor@ianaoconnor.com

www.ingramcontent.com/pod-product-compliance
Lightning Source LLC
Chambersburg PA
CBHW020717130726
47899CB00011B/367